MELANIE ROSE

Down to Earth

This novel is entirely a work of fiction.
The names, characters and incidents portrayed in it are
the work of the author's imagination. Any resemblance to
actual persons, living or dead, events or localities is
entirely coincidental.

AVON

A division of HarperCollins*Publishers*
77–85 Fulham Palace Road,
London W6 8JB

www.harpercollins.co.uk

A Paperback Original 2010

1

A catalogue record for this book is
available from the British Library

ISBN-13: 978-1-84756-107-7

Set in Minion by Palimpsest Book Production Limited,
Falkirk, Stirlingshire

Printed and bound in Great Britain by
Clays Ltd, St Ives plc

Mixed Sources
Product group from well-managed
forests and other controlled sources
www.fsc.org Cert no. SW-COC-001806
© 1996 Forest Stewardship Council
FSC

FSC is a non-profit international organisation established to promote the
responsible management of the world's forests. Products carrying the FSC
label are independently certified to assure consumers that they come
from forests that are managed to meet the social, economic and
ecological needs of present and future generations.

Find out more about HarperCollins and the environment at
www.harpercollins.co.uk/green

My thanks to the following websites for research used in the writing of this book:

On the Number 52 – www.wisdomportal.com/Numbers/52.html

Grass – a deeper look –
www.farm-direct.co.uk/farming/stockcrop/grass/grassdet.html

Cancer Help UK – www.cancerhelp.org.uk

This book is for my clever, elegant, artistic and most beloved Mum, who taught me to put myself in other people's shoes and to see things from their perspective.
I miss you every day x

Chapter One

April 2002

Blood pounded in my head and I thought I might be sick at any minute. The parachute felt surprisingly heavy on my back as I followed Ingrid through the hangar doors and out into the bright, spring sunshine. Ingrid, who had been making little quips and jokes during the six-hour training session, had fallen ominously silent as we followed the jumpmaster towards a light aircraft, which was parked a short way away on the grassy field.

'Maybe we should have waited until more of the group could make it.' I swallowed nervously, wishing I was anywhere but here right now. 'The whole office signed up for this and now there's only the four of us.'

One of my mum's favourite sayings flickered into my mind; *be careful what you wish for, sometimes the cosmos is listening.*

Shaking the thought away with a tremor of unease, I glanced over my shoulder, pausing in mid-stride to let Graham, the red faced, rather rotund chief administrator catch up to us. I wondered briefly if he'd lied on his 'declaration of fitness' form. If not, he must have only just squeezed within the 15 stone limit for a solo static line jump. In Graham's wake dithered the angular Kevin, the youngest and newest member of our group. He'd only joined Wayfarers insurance company a few weeks ago as an IT support technician and had been keen to sign up to what the boss had billed as a 'team-building charity parachute jump'. Looking at his pale face now, I wondered if he was questioning his decision.

Kevin definitely looked as sick as I felt, but before I could commiserate I realised his eyes were fixed miserably on the back of Ingrid's flaxen head. My best friend, in true Ingrid-fashion was sticking close to the jumpmaster and as she turned and tossed her silky hair, I could see her blue eyes dancing animatedly on his.

'She's nervous, that's all,' I managed a weak smile as Kevin lowered his eyes to the ground as if unable to watch his office crush flirt a moment longer.

'Yeah, right,' he mumbled under his breath.

Matt, our instructor and jumpmaster was helping Ingrid into the plane. As she disappeared inside the small white hull, he turned his grey eyes on me and held out his hand. My pulse quickened a little further as I placed my hand in his. He reminded me a little of the French footballer David Ginola, but younger, somewhere in his early to mid-twenties, around my own age, I guessed. He had been kind but thoroughly professional all morning as he'd put us through our paces. He gave my hand a light squeeze.

'Don't look so worried, Michaela, you'll be fine. The first time is scary, but I promise you'll love it.'

Yeah, right, sprang to mind again but as I looked into his eyes I found that I believed him.

'Just remember the briefing video and your roll technique for landing. And do everything I tell you, when I tell you. You have to trust yourself to me, OK?'

He fished a scruffy piece of paper from his pocket and tucked it into the breast pocket of my jumpsuit. 'My phone number,' he whispered conspiratorially. 'Maybe you'd like to have a drink with me sometime.'

I thought fleetingly of my boyfriend Calum, the love of my life, waiting at home, but I nodded anyway; there was no harm in a friendly drink. 'Maybe – if I survive.' I stepped up through the hatch, catching the side of my hand on something sharp as I clambered into the plane and squeezed myself into the seat next to Ingrid who was fastening her helmet in place.

She grinned at me nervously. 'Cute isn't he?'

Gripping my hands in my lap to stop them from shaking I nodded again, realising as I did so that a thin line of blood was seeping from a small cut on the side of my palm. 'I suppose he is.'

Graham and Kevin were scrambling up in front of us and almost as soon as we were all seated the pilot revved the plane into life.

'What the hell was I thinking?' I said louder than I intended, shutting my eyes as the plane jolted and bucked over the short grass. 'I can't believe I'm doing this.'

'You'll be fine,' Matt yelled over the roar of the engine. 'It'll be the experience of a lifetime!'

Tentatively opening one eye to peer out of the open hatch, I glimpsed blue sky streaked with wispy, white clouds. The aircraft engine roared noisily in my ears and I wasn't sure whether my body was trembling because of the aircraft's vibrations or because of my heart, which was thumping wildly in my chest.

The pilot called out to Matt. The ground staff had just reported that the wind and our position were exactly right. We were over the drop zone; it was time to jump.

Graham, I noticed, despite his earlier bravado seemed to be praying silently and under the circumstances I decided that praying wasn't such a bad idea. Scrunching my eyes shut I put aside the fact that I hadn't thought of God for a very long time and entreated the Almighty to forgive me for this folly, praying that I would survive the jump intact.

Whether his silent entreaties to God had given him strength or because he was ever the valiant leader, Graham inched towards the exit with a jaunty thumbs-up, and on the count of three from Matt, jumped blithely out into space.

I watched the wind buffet his jumpsuit as he leapt, catching a fleeting glimpse of his arms and legs spread wide as we'd been taught, before he disappeared from view. But before I had time to register anything else, Matt was guiding Ingrid to the doorway, where she lingered, fingers tightly gripping the edge of the hatch, her body rigid with fear.

'Three, two, one, now!' Matt shouted, and Ingrid leapt out after Graham with a screech of terror that resounded in my ears and rolled around my stomach like an express train.

Matt was beckoning me over but I shook my head. 'No, no way.'

'I'll go,' Kevin slid past me, balanced himself in the gaping doorway, and in a moment he too was gone.

Matt was looking at me.

'I can't do it,' I quaked. 'I really can't.'

'The pilot is coming in for another pass,' Matt called over the howling wind and the drone of the turning plane. 'You've done all the practice drills, you know what to do . . .' He reached out and lightly touched my arm. 'If you don't want to do it you don't have to, but I can guarantee you'll be disappointed with yourself later if you don't.'

Every instinct told me to grab his comforting hand and hang on to it for dear life, but I knew he was right. If I didn't jump I'd be letting my sponsors down. Not to mention the heart foundation who were expecting my contribution.

My colleagues would be on the ground by now, their jumps completed. 'Please, if there is a God,' I mumbled as I scrambled towards the doorway, 'don't let me die.'

'Now!' Matt yelled.

And, with a great gulp of breath, I tumbled outwards into the void.

Chapter Two

I fell like a stone, plummeting earthwards at an astonishing speed, the breath squeezed out of me as I tried to spread my arms and legs out in the free-fall stance I'd been taught. My terrified brain was still panicking; why hadn't the chute opened? Had something gone terribly wrong? But then the static line jerked abruptly and I felt myself yanked upwards as the parachute deployed miraculously above my head.

Opening my eyes I scanned the patchwork quilt of the countryside stretching away for as far as the eye could see. Below me lay bright green squares of young spring growth butting up against brown, neatly ploughed fields and in the distance, the distinct grey tarmac lines of a motorway, speckled with miniature cars moving like brightly coloured ants.

It was stunningly beautiful. My heart was settling back into a regular rhythm and I was thrilled at the feeling of being quite literally on top of the world.

And then the wind came out of nowhere and hit me.

Suddenly I felt the parachute buck and twist. It wasn't simply a blustery gust of wind; more a tidal wave of air, bearing down on me from above and engulfing me as I hung helpless in the sky. Dark clouds appeared and swallowed me up so that I could no longer see the ground.

I hung there, suspended within the giant wave, buffeted this way and that, breathless and terrified. Completely disorientated, I continued my downward spiral towards an earth I could no longer see. The training video certainly hadn't mentioned this eventuality and I had absolutely no idea what to do.

And suddenly just when I thought I was going to die from fright, the airborne tsunami hurled me to the ground, where I lay panting and gasping like a beached fish.

For a moment I lay motionless, trying to still my racing heart, but the wind was plucking at the parachute, threatening to drag my body through the long, damp grass where I had landed. Fuzzily recalling the drill, I unclipped the buckles on the chute and sat up, looking round in confusion. It seemed I was on the airfield, but it was so dark I couldn't make out the aircraft hangar or the adjoining buildings.

Pulling up the sleeve of my jumpsuit I peered through the gloom at my digital wristwatch. Nine thirty. But how could that be? I had left the aircraft hangar at three in the afternoon. Even allowing for the short wait before take-off and the second pass the aircraft had made after the others had jumped, no more than half an hour could have elapsed. Tapping the watch with my finger, I concluded it must have been damaged on landing.

I felt a pang of worry as I struggled to my feet. Even if my watch was broken, why was it so dark? And where were the airfield personnel who were supposed to take me back to the hangar?

'Get a grip,' I admonished myself as I stood trembling in the darkness. The rogue wind had probably blown me off course and I might not be on the airfield at all. Maybe the terror of the jump had confused me or perhaps I had bumped my head and lain here for hours while the parachuting company had been searching the surrounding woods and fields for me. Slowly I realised that if they couldn't locate me, I would have to find my own way back to the airfield.

Taking a deep breath, I turned to gather up the silky folds of the chute, and, finding a depression in the soft earth I stuffed the parachute and my helmet in it, covering it with stones to weigh it down. Drawing another steadying breath, I noticed the outline of trees to my right and set off in what I hoped was the right direction.

Ten to fifteen minutes later a building loomed ahead of me, I could see enough to recognise the aircraft hangar and the one-storey buildings, which housed the small office, toilets and mess room where I'd had lunch several hours earlier.

I decided to check the mess room first. But when I reached out to open the door I found that it was locked. Rubbing at the filthy, cracked window pane with the cuff of my jumpsuit, I squinted into the dark interior. I hadn't noticed the window being quite this dirty earlier in the day and I was pretty sure it hadn't been cracked either, but anything could have happened in my absence. Moving to the next building I located the ladies' loo. The door was swinging gently on its hinges in the evening breeze. Pushing it open I saw that the fittings had been vandalised, the toilet seat was hanging to one side and the wash basin had been wrenched off the wall and was lying splintered on the concrete floor.

Wrinkling my nose in distaste, I decided to use the facilities anyway. This same toilet had been clean and tidy only a few hours before, with brightly coloured curtains hanging in the window which had now mysteriously disappeared.

Zipping up my jumpsuit I stood shivering in the moonlight, unsure what to do next. The hangar looked to be in complete darkness, but I did briefly wonder if this was all some kind of wind-up. Maybe Ingrid, Graham and Kevin were hiding in the shadows waiting to leap out and shout 'You've been framed!' and spray champagne everywhere, while the airfield crew stood laughing appreciatively in the wings.

I walked towards the hangar only to find that the door wouldn't budge. As my eyes adjusted to the darkness I noticed that the door had been kicked in, in one corner, leaving a jagged hole near the ground. Glancing round warily to ensure that no one was around, I lay down so I could spy through the hole into the interior.

The hangar was empty. Everything that had been in there earlier, the television screen on which we'd watched the information video, the padded mats we'd used to practise our rolling falls, the plastic chairs, the parachutes themselves – not to mention two light aircraft lockers, work benches and tools – had all simply vanished.

Completely nonplussed, I crawled onto my knees and scuffled round into a sitting position. Leaning my back against the cold hangar wall, I drew my legs up to my chest, gazing into the oppressive nothingness with wide-eyed fear. For the second time today I found myself muttering a desperate entreaty to the God of my childhood, while staring like a lost and lonely soul into the darkness.

Chapter Three

It took me some time to realise that although my fleece jacket and handbag (including my mobile phone) had probably disappeared along with the locker, I still hadn't checked the car park for my car.

Gingerly getting to my feet, I tried to hold back my tears and slowly walked the short distance to the car park with folded arms and hunched shoulders. I didn't really want to look. The thought of not finding my car sitting waiting for me was so awful that I didn't raise my head to look properly until the very last minute.

It was every bit as bad as I'd expected. Not only had the dozen or so cars disappeared, including my Suzuki Vitara jeep, but the gravel surface had gone too. A rusty tractor stood in the corner of a deserted field, but it might as well have been a spaceship for all the sense things were making right now.

There hadn't been many instances in my life when I'd been at such a complete and utter loss. Once, at school, when I was about ten years old I'd been asked to stand up in class and recite a poem. My mind had buzzed emptily rather like it was buzzing now and my throat had dried to the point where I could barely swallow. But it had been warm in that room and the teacher had come to my rescue by leading me back to my chair and saying kindly that I could try again later.

Here it was cold, and I was on my own. A chilly wind whipped my dark blonde hair around my shoulders, and I shivered, hugging the jumpsuit closely round me, glad of the extra layer of warmth over my jeans and thin T-shirt. I wondered if anyone was likely to come and help me now. I thought probably not. If there was going to be any sort of rescue, then I would have to do it myself. Whatever had happened here, my only recourse was to try and find some shelter, some food and some warmth, a place to collect my wits and plan how I was going to get home.

I remembered passing a village on the way to the airfield this morning. Perhaps I would find help there. I walked down the dark road for what seemed like hours while the wind howled mercilessly and blew dried leaves down from the trees, making me jump with every rustle. When I finally saw the lights of a pub, I could have cried with relief. Pushing open the entrance door, I blinked in the sudden brightness and paused to take stock.

There was a fire burning in the grate against the opposite wall, a long wooden bar counter taking up most of the space to my left and about fifteen people of all ages sitting at tables. Squeezing past them towards the fire, I was surprised by the complete absence of cigarette smoke. I'd always hated the way smoke hung in the air stinging my eyes and throat, making my clothes and hair reek for hours afterwards.

As I took a seat halfway between the bar and the fire, I eyed the couple sitting on bar stools nearby, wondering how I was going to ask for help. I had no money about my person, no personal details or any form of identification. Who would take me seriously?

'Can I get you anything, love?'

I glanced up to find the barman staring at me from behind the bar.

'Er, do you have a pay phone I could use?' I called back.

He pointed his head to the end of the bar. 'There's a phone out by the toilets, but you'll need a phone card.'

'Can I reverse the charges?'

He looked at me long and hard. 'Are you alright, love?'

I felt myself blushing under his scrutiny. The couple at the bar were looking at me now and several of the other customers had stopped talking to glance my way. I suppose I looked a bit out of place sitting in an ill-fitting blue jumpsuit with my tear-stained face and lack of personal belongings.

'I had an accident up the road there.' It wasn't too much of a lie, I thought. 'I need to ring someone to come and fetch me.'

'You look a bit peaky, are you hurt? Do you need an ambulance?'

'No, really,' I shook my head. 'If I could just use your phone I could get my boyfriend to come for me.'

'Where's your car? It isn't blocking the road or anything?' 'No.'

'And no one else was involved?' The barman had come round the bar to get a better look at me. He held out a glass of water. 'Here, drink this.'

He watched as I gratefully sipped the cool liquid. I hadn't realised how thirsty I was.

'You look familiar, somehow.' He looked at me closely. 'Are you from round these parts?'

I shook my head again. 'I drove down from Surrey this morning.'

He seemed to come to a decision. 'Come on round the back and you can use the house phone.'

'I can't pay you; I lost my handbag in the . . . accident.'

'Don't worry about it, love. Come on.'

I rose to my feet and followed him round the bar to a

hallway where a phone hung on a plainly decorated wall. The customers watched for a moment then returned to their drinks. I could hear the kindly barman return to the bar as I picked up the handset and punched in the number for the house I shared with Calum.

Calum and I had moved in together six months ago after a whirlwind romance. He was several years older than me and had a ten-year-old daughter called Abbey. Abbey's mother had died in a car accident eighteen months before I'd met them, and although things had been difficult between me and the resentful young girl for the first few months, we had gradually begun to gel into something resembling a family unit.

As I waited for him to pick up the phone, I thought about Calum's horrified reaction when I'd first told him about the parachute jump. 'Are you crazy?' he had demanded when I'd shown him the sponsorship forms. 'Don't you realise how dangerous it is?'

'People do parachute jumps all the time,' I'd soothed him. 'Nothing will happen to me.'

Over the next few weeks as I gathered sponsorship money, he had realised I wasn't going to back down and had reluctantly added his own name to my list of sponsors. 'I don't think you realise that you are one of the most important people in my world,' he whispered late one evening as we'd lain in bed. 'I just couldn't bear to lose you, Kaela. Promise me you'll be careful?'

I knew he was terrified that history would repeat itself and snatch me away as it had his wife. His reservations were understandable and I'd tried to reassure him the best I could. We'd made love with an intensity sparked by fear and afterwards I'd lain awake listening to his even breathing thinking about how much I cared about him, whilst at the same time yearning for this one last chance at freedom.

At twenty-five the responsibilities I had so willingly taken on were more of a challenge than I'd expected. I was still trying to hold down my job as Graham's personal assistant and would-be apprentice. It had been a smart career move when I'd been single and independent, but now I was doing a daily school run, helping with Abbey's homework, shopping and cooking and cleaning for the three of us. More than once during the last six months I'd feared my parents might have had a point when they'd warned me about taking on a man of thirty four and his child.

'Are you sure he's not just looking for a new mother for his daughter?' my father had cautioned me. 'Is this really what you want to do with your life?'

'He's on the rebound,' my mum added. 'His wife has only been gone a year and a half; it's too soon.'

But infatuation had conquered all. Calum had wined and dined me and had seemed so much more mature and sophisticated than the boys I had dated in the past. He was kind and considerate and we'd taken picnics and long walks by the river discussing all kinds of highbrow subjects, instead of drinking and dancing the night away at bars and clubs.

After I'd moved in with him we'd tried to keep some sort of social life alive, but the pressures of our jobs and being full time parents meant that we rarely went out in the evenings any more.

For all my promise of a lasting commitment, the parachute jump had been a breath of fresh air, an adventure in the making and nothing Calum or anyone else could say would have dissuaded me from taking part. Now, as the phone went unanswered, I wondered if I was being punished.

He must have gone out, I thought, even though he'd said he would be there when I got home. And it was a school night, so Abbey should be in doing her homework. Perhaps Calum had taken Abbey out for a pizza.

Replacing the receiver, I rubbed my hands over my face. I couldn't stay here, that was for sure. Tolerant as the barman was being, I couldn't see him letting me spend the night.

Coming to a decision, I dialled the number for my parents' house. They would want to know why Calum hadn't come for me of course, and I waited for them to pick up with mixed feelings. But the phone rang and rang endlessly there too. Where had everyone gone? Normally my parents ate dinners in front of the television; it was unusual for them to go out unless it was some special occasion. Out of habit I glanced at my watch again, forgetting that it might be broken. Ten thirty. Perhaps they had gone to bed.

I was about to replace the receiver, when it was picked up and a woman's voice said, 'Yes?'

'Mum?' It didn't sound like my mother, but I couldn't imagine who else it could be.

'Who is this?' the voice demanded.

'It's Michaela. Is that you, Mum?'

'I'm sorry you've got the wrong number.'

I repeated the number I had dialled and the woman confirmed it was correct.

'This is Michaela Anderson, are you sure my parents aren't there?'

'Very funny,' the voice snapped waspishly. The phone went dead. I knew it had been unwise to press the point, but I couldn't understand why some stranger had picked up my parents' phone. I stood, rooted to the spot with the receiver in my hand, until someone nudged my elbow.

'Made your call?' The barman was looking at me strangely. He took the phone from me and replaced it gently on its cradle. 'Are you alright, love? You look like you've seen a ghost.'

'I couldn't get through,' I mumbled, trying to shake off

the feeling of deep unease that was creeping up through my body. 'I need to try someone else.'

'Go ahead,' he said, turning away, 'let me know if you need anything.'

I tried Ingrid next, but her line seemed to be out of order. Leaning back against the wall I tried to think. I was over an hour's drive from home and I had no money for a cab, a train, or even a bus – should there have been one at this time of the night – which I doubted. Ice cold fingers of fear tightened around my chest which was feeling increasingly hollow and empty. I thought for a moment that I might actually faint.

Holding onto the wall for support, I clawed my way back towards the bar. There had to be a rational answer to all this. Maybe I was asleep and dreaming the whole thing. As I made my way slowly along the passage I glanced at the walls, which were covered from floor to ceiling with posters advertising various bands I'd never heard of, leaflets and personal messages stuck on top of one another forming a huge collage.

I paused as one particular leaflet caught my eye. There were several copies of it, some partially hidden by more recent stickers, others with pen marks and scribbles obscuring a face. Bold printed words asked: HAVE YOU SEEN THIS GIRL? The thing that made me stop dead in my tracks was the face itself: *my* face peering out from a washed-out photograph. A photo I'd had taken only the week before, and which, to my knowledge hadn't even been developed yet.

But it was not only the enormity of seeing my own face staring wanly back at me from the faded leaflets that made my blood run cold. It was the date printed boldly underneath the picture: 'Last seen 15 April 2002.'

Because 15 April 2002 was today's date. And I wasn't missing at all.

Chapter Four

The pub toilet wasn't the ideal place to hide. Apart from being less than hygienic, customers kept coming in to use the facilities to find me alternately splashing cold water onto my face and slapping or pinching myself in the hope that I'd wake up from this terrible nightmare. Most of the ladies coming in and out averted their eyes, though one or two looked at me sympathetically as they washed their hands or touched up their make-up.

Eventually the barman, who turned out to be the pub landlord, called me out and told me the pub was closing for the night.

'There must be someone you can call,' he said as he cleared the tables of glasses. I watched, perched on a bar stool as he picked up a discarded local newspaper and tossed it into a blue plastic bin.

'Don't throw it away!' I exclaimed, reaching for the paper and smoothing it out.

'I wasn't throwing it away, love, I was recycling it. Look, that's the recycling bin.'

I spread the paper out on the bar top and peered at the date. He hadn't struck me as a save-the-planet type of guy, but I didn't have time to wonder at his idiosyncrasies, because I was staring at the date printed in the top right hand corner of the paper. 'Monday, 20 October 2008'.

'Where did this newspaper come from?' I demanded tremulously.

He shrugged. 'One of the customers must have brought it in.'

'Is it a joke or something?'

He stopped in mid-stride, his fingers full of glasses and stared at me suspiciously. 'In what way might it be a joke?'

'The date,' I whispered. Something in his expression stopped me from protesting further and I backtracked quickly, a plausible lie leaping to my lips, 'Sorry, I lost my reading glasses in the accident and I'm having trouble seeing the small print. This is today's paper is it?'

He came over and took the paper out of my hand. 'Of course it is. Look, love, I've got to close up and you can't stay here. I don't want to throw you out with nowhere to go, but what do you expect me to do with you?'

We stared at one another helplessly for a moment. No amount of prayer was going to help me now, I decided. Tears welled in my eyes and I blinked them furiously back, feeling in the jumpsuit pocket for a tissue, determined not to cry in front of this stranger. But it wasn't a tissue my fingers located – it was a crumpled piece of paper with a telephone number scribbled in pencil.

'Matt,' I breathed.

'Excuse me?'

'There is someone else I could try, if you don't mind letting me use the telephone one more time.'

He waved me towards the back. 'Be my guest, but make it quick will you?'

I dialled the number with trembling fingers. Matt had only given me his number a couple of hours ago, but those few hours seemed to have turned into half a lifetime.

'Please answer,' I begged, shifting from one weary foot to the other as the phone rang in the distance. 'Please, please pick up.'

And then there was a voice at the end of the line. 'Hello?'

'Matt?'

'Who is this?'

'It's Michaela. Michaela Anderson. You gave me your number and asked me to give you a call . . .'

The silence at the end of the line seemed to stretch into eternity. I thought for a moment I had lost the connection, but then his voice came again, hesitant but clear.

'Is . . . is it really you, Michaela?'

'Yes. You suggested going for a drink sometime, but something has happened and I don't know how to get home.'

'Where are you?'

'I'm in a pub near the airfield – the Royal Oak, I believe.'

'Wait right there. Do not move, do not talk to anyone. Give me ten minutes and I'll come and fetch you.'

The line went dead and I turned to find the landlord looking at me. 'Is someone coming for you?' he asked hopefully.

'In ten minutes,' I replied with the faint beginnings of a smile. 'I'll be out of your way as soon as he gets here if you don't mind letting me wait a little while longer.'

The landlord grinned with obvious relief, indicating a seat by the door. 'Be my guest,' he said.

It was nearer fifteen minutes when the door opened startling the landlord, who was leaning against a wall, waiting, key in hand, to lock up and go to bed.

My head, which had drooped wearily onto my chest, shot up as the door swung inwards and I saw a figure emerge through the doorway. A tremor of something indefinable flooded through me.

'Matt?' My voice came out as a hoarse croak. 'You . . . you've had your hair cut.'

I knew it was an odd observation to make, considering the circumstances, but not as odd as the fact that although I could see quite clearly that it *was* Matt, he looked older, had put a little weight on his slim frame and just seemed . . . different.

And he was staring at me as if I were a ghostly apparition.

'My God, Michaela . . . it really is you.'

I opened my mouth to speak, but closed it again in confusion.

He seemed to come to a decision and held out his hand. 'Come on let's get you out of here.'

I rose to my feet, ready to follow him goodness knows where but felt a sudden nagging doubt. What was I doing going off with someone I barely knew? I turned to the landlord, but he was holding the door open for me and I realised that I had little choice but to leave with Matt. 'Thank you so much for letting me wait here, it was very kind of you.'

'Don't mention it.' He yawned widely. 'I just wish I could remember where I've seen you before.'

It was on the tip of my tongue to tell him that he had several posters of my face stuck all over his back walls, but Matt had taken my elbow and was guiding me out into the dark night. He released me as soon as we were outside. I saw a black car parked at the kerb and Matt walked towards it and indicated I should get in.

I would normally never get into a stranger's car, but the alternative was to continue being lost and alone and that was something I could not contemplate a moment longer, so I slid onto the cream leather upholstery of the front passenger seat and clipped my safety belt into place. The driver's door opened and Matt climbed in, started the engine and guided the car out onto the road.

'Where are we going?'

'I'm taking you straight to the police station.'

My insides gave an involuntary lurch. 'Why?'

He risked taking his eyes off the road to glance at me. 'Michaela, you've just turned up out of the blue after all this time. Everyone's been searching for you. We have to let them know you're back so that they can question you.'

So I had come down in the wrong place and they had been looking for me all day and all evening. My theory that I must have bumped my head and become disorientated was right. 'Couldn't it wait until the morning? I'm very tired and I'd rather just go home.'

'I'm not sure that's an option. It's been a long time, things have changed.' He shook his head and whistled through his teeth. 'The press are going to have a field day with your reappearance.'

My stomach clenched at his words and the dread I'd felt earlier began to resurface. 'Things can't have become that urgent in the space of a day, surely?'

Matt slowed down and drew in to a small lay-by where he let the engine idle as he turned to face me. His expression was kind, but his voice firm. 'People are going to want to know where you've been. The whole world is going to want to know what happened to you. Your reappearance is going to cause a sensation. Michaela, it hasn't been a single day. You've been missing without trace for six and a half long years.'

Chapter Five

'I don't believe you.' Even as I said it I pictured the newspaper in the pub dated October 2008; the faded leaflets and posters on the wall.

'Well it's true. Don't you remember anything about what happened?' Matt studied my blank face with an alarmed expression and after a moment swung the car out onto the road again.

I fixed my gaze on the road ahead, the dark tarmac illuminated in the car's headlights, the hedgerows a black blur outlining the road as we sped by. 'Nothing untoward happened,' I insisted softly. 'I jumped out of that aeroplane this morning and when I landed it was dark.'

'I have to let the authorities know you've been found.' He looked at me pityingly and his voice was gentle. 'Whatever has happened to you, you need professional help.'

'No!' I turned to him beseechingly. I was beginning to feel exhausted and didn't know what to think, the physical evidence seemed to support Matt's claim, yet the suggestion that six and a half years of my life had simply vanished since this morning was farcical. 'Please won't you just give me a lift home? My boyfriend must be worried sick about me by now. I said I'd be home before nightfall.'

'It's not going to be as simple as that. After all this time you won't be able to walk straight back into your old life. When you return, it's going to be traumatic – there will be a lot of curiosity, not just from the police but from the media too. It's going to be a shock for everyone, Michaela, your boyfriend particularly. It's been a very long time.'

I fell silent, trying to stay alert despite the weariness that was creeping through me. Forcing my eyes to remain open I stared at the road, thinking about what he'd said. My head had begun to spin and my mouth felt dry. I began to doubt that I could make the journey home to Surrey without being ill. Like a confused and wounded animal, I wanted nothing more than to find a safe dark place where I could curl into a ball and hide. 'I don't want to be questioned; not tonight. If you don't want to drive me all the way home, maybe I could stay at your place . . . just for tonight?'

He sighed. 'I don't think that's a very good idea.'

Despite the fact that all sense of reason seemed to be shutting down, I detected the doubt creeping into his voice and latched onto it with the desperation of someone about to drown. 'Please, Matt, just one night while I collect my thoughts.'

'I ought to take you straight to the police.'

'Please . . . ?'

He rolled his eyes and after a moment or two's hesitation he nodded and I felt the panic inside me subside. Whatever had befallen me, I had one night to rest and to buffer whatever horrors I might have to face next.

'Thank you.'

We hardly spoke for the rest of the journey back to his place, but it seemed that in no time at all he was turning into the shingle driveway of what appeared to be a smart detached house. The house was in darkness save for a single light in the porch. He drove into a narrow garage before killing the engine and turning to face me again.

'It was really kind of you to come and fetch me ...' I began lamely.

He shook his head. 'It was the least I could do. I just wish I hadn't let you persuade me to bring you here instead of taking you to the authorities. I must be crazy.'

'I tried ringing my boyfriend but he didn't pick up and a stranger answered my parents' phone – I'm sure I dialled the right number.'

'Yes, you probably did.'

Raising my eyes to his, I asked the questions that had been foremost on my mind all evening, 'But why? I can't believe what you said about six and a half years having passed, so what's happened to everyone? How come the airfield was deserted, my car gone and a newspaper in the pub said it was October 2008?'

'Do you remember anything, anything at all about where you've been?'

'I remember everything very clearly and I haven't been anywhere. That's why this is all so confusing. I remember the early morning call from Graham saying the jump was going ahead, the drive down to Kent, the exercises and the briefing, the parachute jump ... you telling me I'd regret it if I didn't go through with it, I remember *every* detail.'

He reached out and ran a finger over the material of my jumpsuit as if not really believing I was actually wearing it. 'So you have no memory of anything in between?'

'There has been no "in between". It was only this morning you were teaching me my rolling fall! I didn't want to jump, remember? But I did it and it was all so beautiful once I had got over the terror of falling. You were right, I did love it.

24

Then that strange wind hit me and when I landed it was dark and everyone had gone.'

Matt's eyebrows shot up and he looked sceptical, yet I had the uncanny feeling that he knew more than he was letting on.

'Maybe Kevin has been right all along,' he murmured with a smile.

'Kevin? Oh, so he does exist then?' I countered, thinking he was mocking me. 'I was beginning to think my whole life had been some sort of weird dream and I'd imagined him and my job and my family and friends.'

'No, but something has happened to you and if you don't remember what, then I don't know what to think any more than you do.' He opened his door. 'Look, come into the house and I'll get you a cup of coffee.'

I followed him into a brightly lit, very modern but rather messy looking kitchen. Hovering awkwardly by the door, I watched warily as he filled a see-through plastic kettle and switched it on.

'You look exactly as you did when I last saw you,' he said, shaking his head in obvious disbelief as he pulled out a stool for me at a breakfast bar. 'It's unbelievable.'

'Well, you only saw me this morning.' I was getting a bit fed up with the look of amazement on his face. I slid onto the stool, wrinkling my brow as I took in every detail of his appearance. 'You look different though,' I commented wearily. 'Maybe it's the hair cut, but you look – I don't know – a bit older.'

'That's because I am.' He turned to face me with that penetrating gaze of his. Taking the seat next to me, he rubbed his palms on the knees of his jeans. 'Look, Michaela, I don't want to frighten you, but after you parachuted out of that plane back in April 2002, you simply vanished without trace.

You really have been missing all this time: it was as if you'd been completely wiped off the face of the earth.'

'Stop it!' I got to my feet again, and began pacing up and down, my jump-boots clattering across the quarry-tiled flooring. Eventually I stopped and turned to face him. 'How can you expect me to believe that?'

He shook his head. 'I don't know. But whether you believe it or not your disappearance changed a lot of lives, including mine. I was the last one to see you; I was the one who told you when and where to jump. The mystery of your disappearance has haunted me ever since. At one point the police even had me down as a suspect for your possible murder.'

'But I didn't vanish,' I protested faintly, the anger ebbing away as quickly as it had come. 'I've been here all along.'

He went to the counter and spooned instant coffee into mugs. I watched as he poured the hot water into the mugs and added milk.

'When you didn't land on the airfield we scoured the surrounding fields and woods for you.' He brought the mugs over to the breakfast bar and took a seat. Somewhat begrudgingly I took one of the steaming mugs as he went on. 'We assumed you'd somehow gone off course and landed outside the airfield, but there was no sign of you anywhere. After several hours of fruitless searching we called the police who widened the hunt to farmland, people's back gardens, sheds and outhouses but you were nowhere to be found. The search went on for months with door-to-door questioning and television appeals, but there were no leads. It was if you'd just vanished into thin air. Your parents refused to give up on you long after the police had put your case on the back burner. They had leaflets made and circulated them in the area. That was six long years ago, Michaela. After a year or so everyone except your parents – and Kevin and I – believed you would never be seen again.'

I tried lifting the coffee mug to my lips but my hands were shaking so much I could barely hold it. Resting it back down on the counter I gripped my head in my hands and closed my eyes.

'You must remember something about where you've been?' he pressed again.

'I told you,' my voice came out muffled between my elbows and from under my long hair. 'I remember everything very clearly. Today is 15th April. It's 2002 . . .'

He reached over to the back of the counter and pulled a folded newspaper towards me. Scanning the date in the top corner I closed my eyes again and groaned.

'It can't be . . . it just can't.'

Because this newspaper also proclaimed that today was Monday 20th October, and it was definitely 2008.

Chapter Six

'Wait here.' Matt left the room, returning a moment later with a large envelope filled with piles of posters, leaflets and newspaper cuttings. Tilting my head to one side, I watched as he sifted through them.

The first reports had apparently made front-page headlines; *'Girl vanishes in parachute jump'*, and *'Missing girl in charity jump mystery'*, then, *'Missing jump-girl's parents in TV plea'*, *'Police quiz instructor in parachute puzzle'*, and finally, *'Michaela – abducted by aliens?'*

I read each article with a growing sense of unease. My fingers lingered on a black and white picture of my parents in which they looked haggard and distressed. What must they have been through if what Matt was saying was true?

'I've got to try ringing Calum and my parents again.' I struggled to my feet and stood swaying dangerously. My ears were ringing with a horrible high-pitched buzzing sound and I felt nauseous again.

The floor, which had seemed so solid only a moment before, tipped towards me and I would have gone down hard if Matt hadn't grabbed me and helped me down gently onto the cold floor. My hand hurt where the small cut had grazed against the kitchen tiles.

Matt crouched down so his head was only inches from mine. 'What have you done to your hand?'

'I caught it on the door of the plane as we were climbing in before the jump,' I told him.

He fell very still. 'I remember you doing that,' he murmured, so quietly that I thought he was talking to himself. 'But it can't be the same injury . . . not after all this time.'

'What's happened to me?' I asked faintly as I stared down at the laces of my boots.

'That,' he said firmly, 'is what I intend to find out.'

I decided not to try ringing anyone again that evening. If even half of what Matt had told me was true, then after six and a half years, one more night wasn't going to hurt. I asked him about driving me home to Calum or even to Ingrid's house, but he repeated that it would probably be more sensible if I were to tackle picking up the threads of my life in the morning.

'Think of the shock you are going to give everyone when you return from the dead,' he reminded me. 'If you don't want to go to the authorities or tell the world you're back just yet then I suggest you get a good night's sleep and we'll go first thing tomorrow. No one is going to believe this you know, not until you're standing right in front of them in person.'

After following Matt upstairs I stood back as he held open the door to a good-sized guest room, pleasantly decorated in navy blue and white, with a queen-sized bed in the centre. Crossing to a chest of drawers, he rummaged about and returned with a couple of neatly folded white T-shirts, one with a panda on the front, the other with the picture of a leaping dolphin.

'Here, you can sleep in one of these if you like.'

I took the T-shirts and trailed after him to the bathroom where he produced a clean towel and a brand new toothbrush.

'I'll let you get sorted out then,' he said.

When the door closed behind him, I unfolded the T-shirts and held one against me. It was just long enough to cover my bottom and I decided it would make a decent enough nightdress. Holding the fabric to my face I inhaled the scent, expecting to detect the scent of perfume or some other residual hint of the person this had belonged to, because they certainly weren't Matt's. As I contemplated my reflection in the bathroom mirror, I couldn't help but wonder how many women had passed through his life since he'd invited me for a drink that morning.

It was a relief to get out of the jumpsuit however, and I looked down at the jeans and T-shirt I had on underneath, glad to see something familiar that belonged to me and which hadn't miraculously vanished during the day. After brushing my teeth I emerged onto the landing holding the hem of the T-shirt self-consciously down round my thighs. Matt was waiting outside the bathroom door.

'Have you got everything you need?'

I nodded but as he turned and walked away from me I felt a moment of panic.

What if I closed my eyes and disappeared again? What if I awoke to find another six years had gone by? One of the newspaper articles swam before my eyes; what if I really had been abducted by aliens and they came for me again in the night?

Matt was already halfway along the landing but I called his name and he turned to look questioningly at me. 'Yes?'

'I know this is going to sound pathetic, but I don't want to be left on my own. I don't suppose I could sleep with you

30

in your room, could I?' I felt myself blush as his eyes widened in surprise. 'It's just that I don't want to be alone . . . with all that's happened I'd feel safer sleeping with someone there. Just as a friend, you understand . . . no funny business.'

He hesitated as if thinking things over. 'I'd be crazy to say no to an offer like that,' he laughed easily and I realised how good looking he was. 'There's only one bed in my room, but I promise to be the perfect gentleman or I could sleep on the floor if you want.'

I recalled the undeniable attraction I'd felt towards him this morning when he'd been coaching us for the jump. I'd been surprised and flattered when he'd given *me* his telephone number instead of Ingrid, though the terror of the impending jump and my feelings for Calum had quelled any thoughts of a possible romance.

'You don't need to sleep on the floor,' I murmured sheepishly.

He turned on the lights to his room and I took in the black sheets, black and gold-trimmed duvet and pillows piled high on his king-sized bed and almost changed my mind. Apart from various items of his previously discarded clothing lying about on the floor, the room was reasonably clean. But by the look of the place I got the feeling he was a confirmed Casanova and here I was, begging to be allowed to sleep with him.

Matt disappeared into an en suite bathroom and returned a few minutes later wearing a towelling robe. Sitting on the edge of the bed, he discarded the robe, giving me a view of broad muscular shoulders tapering to a neat waist before he slid discreetly between the covers. I had the impression he was still wearing boxer shorts and I breathed a sigh of relief.

Embarrassed by my neediness, I climbed quickly into the near-side of the bed, turning my back quickly to his. I heard the rustle of the bedding as he reached out to extinguish the light and I lay as still as I could until he asked if I was alright.

'Yes, thank you, I'm fine,' I answered stiffly. I had the duvet drawn up to my chin, my hands crossed protectively over my chest. He murmured 'goodnight' and within seconds I could hear his even breathing turn to a light snoring. I waited until I was absolutely sure he was asleep before carefully moving my foot until it was resting gently against his lower leg.

As the warmth of Matt's flesh seeped into me I felt secure in the knowledge that I was safely anchored to the world by another living, human being and closed my eyes, allowing myself to relax at last and succumb to sleep.

Chapter Seven

I awoke to the tantalising smell of bacon and eggs and lay with my eyes closed, wondering where I was. Calum and I never ate a cooked breakfast. He was a fruit and muesli man, Abbey usually had cereal and I liked fruit, yoghurt and toast. Opening my eyes, I glanced at the empty space beside me, the pillow still slightly depressed where someone had recently slept, and I remembered with a jolt where I was.

With the realisation that I wasn't in my bed, the rest of the previous day's horror reared its ugly head and my heart gave an involuntary flutter of fear. Had I really been catapulted six years into the future? Yesterday the signs had certainly indicated that, but how could such a thing be possible?

In the thin light of morning the idea seemed preposterous, as I lay snug and temporarily safe under the warm covers. I found myself thinking over all the alternatives to the impossible and the unthinkable. People didn't simply disappear for over six years in the blink of an eye and return to find that the world had moved on without them. My task, therefore, was to discover a rational explanation for the strange events of the day before. Somehow, something or someone had altered my perception of what had happened after I'd exited that aeroplane. I merely had to discover who would want to do such a thing to me and why.

Scrunching my eyes tightly closed against the light that was filtering through the gold and black curtains, I curled into a ball, trying to think of at least one credible answer to my list of questions.

My mind began to snatch desperately at various scenarios. From what I'd heard, some con artists concocted elaborate scams to extort money from unsuspecting 'marks'. Apart from the worrying fact that it had been dark when I'd landed, someone could have superficially altered the state of the airfield, hidden my car to ensure I walked to the nearest – and only – refuge, which had been the pub, where they had plastered leaflets and posters of me as 'missing' and left a copy of a specially altered newspaper in a place where I couldn't fail to spot it, with the fictitious date on it.

It wasn't outside the realms of possibility that someone had drugged me before I'd jumped so that I was confused about the timings. Maybe after Graham, Ingrid and Kevin had exited the aircraft the pilot had flown somewhere else and returned to drop me over the airfield hours later to confuse and disorientate me. They'd certainly succeeded in doing that, I thought grimly. The question was why? I didn't have much to offer except my overdraft and credit card bills. So why would anyone want to do such a thing?

But then again, if the pilot had been involved, surely the jumpmaster had to have been in on it too? I recalled Matt's reasonably easy acceptance that it was me on the phone calling him from the pub. If I'd really been missing for six years wouldn't he have been more suspicious at a voice on the end of a phone claiming to be me? And it was Matt who had made sure I had his number in my pocket; he who could have insisted on taking me home last night to Calum or my parents, but didn't. And it was easy enough to get a haircut to give the appearance of having aged . . .

Giving a little groan of despair, I curled tighter into the ball, pulling the bedclothes right up over my head. I wanted to go home to Calum. I knew I would be safe there. I'd throw myself into his arms and he'd laugh and tell me not to be so silly – I was fit and well and had never really been missing at all.

Listening carefully for sounds on the stairs, I decided the safest course of action was to get up and dressed, pretending to Matt that I was still suckered in to his strange fantasy world, and make a break for it as soon as an opportunity arose. Swinging my legs out of the bed, I rested my bare feet on a luxurious wool rug before crossing the polished oak flooring to the bathroom.

Locking the door securely behind me, I spent several minutes in the shower, washing away the grime of the previous day before wrapping myself in a large black towel and padding my way back out into the bedroom.

Matt was standing in the middle of the room with a mug of tea in his hand. I gave a small squeal of fright and nearly dropped the towel. Grabbing it just in time I hung on to it tightly, staring at him with wide eyes. He grinned appreciatively when he saw me.

'Making yourself at home, I see.'

I felt the blood drain from my face and willed myself to sound normal. 'I hope you don't mind.'

He crossed to the bed and placed the mug on the bedside table. 'I'm glad you're already up. I was going to wake you. There's someone downstairs I think you might like to see.'

'Really? I didn't think anyone knew I was here?' I sat on the edge of the bed and sipped at the hot tea. 'Thank you for this, it's just what I needed.'

'I took the liberty of calling Kevin.'

'Kevin?' I was genuinely surprised. If Matt had gone to

all this trouble to lure me here, why would he have called someone I knew? Particularly someone who had been in the plane with me before I had been drugged and possibly kidnapped? It didn't make sense. 'You mentioned Kevin last night, but I honestly don't know him that well. He's only been at the company a few weeks and he keeps pretty much to himself.'

I watched him over the rim of the mug, wondering. Matt couldn't have concocted such an elaborate plan alone, he'd have needed help. Was it possible Kevin was involved too? Matt could have planted the boy at Wayfarer's Insurance company where we worked, to make sure he was with me during the charity parachute jump. A memory of the spotty nineteen-year-old lad shyly handing me a cup of coffee in the mess room half an hour or so before take-off planted itself in my mind. That would have been about the right sort of timing for a drug to kick in. Looking down into the mug in my hand now, I almost choked.

'Six years ago Kevin might have been something of a loner, but we're good friends now,' Matt was saying. 'He's got some wacky ideas, but he's a good guy at heart – and he has an amazing way with computers and technology.'

I handed the mug back to him with the tea half drunk and offered a strained smile.

He grinned at me. 'But I'll let him tell you all about it. Come down when you're dressed and join us for breakfast.'

When he'd gone I tried to remember every detail of the previous day. I recalled thinking how grey and drawn Kevin had looked – not that I could imagine him ever having a ruddy complexion with his pale freckly skin and reddish hair, but I'd put that down to nerves about the forthcoming jump and his hopeless infatuation with Ingrid. Had the pair of them invented some weird alternative reality for me?

Keeping a wary eye on the door, I slid open the top drawer of Matt's bedside cabinet. At first glance there didn't seem to be any clues hidden amongst the few personal bits and pieces, but then I noticed an envelope-sized piece of shiny white card in the corner looking tantalisingly up at me. Hearing nothing outside, I reached quickly in and drew the object out, turning it over in my hand.

A black and white photo of me smiled back at me. My chest tightened immediately and my breath caught in my throat. It was a copy of the snap Calum had taken the week before; the one that I imagined had been used on the posters I'd seen in the pub. With shaking hands I hastily put the offending article back into the drawer, sliding it tightly closed as if sealing the photo back into its place might lessen the impact of what it suggested.

I realised I couldn't sit there forever, I needed Matt and Kevin to think I was going along with their plan – whatever that was.

Eyeing the blue jumpsuit with distaste I pulled on yesterday's jeans and T-shirt, realising I had little option but to put them back on. It was either that or go downstairs looking like a temptress in a dolphin T-shirt. I shuddered at the thought of how easily the scenario they'd invented had had me jumping into the parachute instructor's bed.

'Idiot,' I mumbled to myself under my breath. As an after-thought I stepped back into the jumpsuit, wriggled it over my jeans and zipped it up to my neck.

Once dressed, I crept downstairs to find Matt standing with his back to me poring over a sheaf of papers at the kitchen counter, while a stocky man of about my own age sat at the breakfast bar, hunched over a fried breakfast. My gaze passed over him and rested on the back of Matt's head. I noticed the way his hair curled against his neck, just touching his shoulders, then tore my eyes reluctantly away, reminding myself that he was part of all this . . . whatever this was. And Calum was at home probably anxiously awaiting my return.

Switching my attention to the man, who definitely wasn't the Kevin I remembered, I watched as he scooped egg yolk onto the fried bread and forked it into his mouth with undisguised relish. He had the same reddish, curly hair as Kevin had had and the same pale face, sharp nose and freckles, but there the similarity ended.

Inching further into the room I stood awkwardly, not really knowing what to say. Shifting from one foot to the other, I managed what I hoped was a reasonably bright sounding, 'Hi.'

I couldn't have elicited a more dramatic reaction if I'd pulled the pin on a hand grenade and rolled it into the middle of the room. The man passing as Kevin looked up and stared at me. For a couple of seconds his eyes fixed on mine and then, as if in slow motion he dropped his fork onto the plate with a clatter, splattering drops of egg yolk onto the work top. He shot to his feet, eyes and mouth gaping and backed away from me as if expecting me to explode into a thousand tiny pieces.

Chapter Eight

Kevin stood there, ready for flight, his eyes squinting short-sightedly as though he ought to be wearing spectacles. He seemed to be taking in every minute detail of my appearance; my face, hair, the jumpsuit, right down to my bare feet. Eventually he wiped his mouth on the back of his hand and swallowed hard. '*Michaela*? Is it really you?'

He was a good actor – I had to give him that. His reaction had shocked me almost as much as I had seemed to surprise him. Having recoiled several steps when he'd leapt up, I held my ground near the foot of the stairs and returned his scrutiny, taking in his features and comparing them with the Kevin I knew. There was a little fleshy padding on his face and chin, which seemed to round off a narrow angular jaw. The extra weight on his face and body made him look altogether chunkier and more solid. This was a pretty good impression of what a scrawny teenager might look like as a mid-twenty-something who hadn't taken very good care of himself.

Clever.

Kevin approached slowly, his eyes taking on a gleam of excitement. 'It is you, isn't it? But where have you been? What did they do to you? Have you been kept in some sort of stasis? How did you get away?'

I glanced towards Matt and it was then that I saw what was written on the top of the pile of papers he'd had spread out in front of him. They looked like printouts from computer websites and the words that caught my eye, making my stomach churn afresh, were, 'Unexplained Abductions' and 'People who have disappeared'.

I sincerely hoped that Matt and Kevin were not going to try and convince me that I'd been abducted by aliens.

Kevin was still staring at me with a look of wonder on his face.

'I told you.' He turned to Matt with a grin of triumph. 'Everyone had me down as some sort of weirdo, but I was right all along.'

'Not everyone thought you were a weirdo,' Matt qualified. 'There's still quite a following out there for the abduction theory and the newspapers certainly latched onto the idea for a while.'

'But why didn't you tell me she was back? How long have you known?

'Only since last night,' Matt glanced at me apologetically. 'Michaela rang me from the Royal Oak and I brought her back here so she could get a good night's sleep. She didn't want me to take her to the police station and I thought she needed time to adjust before announcing her return.'

Kevin clutched his head. 'Man, are you telling me no one knows she's back yet?'

Matt shook his head. 'Just you and me and the landlord of the pub, though I don't think he figured out who she was.'

I looked from one of them to the other, wondering how they expected me to believe such nonsense. I cleared my throat. 'Excuse me, but I'd quite like to go home now – if you don't mind.'

'Aren't you going to tell us what happened to you?' Kevin had seated himself back on his stool and was picking up pages of the printouts. He waved a couple at me. 'We've waited six and a half years wondering how the hell you disappeared so completely.'

'I have no idea what you're talking about,' I said huffily. 'Yesterday I jumped out of an aeroplane and when I landed I found the airfield deserted and in apparent disrepair. But then you know that, don't you?'

Kevin looked at Matt, who shook his head. Turning back to me, he raised his eyebrows and his voice came out almost as a squeal. 'You mean you have no idea where you've been?'

I frowned, annoyed with myself for falling into the trap of forgetting to go along with their bizarre stories. 'Look, a joke's a joke, but I really do just want to go home.'

A look of concern crossed Matt's face and he pulled out a stool. 'Come and sit down, Michaela. Have some breakfast at least, you must be starving.'

I sat, partly because my legs were wobbling and partly because I realised I *was* hungry. I hadn't eaten since lunch in the mess room yesterday.

'What would you like, fruit, yoghurt?'

How did he know what I normally liked for breakfast, I asked myself? My eyes wandered longingly to the bacon and eggs however, and Matt laughed, turning to the frying pan where he laid out a row of bacon slices, which began to sizzle mouth-wateringly.

Kevin took the opportunity to push the paper entitled, 'People who have disappeared', under my nose. 'You're not the only one to have vanished without trace over the years'. He ran a stubby finger down the long list. 'Look, people have been disappearing for centuries.'

I felt my eyes stray towards the list. It began with an

account of the disappearance of Nefertiti, royal wife of the Pharaoh Akhenaten of Ancient Egypt in 1336 BC and continued with page upon page of unexplained disappearances right up to October 2008. Sifting through the pages I found an account of my own reported disappearance in 2002.

'Well they'll have to update their list now, won't they?' I shook my head and stuck out my chin. 'Whether or not I was perceived to be missing when this list was compiled, I'm certainly not missing now.'

'This is extraordinary!' Kevin breathed, rising to his feet and peering at me from every angle.

Kevin fished in his pocket and produced a mobile phone. 'Do you mind if I take a few pictures of you, maybe shoot a short film as you are now?'

I was puzzled. 'Where's the video camera?'

Kevin laughed. 'This is the camera. It's also my mobile and I can pick up emails on it too.' He pressed a few buttons and showed me how it worked.

I frowned. How had he got hold of technology like that? And it was all so small, not like my chunky mobile phone which I had left in my bag. Before I could protest, Matt pushed a plate of food in front of me and I picked up the knife and fork trying to ignore the nagging doubts that crowded into my head. Not only had both Matt and Kevin visibly aged, but it seemed technology had moved on too. No matter how I tried to deny it, everything kept pointing to the fact that something terrifying and inexplicable had occurred.

Kevin was holding the tiny mobile towards me, but I held up my hand. 'Please, don't.'

'Enough, Kevin,' Matt's voice was calm but authoritative. 'There's an awful lot for her to take on board. You can collect evidence later. Let her eat in peace.'

I finished the food in record time. Although famished, I kept thinking about Calum and Abbey and my mum and dad. Whether there was any truth in what Matt and Kevin were telling me or not, my family would be worried that I hadn't returned home last night at least. Glancing at my watch again, I pictured Calum trying to get Abbey ready for school; he'd have to make up her lunch box himself and was probably cussing at my absence. Wondering also about why my parents hadn't answered the phone the night before, I pictured Dad getting ready for a day at the bank where he had been manager for ten years; Mum rushing round getting their breakfast so they could eat together before he walked to the station. They would probably be talking about me, wondering why I hadn't reported in to tell them how the charity jump had gone.

I pushed the empty plate away with a sigh. 'I must ring Calum and my parents and let them know I'm OK.'

'Your parents? Didn't Matt tell . . . ?' Kevin began.

He broke off abruptly.

My head shot up. 'What? What haven't you told me?'

'Nothing,' Matt said hastily. 'Look, I'll drive you to Calum's house and we can talk on the way.'

Deciding he'd tell me anything he wanted in due course, I finished the meal with a pile of toast and marmalade and another cup of tea.

'I'm surprised all that stuff I've just eaten isn't banned in the new world of 2008,' I murmured sarcastically as I sat back, replete.

'It's frowned on, certainly,' Matt agreed. 'But I knew the promise of a good old-fashioned cholesterol-rich fry-up would bring Kevin scurrying over here without any questions.'

I almost laughed, but it was short lived. 'Look, I really do have to ring home.'

'You'll be back there before you know it.'

Recalling last night's string of abortive phone calls, I almost capitulated. 'You're probably right, but I have to try again. Can I borrow your phone?'

Kevin shot Matt a look.

'Go ahead,' Matt was holding out his mobile phone.

I punched in Calum's number and listened to it ring and ring unanswered. My parents' number produced the same effect and I began to feel uneasy all over again. I'd call work, I told myself, and if everything seemed normal there, I'd reconsider trying Calum or my parents again in a little while.

The call to Wayfarers confirmed my worst fears. A young girl answered my call but professed never to have heard of me. She reluctantly answered my anxious questions. It seemed she had been at the insurance company for two years and in that time most of the staff had changed. Graham had retired because of ill health several years before, she told me. She had never even heard of anyone called Ingrid Peters.

I disconnected and silently handed Matt the phone.

We left the house half an hour later. I sat in the front passenger seat of Matt's car, with the jumpsuit now folded and resting on my lap. I wanted to curl back into a ball and cry. Yesterday had been a glorious spring day, vibrant with the promise of summer, yet today it looked and smelled like autumn. Matt and Kevin would have had to be pretty amazing illusionists to have changed the seasons I realised. And if not con men, I thought miserably, then what? The feel of the borrowed toothbrush, the one tangible possession I had to my name, felt strangely comforting in my hand.

We sat in virtual silence as the car burnt up the miles towards Calum's house. Every so often I glanced at Matt's profile, taking in his even features with his prominent nose and designer stubble. He had programmed a kind of navigating device with the address and postcode of Calum's house before setting out. The thing was built into the car with a screen showing a map of the route. Every so often a robotic female voice would give instructions and Matt would turn right or left accordingly. I'd heard of the possibility of these satellite navigation gadgets; they already used GPS at sea, but I'd never seen one used in a car before. It was quite unsettling. Eventually however, Kevin, who was in the back seat, leaned forward and broke the silence.

'Are you sure you can't remember anything at all? Not even one itsy bitsy flash of a spaceship or a strange grey figure?'

'The dashboard of this car looks like a spaceship to me, but no, you've been reading too many abduction stories,' I admonished lightly. Turning round in my seat I looked him in the eye. 'I wasn't taken by aliens, Kevin. Those abduction stories were fabricated by the US military to cover up their research into new weapons and aircraft back in the fifties.'

'Try telling that to the thousands of abductees who swear they've been taken and experimented on!'

'Those accounts were probably caused by mass hysteria due to people watching too many science fiction films,' I told him firmly.

'What about all the disappearances that happened long before America was even discovered? According to this list, people have been going missing ever since records began.' Kevin leaned even further forwards. 'If you weren't taken, did you have a good reason to disappear, Michaela?'

'I need to fill up with bio diesel,' Matt butted in suddenly as the sign for a service station flashed by.

'I'm not even going to ask what that is.' I closed my eyes, folded my arms and slid down the seat, trying to stay invisible as he turned into the service slip road and pulled up by a pump. I heard the driver's door open and close as Matt got out and Kevin said quietly, 'You might sneer at it, but the abduction theory is what eventually saved Matt from being hounded by the press for your murder.'

Chapter Nine

My eyes snapped open again and I turned to look at Kevin in dismay. 'Was he really suspected of murdering me?'

'The most popular explanation for your disappearance was that Matt killed you in that plane after Graham, Ingrid and I jumped.' I noticed he kept a wary eye on Matt as he moved about outside the car. 'The theory being bandied about at the time was that once we had left the plane and he had you all to himself, he tried to assault you. You spurned his advances,' Kevin seemed to warm to the drama of his story, 'so he killed you and threw your body out over some water somewhere. As far as everyone else was concerned, what other scenario could there have been? You were last seen in that plane with him, there was no sign that you had landed anywhere, and you were never seen or heard of again. Well, until now, that is.'

For a moment I forgot that I was still trying to refuse to believe a word of what he or Matt was saying. My face paled at the thought of what he'd been accused of. 'I'm so sorry.'

'Once the papers got hold of the fact that he'd been asked to help the police with their enquiries, the media hounded him for months. We'd all been questioned extensively of course, but my alibi and Graham and Ingrid's were water-tight. We were visibly in the air until we landed and once on the ground we were surrounded by airfield personnel. We all swore you had been fine when we exited the aircraft. For a while, every time I set foot outside my door there were flash-bulbs going off in my face, reporters shoving microphones under my nose. But for Matt it was much worse. The police had no evidence of foul play and the pilot absolutely denied that anything untoward had happened inside the aircraft, but the press publicly tried Matt and found him guilty. Mud sticks, Michaela. He had his instructor's licence taken away and he lost his job. It wasn't a good time until I got in touch with the papers and offered them a new theory to sink their teeth into.'

I glanced up at him. 'The abduction theory, I assume?'

'You got it. Aliens have their uses, babe.'

I nearly laughed at Kevin's peculiar use of the English language, but I could tell from his lack of diplomacy that he was still almost as socially inept as he had been as a gangling teenager.

I watched idly as Matt headed across to the pay station, pausing to pick up a newspaper from the display before going inside. I wondered at the strange friendship between these two men. One was handsome, confident and in control; the other, who was busy breathing stale bacon fumes down my neck, was ill-at-ease and seemed uncomfortable in his own body.

'I'm surprised he didn't whisk you off to the nearest police station to clear his name and repair his ruined reputation,' Kevin commented as Matt walked over to us. 'If it was me, I wouldn't just take you home and let bygones be bygones. I'd want you up there on a podium with hundreds of journal-ists, making a statement and shouting my innocence to the world.'

Matt climbed back into the car and tossed the newspaper

onto my lap. Kevin fell silent as I picked it up and looked at the date. There was no doubt about it, it was genuine; I had seen him buy it. The date was Tuesday 21 October 2008. Staring blankly ahead I folded my arms and sat back as he turned the key in the ignition and headed back onto the motorway.

It was only when Matt drew the car up outside Calum's house that the nerves really struck home. Eyeing the familiar tall, thin semi-detached house with its narrow front garden shaded by overgrown shrubs and brambles, I felt a sudden reluctance to leave the safety of the car. The untidiness of the garden struck a jarring chord. Neither Calum nor I were keen gardeners but we did keep the property under control between us. Only the previous weekend we had given the lawn its first cut of the season. Now there was an old banger with peeling paint parked amidst long, tangled grass and overgrown weeds.

'Is Calum alright? Nothing terrible has happened to him, has it?'

'Not as far as we know.' Matt was staring at me. 'I really think it would be better if we went to the police station before you tell your boyfriend you're back. We have to let the authorities know you are safe.'

'I want to see Calum. I want to hear from him that I've been missing for six and a half years.' I'd tossed the jump-suit and the toothbrush onto the back seat some time ago and sat with my hands clenched in my lap, suddenly not sure if I could face him after all. At least it was a Tuesday, I reminded myself, and Abbey would be at school so I'd have Calum to myself for a few hours. He would hold me safely in his arms and everything would be alright again. 'I must go in and see him,' I tried again, this time with a little more conviction.

'You can have two hours,' Matt said firmly. 'After that, we're calling the police.'

'Must the police be involved?' I pleaded. 'I simply want to go home and be left in peace. Surely I'm entitled to that?'

'Matt simply wants to clear his name,' Kevin countered. 'After what he went through surely *he's* entitled to *that*.'

'Leave it, Kevin,' Matt gave him a severe look and Kevin fell silent.

'OK, two hours.' I sighed deeply and rested my hand on the car door handle. My body quaked at the prospect of seeing Calum again. I wanted to see him with all my heart, but that same heart hammered with apprehension. This was the moment of truth, the moment when I discovered whether the last few hours had been some elaborate hoax or whether something truly unthinkable had happened.

The catch on the gate was still as stiff as I'd remembered and it opened with a small familiar clunk. At least something hadn't changed, I thought, biting back a faintly hysterical laugh. By the time I reached the house and climbed the two steps to the front door my hands were clenched clammily at my sides. I glanced back at the sound of Matt's car pulling away and his departure left me with an unaccountable feeling of abandonment. I swallowed and stared impotently at the door. I could hear the doorbell ringing inside the house and waited anxiously. Calum's office was at the top of the house and it would take him a few minutes to come down. When at last I heard footsteps in the passage and the catch being pulled back, my breath caught in my throat with anticipation.

The door opened and I thought at first that the man standing before me was a complete stranger. The Calum I'd left the previous morning had dark unruly hair and blue eyes set in a handsome face. He had always dressed with care, and even when working at home he'd been a stickler for neatness and order; I'd always teased him, it was probably a throwback from his strict Scottish upbringing.

This Calum had dark circles under his eyes, the once glossy hair dull and lacklustre. He seemed pale as a ghost. He peered at me from tired eyes and then those eyes widened in recognition and fixed on me in shock. He clutched the doorframe as if to stop himself from reeling backwards. 'Michaela? Oh my God. Is it really you?'

His reaction was as violent in its own way as Kevin's had been. It sent my last hopes plummeting to the depths of my stomach where the butterflies crash-landed in a sickening heap.

'It's me,' I confirmed, standing stock still. This man was a stranger; I didn't feel at one with him at all. Not only did he look haggard but he also smelled faintly stale and musty as if he'd just crawled out of bed. The gloomy interior behind him didn't look or smell much better.

He stared at me for a moment or two then seemed to pull himself together. His mouth settled into a grim line as he stepped back and beckoned me inside. 'You'd better come in.'

After one last glance at the empty road behind me, I followed the man I had lived with into the house I had called home. It was unrecognisable.

The once cosy sofa in the sitting room, where Abbey and I had sat only a couple of days ago and pored over her homework, and Calum and I had curled up to watch TV together, was covered with a filthy throw; it appeared that someone had spilled tomato ketchup and nacho crumbs over it and no one had bothered to wash it. The coffee table was full of half-eaten pizza in greasy boxes. Beer and coke cans littered the floor. I spotted a couple of empty whisky bottles stashed behind the television set. When I continued to stand, Calum rounded on me with what seemed to be a mixture of anger and confusion.

'I don't know whether to hug you or throw you back out the door. I thought you were dead.' He rubbed his throat where the top button of a blue, checked shirt gaped open, and slowly shook his head from side to side. He sank suddenly onto the sofa as if his legs could no longer support him and sat staring up at me with an incredulous expression on his tired face. 'So where the bloody hell have you been for the last six and a half years?'

'I haven't been anywhere.' I adjusted my weight awkwardly from one foot to the other, uncomfortable looking down at him but not sure if he would want me to sit down. 'I don't know how to explain this, but I've just come back from the airfield.'

He stared at me in silence, his angry eyes roaming from my dark blonde hair to the tips of my toes. 'What do you want?'

'I don't want anything ... at least I don't know what I want, except to come home. I wanted to see you, that's all.'

'You wanted to see me? After all this time? After letting us search fruitlessly for you for months and months, putting our lives on hold as we hoped and prayed you'd turn up alive, never wanting to give up hope of seeing you again? Letting us grieve for you ... ?' He shot to his feet with surprising speed and stood with his face inches from mine. 'Have you any idea what you've put us through?'

I took a step back. 'I'm beginning to realise, yes.'

'You really are something else.' He began to pace up and down in front of me. 'I think I preferred you dead.'

'Look, I'm sorry, Calum. I didn't mean to leave you or Abigail. If you'd just listen, I'll try to explain.'

He stopped pacing and stared at me, waiting. The hurt in his eyes cut me to the core. 'It had better be bloody good.'

Chapter Ten

I twisted my hands together wishing Calum would sit back down so that I could sink onto that filthy couch too. I wasn't sure my legs would hold me up much longer. Swallowing, I cleared my throat. 'Something weird happened during the jump. There was a strange wind, more like a hurricane really. It sort of enveloped me, and when I landed on the airfield it was dark and there was no one there.' I stumbled to a halt, aware that he didn't believe a word I was saying. Taking a deep breath I ploughed on. 'That was only yesterday. I know it sounds far-fetched, but it was truly only yesterday that it happened! As far as I'm concerned I haven't been away at all. I got a lift back here from a pub by the airfield and the newspapers say it's 2008 and I'm so confused . . .' My voice tapered off lamely. 'I just wanted to come home to you and Abigail.'

He reached out and tentatively laid his hand on my arm. I realised that some of the anger had melted away and his shoulders were sagging tiredly. 'I don't know what's happened to you, Michaela, but if you really believe what you've just told me, you should get help.'

'I'm not mad, if that's what you think. Matt and Kevin believe me.'

'Matt? Are you talking about that bloody parachute

instructor?' He dropped his hand as if I might contaminate him somehow. 'I *knew* he had something to do with your disappearance. Your parents were convinced of it too, but the police couldn't pin anything on him.' He furrowed his brow and peered into my eyes. 'Was it him all along? Have you been with him all this time?'

'No! It was nothing like that.'

'Has he been holding you somewhere against your will?'

'No! It happened like I told you. Matt just dropped me back here but he wasn't involved.'

'Where is he now?'

I shrugged feeling rather like a naughty child being confronted by an angry parent. 'I suppose he's gone back home.'

'And would you happen to know where "home" might be for Mr Innocent?'

'Not really.'

'Come on, Michaela. You can't expect me to believe that. Has he tired of you? Is that why you've come crawling back here?'

'I haven't been with him!' I insisted, blushing at the memory of the previous night and my having begged to be allowed to stay in Matt's room. 'Look, I'm sorry for everything you've been through, I'm sorry you thought I was dead, but from my perspective I left here only yesterday morning.' I lowered my voice, trying to regain some semblance of control. 'I tried phoning you from the pub to ask you to come and fetch me, but no one answered. Matt's number was in the pocket of my jumpsuit, so I rang him and he brought me back here.'

I decided not to mention sleeping in Matt's bed; it had been a stupid mistake anyway. 'Where were you when I needed you?'

Calum sank down on the sofa again, this time shaking his head. I decided to risk perching on the arm next to him. We sat in silence for a moment or two and then he turned and looked at me more closely. 'You don't look any older.'

'That's because you only saw me yesterday.'

'Yesterday,' he said bitterly, 'I was at the hospital with my daughter, who was found lying comatose in the park by some boy and taken to the accident and emergency department in Guildford to have her stomach pumped.'

'Oh, Calum, I'm sorry. Is Abbey going to be alright?'

He ran a hand wearily over his eyes and I understood now why he looked so tired and drawn. 'Abbey's in with a bad crowd. They call themselves emo's or something like that. They seem to be into very loud music, alcohol, smoking, self-abuse; you name it. I appear to be enemy number one, and I don't know how to help her.'

I pictured the bright, cheeky child I had said goodbye to and felt a pang of regret that I hadn't been around for her. 'Please tell me this isn't my fault.'

He shook his head again. 'It didn't help, you abandoning her after she'd already lost her natural mother, but I won't lay this at your door. I've been looking after her for the last six years; if there's any fault to be found it's probably mine.' He gazed round the filthy room and shrugged. 'I always encouraged her to bring her friends back here – I thought it was better to know where she was and who she was with – but they use the place like a doss house. I suppose I should employ a cleaner as Abbey refuses to clear up, but money is tight at the moment.'

'Abbey and her friends did this?' I looked round at the chaos with fresh eyes. 'Don't you supervise her at all?'

He shrugged. 'She's not a child any more. When she

bothers to get out of bed in the mornings she goes to college and I suppose I've let her do her own thing. No one supervised me when I was that age. Anyway I have to work to keep this roof over our heads.'

I put a hand to my head. Of course, Abbey's birthday was at the end of October. She'd still been ten and a half in the April when I'd left for the jump, which made her sixteen, almost seventeen now.

I ran a hand over my face. 'Oh, Calum.'

'Don't you dare judge me, not after running out on us like that.' I could hear the anger rising in his voice again.

'I'm not judging you. It sounds as if you've done your best.' We subsided into silence once more but at least he wasn't throwing me out into the street. 'Look, I only came to tell you I'm back before you found out from the police or the newspapers or something.'

'You expect me to believe that?'

I shrugged. 'It's the truth. And I really am sorry. I didn't mean to leave you, Calum. And the parachute jump itself wasn't that dangerous anyway, I survived it, didn't I?'

'It seems so.'

'Look, I think I'd better go.' I got to my feet. 'Could I use your phone to call my mum? She or Dad could come and collect me.'

He reached out unexpectedly and caught my hand. 'Do you really not know about your parents?'

My heart pounded as I looked at him. I suddenly remembered Kevin's comment at Matt's house earlier. 'What about them?'

'There's no easy way to say this. Your father died four years ago; two years after you went missing.'

I stared at him as the words sunk in. Then I gave a strangled cry and put my face in my hands. 'No!' Dad couldn't be dead, I thought; how could that be? He'd always been so full of life, such a constant part of my existence. I thought of the dashing rather handsome middle aged man who had been the centre of my universe when I'd been growing up.

'At the beginning he and your mother flatly refused to believe you were dead.' Calum was continuing as if the bottom hadn't just dropped out of my world. 'After the police enquiry went cold they spent all their waking hours putting up posters and leaflets, asking people if they'd seen you. Your father's heart gave out suddenly one day while he was out for the umpteenth time questioning people who lived in out-lying areas near the airfield. They took him to the hospital but he was pronounced dead on arrival. Your mother thought he didn't put up much of a fight, because he was ready to die . . . to go to you.' It was an accusation. 'I think even he gave up on you at the very end.'

The tears I'd been holding back flowed freely down my face now and were dripping off the end of my chin. 'I must go to Mum.'

Calum lowered his eyes and looked away, his face taut.

'What?' I cried in alarm as I saw the discomfort in his face. 'What else has happened?'

'Your mother never really recovered after losing you. When your father died, it was too much for her and she retreated into a world of her own. She's suffering from clinical depression and is in a nursing home for the mentally ill, Kaela. Your parents' house was sold to pay for it.'

I registered his use of my nickname, the name my family and close friends used.

I looked up at him with my tear-stained face and realised he was observing me with some sympathy now, the earlier hostility gone, or at least tucked away out of sight.

'Where is this home? Can you give me the address?'

'You don't have to go straight away, Kaela. Maybe you should sit a while to get over the shock.'

'I thought you wanted me gone.' I was angry now, my head reeling from his revelations.

He pressed his fingertips to his forehead and shook his head. 'I never wanted you gone, Kaela. There was a time I'd have given anything to have you back, to feel your body against mine again. I just can't get my head round the fact that you've been out there, alive and well all this time; that your parents were right all along.'

'I didn't leave any of you on purpose.' I was furiously sniffing back the tears. 'I cared about you, Calum. I adored you from the first moment I met you.' I lowered my voice an octave. 'Do you remember you were wearing that strange quilted waistcoat under your jacket like Colin Firth in *Bridget Jones's Diary*? I still feel like that about you. As far as I'm concerned I climbed out of your bed only yesterday morning. I don't know where the last six years have gone.' I sighed wretchedly. 'And I'm having trouble assimilating everything you've told me.' I gazed miserably into space feeling almost totally numb.

He lowered his hands and stared at me again as if trying to decide whether I might be telling the truth. I returned his look as calmly as possible, though the tears were still running down my face.

'If you truly believe that, then as I said earlier, you need to see someone, Kaela. And the police should be informed that you are alive and well.'

I found I could barely think, but made a supreme effort to pull myself together. 'Matt and Kevin have given me two hours before they call the police. I insisted on seeing you first.'

He bristled again at the mention of Matt's name, but then seemed to give in.

'And I haven't been very hospitable. I think I'm still in shock. Do you still want to see Abbey before you go?'

Tearing my thoughts away from the plight of my parents I tried to stay focused. 'What will Abbey make of me being back?'

'At the moment she's not in any state to say anything. She's still sleeping off the effects of last night.'

'And when she wakes up?'

'She'll probably hate you,' he said with the beginnings of a sympathetic smile. 'She seems to hate everyone at the moment, but deep down she really misses you. I think she thought you'd left because of her behaviour towards you.'

'Have you taken her to see anyone, to get professional help?'

Calum looked at me blankly and I assumed he hadn't. That poor child, I thought. First losing her real mother and then being left to think I'd abandoned her because of something she'd done.

At that moment the door to the sitting room opened and a strange apparition appeared in the doorway. The creature was dressed in a long, black, jagged hemmed skirt, which ended above the ankles, revealing what looked like army issue boots. Her top half was barely covered by a skimpy black and purple top. Her hair, part of which was piled high on her head in a messy fifties bee-hive, was dyed jet black with purple streaks. But it wasn't so much the hair or the deathly make-up and eyebrow and nose piercings that made me stare, but the terrible self-inflicted scars and tattoos which were etched into both her arms.

'Abbey?'

Her eyes rested on mine beneath their thick kohl liner

and widened in shock. Her already chalk white face blanched even further, and clutching one hand to her mouth and the other to her stomach, she turned and threw up all over the carpet.

Chapter Eleven

The mop and bucket were exactly where I'd kept them when I'd lived here a day – or was it six years – ago.

After helping Calum hoist Abigail to her feet and over to the couch, where she watched me in shocked silence, I set to cleaning up the mess on the floor. Presumably because she'd already had her stomach forcibly emptied at the hospital, it didn't take too long before the only evidence of her sickness was nothing more than a damp, rather brighter patch on the otherwise filthy carpet.

Once I'd washed my hands in the kitchen sink, I went over to the girl and squeezed down beside her as she lay on the couch with her knees drawn up to her chest.

'Abigail?' I ventured.

She turned her head away, ignoring me.

'I want you to know that I didn't mean to leave you,' I tried. 'I was happy living here with you and your father. I would never have done that to you on purpose . . .'

With shaking hands she picked up the TV remote control, turned the box on and flicked through the daytime channels, cranking the volume up high.

I sighed, realising that attempting to reason with her was a losing battle.

'Abbey!' Calum strode over to his daughter and tried to

snatch the control out of her hand, but she evaded him deftly. He tried once more then turned to me defeated, and shrugged helplessly over the noise, 'Shall we go to the kitchen?'

I could see from that short exchange that Calum had definitely lost the battle to keep control of his daughter. Following Calum to the kitchen, I realised that my one-time family need no longer be my business. In the space of a day my mature hero-figure had turned into a stranger. His daughter, my one-time nemesis, was in the throes of killing herself. Pausing in the passage, I glanced towards the front door. All I had to do was walk through it to be out of their lives forever.

Glancing back through the open living room door to where Abbey was slouched weakly on the sofa, I caught her watching me. As soon as she realised I'd seen her, her eyes flicked back to the television, but not before I'd seen the pool of stark despair in them.

I thought of yesterday morning when I'd woken her up with a glass of orange juice and told her that her father would be taking her to school as I had to leave early for my journey down to Kent – and her shrug of feigned indifference as she'd turned over to go back to sleep. But minutes before I'd climbed into my jeep, she had appeared at my elbow in the driveway with her homework diary in her hand.

'Will you sign it, Kaela?'

I'd been nervous about the jump and a little short with her as I'd thrown my bag and fleece jacket onto the passenger seat. 'Can't your father do it?'

She'd shrugged. 'My friends' mums all sign theirs.'

I'd narrowed my eyes as I searched her face, which was fresh and innocent from sleep, hope filling my heart with her words. Had she accepted me at last? But time and the promise of adventure were pressing.

I'd smiled at her as I'd scribbled my signature, thinking that maybe at last we had the foundations of something we could build on. 'I'll see you later, off you go and finish getting ready or you'll be late for school.'

She'd stood for a moment, watching my car creep down the long narrow drive, and then I was out into the traffic, forgetting everything but the adventure that lay ahead of me, never thinking that I would return anywhere but here to the two people I had intended to remain with for the rest of my life.

It was unbelievable that Dad was gone and Mum was languishing in a nursing home somewhere. As soon as Calum and I had thrashed out whatever was left between us, I would go to see her, though what I would say, I didn't know.

As it happened I didn't have the chance to continue where Calum and I had left off. I was halted in my tracks halfway across the passage by an urgent pounding on the front door. The noise even surpassed the racket Abbey was listening to in the room behind me. Rooted to the spot, I watched as Calum hurried past me and threw the door open to reveal two burly uniformed police officers standing, fists raised, on the front step.

'Mr Calum Sinclair?'

I watched as Calum took an involuntary step backwards. 'Yes.'

A slim blonde woman, wearing a plain grey skirt suit swept past the two officers, brandishing an identification card. 'DI Sandra Smith,' she announced. 'We have reason to believe you are holding a young woman on the premises . . .' She stopped in mid sentence and peered at me through the gloom of the hallway, a note of surprise creeping into her voice. 'Michaela Anderson?'

I nodded and the woman blinked behind a pair of rimless glasses as if having to reassess the situation. Frowning she held out her hands in a placating manner, palms down, neatly manicured fingers splayed. 'Don't be afraid, Michaela. We have come to help you.'

'How did you know I was here?'

'The Kent police received a tip off from a member of the public early this morning. Because your disappearance was originally handled jointly by both forces and is now considered a cold case, they handed this end of it to us.'

I pictured the friendly barman waking up and suddenly realising where he'd seen me before.

'It took us a while to authenticate the report and look up your file, but I personally decided that after all this time it might not be another hoax sighting.' She lowered her voice, presumably to make it less intimidating. 'You are safe now. We need you to come with us, Michaela.'

The two uniformed officers stepped into the hall and confronted Calum, who was standing with his mouth slightly open. 'We'd like you to accompany us to the station please, sir.'

'What?' Calum was spluttering and despite everything, I felt desperately sorry for him. The last six years had not been kind to him. It was obvious he'd had very little sleep the night before while Abbey had been in the hospital, then there had been the shock of my reappearance, and now it seemed he was under arrest.

'He had nothing to do with this,' I told the DI. I had no idea what 'this' was exactly, but I did know that I didn't want Calum getting the blame. 'I've only been here an hour. This has nothing to do with him.'

'We'll take your statement later, Michaela,' the DI said, taking my arm. 'Don't worry about it now.'

The DI guided me towards the door. The two police officers were already marching Calum out of the house.

He was protesting, trying to twist free of the police officer's grip. 'Wait! I can't leave Abbey – that's my daughter. She's only sixteen and she's not well.'

The sitting room door flew open and Abbey stood in the doorway, clutching the doorframe for support. 'What's going on?'

The DI paused, taking in the girl's pale face, multiple piercings and tattoos. 'Who are you?'

'I'm Abigail Sinclair. That's my father! What are you doing to him?'

'We need your father to help us with our enquiries into the disappearance of Miss Anderson,' the DI said shortly. 'We are taking him to the station for questioning.'

Abbey turned wide beseeching eyes on her father. 'Dad?'

'It'll be alright, Abbey,' Calum said, although he certainly didn't look too confident at that moment, his thin frame flanked by the two officers. 'I'll be back in no time at all.'

'Is there anyone who can stay with Miss Sinclair?' DI Smith asked of the captive Calum.

'No there's only her and me.' He shot an accusing glance at me. 'I'm all she's got.'

'Very well,' The DI turned to Abbey. 'You had better come with us.'

A woman police constable was waiting outside by two police cars, which were parked across the end of the driveway. The two male officers stowed Calum into the back of the first one, while Abbey and I were helped into the rear seats of the second. DI Smith climbed into the front seat, the WPC took the wheel and the police cars nosed away from the kerb in tandem and out into the traffic.

All the way to the police station, Abbey stared fixedly out of the side window, her face turned away from me. I could feel the tension emanating from her thin frame. The residual sickly sweet smell of stale marijuana smoke seeped from her hair and clothing and I wondered if DI Smith would notice. When the cars drew up outside an ugly rectangular building, both Abbey and I faltered as we climbed out into the chill autumnal air.

I felt Abbey shiver and reached out to her but she threw me a murderous look and stepped out of my reach. The DI took my arm and guided me towards the glass cubicle which served as an entrance. Once inside she pressed a buzzer, a door opened and as it swung closed behind us I had the ominous sensation that I was a prisoner.

We were taken down a long corridor, lit by overhead fluorescent lighting. Doors opened off on each side and as we passed one which was ajar, I glanced inside and almost gave an exclamation of recognition, because in that fleeting glimpse I saw Matt sitting slumped at an interview table, his head in his hands. I paused in mid stride, but the WPC whisked me quickly past and I heard the door slam behind me.

The sound rang in my ears like the clanging shut of a prison gate and my stomach gave a lurch of unease. Perhaps if I closed my eyes, I thought, this would all go away. I would wake up in my own bed; the double bed I shared with Calum, and it would be yesterday morning again and I would decide not to do the stupid parachute jump after all. I would call in sick like my other colleagues had done, and I'd take Abbey to school like a proper step-mum and then spend the day with Calum or visiting my parents; a nice normal day in which the world wouldn't suddenly turn upside down so I didn't know which way was up.

Chapter Twelve

An hour later I found myself sitting on a squishy sofa in a deceivingly comfortable room, nursing a colourful mug of hot, sweet tea. I had been taken from the police station by a second WPC and driven to what looked from the outside to be a small residential house where I had been issued with a disposable all-in-one suit while my clothes were sent to forensics for checking. There was a watercolour picture of a group of shells on the wall, which my eyes kept straying to; pink and beige spirals that interlinked and overlapped. I remembered reading about the Fibonacci sequence and how everything on the planet was designed to the exact specifications of the golden rule: phi or 1.6181. The pattern made by sunflower seeds, the measurements of a dolphin from snout to tail, and those spiral shells were just a tiny example. I was glad to have something other than my present dilemma to occupy my mind and fell to thinking that if there was a grand designer of that pattern, then what else could they be responsible for?

The shell painting, I was sure, had been specifically designed to put traumatised young women using the rape suite at ease, but my mind was far from easy. By what great design had I possibly lost six years of my life in the space of a day? Was it design, I wondered, or an accident?

I wanted to go home, but with my parents gone and Calum believing that I had abandoned him, I wasn't sure where home might be for me now. It was a sobering thought to add to the rest of my problems but I refused to allow it to overwhelm me. I had to try and keep some semblance of control or I might go mad.

To keep my mind from dissolving into self pity I looked at the shells again and remembered the holiday Calum and I had taken the summer before, when we'd first been dating. He had been a keen body-boarder and had wanted me to experience the adrenalin rush and the powerful feel of conquering the might of the sea. I had loved the idea and we had taken Abbey with us to Cornwall, and watched her build sandcastles on the beach as we paddled out on our boards through the bracingly cold water.

The first couple of runs had gone well and we had whooped for joy as our boards flew towards the beach, turning and hurrying back out with each successful run to catch the next big wave. But then the sea had become choppy. A few of the bigger waves ran into each other and I felt myself caught in one of the undertows for which the area was renowned. No matter how hard I paddled my board, the sea was stronger. I was soon swallowing salt water, gasping for breath and tiring quickly in the cold water, despite my wet suit.

And then Calum had been at my side. 'Just keep your head above the water,' he'd told me as my limbs began to numb with cold. 'You have to fight until the lifeguards come and rescue us.' And I realised he'd risked his own life by coming to my aid. We trod water, spitting salt, concentrating on keeping our heads above the breaking waves, while the current bore us irrevocably further from the beach.

Eventually the rescue dinghy came for us and we were hauled aboard by two strong life guards, shivering, exhausted and grateful to be alive. When we got to the beach I could barely stand, but I was aware of the crowd that had gathered to watch, and Abbey crying inconsolably.

Calum, Abbey and I had clung shakily together. Looking back, I wondered if almost dying together was what had cemented our fledgling relationship into something more solid so quickly after our first meeting. Within two months I had moved in with him and we became a couple, but it was the last time we had gone body-boarding; the last time Calum and I had taken any sort of risk – until I had done the parachute jump. And look where that had got me.

The door opened and DI Smith walked in followed by a woman of Asian descent, wearing a skirt suit very similar in design to the DI's but in a pale lilac colour, which flattered her dark complexion. I had intended to remain aloof and distant, knowing that no one was going to believe what I had to say anyway, but when the DI introduced me to Dr Soram Patel I warmed to her immediately, with her soft compassionate eyes and gentle smile.

Dr Patel was a police doctor and SOTO officer, which apparently stood for Sexual Offences Trained Officer. I wasn't sure why they were treating me as a possible rape victim, when I'd made no comment or complaint that I had been abused by anyone. I'd tried telling DI Smith that several times, but she'd merely smiled patiently and told me it was best to get me properly checked out so they knew what they were dealing with. 'We would like you to tell us everything you remember about the last six and a half years,' DI Smith said shortly.

'In your own time,' Dr Patel added with an encouraging smile.

So I told them mostly what I remembered from the moment I left Calum's house on the day of the jump, to the time DI Smith had come banging on his front door, discreetly leaving out the bit about my having spent the night in Matt's bed. 'So you see, neither Matt, nor Calum had anything to do with it,' I finished, settling back into the softness of the sofa, relieved that for better or for worse, my story had been told.

'How did you come by the cut on your hand?'

'I told you, I nicked it on something when I climbed into the plane just before the jump.'

The two women exchanged glances.

'Have you heard of hostage dependency syndrome?' Dr Patel asked softly.

'You mean when a person who has been held against their will, becomes emotionally fixated on their captor?' I felt the first tug of the underlying current snatching at me.

The two women nodded in unison.

'One would have had to be kidnapped for that to happen,' I replied, eyeing them both with suspicion. 'I've just told you I wasn't kidnapped, held anywhere against my will or even beamed up by a spaceship. I don't know what happened to me.'

'We have to allow for the possibility that your perceptions of recent events have somehow been altered.' DI Smith said shortly.

'The human mind is complex and works at more than the one level of consciousness,' Soram Patel explained more gently.

Icy waves began to wash over my head. What were they getting at?

'You mean I could have been brainwashed?'

'Not brainwashed. Though there is the possibility of self-induced amnesia caused by prolonged trauma,' the doctor replied. 'With your permission, I would like to do some psychological tests on you. It may help establish your mental state and give you some much needed answers.'

'And if I don't give my permission?' I could feel the current tugging me forcibly out to sea.

'It would be much easier for us and for you, if you co-operated fully.' DI Smith crossed her arms over her chest and sat back in her chair.

I glanced at the door, remembering that I had nowhere left to run. Calum and Abigail obviously didn't want me back, and if Calum had been telling the truth, my family home had been sold when my mother had been committed to the institution.

'I haven't even seen my mum yet,' I said out loud. I was grabbing at straws, hoping to elicit their sympathy. 'Calum told me that my father died four years ago and my mother is in some kind of nursing home.'

Dr Patel nodded, tapping the notes in front of her. 'That is the case I'm afraid.'

'Could I speak to Calum?' I assumed he was still being questioned at the main police station and hoped they'd take me back there. No matter what he thought of me, I had hoped to find him by my side, being there with me even at the expense of his own safety.

'Mr Sinclair has been allowed to leave,' DI Smith replied. 'We haven't charged him with anything so he left with his daughter.'

I could see from her expression that this must have been a disappointment to her. It was a severe disappointment to me; he had left me on my own to sink or swim.

I remembered that Calum hadn't been the only person dragged off to the police station because of me. 'What about Matt?' I asked in a tremulous voice.

'Mr Matthew Treguier is still helping us with our enquiries.'

I realised with a jolt that I hadn't even known Matt's surname. Matt Treguier . . . I toyed with the name, letting it flow over my lips. Then I saw Dr Patel watching me intently and I closed my mouth with a snap. Matt was in enough trouble because of me.

But it was too late. Like the vastness of the ocean, this institution was bigger and infinitely more powerful than me. DI Smith narrowed her pale eyes behind those glasses, her expression intent. I remembered what she'd said about hostage dependency and realised I'd been swept right into her clutches.

'Can you tell us about your feelings for Mr Treguier?' Dr Patel asked in that deceptively soft voice. 'Do you feel responsible for him, protective of him, perhaps?'

'I hardly know him,' I replied.

'Then how do you account for the fact that the jumpsuit you were wearing when you went missing over six years ago has been found, along with a toothbrush, which we are currently testing for your DNA, in the back of Mr Treguier's car?'

I felt as if a particularly icy wave had slapped me in the face. I'd forgotten to mention in my statement that I'd brought the jumpsuit back with me from Kent when recounting the incredible events of the previous day.

'I put them there.' I tried to regain some semblance of control. 'Matt hasn't done anything wrong. Ask Kevin – he was with us.'

'Would that be Mr Kevin Wheeler?'

'Yes.'

Dr Patel leaned towards me, her expression intense. 'And what can you tell us about your relationship with Kevin?'

The DI gave a triumphant smile as I reeled backwards, shocked that every word that escaped my lips seemed to implicate someone else. 'We were rather hoping you would mention Mr Wheeler. He's been of interest to us for some time. He was one of the last people to see you before you disappeared, I believe?'

I nodded reluctantly. My case had been left open and now they could see a chance of solving a six-year-old mystery; a statistic to add to their end-of-year clean up rate.

'Can you tell us why Mr Wheeler might be in possession of an unusual amount of documentation concerning your disappearance?'

'He was interested in what happened to me, I suppose. It seems my so-called disappearance did make quite an impact on his life.'

'An *obsessive* amount of documentation,' DI Smith declared as if I hadn't spoken. Her eyes watched me closely for a reaction. 'Newspaper cuttings, photos of you, computer printouts of other disappearances; the sort of collection someone with an unhealthy interest in your case might accumulate. He and Mr Treguier are friends, I believe?'

'I think they have become friends recently – since the jump. They had never met each other prior to the day ... it ... happened.'

The DI leaned forward, her eyes fixed on mine. 'Would you be surprised to learn that Mr Wheeler *did* know Mr Treguier before you and your other colleagues went down to the airfield that day?'

A picture of the four of us – Graham, Kevin, Ingrid and me – arriving at the airfield and being introduced to our instructor swam before my eyes. Neither Matt nor Kevin had given any indication of having already met.

'I don't believe it.'

'We have records showing that Kevin Wheeler had already completed a static line jump the week *before* he went with you to the airfield on the day you vanished. According to the parachute company's log book, Mr Treguier was his instructor.'

Calum had told me to fight, but the breakers just kept toppling over my head. No matter what I said, no one was going to believe me. They'd decided I'd been kidnapped by Matt or Kevin, or both. I gulped in a desperate breath of air. Hadn't I fleetingly suspected both Matt and Kevin myself? Perhaps it was time to give up the battle and simply sink beneath the waves. Maybe DI Smith and Dr Patel's theory was right and I had been drugged and abducted by Matt and Kevin and simply couldn't remember anything about it. After all, it wasn't as if I had a better explanation . . .

Chapter Thirteen

The defeated, sinking feeling lasted no more than a few minutes. Pulling myself upright, I lifted my chin and looked DI Smith in the eye. Fight, Calum, my one-time hero had said. He might not be fighting in my corner any more, but that didn't mean I had to give up.

'I've always prided myself on being a good judge of character,' I said stubbornly. 'Whatever happened to me during that parachute jump, I don't think either Matt or Kevin had anything to do with it. If Kevin sneaked a surreptitious lesson before the rest of us went down, it was more likely that he didn't want to make a fool of himself in front of Ingrid.'

'Ingrid?

'Ingrid Peters. We work . . . worked together. I think Kevin has . . . oh, for goodness sake *had,* a crush on her. In all likelihood he probably thought if he had already completed a jump he would be one step ahead of the rest of us.'

'Do you think Kevin Wheeler had a fixation with Ingrid?' Dr Patel was leafing through notes, which I assumed had been made by whichever officer had investigated the case six years ago. 'It would have been a lot of trouble to go to, to book and complete a parachute jump only a week before the one scheduled by your office manager. Some people can become obsessed by a member of the opposite sex whom they deem unobtainable.' She scrutinised me over the open file. 'Did Matt Treguier indicate at any time that he had met – and in fact already trained – Kevin Wheeler prior to that day?'

I shook my head. 'No. But he was probably being kind to Kevin and keeping his secret.' I recalled Matt distancing himself from the flirtatious Ingrid. 'Perhaps he didn't want to tread on Kevin's toes romantically speaking. I'm no psychologist, but I think Kevin is completely harmless.'

'As you say, you are not a psychologist.' Dr Patel closed the file with a rustle of papers and a small thud. 'But I think you are unduly trusting of people, which is not always a wise or safe option.'

I thought of how the wise or safe option didn't always appeal. I'd taken quite a risk moving in with Calum and his traumatised daughter six months ago, despite my parents' advice. I'd loved the sense of adventure with which I had embraced Calum's hobby of body boarding, and the stubbornness with which I had pursued my aim to complete the charity jump, despite Calum's pleadings. Perhaps there was some daredevil streak in me which shunned the 'safe option' as Dr Patel put it. I wanted comfort and security, but that security had to be tempered with a bit of mild adventure or I'd go mad.

I decided I'd had enough of the doctor's probing and began to lever myself out of the pillow-like sofa. 'Am I free to go now?'

Dr Patel shook her head. 'I would like to perform a series of psychological tests on you. It will help us to understand your state of mind and give us more of an insight as to whether you are suppressing certain memories.'

77

I hesitated. I didn't much like the idea of the tests, but if they helped in any way to find out where the last six and a half years of my life might have gone, they had to be worth a try. I nodded reluctantly and DI Smith took her leave as I followed Dr Patel into a small office and seated myself at a desk while she opened a second file. She held up the first of a sheaf of papers printed with abstract drawings.

She took a deep breath as I made myself as comfortable as possible on the upright chair. 'What do you see when you look at this, Michaela?'

Two hours later I leaned back in the hard chair and rubbed my eyes. My mind was swimming with images, all of which had been completely open to interpretation. By the end of the session I had realised that nothing Dr Patel had shown me could possibly help me in any way.

'Am I free to leave?' I asked as the doctor finished scribbling her findings.

'We would rather wait until the lab test results have come through.' She glanced up at me. 'Do you have anywhere to go?'

I mulled over my options once more. The only things I'd taken to the airfield were the car I'd been driving, my fleece and my handbag, everything else had been in Calum's house in Leatherhead. At present I had no money, no clothes, no identification – and nowhere to go.

'What happened to the things I left at the airfield, my jeep for example?'

She frowned and pushed a strand of silky, black hair from her face. 'They would have been impounded as evidence. As the case was officially left open, they are probably still in police possession.'

'Can I have them back?'

'I doubt they will be released to you until the case is closed.'

'But no crime has been committed! I'm here and I'm unharmed. What case is there?'

'You may be physically unharmed . . .'

'Have you finished with my T-shirt and jeans at least?' I cut her short. All I wanted was to get out of there and have my life back.

'I will see what I can do.'

'Could I make a phone call? I need to speak to Calum and find out if he still has all my other things.'

Dr Patel nodded. 'You may use the telephone here while I go and locate your clothing.' She got up and headed for the door before pausing and glancing back. 'I am on your side you know, Michaela. I know you think all this is a waste of time, but something has happened to you whether you want to accept it or not and it is our job to find out exactly what that something is.'

As soon as she closed the door behind her, I dialled Calum's number. He answered on the second ring and I felt my eyes tearing up at the sound of his voice. I swallowed and tried to make my voice sound matter-of-fact. 'Calum, it's me, Michaela.'

'What do you want?' I could hear the weariness in his voice.

'I wanted to say sorry for what happened today. I told them you hadn't done anything wrong.'

'Well, we're home now and Abbey's sleeping. Where are you?'

'I'm still at this house they've taken me to. I was wondering what you did with all my things. I don't have any clothes or anything.'

There was a long silence at the end of the line and for a moment I thought we'd been cut off. 'Calum?'

'Yes, I'm here. I packed everything up and took it to your parents about a year after you vanished . . . when it became obvious you weren't coming back.'

'Everything?'

'Yes.'

So he'd given up on me after a year. I felt a chill run through me. When I'd moved into his home six months ago his wife had been dead less than two years, but there had been no possessions of hers lying about, no photos or mementoes of any kind, no forgotten clothes lying hidden at the back of the wardrobe. It was as if he had erased her memory completely from his and Abbey's lives.

We had never talked about her much. After him initially telling me he was a widower, Grace's name had hardly been mentioned again and I realised that I had been grateful for that. Now it suddenly seemed like a betrayal. It was as if the years they had spent together meant nothing to him, not even worth an occasional thought. I realised with a shudder that to Calum it was as if she had never existed. Now he was doing the same to me.

I gave myself a mental shake. He wasn't going to get away with sidelining me that easily. 'Do you know what happened to my things when Mum went into the home?'

'I'm afraid not.'

'Thanks a lot, Calum.'

'Well, what did you expect?' His voice was suddenly angry. 'You weren't here, Michaela. You weren't here to see Abbey grow up, you left her motherless and grieving. And you left me to cope on my own!'

I wondered if it was me he was angry with, or Grace, or both.

'I told you I didn't leave you on purpose. I wouldn't have hurt you or Abbey for the world.'

'That's what Grace said during those few hours when she was in the emergency room after the accident,' he said bitterly. 'She said she didn't want to leave us, but she did. And so did you!'

'I'm sorry.'

'So am I, Michaela. I had hoped we'd grow old together, but it was not to be, was it? Look, I hope you find your things. I hope everything works out for you, really.'

It was a dismissal; he wasn't going to help me. I felt bereft. Yesterday morning we had been a happy couple chugging along with our daily lives, today we were strangers. 'At least tell me where my mother is. Which nursing home is she in?'

He gave me the address and I scribbled it down on a notepad on the doctor's desk. 'Thanks,' I paused but he said nothing more. 'Goodbye then, Calum.'

'Goodbye, Michaela.'

It was another full hour before I was able to leave the police house. Dr Patel had returned my clothes and boots, for some reason minus the socks, given me the address of a women's refuge where I might stay and enough money to catch a bus and train back to Leatherhead, where my mother was apparently ensconced in a secure nursing home called 'Acorn Lodge'.

As I stood at the bus stop shivering in the dull light of a chilly late autumn afternoon, I had the strangest, fleeting feeling of freedom. It could have been scary, standing there owning only the clothes on my back, with no bag, no possessions, no money or identification and my bare feet stuffed into hard brown boots. Cars sped by, their occupants intent on the journey ahead of them, like shoals of fish in an endless silver stream. I felt strangely out of sync with everything, outside of it all. I wanted to run wildly up and down the grass verge screaming my frustration to the sky, but I had the strangest sensation that if I did no one would even see me.

Chapter Fourteen

A black car drew up at the kerb next to the bus stop and I glanced over to see Matt sitting in the driver's seat. He rolled the window down and grinned at me.

'Need a lift?'

I found myself smiling back. 'You're still speaking to me then?'

'Why wouldn't I be?'

I edged over to the car and saw Kevin watching me from the back seat. 'A small matter of being incarcerated in a police interview room for most of the day, perhaps,' I suggested.

'Just like old times,' he said flippantly. 'It took me back six years. Only the interview rooms have been repainted and the coffee is better.'

'I'm really sorry.'

I *was* sorry and yet I wasn't. The relief I felt at Matt's appearance was palpable. The feelings of being so completely alone and at odds with the rest of the planet had melted away as soon as I'd seen him. I'd felt the same when he'd come for me in the pub, I realised. He was the only one with the possible exception of Kevin, who wasn't treating me with hostility and suspicion. And just like the previous night when I'd insisted on sharing his bed, I felt an overwhelming desire to connect physically with him, as though he might be able to anchor me securely to the world.

Kevin ran his window down and stuck his head out. 'Are you getting in, or what?'

I realised they had been waiting for me. Kevin had apparently even left the front seat vacant, so I scurried round to the passenger side and slid onto the cream, leather upholstery.

'Where to, Milady?'

'I was going to find my mother. She's in a nursing home – but you knew that didn't you?'

Matt nodded. 'I thought you had enough to cope with this morning, without us telling you about your parents.'

I read out the address of the nursing home and swivelled to look at his profile as we headed back towards Leatherhead. 'How come you know so much about me and my family? I understand that you were sucked into the aftermath of what happened to me all those years ago, but my father died a whole two years later and my mother went into a home some time after that. After the police released you, why didn't you simply put it all behind you?'

'I told you. I felt responsible for you. What happened to you seemed like my fault. I convinced you to jump, I asked you to put your trust in me and promised you'd be OK. When you vanished I felt like I'd failed you. Kevin and I have considered every possible scenario for your disappearance, including keeping watch on what was happening to the people in your life.'

It made sense to me. But DI Smith's voice echoed in my head. 'An unhealthy interest, an obsessive amount of documentation . . .'

'I still don't understand why.'

Matt sighed. 'It isn't every day something inexplicable happens. Maybe I just needed an explanation as to where and why you vanished, to make my own life worth living. It seemed a scandal that you had your whole life ahead of you and the police gave up with the investigation.'

'The trouble with the police,' Kevin put in from behind me, 'is that they have no imagination. They deal in the here and now and what's right in front of them. Lateral thinking is beyond them.'

I watched the imposing rise of Box Hill looming against the darkening skyline on our right, and settled more comfortably in my seat. The two of them sounded completely nuts, yet however crazy it was, I felt increasingly relaxed in their company. On the pretext of watching the shadowy scenery, I studied Matt's profile and resisted the urge to reach out and brush my fingers along his jaw. Glancing in the mirror I realised that while I'd been watching Matt, Kevin had been watching me. What was it with these two, I asked myself?

The nursing home was in a big old house on the corner of a large plot behind a church. Matt drew the car into the kerb and turned off the engine. 'We'll wait right here for you.'

I paused as I climbed out of the car, trying to keep the doubt out of my voice, 'I'm not keeping you from work or anything, am I?'

Matt shrugged. 'I don't have a flight for a few days and Kevin's between trouble-shooting jobs.'

Hesitating with one foot on the kerb and the other in the car, I stared at him in surprise, 'Flight? Trouble-shooting? What do you do?'

'Kevin's a freelance IT expert and I'm a pilot.'

I felt my eyes open wider. 'A pilot?'

He grinned at me. 'I fly cargo planes for a living, and I can tell you that flying the things definitely beats coaxing terrified people to jump out of them.'

Half of me wanted to get back into the car and hear about how Matt had become a pilot, but it had been a long and traumatic day – and it was now nearly twenty four hours since I had landed in the airfield and found that my world had fallen apart. I shook my head, there was so much I wanted to find out. But first, I had to see my mother.

The nursing home was in semi darkness as I stood on the wide-stone step and rang on the bell. A few minutes passed before I heard soft footsteps and the front door creak open, revealing a girl of about my own age dressed in a nurse's uniform, black Afro hair swept up in a tight knot.

She looked me up and down. 'Can I help you?'

'I'm Michaela Anderson. I've come to see my mother, Susan Anderson.'

She glanced at her watch. 'It's rather late. We've started getting the patients ready for bed. Can you come back tomorrow?'

'I really need to see her now.'

She pursed her lips but stood back to let me pass. 'I'll have to talk to her first. A lot of our residents get upset when their routine is disturbed.'

I stepped into a wide hallway, lit softly by a yellow light, with a wide central staircase sweeping upwards. It would have looked like any other large house, except for the sterile looking office which opened off to one side and the faint smell of stale urine and antiseptic in the air.

'You'll need to sign the visitor's book.' She led me into the office and turned a hefty tome towards me so I could add my name to the list of daily visitors. She eyed me appraisingly. 'I haven't been here long myself, but I don't remember having seen you before.'

'I've been away,' I said vaguely, following her round the

corner where she paused at a lift door. 'She won't be expecting me.'

We stepped into the lift and waited in silence while it took us to the second floor.

'Wait here, while I go and talk to her.' The nurse turned to walk down a carpeted corridor, but I caught her arm.

The nurse stared at me and I read the name on her badge in the dull light. 'Please, Zenelle. It would mean a lot to me to be able to tell her I'm here myself, in person.'

The nurse looked doubtful.

'How is she?' I asked. 'Is she very down?'

'She has good days and bad days. Today she has been quite calm. It would be a shame to get her over-excited so close to bedtime.' Zenelle looked into my pleading eyes and seemed to relent. 'Very well, you can come with me while I talk to her, but if she doesn't want to see you, you will have to come back tomorrow when we have more staff on duty.'

I nodded and followed her as she went to a door which surprisingly was standing ajar. I found I was inexplicably nervous of seeing my mum in these unfamiliar surroundings. I don't know what I expected – locked rooms with bolted doors or something. Calum had said my mother was in a secure nursing home after all. I peered inside to see a slender woman with short, cropped brown hair sitting slumped on the edge of a single bed staring into space. She seemed listless and tired, her shoulders hunched miserably forwards as if even sitting up straight was too much of a bother. Zenelle walked over and spoke softly to her and the woman looked up.

I felt the tightening in my stomach which had become all too common in the last twenty four hours. The woman looked like a stranger and yet was heart-rendingly familiar. My mother had been all elegant curves, while this woman was painfully thin. The mother I had seen the week before had only been in her late forties, whereas this person must be in her mid-fifties.

Willing my legs to move, I inched towards her, noticing the agitated look on her face as she stared at me in disbelief. This was a pale imitation of the woman I had gone to with my problems, the chair-person of the Woman's Institute, charming hostess to my father's colleagues and the woman behind the powerful, dynamic man my father had been.

'Mum?'

'It's not you,' she said, her voice coming out in a thin wail of distress. 'It can't be. They say my daughter is dead.'

She began to rock to and fro on the bed, her eyes darting about the room as if looking for a means of escape from something she didn't understand. 'You're not real. They tell me you're never real – just an illusion I've conjured up.'

I went to her and rested my hand on her shoulder but she shrugged me off. 'Mum, it is me. It's Michaela.' I tried to take her hand but she wrapped both arms protectively round her body, her hands wedged firmly under her armpits as she continued to rock, her red-rimmed eyes avoiding my face.

'I hurt,' she whimpered. 'I ache all over and you're making it worse. Go away and leave me alone . . . I know you're not really here.'

Chapter Fifteen

My mother, it seemed, spent most of her time in the nursing home trying to kill herself and was apparently on constant suicide watch.

I sat shakily in the office as Zenelle made a cup of tea and handed it to me. I don't think she realised I was the cause of my mother's grief.

'Susan is not allowed laces on her trainers or a belt on her trousers. Where you or I would see an ancient beam or a harmless tree, she thinks only of hanging herself. We might see a simple glass of water or a mirror, but to your mother they are a means of cutting her wrists.'

'Surely she could be given anti-depressants or something to help her?'

'Susan has been on a variety of different medications, but she suffers from side-effects. Look,' Zenelle said kindly. 'If you want to know more about your mother's treatment you should come back tomorrow and see the doctor.'

'I can't leave her here like this,' I told the nurse, resting the tea down on the corner of the desk. I felt tears of helplessness welling up. 'There must be something I can do.'

'She's getting the best possible care,' Zenelle assured me. 'And you couldn't take her home even if you wanted to. Susan is here under the mental health act.'

'Could I see her once more before I go?'

Zenelle pursed her lips and I was sure she was going to say no, but she nodded briefly. 'You can go in to say goodnight and tell her you'll be back tomorrow, if you like. But I warn you, you may not get a positive response.'

I stood in the doorway to my mother's room for several minutes, watching as she rocked back and forth and plucked at her short hair. I wanted to take those few steps across the carpet towards her, fling my arms round her and inhale the comforting smell of the mother of my childhood, but I felt sure she would flinch away from me. 'I'll come back and see you again tomorrow, Mum,' I promised, my voice breaking with emotion.

'You won't come back,' my mother whispered. 'I've seen you before and they just give me more pills to make you go away again. You always go away and then they tell me you're dead.'

'Don't upset yourself, Susan. Michaela is here to visit you,' Zenelle told her. 'Why don't you sit together for a while and I'll go and see to Ethel in the next room.'

Mum looked up at the nurse, a glimmer of hope crossing her face. 'You won't give me more pills?'

'Your next tablets are due in an hour,' Zenelle told her, glancing at her watch. 'Just enjoy your daughter while she's here.'

I crossed the room slowly, afraid to make Mum shy away from me, but when I drew close enough she reached out and clasped my fingers so tightly that it actually hurt. Leaving my hand in hers, I put my other arm round her shoulders and sank down on the bed next to her.

'Is it really you?' she asked tremulously.

'It is Mum.'

'I'm not imagining you?'

'No, it's really me.'

She turned teary eyes towards me. 'And you won't leave me again?'

I thought fleetingly of Calum's accusation that both Grace and I had abandoned him and Abigail and the pain they had suffered. My mother had lost first me and then my father and had obviously never recovered from the shock. 'I won't leave you, Mum, I'm back,' I said. 'I'm right here with you.'

My mother looked down at her lap and avoided eye contact with me for some time. I fell to making polite conversation about the nursing home, asking what she did during the day and how the food was. After a while she seemed to relax and her grip loosened on my hand. Her gaze wandered over my face and she smiled a hesitant smile, as if reluctant to believe her own eyes.

She brushed a tendril of hair from my face. 'They told me you were missing, but we knew you weren't dead. Leonard and I searched for you, you know. We never gave up hope . . .'

I returned the smile, ecstatic that she seemed to believe it was truly me at last. It was as if an aperture had opened in her drug-filled mind and my words came out in a jumble, knowing I had to get them out quickly in case the window closed again. 'I don't know what happened, Mum. I was doing the charity parachute jump and I got caught up in this strong wind. When I landed I thought I'd been blown off course, because the airfield was completely deserted! I walked to the nearest pub and saw the posters that you and Dad had made. I never meant to cause you all this grief; I don't understand where the last six years have gone.'

She shook her head and I realised my excitement had been premature. Mum was still very confused. 'I keep telling them; I don't know where the last six years have gone either.' She

91

began to stroke my hair as she had done so many times when I was a child. 'My little girl,' she murmured. 'Was it only last week I saw you last?'

And then the shutters seemed to come down again and she was struggling to her feet and walking to the firmly closed window. She put her hands over her ears, closed her eyes and began to wail – a long keening sound intended to shut out the illusion she thought was me.

Looking on helplessly at her thin frame draped in the loose, grey jogger bottoms and shapeless sweatshirt I couldn't help but recall the elegant woman she had once been and it tore at my heart. Mum had loved to shop and was always decked out in the latest fashions and here she was, a mere shadow of her former self and in such obvious mental torment.

I tried to go to her but she shrugged me off and I stood a few paces from her, swallowing my tears as I tried to soothe her. 'It'll be alright, Mum. We'll get you some new clothes when you're better,' I promised her. 'We'll go shopping together like we used to and buy you a whole new wardrobe!'

She sank without warning to the floor and crouched down with her head in her hands. 'I want it to be like it was before,' she moaned, as she rocked back and forth, on the balls of her bare feet. Tears were pouring down her face. 'I want Leonard, and I want Michaela. I want my little girl.'

Kneeling next to her, I rested my arm around her trembling shoulders. 'Don't cry, Mum, everything will turn out OK.'

Footsteps sounded across the carpet and I looked up to see Zenelle hurrying towards us. 'Come on, Susan. Let's get you into your chair, shall we?'

Sobbing, my mother attempted to push her away. 'My daughter is dead and no one cares.' I watched in horror as she lashed blindly out but Zenelle stepped deftly to one side, catching the flailing hands and pinning them in hers.

I stood up and looked on helplessly as Zenelle expertly guided my mother to her feet and escorted her over to the bedside chair. 'It's nearly time for your sleeping pills. You'll have a good night's rest and your daughter can visit again in the morning.' Zenelle turned deep brown eyes on me. 'Better if you go now, I think.'

Biting back tears I nodded wordlessly and left the room.

Matt and Kevin were waiting where I'd left them and I climbed wearily into the passenger seat feeling like the very old woman my mother had become.

'Bad?' Kevin asked.

I nodded, still close to tears.

Matt reached out and patted my jean-clad knee. 'Where do you want to go?'

Like my mother, I wanted to go home. But if Calum didn't want me and my family home had been sold, such a place didn't exist for me any more. 'I meant to ask Mum what happened to all my things,' I said. 'I have hardly any money, but I could go to the women's refuge Dr Patel found for me.'

The two men exchanged glances and I knew they had been discussing me in my absence.

'You're welcome to come back with me, if you want to,' Matt said.

'That would give DI Smith something to think about,' I said with a faint smile. 'It isn't the wisest of ideas.'

'I'm not sure there are any other viable options,' Kevin commented. 'You don't want to go to some women's refuge, surely? Apparently the Kent constabulary have already searched Matt's place while we were supposedly helping the police with their enquiries today.'

'Oh no, I'm sorry.'

'They probably found your DNA all over my bedroom,'

Matt said with a snort. 'I could have saved them the trouble if they'd bothered to actually ask me. The Surrey police apprehended Kevin and me only a short distance from your boyfriend's house and I told them you'd slept in my bed when DI Smith – who appears to be running the case from this end – eventually thought of putting that question to me.'

'Oh.' I was embarrassed, not only because he'd told them I'd stayed in his room and I hadn't, but because I'd been in his bed at all.

'You can't stay at mine,' Kevin continued almost cheerfully. 'It's full of computer components. I've been building a computer from spare parts and it's kind of taken over my flat.'

I sat and twisted my hands together in my lap. Kevin was right; there weren't many other options open to me. There was Ingrid of course, but I had no idea whether she still lived at the same address. Her phone number had been unobtainable when I'd tried calling her from the pub.

'I could go and stay with Ingrid,' I glanced apologetically at Kevin remembering his infatuation with Ingrid. 'Do you know if she still lives in the same place?'

'I don't think so.' The reply came a little too fast. 'She left her job at Wayfarers soon after I did and apparently moved away. I did contemplate asking around a couple of years back but decided if she hadn't told anyone where she was going she probably didn't want to be found.'

'Oh.' I looked back at Matt. 'It looks like I might be taking you up on your offer. I'm sorry to put you to all this trouble.'

He grinned and turned the key in the ignition, pulled smoothly away from the kerb and headed towards the M25. Fortunately the dark roads were fairly free of traffic and we made it to Matt's house in Kent in only an hour and a half. We spent most of the journey in silence; the two men

apparently sensing that I needed time to assimilate everything that had happened during the day. I sat hunched down
in the seat thinking about Mum, Dad, Calum, Abbey and the
fateful jump. When the car drew into Matt's driveway and
he opened the garage doors I felt a certain amount of relief
at having reached some sort of sanctuary. It was almost like
coming home.

Kevin took his leave of us, collecting a battered white van
from where he'd parked it in Matt's drive that morning. After
following Matt into his kitchen, I climbed onto one of the
bar stools and rested my elbows on the counter. Twelve hours
had passed since I had sat here and breakfasted on bacon
and eggs, yet so much had happened, it felt like a lifetime.

'You must be hungry.' Matt had reappeared at my shoulder.
'I was thinking of making a stir fry. Would you like some?'

I nodded. 'Do you want some help?'

'No, I'm fine. You just sit and talk to me, it won't take
long.'

I watched as he took out a couple of packets of ready-
cubed raw chicken and vegetable stir fry ingredients from his
fridge and poured them into a large wok with a little olive
oil. He stirred the contents round with a spatula, his movements efficient and assured. I allowed my gaze to linger on
his face, watching the place where his hair curled slightly into
the nape of his neck.

'How did you become a pilot?' I asked, trying to keep my
mind off the well-toned muscles in his upper arms and the
neatness of his bottom in the close-fitting black jeans.

'After your disappearance I was asked to leave my job as a
parachute instructor. The bad publicity had virtually closed
the parachuting company down. No one wanted to do a jump
with a company that had managed to lose one of its clients,
despite the fact that no charges were ever brought against the

company.' He shook some sauce into the wok and continued to stir. 'I had always wanted to be a pilot, so after a few months of trying this and that I decided to take flying lessons.'

'The bad publicity didn't stop you from getting a flying job?'

He shrugged. It was a typically Gallic gesture and I found myself wondering about his French sounding surname. 'The stigma of being connected to your case did follow me. I wanted to fly passenger planes but of course none of the big airlines would touch me. I eventually found a small company which specialised in flying freight, who were looking for a good pilot. They took me on and I've been with them ever since.'

So my disappearance hadn't completely ruined his life, I mused. But it had changed it. I thought of the photo of me I had found in his bedside drawer. It didn't seem normal to keep a photo of someone he'd barely met. It seemed he'd been holding a candle for me, but there was something else, something about him and Kevin and what had befallen me that I couldn't quite put my finger on.

And despite everything, I was determined to get to the bottom of it.

Chapter Sixteen

'And you kept in contact with Kevin?' I asked nonchalantly.

He gave me a sideways glance and nodded. 'Kevin also lost his job a few months after your disappearance. I suppose you could say he became a little fixated on what had happened to you and spent more time concentrating on your case than on his work. The insurance company you all worked for fired him for poor attendance and he concentrated his skills on what he does best. He works freelance now, fixing people's computers for them, but his main passion is a website he set up about you and your disappearance. It became something of a cult thing soon after he launched it. Kevin persuaded me to become a sort of celebrity figure, as I was the last one to see you before you vanished. Can you get me two plates from that cupboard there?'

I slid off the stool, went to the cupboard he had indicated and handed him the plates. With the spatula in one hand he went to take the plates from me, but paused, his eyes lingering momentarily over my face and neck, which I could feel flushing under his gaze. The hunger in his eyes had nothing to do with the food he was preparing and I released the plates quickly slipping back onto the stool, fearing my legs might no longer support me.

'DI Smith thinks that you and Kevin have both

been unhealthily obsessed with my disappearance,' I said rather breathlessly, trying to keep my mind focused as he turned quickly back to the cooker. His closeness was unnerving. It was almost as if an underlying spark of desire had been ignited and was simmering in the small space between us.

When he turned round with the plates of food I saw that his hands were shaking so much that he had to slide the plates quickly onto the counter to steady them. He glanced at me then sighed deeply and looked away as he took the seat next to mine.

He paused. The sigh had been almost a groan. I wondered what would happen if I reached out and touched his hand. He shook his head and I thought for a moment that he'd read my mind.

'I suppose you could say we both became a little obsessed.' He took a deep breath, trying to compose himself. 'Your disappearance changed our lives so dramatically, but it wasn't just that. For Kevin it was the challenge of discovering what had become of you. For me it was something else . . .' He glanced sideways at me. 'It's hard to explain without sounding corny and pathetic, but I'd felt an immediate connection with you that day at the airfield.'

'I bet you say that to all the girls.'

He smiled faintly, but shook his head again. 'No, no I really don't. It's difficult to put into words but I've come to realise that what I felt for you was more than just a physical attraction, it was almost as if I knew you – that I had recognised you at some unconscious level as someone who should mean something to me.'

I watched him while he fidgeted with the cutlery he'd laid out, turning a fork over and over in his fingers, until I wanted to snatch it from him and throw it across the room.

He swivelled suddenly on the stool so he was looking directly at me again. 'Do you believe in love at first sight?'

I had never really considered it, but if the fizzy feeling suffusing my belly and the tightness in my chest was anything to go by, then I was prepared to give it some serious thought now, despite my earlier reservations. Maybe this was simply his favourite chat-up line, but from the look on his face I didn't think so. Still I was cautious. 'How can you tell what's love and what is merely sexual attraction?'

'Maybe it *begins* with a basic physical attraction.' He sucked in a breath, his voice gruff. 'During the training day I thought that's all it was, but when you were in that plane with me and so very scared, I found I wanted to gather you up and hold you close so that nothing would ever frighten you again . . .'

Warning signals sounded in my head, reminding me that I was trying to unearth more about his real intentions. If DI Smith was looking for someone who seemed obsessed with me, then Matt certainly fitted the bill. If I hadn't been feeling the same way myself, I think I would have got up and left the house right there and then. The women's refuge had to be safer than this. I didn't get up to leave, however. Even before Calum had turned his back on me, he had never vocalised his feelings like this virtual stranger was doing. On top of the obvious sexual attraction, I was finding Matt's openness completely irresistible.

'But then I vanished,' I prompted him. 'And you felt as if it was your fault?'

'Completely. I should have taken you back to the airfield and we could have done a tandem jump instead, or no jump at all. Not a day has passed that I haven't berated myself for my stupidity.'

I wondered if his misplaced feelings of guilt had clouded

his judgement over the years. Maybe what had begun as physical desire had escalated out of all proportion into something else.

With my heart in my mouth, I reached out and touched his arm. Even through the fabric of his shirt I could feel the heat of his body. My fingertips seemed to burn from even that slight contact. 'It wasn't your fault. I could have refused to make that jump.' Just as I could refuse to go any further with this now, I thought. 'In the end, it was my own decision.'

He looked deeply into my eyes and rested his hand on top of mine. A current passed between us and suddenly I knew crazy or not, that I wanted him more than anything I had ever wanted in my life. We stared at one another, and time, which seemed to have taken on a life of its own, seemed to slow to nothing. He brought his face close to mine and I inhaled the scent of him, the food quite forgotten. Lifting my chin in anticipation of that first contact with his lips, our mouths found each other and suddenly there was no one else in the world but him.

It was strange, I thought as I lay nestled several hours later in his arms in the black and gold bed, how in films lovers kissed once and ended up almost immediately making frantic love. Matt and I had contented ourselves with kissing until our lips had actually become sore, both unwilling to rush to the next stage. We had explored one another's bodies with sensual delight and when at last he had carried me to his bedroom and stripped me completely naked, I wondered how I had ever existed as one person without him beside me.

I awoke at dawn to the sound of birdsong and Matt's gentle snoring next to me. Sleep had eventually overtaken us and we'd drifted off in a tangle of limbs, our bodies bathed in sweat, and too exhausted to move.

Easing myself from his arms, I leaned up on one elbow and ran my gaze over his sleeping form, thrilling in the way his chest rose and fell with each breath, the way his eyes looked when they were closed and his features relaxed in sleep. Resisting the urge to kiss him again and risk waking him, I slid my feet out onto the rug and then tiptoed across the cold floor to the bathroom.

Whilst standing in the shower I realised three things. One, I had fallen hopelessly for Matt. Two, on a more practical note, I couldn't put those same dirty clothes back on yet again and three, I was absolutely starving. Last night's stir fry had congealed on the plates; our appetites had melted away as our passion had intensified. Now, however, my stomach was rumbling. As soon as I had finished my shower I gathered up the remnants of my discarded clothing, helped myself to Matt's towelling bath robe and wandered downstairs to the kitchen, where I searched in vain for his washing machine, intending to pop my clothes onto a quick wash whilst making us some breakfast.

Pausing, with the clothes bundled in my arms, I stared round the kitchen. He must surely have a washing machine. After a cursory wander around, I noticed the door under the stairs. Perhaps his washing machine was hidden in there. Trying the door knob I found the door unlocked. There was a light switch to one side of the door and I flicked it on, opening the door to find a flight of steep wooden steps leading down into a basement. The light, was supplied by a single dull bulb hanging in the centre of the room, but it was enough to see that the basement had a stone floor, and breeze block walls. On one side was a wine rack stacked neatly with bottles, and along another wall stood a washing machine and tumble dryer, all very clean, tidy and minimal. I found a box of washing powder and set my clothes to wash, re-tying the robe tightly round me and walking back towards the stairs.

Pausing with my foot on the bottom step, I peered through the slats of the open staircase and saw that an accumulation of odds and ends, boxes of tools, an old vacuum cleaner and broom, a bucket and a cardboard box filled with some kind of fabric with a pile of papers tossed on top had been stashed behind the stairs. Something about the fabric hanging out from under the heap of papers seemed oddly familiar. Backtracking, I crept round the staircase and peered into the box. The papers on the top were a wad of the leaflets my parents had had made, asking, HAVE YOU SEEN THIS GIRL?

Pushing the pile of leaflets to one side, I stared at the object, which was partially hidden beneath them; a navy-blue something with an embroidered motif proclaiming, 'Surf's Up'. Cold fingers prickled down my spine as I pulled the remarkably dust-free, fleece jacket from the box and held it out before me. It was without doubt my jacket, the one I had bought in Cornwall when Calum and I had taken our boarding holiday and I'd got really cold on the beach.

Bringing it to my face, I held the soft fabric to my cheek. This was the jacket I had taken with me on the day of the jump in case the spring day had turned cold. I'd left it with my handbag in the locker at the airfield and had assumed it was in police custody with my other belongings.

Footsteps sounded at the top of the stairs and Matt's voice filled the basement. 'Michaela? Are you down there?'

With shaking hands I stuffed the jacket back into the box, pulled the robe more firmly round me and started up the stairs. He reached for me as soon as I set foot into the kitchen, gathering me into his arms and holding me close against his bare chest.

'What were you doing down there?' The words were muffled in my hair.

'I . . . I wanted to wash my clothes.'

'Oh . . .' there was a moment's hesitation. 'And you found everything alright?'

I nodded against his chest, feeling sick to my stomach. I had certainly found something alright. I just hadn't worked out exactly what that something might mean.

Chapter Seventeen

I pulled away from Matt with the excuse of needing to make breakfast. 'I hope you don't mind me making myself at home in your kitchen,' I said lightly, trying to shake off the questions that were crowding my head.

'Go ahead.' He was only wearing a pair of denim jeans and had folded his arms protectively across his chest when I'd moved away, watching me with a confused expression on his face. Only half an hour earlier we had been curled contentedly in one another's arms; now I was trying to keep the hurt out of my voice as I asked him where he kept his omelette pan, wondering how the hell my fleece had got into his possession.

As I whisked eggs, I found myself watching him surreptitiously. DI Smith's warnings sounded in my head. Dr Patel had suggested amnesia caused by prolonged emotional trauma. I'd vehemently denied it, but six and a half years had gone somewhere, hadn't they? I realised I was whisking the eggs so hard that globs were splashing out of the bowl and making little yellow puddles on the counter. Matt, who had been solemnly grating cheese, stopped and gave me a hard stare.

'What's the matter, Michaela?'

I found I couldn't look at him as I went to the sink to get a cloth to wipe up the spills. He dropped the metal grater down with a clatter and walked round the breakfast bar, put his hands on my shoulders and gave me a little shake. 'Talk to me godammit.'

I looked down at my feet. 'I found my fleece in your basement.'

'Damn.' He dropped his hands to his sides and stood chewing his lip. 'It's not what you think.'

Raising fearful eyes to his, I found I could barely find my voice. 'What then?' I mumbled. 'What possible reason could there be for you having it here? It was locked in the locker at the airfield.'

Taking the cloth from my hand and dumping it on the counter, he guided me through the kitchen and into the little sitting room, which was decorated in creams and blacks with dark mahogany furniture. Seating himself on a cream-coloured couch, he pulled me down next to him and turned to face me.

'A master key to the lockers was kept in the office at the airfield. When we couldn't locate you after the jump, everyone was desperately looking for clues. Kevin suggested going through your locker – this was before we'd realised things were way beyond our control. Kevin thought maybe you'd landed somehow without anyone noticing you and he had the idea of checking to see if your things were still in there.'

'As soon as you saw my things *were* still there you should have left them to the police, surely?'

'I know. But it's easy to be wise after the event. Kevin had pulled all your things out and they tumbled onto the floor. The fleece was the last thing I picked up and I was still holding it when my boss walked in and Kevin slammed the locker shut before he could see that we'd been rifling through it. It was too late to put the jacket back without looking guilty as hell. So I stowed it away in my own locker and no one was the wiser.'

'Why did you bring it back here?'

'When I was dismissed from my job I brought everything that belonged to me back here, including your jacket. I didn't want to throw it away.'

'Why didn't the police find it yesterday when they were conducting their search?'

He shrugged. 'You didn't wear it to the airfield that day so everyone's description of you was just that you'd been dressed in T-shirt and jeans. They didn't know to look for it, I suppose.'

'Calum didn't tell them it was missing?'

'Maybe he didn't notice one item of your wardrobe had gone; not that surprising considering how upset he was over your disappearance. Did he see you leave with it?'

I thought back and remembered that Calum had still been in the shower when I'd left. Even Abbey hadn't seen it as I'd tossed it into the car with my bag.

Frowning, I pursed my lips, sighed and closed my eyes. 'This is like a nightmare. Why can't everything be as it was before?'

Matt tightened his grip on my hand. 'Everything? Are you sure?'

I knew he was referring to our night together. 'I'm so confused. I thought I loved Calum and that he loved me and now I find he doesn't want me back. He got rid of everything that reminded him of me. How could he have done that if he'd truly cared about me?'

'I don't know,' Matt's voice was soft. 'I found I couldn't.'

His comment stilled me. I was berating him for the very thing which had upset me about Calum. I wondered if Dr Patel would have added his keeping an item of my clothing to her list of possible psychological problems.

'I'm sorry for leaping to conclusions.'

'I'm sorry you don't trust me.'

We lapsed into a silence which was broken by the sudden ringing of the front door bell. Our heads shot up.

'Police?' I whispered.

'I don't know. I'd better answer it.' He got to his feet and I realised I was still clad in the towelling robe. If it was the police, they would reach all sorts of unsavoury conclusions after finding me in their number one suspect's house with no proper clothes on.

Matt returned a few seconds later with Kevin at his heels. Kevin was holding a piece of paper and looking rather pleased with himself.

'Am I in time for breakfast?'

I remembered the eggs in the kitchen and rose to my feet, aware as I did so of Kevin's eyes following me with interest. 'The only clothes I own are in the wash,' I told him shortly as I slid past him. 'Do you want an omelette?'

'I wouldn't say no.'

Ten minutes later the three of us were sitting in the kitchen eating cheese omelettes. Kevin was having trouble keeping his eyes off my bare legs and I shifted uncomfortably, re-tightening the robe and pulling it over my thighs as I sat on one of the high stools.

'This,' he said triumphantly, holding out the piece of paper, 'is Ingrid Peters' new address.'

'Really?' I was surprised and pleased he had taken the trouble to find it for me. Holding out my hand for the paper I read the address with surprise. 'Brighton? What's she doing down there, I wonder?'

Kevin shrugged. 'Search me, babe. It took me quite a while to locate her. I had to do some serious hacking to find her social security number and from there I got her most recent place of residence.'

'Is there a phone number?'

He gave me a terse look. 'What do you want, her dress size as well?'

'Just her phone number would have been nice,' I replied evenly. 'But the address is great. Thank you, Kevin.'

He looked away but his freckled face and neck were suffusing with colour. I realised that weird though he was, he seemed genuinely gratified to have been able to do something to help me.

After finishing off a glass of orange juice, I left the men talking and eating toast while I ventured down the stairs to transfer my clothes to the dryer. Standing on the cold basement floor in my bare feet, I hopped from one foot to the other to keep them from freezing. The air itself had been partially warmed by the dryer, but there was a dank musty smell in the air. Where had I smelled that smell before, I wondered?

Wandering over to the box behind the stairs, I took out my fleece jacket and zipped it up to my chin. I might as well wear it, I thought. Climbing the stairs, I stopped to listen to Kevin and Matt talking in the kitchen.

'It's amazing. She seems to have no recollection of anything that happened,' Matt was saying quietly.

'Maybe it's just as well,' Kevin replied. 'We don't want her suddenly remembering stuff that might send her over the edge.'

'Do you think the police tests will show drugs in her system?'

Kevin mumbled a reply, but I couldn't catch it. Had they said anything which could mean they had been implicated in my disappearance? I wasn't sure. Their conversation could be taken either way.

I coughed to let them know I was back in the kitchen and

Kevin jumped guiltily when he saw me. His eyes widened as he took in the jacket I was wearing. 'She knows then?'

'That you rifled through my locker? Yes,' I said as I came fully into the kitchen. 'Your idea I believe?'

'Raiding lockers is my speciality,' he said blandly. 'I used to do it all the time at school. It's amazing what you can find out about someone from the contents of their locker.'

'Dr Patel must have had a field day with you.' I slid back onto a stool. 'I'm surprised they let you go. Do either of you have to go to work?'

'I'm self employed,' Kevin said. 'I can do pretty well as I please.'

'Nice for some,' Matt commented dryly. 'But no, I don't have work today. I'm not booked for a flight for another couple of days. Why?'

'I wondered if you'd mind taking me to see my mother again some time this morning. I did promise her I'd go back to see her.'

'Will she even have remembered you visited her? From what you told us, she sounded pretty confused.'

'I can't risk that she might have done and not turn up. I'm sorry; I know it's a lot to ask.'

'I'll follow in the van if you don't mind stopping at Redhill to drop it off at my place,' Kevin said. 'It's a nuisance to have to come back here to fetch it.'

'You don't need to both come.'

'What? And let you out of my sight?' Kevin exclaimed. 'You are a famous person, a returned abductee. I'd quite like to film you if you have no objection now you've settled a bit.'

I shot Matt a quick grimace and he hid a smile from his rather wacky companion.

'I'd better go and see if my clothes are done.' I slid from

the stool, anxious to get away from them both for a moment. 'You are certainly not filming me like this.'

I hurried down the basement stairs, my mind whirring anxiously. Once dressed, I stood and looked closely around the small, underground room. Was it possible that I had been locked in here for six and a half years and not remembered a thing about it? Was I letting my imagination run wild? I shook my head and ran my fingers through my tousled locks. No, no way. Matt and Kevin may have been stupid to have rifled through my locker, but they weren't kidnappers – or at least I sincerely hoped not.

Chapter Eighteen

I reached Acorn Lodge two hours later. On arrival Dr Stephen Hewitt talked me through my mother's condition before I was allowed to see her.

'Take your cues from your mother,' he advised me. 'Don't rush her and don't expect too much. If she becomes agitated you must leave her to the ministrations of the medical staff.'

After my chat with Doctor Hewitt I was taken to a spacious day room. Mum was perched in front of a large easel with a paintbrush poised above a canvas filled with abstract splodges of acrylic paint.

I watched her from across the room for a while, noticing that she still had a trim figure despite the unsightly jogging trousers. Her brown hair was shorter than she used to wear it, but I noticed it was stylishly cut, not just hacked off, and there was an air of calm about her this morning, which gave me hope.

I approached her slowly from the side, taking in her features which were so like my own. She was concentrating, holding the paintbrush in mid air as if deciding where to put the next stroke.

'What are you painting?' I asked softly as I peered at the livid purple and brown swirls.

'It's my daughter.' She didn't even glance up at the sound of my voice. 'This is what I see when I think of her.' It seemed she had slipped back into her other world and my heart sank. But she seemed happy enough and I watched quietly as she guided the brush over the canvas. 'Michaela's here, look.'

Staring at the canvas I tried to see something of myself in there, but there was nothing which looked remotely like a person, let alone me.

'This is where Michaela lives,' she explained, as if my silence was a criticism of her art. 'This is the world between worlds. One day I'll join her there and we'll be together again.'

I looked again at the painting and back to my mother's momentarily contented expression. Whatever this place was that she had drawn, it obviously brought her comfort. 'Is Dad there too?' The question slipped from my lips before I had time to think of the consequences.

She turned slowly to me and her eyes searched my face. The paintbrush fell from her fingers and she stood up abruptly, the stool falling with a crash. One of the care assistants who had been supervising the art session, dived forwards and tried to take her arm, but Mum shook him off and held her arms out towards me with such anguish that tears sprang to my eyes.

'Is it you?' she asked me in a quavering voice. 'Or am I imagining things again?' she extended a trembling fingertip towards my face.

'It's me, Mum,' I told her and she let out a wail before throwing her arms around me and crushing me into her embrace.

The carer had backed off a little but still stood within reach. He shook his head and I lapsed into silence, overjoyed that she seemed ready to believe it really was me. Eventually she let go of me and stood back. 'So you are really here. I'm afraid to believe it.' She looked past me towards the door. 'And where *is* your father?' she asked, apparently in response to my question. 'Is he here too?'

Glancing round the room I saw that several other patients had stopped their painting and were watching us with curiosity. Mum was looking at me, waiting for an answer. Unsure what answer to give, without sending her spiralling back into a dark world of despair, I nodded towards her painting.

'He's there,' I whispered huskily. 'He's waiting for you in the world between worlds.'

A shadow crossed Mum's face, as if some unwanted memory had stirred in her mind, but she pushed it away and nodded, apparently content with my answer. She bent to right her fallen stool and picked up her paintbrush. 'Everyone returns there in the end,' she said as she turned away from me. 'People think heaven is above us and hell is below, but there is only the place beyond – it is the place we come from and the place we go back to.' She dipped the paintbrush in a purple splodge of paint and made a long sweeping movement on the canvas. 'Soon I will become one with everyone who has come before and everyone who is yet to be born. And then,' she gave a great sigh, '. . . then I will be home with my family.'

Dr Stephen Hewitt leaned back in the padded leather chair in his office, his fingertips pressed to his chin. The walls were lined with bookshelves, groaning under the weight of medical journals and volumes on psychiatry and psychology.

'Ah, here we are.' He leaned forwards, his thinning hair revealing an almost bald pate as he scanned his computer screen. 'Your mother was placed in our care by the very specific instructions of your father's will. It seems that even before your father passed away, your mother was showing signs of severe depression, probably brought on by the grief of losing her only child.' He shot me an accusing glance.

'Although your father stated that everything was to be left to your mother should he pass away before her, he put a codicil in place. In the event of her being diagnosed with clinical depression which might require long term care, the family home was to be sold and the proceeds of his estate used to give her a permanent home here. Your father's solicitors acted as his trustees and complied with your father's wishes to the letter.'

So my father had put his trust completely with his solicitors. It occurred to me that perhaps I should follow his lead. I leaned forwards. 'Do you have an address for these solicitors?'

Dr Hewitt scrolled down the screen. 'Yes, here it is.' He scribbled an address onto the page of a note block, tore it off and handed it to me.

I glanced down at his neat handwriting. *Armstrong and Brent, Solicitors. High Street, Putney.* Not that far away if I had suitable transport. I stowed it along with Ingrid's address and rose to my feet, hoping that Matt might be inclined to continue to act as my personal chauffeur. 'Thank you for your time, doctor.'

But Dr Hewitt was no longer listening to me, he was looking at someone or something behind me and I turned to see an apparition framed in the office doorway. The vision had dyed hair, which hung loose around a pale face, the eyes heavily outlined in black as they had been when I had last seen her at the police station the day before. My gaze took in the thin legging-clad legs poking out from an alarmingly short black skirt and a black sleeveless smock revealing tattooed and scarred arms. Before I could open my mouth, Dr Hewitt beamed and rose to his feet, his hand outstretched in greeting.

114

'Abigail. How nice to see you again. Have you come to see Susan?' His eyes flicked uncertainly towards me. 'She's just had a visitor and may be rather tired, I'm afraid.'

'That's alright, doctor.' Abbey fixed her eyes on me. 'I haven't come to see my grandmother today. I've come to see Michaela.'

Abbey led the way with the ease of someone completely familiar with the home's layout, to a small sitting room where red velour armchairs were arranged around polished coffee tables covered with glossy magazines. We perched on the nearest of the chairs and I tried not to stare at the silver hoop which threaded through her left eyebrow or the stud at the side of her nostril which flared out as she breathed.

'How did you know I'd be here?'

She shrugged, making it an unnecessarily sullen gesture, since it was she who had sought me out. 'I thought you'd probably turn up here sooner or later.'

'How did you get here? Shouldn't you be at college?'

'What is this, the Spanish frigging inquisition? God, you are *so* like my dad.'

I lapsed into silence, nonplussed. Why had she come to find me when she was apparently so angry with me, I wondered?

'Bus.'

'Pardon?'

'I came on the bloody bus, what do you think?'

'Look . . .' I decided to take up the conversation where we'd left off the day before, trying to diffuse her anger. 'I tried to explain to you, Abbey – when I said I didn't leave you on purpose, I meant it.' I sighed, knowing that whatever I said she wouldn't believe me. But I had to try. 'As far as I'm concerned I said goodbye to you only two mornings ago.

I don't know where the six and a half years in between have gone to. I never left you or your father. Something or someone stole those years from us.'

She wrenched her eyes away from the view beyond the window and gave me a measured stare. 'You're mental. You should be here as a patient, not a bloody visitor.'

Her words struck home like a hammer blow and I felt my heart thudding in my chest. My gaze went automatically to the door, which had closed behind us and I wondered what it would be like to be shut in here against my will. What, I thought with the first flicker of real fear, if Abbey was right?

Chapter Nineteen

'I'm not mad, Abbey.' I hoped I was right and that my mother's mental instability wasn't hereditary. 'I'm finding it pretty hard to believe myself,' I pressed on. 'If it wasn't for the evidence of having you sitting in front of me looking six and a half years older, then I wouldn't believe it either, but it's the truth. How often do you visit my mother?' I asked after a few minutes of awkward silence. 'I'm surprised you've kept in touch with her all this time.'

'Well, I thought she was going to be my step-grandmother, didn't I?' The aggression with which she answered my questions took me aback, but I waited for her to go on. 'I always liked your mum; she was kind to me after you buggered off and left us. I think she felt a bit sorry for me, but she always insisted you hadn't gone off on purpose. She thought someone had kidnapped you or something.' Abbey raised her eyes to mine and I saw the hostility was being tempered by a tinge of sorrow. 'I didn't. Believe it, I mean. I hoped you were dead.'

I stared at her, wondering how she could be so cruelly candid. But she had convinced herself I was dead because that would mean I hadn't left her on purpose after all. 'It must have been a terrible shock when I showed up yesterday. I'm so sorry.'

She shrugged again, a gesture of defiance and not giving a damn, when I knew she cared very much.

'Why did you come to find me, Abbey?'

'I wanted to ask you to come home.'

Did I want to go back with Abbey? I wasn't sure any more. 'I don't think your father would be very pleased. He made it pretty clear on the phone yesterday that it was over between us.'

She glanced up at me from under long lashes thick with mascara. 'He was just tired and angry from being treated like some sort of criminal all day, he didn't mean it.'

I thought of Matt waiting for me outside. Thinking of the intensity of my feelings for him, I didn't think it was a good idea to contemplate going back to Calum. I shook my head. 'I can't.'

'Why not?'

'It's complicated, Abbey. For your father it's been over six years since we were together. We can't just pick up where we left off and pretend nothing happened.'

'You wanted to come back yesterday.'

I sighed. She was bright, this girl, older and wiser than I'd given her credit for. She pulled a cushion from behind her and hugged it to her chest. 'I think there's something wrong with him. He needs you, Kaela.'

'Wrong? In what way?'

'He pretends to go to work but when he thinks I'm safely at college, he just goes home and lies in the chair.'

'Well, he works from home. He isn't always out on sales calls.'

'They cut the phone off last week and he needs that for work, doesn't he? He got it put back on, but I'm worried we might not have enough money to keep the house.' Her voice had risen with her anxiety and I nodded to show that I understood.

'How come you know about what your father does during the day? Have you been skiving off college?'

She hung her head. 'I couldn't tell Dad. He'd be so mad with me.'

'This is only your first term there, surely? You've hardly given it a chance. Aren't you enjoying the course you're taking?'

There was a long silence and then she rested the cushion on her knees and looked up with an expression of such misery that I wondered what on earth she was going to say. 'I lied to him, didn't I? I never got offered a place at frigging college. My GCSE results were crap and they wouldn't take me.'

'Oh.' I pressed my lips together as I absorbed this information. 'That's quite a secret you've been keeping. Where on earth do you go every day?'

She gave that sullen shrug again. 'Sometimes I come here to see your mum, sometimes I hang out with people and do stuff. I thought I could sneak back home once Dad was out on his calls, but now he's home all the time too.'

'It must be hard living a lie. You'll have to tell him, you know.'

She gave me a pleading look, suddenly a child again. 'I rather hoped you might do it.'

'Oh Abbey, I don't think he'll listen to me any more.'

We stared at one another in silence until she tossed the cushion angrily to one side and leapt to her feet. 'You say you didn't leave us on purpose, but you're leaving us now, aren't you? You don't care about me or Dad, you just care about yourself.'

'That's not true.'

'No? Then come home with me now and talk to Dad. I can't face him again unless you do.'

I tried not to notice the desperation in her voice; the

119

veiled threat that she might do herself some harm. 'I can't, Abbey, I do care about you but I have to go and find my mother's solicitor. There are questions I need to ask, things I need to know.'

She glowered at me, her long fingernails picking at one of the scabs on her arm. 'Well, if you won't come home and you really care about me like you say, then take me with you.'

I glanced back towards the road and wondered what Matt and Kevin would say if I appeared with the truculent Abbey at my heels. Then I looked again at her scabbed arms and realised that the self inflicted wound she was picking at was a word . . . no not a word, but numbers; the numbers 666.

Before I had a chance to dwell on the morbid significance of these, Abbey let out a squeal of fright. 'Oh my God, Kaela, I've got to get out of here.'

'What?' I glanced at the door wondering what had agitated her so.

'It's Dad, he's here. See there, look between those bushes to the road, you can see him getting out of his car.'

I followed her gaze through the window and saw a figure stooping to lock an ancient Volvo. I remembered that Volvo well; Calum had been driving it when I'd first met him and it hadn't been anything like new, even then.

Glancing round anxiously, I breathed a sigh of relief that Matt and Kevin were parked in the side road, where Calum wouldn't see them. I didn't know why I was bothered if he spotted them or not, except for the feeling of guilt that I had betrayed him in some way. I realised I didn't want to come face-to-face with Calum today any more than Abbey did.

Abbey was white-faced and wide-eyed. 'He can't see me here when he thinks I'm at college! If you're not going to tell him for me, then I've got to get the hell out.'

'What on earth could he be doing here?' I asked of no one in particular.

'Come to find you, I expect. It's the one place he'd know you'd come, just like I did.' Abbey thrust her fist against her mouth and I wondered if she was going to be sick again.

'Look, if you really don't want to face him, we'll wait until he's gone into the office and slip out of the front door – presumably he'll have to stop and check in with Dr Hewitt.'

'There won't be time! He'll see us!'

'Is there a way out the back?'

She thought for a moment and nodded. 'We can get out through the kitchen. They keep the back door locked in case one of the patients tries to escape but I know Tommy, the cook here; he'll let us out if I ask him.'

Feeling like a fugitive, I followed Abbey back through the hall just as the front doorbell rang. The sound seemed to reverberate through the high-ceilinged room and I found myself breaking out into a sweat.

'Quick!' she squealed as she headed down a passage beside the lift and staircase.

We shot along it like a couple of scared rabbits and I followed Abbey as she flung open a polished wooden door at the far end. A young thin-faced man wearing black-and-white checked trousers and a white tunic looked up from the work surface in surprise.

'What the . . . ? Oh, it's you, Abbs. What's the hurry?'

'It's my Dad,' Abbey was panting and looking over her shoulder. 'He's just arrived and he can't find me here.'

'You want a quick exit, yeah?'

'Yes.' She glanced over her shoulder at me. 'And her too, she's not a patient or anything, but she doesn't want to see my father just now either.'

'OK then, anything for you, Abbs. Let's get you out the

back way.' He led us through the stainless steel kitchen to a side door, which he unlocked with a swipe card. 'Don't tell anyone I did this,' he said with a grin as we dived past him. 'Next time you come over you can read my cards for free and we'll call it quits.'

'Sure, Tommy, and thanks.'

Abbey and I slipped through the door and walked out onto the quiet side road. 'There's Matt's car,' I told her. 'I'll ask if he'll drop you at the bus stop.'

She stopped in her tracks and threw me an accusing look. 'Matt? The one they thought killed you? Have you been with him all along?'

I remembered Calum asking the same question the previous day. 'No, Abbey. He came to fetch me when I called him, that's all.'

I could see the indecision in her face. She wanted to believe me, but was finding it hard. 'I don't want to get the bus home, I want to come with you.' She folded her arms tightly across her chest as if to protect herself from further rejection. 'Please, Kaela?'

I looked into her pleading eyes and felt my resolve to leave her behind weaken. 'Well OK, but I'll have to ask Matt if he minds.'

Matt and Kevin were lounging in the front seat of the car, listening to some music I didn't recognise. Matt looked up when I tapped on the window and opened the driver's door.

'Hi. How was your mum?'

'Confused,' I replied with a sigh. 'She doesn't know whether to believe it's really me or just another hallucination.'

But he was already looking past me to where Abbey was standing. 'You're not alone then.'

'No. Look, I need to go and see my mother's solicitor in Putney. I'm hoping he'll have some idea what happened to things like my birth certificate, passport, driving licence and bank account. Are you still OK to be driving me around?'

He nodded. 'Of course.'

'And can Abbey tag along?'

He looked dubious. 'Is she who I think she is?'

'She's Calum's daughter, Abigail, yes.'

'Is this a good idea? I don't think your boyfriend would like her hanging around with us.'

I was about to say, *ex* boyfriend, when I realised what that admission might do to Abbey, so I merely shrugged. 'Her father thinks she's at college – and we've just missed bumping into him. For some reason he turned up at the nursing home.'

Matt looked over his shoulder, presumably hoping to avoid a confrontation.

He seemed to come to a decision. 'Come on then, you'd both better get in.'

Chapter Twenty

I climbed into the back seat and scooted over to the passenger side behind Kevin while Abbey slid in alongside me, slamming the door unnecessarily hard behind her. I made the introductions as Matt turned the key in the ignition and the car pulled away from the kerb.

Kevin reached his arm through the gap between the front seats and held out a hand for her to shake. Abbey took it warily, but he tightened his grip as soon as he had her hand, twisting her arm so he could get a close-up view of her self inflicted wounds.

'Six six six, that's a devil of a number. What's it doing on your arm?'

She wrenched her arm out of his grasp. 'None of your frigging business.'

'Nice language, toots,' Kevin intoned with a grin. 'I can see we're going to get along famously.' He narrowed his eyes at one of the tattoos visible on her upper arm. 'What's that, a five point star within a circle; a witch's pentagram, eh? Not very imaginative is it?'

I could feel Abbey tensing up beside me. 'Go to hell,' she told him shortly.

'A more likely destination for you, by the looks of things,' he replied.

Abbey fell silent and Kevin slouched down in the front seat, while I glanced towards the rear-view mirror to see Matt's eyes twinkling back at me. I could see he was trying to suppress an exasperated smile at the eccentricities of our travelling companions. 'Do you have the exact address for this solicitor?' he asked neutrally.

I read out the address Dr Hewitt had given me and he nodded. I found I was drawn to his eyes in the mirror and couldn't stop looking at him.

'Actually, 666 is a very meaningful number,' Abbey said suddenly. 'Even if you forget the devil worship element for a moment.'

'It's not that important a number,' Kevin shot back. 'There are other numbers that are far more interesting.'

'The three sixes represent the secret symbol of ancient pagan mysteries, I'll have you know. In the Greek alphabet it is represented by an "S" making six, six, six, "SSS", which is the symbol of the goddess Isis.'

'Not as interesting in my book, as the number 52,' Kevin countered, still looking idly out of the window. 'Now that *is* a number.'

'I thought *42* was supposed to be the meaning of life,' Matt murmured dryly.

'You mean from the *Hitchhiker's Guide to the Galaxy*?' I smiled, 'the quest for the Ultimate Question?'

Matt nodded, but Abbey wasn't having her point brushed to one side by the vagaries of a TV programme.

'Six six six is related to the golden ratio,' Abbey threw back angrily as if Matt hadn't spoken. 'You can't get more important than the Fibonacci sequence, for goodness' sake. The golden ratio or Phi is the equation that forms the very building blocks of the universe.'

'We've all read the *Da Vinci Code*, toots. It doesn't mean

we have to carve a minor relation to Phi into our skin,' Kevin pointed out.

'Don't you "toots" me!' Abbey squealed, sitting forward, her seatbelt straining as she tried to make her point. 'What do a couple of wackos know about anything? You're probably the ones who took Kaela away from us in the first place!'

'You ought to check out my website,' Kevin replied. 'Then you'll hear all the theories about where Michaela has been for the past six and a half years.'

'I suppose it's like that weird website I've logged onto by someone calling himself Space Dog,' Abbey snorted.

'You got it, babe.'

'I wasn't abducted by aliens,' I protested, but my words were lost on the two combatants.

'How often have you logged onto that site?' Kevin asked.

'A few times, I suppose. I have to do something to stop me from going crazy.'

Kevin turned round in his seat again and grinned at her. 'Space Dog says hello.'

'What?'

'I'm Space Dog. I run the website.'

'You're kidding me?'

'I kid you not, toots. And for your information, I don't believe she was abducted by aliens either, but it let Matt off the hook six years ago and it brings in the bread. We sell Space Dog T-shirts, hoodies, bracelets and all kinds of abduction-theory memorabilia.'

'Shit, I've got a Space Dog pendant at home.' Abbey lapsed into silence and Kevin returned his gaze to the windscreen as we passed Chessington and headed for the A3.

I occupied myself with gazing at Matt's back, wishing I could reach out and touch him.

'What's so special about the number 52 anyway?' she said

126

suddenly, throwing down the gauntlet again. 'I mean, I know it's the number of weeks in a solar year and the number of playing cards in a pack and the number of white notes on a piano . . .'

'I could tell you a hundred interesting facts about the number 52, starting with the Fibonacci sequence as you're so interested in it.'

'Go on then smart arse Space Dog, surprise me.'

'Fifty two is the sum of the third through the eighth of the Fibonacci numbers. And in Pythagoras's "Golden Verse", the fifty second verse reads "Thou shalt likewise know that according to law, the nature of this universe is in all things alike."'

Abbey made a small snorting noise but Kevin ploughed on. 'Fifty two is also the atomic number of the semi-metal Tellurium, the Mayan calendar moves through a complete cycle every 52 years, the Morden Blush rose and the Yin Hehuan lotus have 52 petals each . . .' He took a breath before continuing. 'In symbolism, as you obviously like that kind of thing, 52 stands for being able, determined and a lover of mountains, which is interesting as chapter 52 of the Holy Koran is titled "The Mountain"– you should read it, it's enlightening stuff.'

Abbey fell silent beside me and I knew she was listening now.

'And you'll like these – number 52 is not only the number of chapters in Jeremiah in the Old Testament but it's also the number of the set of religious and philosophical texts found hidden in an earthenware jar which include the lost Gospel of Thomas and the secret sayings of Christ.'

'Those things are all ancient history,' Abbey pointed out, wriggling in her seat beside me. 'The numbers 666 are still relevant today. I suppose you know that the central computer that ties all the national computers together is housed in

Brussels and is so huge that it's actually nicknamed "the beast"? It has a 6 core memory with 60 bytes per word and 6 bits to character; that's 6, 60, 6.'

'If you bothered to read the Bible before deciding to go off on some uninformed satanic journey, you'd have saved yourself the indignity of walking round with that rubbish carved into your arm for the rest of your life. I'll bet you didn't know that the fifty second word of the King James version of the Bible's Old Testament is . . . God.' I half listened to the two of them, wearying of the numerical sparring as I watched Matt navigate the traffic, but then Abbey, rising to the challenge anew, announced, 'You have realised, I suppose, that Kaela went missing on 14th April 2002 and turned up again on 20th October 2008?'

Kevin was nodding, 'Yeah, of course, what of it?'

'That's 6 years, 6 months and 6 days,' Abbey announced triumphantly. 'Kaela's disappearance obviously has something sinister about it because those are the numbers of the beast: 666. Beat *that* smart arse.'

Chapter Twenty-One

Mr Archibald Brent of Armstrong and Brent Solicitors deemed to give me fifteen minutes of his precious time so Matt and I left Kevin and Abbey in the car still warring over symbolic numbers while we climbed the short flight of stairs to his office.

After formal introductions the middle-aged man with a comb-over of thinning black hair waved us towards two hard-backed chairs and took his own comfy swivel chair on the opposite side of a wide cluttered desk.

'So what you're asking is if your parents left any legal documents pertaining to you in my possession?'

I nodded as my eyes roamed the messy office, taking in a row of antique bookshelves on the far wall and a computer sitting half hidden amid heaps of papers on a long shelf. 'My boyfriend, who I was living with at the time, says he sent all my things back to my parents. With my father dead . . .' I took a deep breath and tried to close my mind to the actuality that I would never see my father again. It was something I had been trying to block out since I'd first heard about it. On the practical front I needed to deal with the consequences of the fact that he had gone, but on the emotional front I simply didn't believe it. 'And with my mother in the nursing home, I need to know where my birth certificate, passport and driving licence are. And I need to know if I still have a functioning bank account.'

'The problem we have,' Mr Brent leaned forward and regarded me earnestly from under bushy eyebrows, 'is that for me to be able to deal with you on this matter, I will need proof of your identity. Anyone could walk through that door and claim to be the long lost relation of one of our clients.' He wrinkled his nose distastefully. 'I don't mean to be rude, my dear, but you could be simply anybody.'

I felt my shoulders sag. 'Don't tell me, you'd want to see a birth certificate, passport or driving licence.'

The solicitor nodded and I felt Matt bristle beside me. 'If you have any of those documents you could see from the passport photograph that she is who she says she is,' he insisted. 'Surely that's the whole point of having photos on the things?'

'Anyone of similar build and face shape could make themselves up to look like someone they're not. We have a duty to our clients to protect their possessions. If we took your word that this young lady is the long-lost daughter of the late Leonard and Susan Anderson and it turned out she was not that person, it would not reflect well on our competence as a company, now would it?'

'The police have accepted that I am Michaela Anderson.' I tried to reconcile this pedantic, obstructive man with the person who had found a place in the nursing home for my mother and who was overseeing her future with such care. 'And Matt here has confirmed I am who I say I am, so why won't you accept his word for it?'

He leaned back in his chair and regarded me thoughtfully. 'I believe Mr Treguier was at one time suspected by the police of your abduction. For all I know he has some ulterior motive in confirming your identity.'

I sighed, realising that for some reason the solicitor was not going to make this easy for me. I contemplated bringing Kevin or Abigail up to identify me but Kevin had also been suspected of being involved in my disappearance and one look at Abbey would probably confirm the solicitor's suspicions that we were a group of nut-cases. 'Why don't you just ring DI Smith and ask her?'

'I might just do that, yes indeed that would be a splendid idea. If you could make an appointment with my secretary, I will try to see you again early next week.'

'Next week? How am I supposed to survive until then? Unless I have means of identifying myself or access to my bank account I am completely unable to survive without relying on the charity of my friends!'

His eyes narrowed giving me a brief glimpse into the workings of the mind of the man beneath the professional façade. 'It is fortunate for you that you have such friends, young lady. Miss Anderson's father was a business associate and colleague of mine. I had to stand by and watch him grieve for his lost daughter. He became a mere shadow of the rather dashing man I had once known in the banking world, desperate and in deep emotional pain. News of his eventual death, although a shock, was in its way a blessing. I hope and pray you are an impostor, because the alternative – that you chose to remain in hiding while he suffered so badly would be very hard to bear.'

Maybe Abbey's triple sixes had some significance after all, I thought, maybe I was some kind of monster. The blood, which had rushed to my head in response to his cutting words, now drained just as quickly. As if it wasn't bad enough that I had lost six years of my life, my supposed disappearance was directly to blame for my father's death, my mother's decline, Calum's loneliness, Abigail's insecurities and Matt's persecution. The buzzing in my head which had started on the deserted airfield two days ago rose to a crescendo. A sepia-coloured wave seemed to roll towards me and I fell forwards, then down, down into a musty-smelling pit. And saw only blackness and despair.

I stirred to find Matt leaning over me. Someone thrust a glass of water in my hand and I clutched at it, trying to remember where I was.

'Can you stand?'

I nodded and allowed Matt to help me to my feet where I stood, swaying dangerously. I was in the ante room of the solicitor's office but Mr Brent was nowhere to be seen. His secretary, a small mousy looking woman in her fifties, hovered anxiously then took the glass of water from me as Matt directed me towards a chair. I took a few deep breaths and tried to steady my pounding heart.

'I have to make an appointment for next week,' I whispered, as my memory came back to me, 'as soon and early as possible.'

The secretary returned to her desk where she flipped pages in her diary before looking up. 'Would eleven thirty on Monday morning suit you?'

I nodded and after a few more deep breaths, I got to my feet. We descended the steep stairs to street level with Matt's arm fastened securely round my waist, and as soon as we were outside I gulped gratefully at the cool air and leaned against him for a moment while I regained my senses.

'I'm so sorry.' I gave him an apologetic smile, thinking how I had nearly collapsed at his house the evening he had collected me from the pub. 'I'm not prone to fainting, honestly. I always thought women who swooned at the first sign of trouble were pathetically weak creatures.'

He gave me a reassuring squeeze. 'You have been through

quite a bit in the last couple of days, I think you can be excused a little weakness.'

'You don't have to be lumbered with me,' I offered shakily. 'I could still go to the women's hostel for a few days until Mr Brent has satisfied himself as to my identity. Once I've got some means of identification I can look after myself.'

'There's no way you're going to the hostel.' We'd started walking slowly back to the car, his hand supportively under my arm. 'I've waited over six years for you, Michaela, and I'm not letting you slip away from me again that easily.'

The car was parked where we'd left it and surprisingly Abbey and Kevin were sitting together in the back, their heads bowed in concentration over something on the seat between them. We'd been gone about an hour in all and I'd half expected to see them at each other's throats. Kevin looked up as Matt opened the front passenger door and grinned. 'You back already?'

'Our friend Mr Brent wasn't overly cooperative,' Matt told him as he slid into the driver's seat. 'He won't accept Michaela's word – or mine for that matter – as to who she is.'

'He's punishing me.' I leaned my head back against the head rest and closed my eyes. 'He was a business associate of my father. He holds me responsible for Dad's death and I can't say I blame him, given the circumstances.'

'Well, according to these cards of Abbey's, you've got a lot more difficulties to come,' Kevin announced, almost gleefully. 'There are trials and tribulations ahead of you that would keep fans of my website agog for weeks.'

I opened my eyes and glanced sharply into the back, where a set of cards was splayed out in the shape of a cross on the leather seat. I recognised them immediately as tarot cards and my mind went back to the cook in my mother's nursing home. *You can read my cards for free . . .*

'Don't tell me you believe in that stuff,' I groaned.

'It is rather fascinating,' Kevin told me with a grin. 'Abbs definitely has a way with the cards.'

'It's rubbish,' I protested, gazing distastefully at the cards on the seat between them. 'And even supposing for a moment that the cards do tell the future, surely we're better off not knowing what lies in store? I for one do not want to know.'

Matt reached out a hand and rested it lightly on my knee. 'I had my cards read at a fairground once, just for a laugh – and the reader told me I was going to find the woman of my dreams; that I would lose her, but that all I would have to do was wait patiently and she would come back to me one day. I thought it was rubbish at the time.'

'I think people who go to have their cards read are open to suggestion in the first place and simply interpret what happens to them in terms of what was foretold.' I turned back in my seat but not before I'd seen the look in Abbey's eyes. I was pretty sure she wasn't simply miffed at my dismissal of her card reading abilities; she hadn't missed the meaning of Matt's words or the familiarity of his touch. I pulled my leg away from him, partly to appease Abbey and partly because I was disappointed that Matt had not only been to a tarot reader but actually set some store by what he'd been told. 'Can we just get out of here?'

Matt sighed and started the engine. 'Where to?'

'We should go home,' Abbey announced in a tight voice. 'According to the cards you're going back to Dad anyway, so you may as well get on with it.'

'I am not going to have the direction of my life dictated by a pack of cards.' I stared pointedly out of the side window while Matt hesitated, the car in neutral. An awkward silence grew between us as Abbey mumbled something unintelligible under her breath, scraped the cards together and thrust them

134

back into the pack. Kevin rolled his eyes to the car's ceiling as if silently questioning the vagaries of women but for once, he kept quiet. I considered the options that were open to me, wishing I could just have things back the way they were before I'd made that ruddy jump. A women's hostel, my mother's nursing home, little Abbey playing with tarot cards, Calum's rejection, Kevin's weirdness, the feelings for Matt I had to hide from Abbey – not to mention the six missing years and my lack of proven identity all jostled for precedence. And then suddenly, as if the flood of terror and disillusionment had come to a head, the dam burst wide open. The pressure which had been building behind my eyes released and I found the whole thing terribly, mind-shatteringly hilarious.

I made a snorting noise as I tried to suppress a torrent of mirth, but it was too late; the laughter bubbled up out of my throat. Giggling, my shoulders heaving, I fumbled in the pocket of my fleece for a tissue to clamp over my mouth. Matt was smiling at me nervously but both Abbey and Kevin remained silent, seemingly bewildered by my sudden change in mood.

'Oh, I'm sorry.' I was gasping for breath, barely able to talk, still rummaging for a tissue. 'It's just all so awful . . . and so . . . funny.' A piece of paper slid into my groping hand. My eyes were streaming but I could make out a name and address and I, who had never set any store on omens or premonitions of any kind, had an answer to Matt's question written before me in Kevin's angular writing. Ingrid.

Wiping my eyes on the back of my hand I leaned round to look at the other two through a blur of tears. 'Anyone fancy a trip to Brighton?'

Chapter Twenty-Two

It took over two hours to get to Brighton in the end and by the time Matt had parked the car in a multi-storey car park it was almost three o'clock in the afternoon. Having grabbed some sandwiches at a service station we were ready to start looking for Ingrid's flat almost immediately, though I was concerned that Abbey should let her father know that she was safe and would be home late.

'What time does he think your college day ends?' I asked as Matt locked the car and we headed out into a side street between tall grey buildings. Abbey wrapped her arms around herself and shivered.

'He won't care what time I get in.' She spoke through clenched teeth and I felt a maternal concern that she should have brought a coat. 'I'm sure he worries about you more than you realise. If you want to stay with us, I'd rather you rang him.'

'Here.' Kevin removed his zip front jacket and draped it round her bare shoulders as she fished her phone from the bag. 'It's freezing down here.'

Abbey made the call, telling Calum she would be hanging out with a friend after college and not to worry if she was late coming home. I gave her an approving smile as we crossed the road and walked along the sea front, heads bowed against the wind. I inhaled the sea air, tasting its saltiness on my lips and marvelled at how the brown waves crashed constantly and rhythmically onto the pebble beach below us.

As we made our way inland, the wind lessened and I tugged my fingers through hair that felt sticky with salt. Abigail still looked blue with cold, even with Kevin's jacket zipped up to her chin. Her bare ankles looked white, sticking out from thin legging-clad legs, her feet thrust into flimsy flats and her short skirt completely invisible beneath the jacket. Matt had been walking, head down, hands thrust deep in the pockets of his jacket, and only Kevin with his short, wiry red hair and clad in a baggy T-shirt emblazoned with the name of a band I'd never heard of, looked relatively un-windswept and at ease.

'Regent Gardens,' I read out. 'I think we should carry on inland a bit longer.'

After twice asking for directions we found ourselves at the foot of some stone steps leading to a long row of terraced Regency-style houses. The black painted front door was faded and chipped and the line of buzzers had long ago lost their name tags. 'Flat eight, number twenty four, Regent Gardens,' I intoned. 'This is it.'

We climbed the steps and Matt pressed his finger to the top bell. After a brief pause there was a buzzing sound and we were admitted into a gloomy hallway. Although it hadn't been particularly bright outside, we stood blinking in the dull and shabby hallway, noticing how threadbare the hall and stair carpet were; the once grand wallpaper peeling and dotted with graffiti.

There were four doors leading off the ground floor, marked with the numbers one to four, so I started up the stairs to the first floor.

Matt hesitated. 'I think we should wait for you here, your friend isn't going to want to be inundated with all of us at once.' He sat down on the third step and fished his phone from his pocket. 'I've got some calls to make anyway.'

Abbey settled herself on the stair below him, but Kevin grinned wickedly and stepped around them. 'I for one, would love to set eyes on the delectable Ingrid again.'

'Come on then.' I rolled my eyes as he trotted up ahead of me. Once we found number eight Kevin took a step back while I stared at the grey painted front door before ringing the bell.

A few moments passed, as someone scrutinised me through the peephole, then the door opened as far as a security chain would allow.

'Ingrid?'

'Who wants to know?'

'It's me, Michaela. I'm back and I need to talk to you.'

'Don't be ridiculous, Michaela's dead. Who are you?'

'It really is me, Ing.' I fidgeted from one foot to the other, hoping she wasn't going to slam the door in my face. 'Are you going to let me in?'

There was a long pause and then the safety chain was removed and the door opened to reveal a skinny woman in her mid thirties, with stringy, bleached-blond hair showing mousy roots at the centre. She wasn't wearing any make-up and her face seemed grey and drawn, with deep wrinkles round her eyes and mouth. She was wearing a faded denim mini-skirt with a low-necked T-shirt revealing a deep cleavage. Her mouth had dropped open when she saw me and she clamped a hand to her throat as if to protect herself from the shock.

'My God, it is you.'

'Can I come in?'

She looked past me to where Kevin was standing in the shadows and her expression became wary. I could see she was fighting some internal battle of indecision, but then her shoulders slumped a little and she gave a minuscule toss of her head. 'Just you, he can clear off,' she said rudely.

I turned apologetically towards Kevin. 'Would you mind? Can I meet you and the others at the car later on?'

'I suppose so.' Kevin sounded disappointed. 'I guess we could go and find ourselves a cup of tea in one of the café's on the front. He started to turn away, then stopped and handed me his mobile phone. 'Matt's number is listed, just give us a call when you're ready, OK?'

'Thanks.' I watched him turn away towards the stairs and followed Ingrid inside the flat. She slammed the door behind me and put the safety chain back in place. 'You can't be too careful,' she commented as she turned to stare at me. 'God, you don't look a day older. How have you done that? Where the hell have you been anyway? We all gave you up for dead.'

We were standing in a sparsely furnished and very dilapidated room. She walked past me, her pair of fluffy pink slippers slapping at the old carpet as she moved to pick a couple of tattered magazines from a stained and grubby sofa. I'd thought Calum's house had been badly neglected but this was something else altogether. Whereas Calum's place could have been put to rights with a thorough airing and a good clean, Ingrid's flat was damp, with peeling paint and wallpaper. The high-ceilinged Regency walls were permeated with the smell of mildew and decay.

She dropped down onto the sofa and unscrewed the top of a bottle of vodka. 'Drink?'

'Not for me thanks, Ing.' I looked round for somewhere to sit, but there was no other furniture in the room so I sat down on the sofa next to her. 'Why did you move all the way down here? What's happened to you? Have you got another job?'

Her eyes flashed and then she nodded abruptly, bottle

poised in mid air. 'You could say circumstances beyond my control brought me here and yes, I work. But what about you? You can't just turn up here with no explanation. What the hell happened to *you*?' She poured a measure of the vodka into a glass that seemed to have been tucked down the side of the couch and took a mouthful.

I toyed momentarily with the idea of making something up, but found I couldn't lie to her. Ingrid had been my best friend since we'd met at Wayfarers a few years back – a few years from my perspective anyway, and we'd shared lunch breaks and girly evenings out and talked about everything from the latest fashion to our latest men. I remembered with a jolt that while I'd had promotion in mind and advancement within the company, Ingrid's aim had only ever been to find the perfect man and settle down. Her pursuit of that goal had involved dating every available man within the company and had earned her a bit of a reputation.

I took a deep breath and plunged ahead. 'The thing is . . . I haven't been anywhere, Ing. As far as I'm concerned we did that parachute jump a couple of days ago. I feel like I only saw you the other day.'

She stared at me, studying my face carefully as if searching for a hint of something in my expression. 'You're talking rubbish. Are you on something?'

I shook my head. 'No. I don't know what's happened to me. I thought at first it was some sort of prank, a trick, but then I realised that no-one could make the seasons change or people I know grow older. The police think I was abducted and held somewhere against my will and that I'm blocking out the memory of it.' I smiled apologetically. 'Kevin thinks I was abducted by aliens.'

She snorted. 'I thought that was him in the hallway; he always was a prat.'

The derisive comment should have been offensive, but Ingrid had always been quick to judge and liked to reduce people with her dry humour.

If I hadn't known about her background and what her childhood had been like I might have disliked her, as did many of our female colleagues. But Ingrid had drunk too much one evening and confided in me the details of her miserable childhood. Too pretty for her own good, she had been abused by one, then another of her mother's boyfriends and even after being taken into care she had been singled out by one of the staff who preyed on her vulnerability by systematically violating her.

Shocked, and feeling guilty that my own childhood had been idyllic in comparison, I had made it my business to befriend her. And the Ingrid I knew and loved could be outrageously funny when she set her mind to it.

But now Ingrid's expression was serious, her head tilted to one side as she looked at me. 'Do you really not remember where you've been?'

I shook my head, wishing I had something to confide to her.

'Is it possible you might have been kidnapped? I mean, surely you have *some* feeling as to what might have happened?'

'I really don't. The last six and a half years are a complete blank.'

There was a small spark of interest in her eyes, now overlying the suspicion and desolation that had been there a moment ago. 'You're sure Kevin wasn't involved in some way? He was always a bit too smart, if you ask me. And he's weird round women.'

I remembered my initial fear that Matt and Kevin had been involved in my disappearance, but I shook it away. 'I think he's harmless enough. He just doesn't know how to

141

behave with the opposite sex unless they can discuss computers or some of his more wacky theories with him.' I thought of the numerical sparring he and Abigail had indulged in and decided that was a case in point.

'Hmm,' she didn't sound convinced.

We sat for a second or two in silence while she sipped at her drink and I stared around the room. 'Why did you leave Wayfarers?' I asked at last. 'You seemed so happy there.'

Ingrid gave a deep, heartfelt sigh. 'Nothing was the same after you left. We were questioned by the police and then the press got hold of your sudden disappearance and pestered the life out of us. I couldn't go outside my own front door for flashbulbs going off in my face.' She took another swig of her drink. 'After a couple of years or so everything seemed to go wrong with my life at the same time. I had to leave the job and couldn't afford to keep up the payments on the flat. I had no one to turn to for support so I moved down here to make a fresh start.'

I glanced at the tattered curtains hanging at the front window and the piles of rubbish heaped in the corners of the room. There wasn't even a television or a telephone in sight. 'How do you live?'

'I get by.'

We lapsed into an uneasy silence again. I didn't want to leave her but wasn't sure if she really wanted me to stay. After all, it seemed it was unwittingly my fault she was in these circumstances in the first place. That all-too-familiar feeling of guilt rolled over me. I'd not asked for whatever it was that had happened to happen, but still, the dramatic changes in the circumstances of my family and friends were somehow connected to me. I felt my hands grow damp and my mouth felt dry.

'Could I have a drink of water?'

'Help yourself.' She nodded towards one of the two doors to the right of us.

I got up and went into a tiny kitchen, trying not to shudder at the sight of unwashed plates piled in the sink, and the general dirtiness of the cupboards and work surfaces. There was a plastic beaker on the side which appeared to have black-currant in it and a saucepan on the hob containing the remains of spaghetti hoops. In one corner of the room a pile of blankets and a duvet had been tossed in a heap; it looked as if someone had been camping out on the floor.

Grabbing a semi-clean glass from a cupboard I poured myself some water and was about to return to the living room when curiosity made me pause to look more closely at the mound of grubby bedding. There was a small pair of scuffed trainers sticking out from one corner of the blanket. Puzzled, I bent to pick them up and as I did so, I heard a movement behind me and saw Ingrid framed in the kitchen doorway.

'Nosy cow, aren't you?' she said coldly.

Straightening up I turned to face her, but she wasn't alone. Standing a few paces behind her stood a small boy with a pale face and tousled, light brown hair. He looked as if he could do with a good bath, but was a handsome child. He regarded me suspiciously through anxious blue eyes. I'd seen those eyes before; they were Ingrid's eyes.

'Good grief, Ing . . .' I struggled with the knowledge that since I had seen her only two days ago, she had acquired a child who looked to be around four or five years old. 'Is he yours?'

She nodded abruptly. 'Of course he's bloody well mine. This is Tristan Matthew Peters – my son.'

143

Chapter Twenty-Three

I stared at the child who had one hand round his mother's leg, while the other clutched at a filthy piece of frayed blanket.

'And before you ask, I'm not married,' Ingrid announced in that same defensive voice. 'His father is no longer around.'

Suddenly a little of my friend's struggles became clear. This child was possibly the reason Ingrid had been forced to leave her job at the insurance company.

The boy was watching me warily and I smiled tentatively at him. He dropped his gaze immediately and hid behind his mother. Ingrid grew impatient and pulled his hand away from her leg, before marching back into the living room where she flopped down on the couch again. The child followed her and stood next to her.

As I drew closer, he backed away from me making sure the couch was firmly between us.

Ingrid gave him a none-too gentle shove. 'Stop being silly, Tristan. Say hello to Kaela.'

Tristan managed a small noise that I took to be a greeting as I hunkered down so I was on his level. 'Hi Tristan, I'm Kaela. I'm a friend of your mummy.'

'A long time ago, maybe,' Ingrid amended curtly. 'Whether you were kidnapped or not, you haven't been much of a friend for the last six years have you?' She picked the bottle of vodka off the floor and poured herself another hefty measure. 'Where were you when I needed you?'

'I'm sorry, Ingrid. I can't do more than say how sorry I am. Is there anything I can do for you now? Anything you want?' I remembered my own circumstances and wondered what I thought I could do for her. I had no money, no clothes, nowhere of my own to stay.

'You can't resurrect our friendship after everything that's happened; it's not possible.' She tilted her head to look up at me. 'When I was giving birth to Tris I prayed you'd appear out of nowhere to hold my hand or rub my aching back. I was the only mum on the ward who had no visitors, no cards of congratulation, or relatives bearing bunches of flowers.' She paused and I watched her eyes moisten slightly. 'Do you remember that time I was dumped by Greg at the office? I'd thought he was the One, the love of my life, but he dumped me for that frumpy cow from finance, and you came over with an enormous box of chocolates and a bottle of wine and we stuffed our faces and got completely pissed?'

I nodded, trying a hopeful smile. 'We could be like that again.'

She looked away abruptly and fumbled for the vodka bottle. 'It's too late for that now, Kaela.' She took a swig, not bothering with the glass this time, despite the fact that her son was watching her closely. She gave a harsh laugh. 'I was always the bad girl, wasn't I?'

'It wasn't your fault. You had a lousy start in life, but you were fun to be with.'

'Fun for you maybe, shit for me.' Her face took on a grim look. 'I hated you sometimes, do you know that? Miss goody-two-shoes with respectable parents and a comfy middle class home. Smart, organised, good looking . . . God, Kaela, you had it all. What did you ever see in me?'

'You were my friend . . . are my friend. You were there for me as much as I was there for you.'

She shook her head. 'I was hanging on your shirttails, hoping a bit of you would rub off on me. I wanted what you had and . . . and I liked the way you seemed to think I was worth something.'

'It went both ways, Ing. I'll never forget my first day at Wayfarers. I was trying to hide my nerves when I went into the cafeteria and my hands were shaking so much, my roll and juice slid off the tray.' I smiled at her, willing her to remember. 'Everyone seemed to be looking at me and I felt like such an idiot. And you came over and took my tray, so I could scrabble about on the floor to clear up the mess, and then you invited me over to share your table. You were friendly and kind and I was so grateful to you.'

I took a step towards her, but she held up a hand and shot me a venomous look. 'I was never really your friend. It's best you believe that now before you try to recapture something that never existed.'

I felt my eyes fill with tears. 'You're just down and upset, but you will always be my friend, Ingrid.'

'You don't abandon a friend for six years without so much as a word.'

The conversation had gone full circle and I could see I wasn't achieving anything by being here. Ingrid was lonely, bitter and rather drunk and there didn't seem to be anything I could say to console her.

'Look, I'd better go. Matt, Kevin and Abbey are waiting for me.'

Her head shot up and her eyes narrowed. 'Matt? You don't mean Matt Treguier, surely?'

I nodded. 'After I found myself wandering around the deserted airfield, I called him. He came to fetch me.'

'Oh, I'll bet he did. He was always going on about you, Michaela this and Michaela bloody that . . .'

'You saw him again? After I went missing?' I interrupted her.

She shook her head, as if wondering how I could be quite so stupid. 'Of course I saw him. We were all thrown together, Graham, Kevin, Matt and me. We went through hell. We were the only people who understood what it was like to lose you like that and at the same time to be suspected of having something to do with your disappearance. It made us really close.'

I thought of her abrupt dismissal of Kevin and wondered if her recollection of that time was rather different from theirs.

Her eyes flickered towards her son and settled back on my face. 'And did you say Abbey? Are you back with Calum then?'

'No. Abbey wants me to go back, but I don't think Calum wants me after all this time.'

Ingrid drained the remains of the bottle and dropped it beside her on the couch. She stared off into space and for a moment I thought she had forgotten my existence. Tristan stood quietly, his eyes moving from his mother to me as if he'd seen her like this many times before and was waiting for some inevitable outcome. And then she gave me a bitter smile.

'Just remember one thing; a word of warning from your old pal . . .' She hiccoughed and pressed the back of her hand to her mouth, before uncurling an index finger and wagging it at me. 'All men, Kaela, and I do mean *all* men . . . are complete bastards.'

Matt, Kevin and Abbey were sitting in a café below the promenade, when I eventually tracked them down. Abbey was wrapped tightly in Kevin's jacket but her long hair was being blown across her face by a stiff, sea breeze and she looked blue with cold. Her hands were clasped round a polystyrene cup of hot chocolate. Matt and Kevin were nursing beers. Matt leapt to his feet when he saw me and pulled out a chair.

'How did it go?'

I wasn't sure if I was imagining the anxious look in his eyes as he asked the question. What did he think Ingrid had told me? Her parting words niggled me as I sat down. I glanced at a nearby couple locked in one another's embrace and wished my life was as simple as that. Why did everything have to be so damned complicated?

'She's in a bad way.'

Kevin nodded sagely. 'I met a guy on my way out of Ingrid's building. He was coming up the stairs and asked if I'd just come from her flat. When I said I might have done, he winked and asked if she was any good.'

I stared at him, eyes wide with shock. 'You don't mean . . .? What did you say?'

'I told him she was busy at the moment. He said he'd wait.'

'Oh poor Ingrid! She said she worked and I did wonder what she did, but I never imagined . . .' I pictured the child's bedding bundled in the corner of the kitchen. If the flat only had one bedroom and Ingrid entertained there, did that mean Tristan slept on the kitchen floor? I grabbed Matt's beer and took a long drink, wiping my mouth with the back of my hand while Matt and Kevin looked on in silence.

Abbey glanced up from her hot chocolate and grimaced. 'What . . . is this friend of yours a hooker?'

I stared at her in horror. I was still thinking of Abbey as the little girl she had been and the question, asked in such a matter-of-fact way, left me reeling. I shook my head, quite

148

dazed. 'I don't know. But she has a child to support and things are obviously very difficult for her.'

'Still, to go on the game is a bit drastic. I mean, all those strange men, ugh!' Abbey swallowed the last of her chocolate and gave a heartfelt shiver.

I shook my head. The world I had left only a few days ago had changed so dramatically that I felt completely at sea.

I didn't have long to wallow in self-pity, because Abbey had leapt to her feet, crumpled her polystyrene cup and was glowering at me accusingly. 'What are you going to do now? You're not going home with him, are you?' She shot Matt a venomous glare.

'I don't know that I have much choice.'

'You have to come home with me. Dad needs you.'

'Oh, Abbey, we've been through this. I told you, your father made it clear our relationship was over.'

She faced up to me, her head down but her eyes fixed on mine. 'You're no better than your whore of a friend! I told you Dad was only tired and annoyed and you're just using it as an excuse to run out on us.'

'Abbey, that's not true.' But even as I said it I wondered if she was right. I had wanted to be with Matt from the moment he'd come for me at the pub. The trouble was, I knew, deep down that I also still cared a great deal for Calum.

She latched on to my moment of doubt immediately.

'Come back with me, Kaela,' she pleaded, gripping my arm with her purple-tipped fingers. 'Please?'

Matt had put down his beer and was watching the proceedings intently. I wanted to turn and huddle in his arms, but the touch of Abbey's cold hand and the pleading look in her eyes was weakening my resolve.

'What if I said I'd at least speak to your father? When we

drop you off, I suppose I could come in so we could have a proper talk. If you like, I'll tell him about the fact that you're not actually going to college.'

I felt Matt stiffen beside me and Kevin muttered something I couldn't quite catch, but Abbey's eyes had filled with hope and I knew that I'd made the right decision. I was pretty sure Calum would confirm that our relationship was well and truly over, Abbey would see that I had made one last effort for her, and I'd feel absolved somehow, from running out on them the minute I was back.

But life, it seemed, wasn't going to be made quite that easy.

Chapter Twenty-Four

The journey back to Leatherhead seemed to take forever despite the miles flashing by outside the car window. As if my bizarre situation wasn't bad enough, there was the deep, raw grief for my father gnawing at my insides that I was trying to push unsuccessfully to the back of my mind. I gripped the hand rest, took deep breaths and realised I felt quite sick.

Running the window down a couple of inches, I leaned my face against the glass and let the cold evening air rush past me, swallowing as the uneven pressure in the car battered against my eardrums. I tried to recall any instances over the years which might indicate why my supposedly best friend should profess to have hated me. Was it envy, or had I never really understood her? I thought about what she'd said about my having such a settled home life and that led me to the dark area I'd been trying to avoid– what my six year disappearance had done to my parents.

I tried to remember what Dad had said the previous weekend when I'd popped in for a chat and told him and Mum about the impending parachute jump. What words had I chosen for our last conversation together on this earth? Why hadn't I told him I loved him? Had I ever actually said the words? I recalled the weekends when he read the newspaper from cover to cover, reading out titbits of some silly article that we'd spar over until Mum came in telling us not to take things so seriously. When they'd entertained he'd been the perfect host; a good story-teller and a bit of a flirt. He'd seemed so healthy, so permanent. I couldn't get my head round the fact that I'd never do those things with him, never see him again.

I gave a small sob which I tried to turn into a cough when I realised I was still sitting in the back seat of the car. Abbey paused in her declaration to Kevin that he was a moron and looked at me closely and frowned.

'Are you alright?'

Kevin, in his usual insensitive way, was still bumbling on, 'Tarot cards are complete crap, toots. Look at the symbolism of a normal pack.'

'Shut up,' Abbey said briskly. 'There's something wrong with Kaela.'

'I'm fine,' I lied. 'It's just that everything has changed so much since . . . last week. It's hard to get my head around it all.'

'Not so hard as her bloody tarot cards,' Kevin mumbled. 'I mean . . .'

'Shut up, Kevin.' Matt was looking at me in the mirror. I wished I'd sat in the front with him again.

'Is it because I called your friend a hooker?' Abbey asked. Her voice was still confrontational but I noticed she was looking anxious and I wondered if she thought I might have changed my mind about coming to talk to her father. 'If what you, Matt and Kevin say is true, then you must be feeling pretty weird, not being able to remember the last six years and everything,' she conceded.

'It is weird.' I decided not to mention my parents. 'You've all had time to grow accustomed to everything as it is now.

152

It was a shock seeing Ingrid like that. And Tristan ... the poor little mite didn't look that well cared for. He seemed so quiet and withdrawn, goodness knows what he's seen if his mother really is ...'

I petered off, not wanting to say the words.

'At least he *has* a mother.' Abbey had stuck her bottom lip out in a pout. 'It's pretty crap growing up without one.'

The thought drew me up short. Abbey had been ten and a half when I'd disappeared, but she'd been even younger – only a few years older than Tristan – when her real mother had died. No wonder the girl had been searching for something with her tattoos and her defiant lifestyle.

She was looking at me strangely. 'I hated you when Dad first brought you home.'

I felt my stomach churn. This was the second time today someone I'd cared for had told me they'd hated me. 'I didn't realise,' I stammered.

'It wasn't so much you, exactly. I would have resented anyone who tried to take Mum's place.'

'I never meant to replace her.' I reached out to touch her but she pulled back as much as the confines of the back seat would allow. I dropped my hand back into my lap. 'I could never have taken her place.'

Abbey was staring fixedly out of the dark window presenting me with a view of the back of her dyed and tousled hair.

'After you came to live with us, I realised I was forgetting her. Now, I can't even recall what my own mother looks like, how un-loyal is that? I feel like I've let her down.'

I found I was shocked. 'Surely you have photos, some memento of your mother?'

'Do you remember seeing any in the house?'

I shook my head, realising that I'd mulled over this when

153

I'd rung Calum from the police house. It hadn't occurred to me that he hadn't even allowed Abbey to keep anything that belonged to her mother.'

'I have nothing,' Abbey said so quietly I could barely hear her. 'She never left me anything. It's as if she never existed. I feel like she never loved me at all.'

'She gave you life,' I whispered, the words popping unbidden into my mind, as if planted there by some unseen hand. 'And she must have loved you with all her heart.' I wished we weren't having this conversation in the back of a car, with Matt and Kevin listening in. 'She didn't leave you on purpose after all, and I'm sure she would have wanted you to be happy.'

I shivered, unsure where the certainty of Grace's love for her daughter had come from.

Abbey didn't seem to notice. 'I used to read stories about people whose mothers had died. They left their children letters, or lockets or precious little boxes full of meaningful things.' She turned to face me suddenly and I saw, in the flickering light from passing street lamps, that the quiet whimsical sorrow had been replaced by an angry hurt. 'Mum must have known she was dying, I mean I know she was in that accident but I don't think she was killed on the spot. Dad wouldn't let me see her but she might have had hours, maybe days to say goodbye . . . yet she didn't.' Abbey was crying now and I wished she'd let me comfort her.

I tried to block out what Calum had told me about Grace's final moments. 'I'm sure if she'd been able to see you one last time your father would have taken you to her. And maybe after she passed away your dad couldn't bear being reminded of her and threw everything out in a fit of grief. Look, we'll ask him. Perhaps he still has some of her things hidden away somewhere.'

'He hasn't. I asked him a few years ago. He was throwing out all your stuff and I plucked up the courage to ask him then. He said she didn't leave me anything at all.'

Her body was shaking now with huge sobs. Matt and Kevin were silent, both studiously looking out the windscreen as we rounded the corner of Abbey's street – my street only a few days before.

'Maybe he made a mistake.' The words were spilling from my mouth as if they were being directed from somewhere outside my head. 'Perhaps there's something she wanted you to have.'

The girl had choked back her tears and grown silent now, her face pressed to the window. I wished there was something I could do, some way of showing her how much she must have meant to her mother – how much she had begun to mean to me.

The car had drawn up to the kerb outside the house and an awkward silence descended on the four of us. Matt turned off the ignition and the engine whirred quietly as it cooled. I thought what a mismatched group we made, the handsome pilot with the soft heart, the geeky computer buff, the teenage Goth – and the woman who had reappeared from the dead after six years. I stared at the tall, narrow house I'd thought of as home and realised it had an air of waiting; waiting for events to unfold, or the earth to turn one more time and tip us all on our heads.

I squared my shoulders and took a deep breath.

Because I realised that whatever happened next would largely be up to me.

Chapter Twenty-Five

The front door opened before Abbey had time to put her key in the lock and there stood Calum, outlined against the single light spilling from the hallway.

'I've been waiting for you.' He pulled his daughter inside and turned to me. 'Has she been with you?'

I nodded.

'Do you want to come in?'

'I want her to come in.' Abbey had turned to face him in the hallway.

Calum looked long and hard at his daughter then stood back and let me slide past him into the hall. I could smell the familiar scent of him as I passed and felt a pang of something deep within me. Did I still love him, or was it just the comfort of finding someone familiar from my previous life? Abbey turned and walked into the sitting room and I followed her, trying to keep my heart from fluttering, my thoughts grounded.

Abbey had paused by the window and was drawing abstract lines in the dust on the cluttered, window ledge. She looked unsure of herself, her eyes flickering from her father to me. Calum turned to face us.

'Well?'

I stared at him, surprised to find he didn't look as old as

I'd thought when I'd seen him the day before. He had washed his hair and the fine scattering of premature grey round his temples didn't look as pronounced. If anything it made him look quite handsome.

'We went to see Ingrid,' I said.

He went very still. 'And why did that involve taking my daughter?'

'I wanted to go, Dad. I wanted to stay with Kaela.'

'You should have been in college, my girl, not gallivanting round the countryside with someone who walked out on us six years ago.'

'I didn't walk out on you.' We were having the same conversation we'd had before. 'You know the police don't believe that.' I noticed the room looked a little tidier than the first time I'd come back. The throw had been washed and put neatly on the couch, the beer cans and pizza boxes removed and the carpet vacuumed.

Calum rubbed a hand tiredly across his face. 'Do you want a drink or something?'

I nodded. 'Maybe a cup of tea? It's been a long day.'

'I . . . I could make it if you like.' It seemed Abbey needed something to occupy her hands.

Calum looked at her, askance. 'I didn't know you knew where the kettle was.'

'You don't know very much about me at all, do you?' she retorted. Her offer had been conciliatory but Calum hadn't understood. His off-the-cuff joke had obviously cut her to the core. 'You don't know because you don't give a damn!'

'Abbey.' Calum tried to soothe her but she was beyond shushing.

'You don't even know what I do and where I go every day because you've never bothered to ask!'

'What are you talking about?'

'I'm talking about the fact that Kaela has only been back two days and she already knows more about me than my own father!'

I watched as a veil of incomprehension came over his face. He looked nonplussed. With a shrug in my direction he walked out of the room.

'You never listen!' Abbey screeched after him. 'You never listen to anything I say. I hate you!'

'Let me talk to him,' I said to her. My hands were shaking. I whole-heartedly disliked confrontation, but I could see that someone had to explain his daughter's feelings of rage and frustration to him. Abbey bit her lip, turned and ran out of the room.

I followed Calum to the kitchen where he was pouring water into the kettle. He gave me a wan look.

'She's quite a handful. I don't seem to be able to get through to her.'

'She's a lovely girl, just a bit upset and angry at the moment.'

I decided not to launch straight into an accusation that he had not been a good father. Diplomacy seemed the better course of action for the moment.

He indicated a kitchen chair and I sat down amidst piles of unopened post and a dying plant while he fiddled about with tea bags and milk.

'How's work these days?' I asked, hoping to stay on neutral territory.

He brought over two cups of tea to the oak finished table, kicking a pile of old newspapers aside with his foot, which revealed an unwashed floor in tiles of dull yellow.

'The pharmaceutical industry isn't what it was. Doctors and pharmacists don't want to give me their time any more.' He shook his head in a defeated manner.

I recalled the fighter I had known, the man who'd probably saved my life by telling me not to panic, to never give up.

Resisting the urge to grab hold of him and give him a good shake, I searched his eyes for the Calum I had known and cared so much for. 'What's happened to you, Calum? You were good at selling, you took pride in your appearance, the house . . .'

His eyes flashed angrily and I saw where Abbey got her quick temper from. 'Don't you judge me, Michaela. You disappeared without a word, leaving me and Abigail, and your parents all to think you were dead.' He stood up abruptly and ran a hand over his stubbly chin. 'When I rang the airfield and they said you were missing, I couldn't believe you'd really gone. And then there was the police search and the accusations and the agonising wait and worry and the eventual realisation that you weren't coming back . . .' The anger went out of his voice leaving it low and sad. The grief in his eyes cut me to the core. 'After Grace died I thought I'd never meet anyone I could care about again. When I met you everything changed. For those six months that you were living here I was happier than I'd dared imagine.' Calum gripped the draining board hard. 'How could you do that to us?'

I could feel my cheeks blanching. I supposed he had a right to be hurt and angry. But what no one seemed to understand was how awful this situation was for me too. I still felt the closeness of our recent relationship and though I realised my feelings for him were bound to be stronger than what he must feel for me after six years, I was still hurt. I was being accused of ruining everyone's lives as if I'd done it all on purpose. Pushing back my chair I stood up. 'I'm so sorry, Calum. Perhaps I'd better leave.'

Calum crossed the kitchen and stopped in front of me. He lowered his voice to a gruff whisper. 'Don't go, Kaela.'

The world paused, and an eternity seemed to slip by, his tall, familiar frame inches from mine. My eyes took in the face that had once been so strong; the blue eyes, square chin, the thick unruly hair and skin that smelled of soap . . . and of him. I wanted him as he had been before. And suddenly I was in his arms. I buried my head in his shoulder and found I was crying.

He held me close and stroked my hair, telling me he'd missed me so much and that he still loved me, and that Abigail had loved me and it seemed she still did.

When at last I raised my head, he pointed to a faded picture pinned to the side of the cupboard beside the fridge. I extracted myself from his arms and walked over to stare at the child's yellowing drawing of three people standing in front of a house. Running my finger over the neatly coloured-in figures, I felt the tears start again.

'Abigail did that at school the day you disappeared.' Calum had come over and was standing at my shoulder. 'We pinned it up and waited for you to come home so she could show it to you. It was the first time she'd drawn us as a family and I remember thinking that she had accepted you at last.' He grimaced. 'When you didn't come back I wanted to rip it down and throw it away but she insisted on keeping it there.'

Reaching out, I traced the outlines of our figures, remembering that last morning when Abbey had stood in the drive with her homework diary. How unfair that the very morning she'd decided to trust me, I had been torn away from her.

I looked up into the achingly familiar face of the man I had once loved. I tried not to think of Matt sitting patiently outside in his car. 'Do you still want me to leave?'

He smiled wanly. 'When I think of the nights I lay in

the dark, wishing you were beside me, when I would have given everything I had to have you back, to hold you in my arms one more time, it seems crazy to let you slip away again.'

'But?'

He reached out and touched my hair as if to reassure himself I was really here. 'But six years is a long time. Things have changed. Even if I believed you didn't leave us on purpose, things could never be exactly as they were before.'

'So you're saying we're finished?' I tried to keep my voice neutral but it was a sorrow tinged with hope. I had promised Abbey that I would make sure that my leaving was what her father wanted – that it was what I wanted, but my thoughts kept drifting back to Matt.

'You're good with Abbey. You were when she was little and I can see she's still very attached to you.' He bit his lip and looked away as if trying to come to a difficult decision. 'There's something I must tell you. You won't like it, but I need to tell you the truth.'

My skin prickled with apprehension, but I nodded faintly. 'Go on then.'

'There was a time during the last six years when I hated you, Michaela. I know that sounds childish and immature, but I resented you for what your disappearance did to us. I felt badly betrayed by both you and Grace.'

He looked up and held my gaze. 'I want you to know I'm sorry. I still love you and I know Abbey does too.'

This was the third time someone I thought had loved me had confessed to hating me and it wasn't something I wanted to get used to. But my heart went out to him regardless, 'Oh, Calum.' He had suffered and it was because of what had happened to me.

'There's something else.'

A picture of Ingrid elbowed its way into my mind's eye. Was he going to confess he'd found solace elsewhere?

'You're going to find this difficult. I'm not sure I should burden you with it at all . . .'

I closed my eyes and took a deep breath. 'Tell me.'

Calum backed away from me, hugging his arms around his body as if shielding himself from what he was about to say. 'I'm ill, Kaela. I've been ill for some time. I've been keeping it from Abbey – but I think I'm going to die.'

Chapter Twenty-Six

I felt my heart give an involuntary lurch, my senses reeling. 'Ill?' I echoed stupidly.

I recalled what Abbey had said about coming home and finding her father slumped in a chair and he'd told me himself that finances were tight. 'What is it, Calum?'

He gave a low groan and stared at me for several seconds before saying softly, 'It's prostate cancer and the doctors say it's serious.'

My mouth dropped open. Of all the things I'd been thinking, this hadn't been one of them.

'You can't . . . I mean, are you sure?'

'I'm afraid so. It's what they call a high risk localised cancer. They wanted to surgically remove the prostate but I wouldn't let them; because of Abigail, you see. I didn't want a general anaesthetic, in case I didn't survive it and I didn't want the op anyway because then she'd have to know.' He held up a hand to stop any protestations to the contrary. 'I've never had an operation before and I just didn't want to risk it. I would have needed post-operative care and there wasn't anyone to take care of us, and anyway, I didn't want her to worry . . .'

'But if you wouldn't let them operate, how are they treating it?'

'I've been having radiotherapy and hormone treatment. I think that's why I'm so tired and finding it so difficult to work.'

All this time he had been worrying in secret with no one to talk to, suffering in silence to protect his daughter from pain. I crossed the space between us in two strides and wrapped my arms tightly round him. 'I'm so sorry, Calum.'

I felt his body grow taut within my arms and then he relaxed and lowered his face to my hair. I heard him inhale deeply and then he went on, 'I lie in bed at night and worry about Abbey and what will become of her. First her mother dying, then you disappearing and then this. It's more than a young girl should have to suffer.'

I was glad I hadn't found the right moment to tell him that his daughter wasn't even going to college as he believed. It would have been the worst time to tell him that his daughter was drifting aimlessly and mingling with the wrong kind of people.

'Is there anything I can do?'

He unwound my arms as if thinking he'd overstepped the mark. 'You can be here for us, if you can bear it. I still love you, but I know it's a lot to ask of you.'

I led him towards the hard kitchen chairs and he allowed me to guide him. We sat opposite one another with our knees touching, our hands linked together. He leaned forward and rested his forehead against mine. I closed my eyes feeling the warmth of his breath and knew that I cared too much to let him suffer this alone. We remained like that for some time. There wasn't really a decision to be made. Whatever feelings I had for Matt – and he for me – would have to be sacrificed for what I saw as the only path open to me. Staying with Calum was the right thing, the honourable and humane thing to do. But it was the hardest decision I would ever have to make.

I told Calum I needed one more day to get things clear in my head and that I would be back tomorrow to sort things out properly. I'd popped my head into Abigail's bedroom before leaving, to find her sitting on her window sill, with the window flung open beside her. Sniffing the air, I'd realised she was smoking something suspicious, but it didn't seem either the time or place to caution her. Nor did I have the right, I realised.

She didn't speak, though I knew she'd sensed my presence, so I clambered across the bed and perched next to her, looking out over the dark back garden.

'It's been quite a day,' I offered quietly.

She merely shrugged and took a drag on the joint, holding the smoke down in her lungs then blowing it slowly out into the night air. 'It's been a bloody weird *couple* of days, ever since you came back really.'

'I'm glad you were with us today.'

'Cut the crap, Kaela. Did you tell Dad I've been skipping college?'

'Not yet. We had other things to discuss.'

She turned to face me and her eyes seemed huge, her pupils dilated from the drug. 'Are you coming back?'

'I haven't completely decided, but it looks that way. Do you want me to come back?'

'Does my opinion count for anything?'

'Of course it does.'

'At least you've noticed I'm alive, which is more than Dad has. He doesn't care what I think. I don't think he gives a damn about me any more.'

'He cares a great deal about you, Abbey. More than you could possibly know. He just finds it difficult to show it, that's all.'

She shrugged again as if she didn't believe a word of it then held out the joint. 'Want a drag?'

I shook my head. 'I need to keep a clear head. I've got some thinking to do. I popped in to tell you I'm going back with Matt and Kevin tonight, but I'll be here tomorrow, possibly to stay.'

She thought about this for a moment then nodded briefly before turning to look pointedly out the window once more. The discussion was over.

I could see Matt's car in the glow from a streetlight as I walked down the front drive. I'd been an hour and a half with Calum and Abbey – and Matt was still waiting patiently for me.

And now I was walking towards the man with whom I had just begun something pretty amazing: love, passion, a desperate need – I wasn't sure which – to tell him it was over before we had barely had the chance to get used to the idea.

Damn.

Matt leaned across and opened the passenger side door and I slid in beside him. He smiled at me. 'Everything OK?'

'Not exactly.'

'Abbey OK?' Kevin was leaning through from the back, resting his elbows on the sides of the seats.

'I left her smoking a joint in her bedroom.'

'Way to go, man.'

'She's not even seventeen yet,' I said, rather more tersely than I'd intended.

Matt started the engine. 'I assume you're coming back with me tonight?'

There was an edge to his voice now, as if he realised something was very wrong but was afraid to hear me say it.

'I think so.' I took a deep breath and tried to infuse some sort of life into my voice although it felt as if I was wilting inside. 'I need to talk to you. And I'm sorry I was so long in there. Thank you for waiting.'

166

'We didn't wait – I mean not all the time, you know.' Kevin produced a carrier bag from the back seat. 'We've been doing some really pervie stuff, looking at ladies' underwear and women's clothing . . .'

'We went to buy you some clothes,' Matt explained, cutting Kevin short. 'I thought you'd need some things, so we went late night shopping. I hope that's OK with you.'

Peering into the bag, I bit back tears. There were jeans, T-shirts, a jumper, a bra, knickers and even a pair of pumps.

'We found a sales girl who looked to be your size and asked her what she reckoned you'd need to tide you over for a couple of days. We let her choose,' Matt was shooting dagger looks at Kevin in the rear view mirror, 'we didn't spend the evening drooling over women's underwear or anything.'

I would have laughed at Matt's discomfort if the situation hadn't been so sad. As it was, I wanted to hug him. 'It's a really kind thought. I'll pay you both back as soon as my finances are up and running.' I spent the remainder of the journey listening to Kevin prattle on about his dream shopping trip and how he'd once bought a blow-up doll clad in a G-string in a sex shop by mistake. I wasn't sure how he'd managed such an error and was beginning to think that with Kevin anything was possible.

We dropped him off at his flat and he paused at the kerb. 'Don't do it, Kaela. Abbey and her father will work things out. Just don't do anything you might regret for the rest of your life, OK?'

And I realised in that moment that Kevin wasn't quite the buffoon I'd taken him for.

Chapter Twenty-Seven

As Kevin disappeared, Matt turned to face me, the engine idling.

'You wanted to talk to me?'

I felt my hands shaking. I didn't want to talk to him; I wanted to feel his body against mine, his fingers wound tightly in my hair. I wanted to slide my lips and tongue over his skin, tasting the very essence of him and lose myself in his embrace. I wanted him to wrap me in his arms and tell me everything would be alright.

I let out a long breath. 'I have to go back – to Calum, I mean.'

He remained silent for several seconds then raised his eyes to mine. 'Now? Tonight?'

I shook my head. 'I told him I'd go back and talk to him about it in the morning, when we'd both had a chance to think things over.'

Matt guided the car away from the kerb and headed out into the night. 'I'm not driving all the way to my place,' he said shortly. 'I know a small hotel not far from here where we can get a room and talk. Is that OK with you?'

I nodded dumbly, blinking back tears as I looked out the window into the darkness, wishing it would swallow me up whole.

Fifteen minutes later we were standing in the tiny carpeted reception area of a hotel just outside Reigate. Matt had his credit card swiped by an elderly woman who peered over her glasses at me with just a hint of disapproval, as Matt signed the guest register.

'Do you have any luggage, sir?'

When Matt shook his head the receptionist clucked her tongue very slightly.

'Take no notice,' he whispered consolingly.

I waited while Matt unlocked the door to a small, but comfortable looking room. There was a double bed with bedside tables either side and a wardrobe stood drunkenly against one wall.

'Home from home,' I said with an attempt to lighten the sombre mood between us.'

He sat on the edge of the bed and reached out to take both my hands in his own. Why did I feel so bereft at the thought of finishing things with him when I'd known him for such a short time? It didn't make sense.

'I feel like I've known you forever,' he said, echoing my thoughts. 'It's as if I had been waiting for you all my life, way before I met you at the airfield on the day of your jump. And once I had met you, I fantasised about you and worried and grieved for you – and we've only had one proper night together. Please tell me this isn't all we are to have, Michaela.'

Dropping to my knees I buried my face against his chest. He drew back and pressed a finger under my chin, tilting my face up to his, then he lowered his head and his lips found mine and for a moment, the rest of the world was forgotten. When at last we surfaced, he pulled me up onto the bed next to him, his brows knitted in perplexity.

'I don't understand. If you feel like this, then why the hell are you even thinking of going back to Calum?'

I grasped his hands and tried to steady myself. 'He's sick. Calum has cancer. He needs an operation but he's all alone and he's afraid.'

'That's terrible. I'm sorry.' The anger that had begun to surface subsided again as he studied my face. 'You feel you should be there for him, is that it?'

I nodded. 'I can't leave him to face this on his own.'

Matt was silent for a few minutes while I threw him anxious glances. Eventually he sighed deeply. 'I know he meant something to you, Michaela, but only yesterday you seemed pretty sure things were over. Six years is a long time. Are you sure you still owe him this?'

'The time thing is the problem,' I explained. 'For me it hasn't been six years. As far as I'm concerned I was with Calum only a few days ago.' I took a deep breath. 'When you found me I was confused, I took advantage of Calum's harsh words to assure myself that being with you was OK. But deep down I felt guilty, because it was like stepping straight from his bed into yours.'

'So you're going back to him because you feel guilty.'

I could sense the anger bubbling up in him again and tried to explain. 'You make it sound like a bad thing, but I do care for Calum. He says he'd settle for friendship but I know that wouldn't work. I have to make a choice, Matt, and it's the hardest thing I've ever had to do.'

'Come here,' he pulled me to him and hugged me close before planting little kisses over my eyebrows, down my face and over my neck. I responded by clinging tightly to him. Rather like that first night when I'd rested my foot against his, I felt myself drawn to him, wanting to be part of him. I didn't want to let him go, not ever.

'If you go to Calum because he's ill, what will you do when he gets better?' He murmured the words into my hair. I thought of Calum holding me and stroking my hair earlier this evening and felt wretched inside. 'Would you come back to me then?'

'I don't know. It would seem so disloyal to leave him as soon as he's no longer sick, it would be as if I'd never meant to stay. Maybe I'm an old-fashioned girl, but I feel I have to make my commitment fully, or not at all.'

'I wish you weren't so bloody loyal . . . but then maybe that's part of what I see in you.' He nibbled my neck and I felt my pulse race.

'Matt, I can't do this. I've already half made my decision to stay with Calum and I can't sleep with you, I'm so sorry, but it wouldn't be right.'

He pulled back and stared at me and I was surprised to see not frustration or annoyance, but a deep sadness in his eyes.

'Will you still spend the night with me? If I promise just to hold you?'

I remembered the first night I'd spent in his bed, when he'd promised to be the perfect gentleman, and how he'd kept his word. I wasn't sure I trusted myself with him, given the way I felt, but the thought of spending one more night in his company was more than I could have hoped for. I nodded, biting back the tears.

'How about something to eat?' he asked with a forced cheerfulness. 'They might still be serving dinner.'

It turned out that dinner was finished, but the proprietor said they could send sandwiches and a bottle of wine up to the room. And so, feeling like an inmate on death row, I ate what might be my last meal with Matt and sipped at the wine and watched his every movement, drinking him in and committing everything he said, everything he did, to memory.

After the meal we undressed slowly and climbed between

171

the clean sheets of the double bed, then he moulded his body to mine and held me against him, my head nestled against his shoulder, until at last I fell into an uneasy sleep.

I dreamt that I was in a small, dark place. The walls were spinning and I was being thrown about like a piece of tumble weed. Faces loomed out of the gloom; Matt's, Kevin's and even Calum's. I cried out and heard Matt shush me. He was holding me and I couldn't get my breath. I felt as if I was swimming through black, brackish water and the musty stale smell of it was in my mouth and nostrils, threatening to choke me.

Abbey appeared holding a fan of tarot cards, the wind caught the cards and tossed them up and suddenly they were spinning with me, trapped with me inside the vortex of the tornado, sucking me to a place I didn't want to go. And as I spiralled upwards I saw my mother smiling. She was holding a paintbrush in her hand and I realised she was painting this whole scene and I was trapped inside, but unable to make her realise it was me, her only daughter and that I was still alive.

I awoke sweating, to find Matt leaning over me, his face white in the gloom. 'It's only a dream,' he whispered as I clung to him, shaking and gasping for breath. 'Go back to sleep, everything will be alright.'

I felt him place a kiss on my brow and as the dream receded I turned into him, holding on for dear life.

In the morning we dressed without saying very much to one another. There didn't seem much more to say. We ate a light, continental breakfast in a dimly-lit dining room then Matt paid the hotel bill and we walked to his car like a couple of condemned prisoners walking out to the gallows.

'I'm not taking you back.'

I glanced at him half afraid he was going to carry me off somewhere, half hopeful that he would.

'I'll take you to Kevin's and he'll drive you to Leatherhead,' Matt said as we approached his car. 'I rang him while you were in the bathroom and he said he'd be glad to take you.'

I nodded and climbed into the car, staring miserably out the window while he drove back to Redhill. The sun shone down on trees that seemed to have turned from yellow and orange to red and gold. A man I barely knew had stolen my heart and whose absence from my life would leave my world empty and grey.

I paused and looked back at Matt, my heart aching. He was smiling at me, it was a sad smile but a smile nonetheless.

'You know I'll always be here for you, don't you, Michaela; no matter what you decide?'

'You mustn't waste your life waiting for me.'

'That's what my friends told me when you first went missing. After six long years I was beginning to believe it, and then you rang from nowhere and came back.'

'I don't see how I can leave him. I can't abandon Calum.'

'And I won't abandon you. Remember me sometimes, won't you?'

I nodded and climbed out of the car just in time to see Kevin waving a greeting and jangling a bunch of keys at me.

Chapter Twenty-Eight

'Morning, babe. Your taxi awaits.'

'Hi, Kevin.'

Behind me Matt's car pulled away from the kerb into the stream of traffic and I risked a final glance over my shoulder, but it was too late, he had gone.

'The van's round the back in my parking space,' Kevin announced briskly. 'Come on, let's get on with the "sacrificial maid to the dragon's lair" thing.'

I felt myself bridle at his words. 'How can you joke about this? You don't know anything about Calum and me!'

'That's true. But I do know about Matt and you, and you were clearly made for each other.' He gave me a quick grin to show there were no hard feelings, but proceeded to undo the partial apology by reciting every great twosome he could think of. 'Adam and Eve, Antony and Cleopatra, Romeo and Juliet . . .'

Kevin went on about who he considered to be perfect couples for the whole twenty minutes back to Leatherhead but I wasn't really listening and was happy enough for him to drone on. Occasionally he flicked me a concerned glance but I was content to sit up high and watch the scenery unfolding from my lofty position in the front seat of his van.

'What do you keep in the back?' I asked at one point, as

he took a bend rather sharply and swore as something large slid and banged in the rear of the van.

'Electronic equipment, computer components, all sorts.'

'Aren't you afraid someone will steal it from the van?'

'What, break into a rust bucket like this?'

I saw his point and almost laughed. And then I realised we were turning into Calum's road and my stomach flipped over with apprehension.

I turned to him and mustered a grateful smile. 'Thank you for everything, Kevin. You will keep in touch? Let me know how . . .' I wanted to say, how Matt is, but simply finished with, 'well, how things are – you know.'

'Sure, babe. I was rather hoping you'd consider making a guest appearance on my website, via a webcam. What do you think?'

I was about to say I wasn't sure, when someone knocked on the van's window, making me jump. Looking out I saw a ghostly face and wild hair and realised it was Abbey.

Kevin came round to open my door and gave Abbey a wink. 'How's the tarot stuff panning out, toots?'

Abbey looked pointedly in my direction. 'Your answer is right here in front of you. The cards said she'd come back to Dad, didn't they?'

He gazed thoughtfully at me. 'I guess they did.'

I looked away from Abbey, unwilling to tell her I still wasn't completely sure and glanced down at my watch; it was nine o'clock. 'Is your dad up yet?'

'He's just got me up for *college*.' Abbey grimaced theatrically. 'You will tell him, won't you, Kaela? I could have had a lie in. Keeping up the pretence is getting to be a bore.'

She looked so confrontational with her eyebrow and nose piercings, yet somehow fragile with the dark hair framing her pale face.

'I think you should tell him yourself, but maybe not just yet. Let me talk to your dad for a bit before we have any fireworks, OK?'

She scowled, but then her gaze alighted on something a little way down the road. I followed her gaze and saw a man, dressed in a tracksuit and hoodie, lurking on the corner. Abbey was suddenly jittery. 'Look, I've got to go.'

Kevin was peering down the road now, his eyes narrowed. 'Who's he, your dealer?'

Abbey was immediately defensive. 'What if he is?'

'I thought you had more brains than to mess with guys like him.'

'What would you know about it?'

'I've been there and done it and I can tell you it's a mug's game, toots.'

Abbey stood indecisively with her mouth open then closed it briefly. 'You can mind your own frigging business,' she said tightly, walking off in the direction of the hovering guy.

'Now you see part of the reason I have to come back,' I grimaced.

Kevin turned to face me and for the first time since my return, actually studied me, as opposed to the quick embarrassed glances he normally flicked at me. He nodded briefly then started back to his van. As he opened the far door, he lowered his voice to Arnold Schwarzenegger pitch and said: *'I'll be back.'*

I walked up the drive trying not to laugh and was still smiling when Calum opened the front door a moment later. He was dressed in smart trousers with a white open necked shirt and looked lovely, and I remembered why I'd first fallen for him. If it hadn't been for meeting up with Matt, I know I would have been perfectly happy to have come back home to him.

We stood either side of the front door and I suddenly felt awkward. After a moment, he stood back to let me pass. 'Welcome back, Kaela, I wasn't sure you'd come.'

He made us tea as he had done the evening before and we sat in the kitchen with the autumn sunshine filtering in through the grubby windows.

'You look exactly as I remember you,' he said wistfully.

'You only saw me yesterday.'

'I mean before you disappeared. You really haven't changed at all.'

His comment reminded me that I still wasn't any closer to finding out what had happened to me. So much had occurred since my return that there didn't seem to have been time to dwell on the most mystifying question of all.

Wrenching my mind back to the present I took a sip of the hot tea. 'How are you feeling? You seem better today.'

He gave me a quick smile. 'I think it was the thought of you coming back. When I got up this morning I felt better than I have for months. I thought after we've talked I'd fit in a couple of sales calls before my hospital appointment this afternoon.'

'What time do you have to be at the hospital?'

'I'm scheduled for radiotherapy at three thirty.'

'Would you like me to come with you?'

He shook his head. Resting his mug on the table he leaned forward to look at me.

'No need. But I'm glad you came back.'

'We need to work out how we're going to do this,' I said, getting down to business. 'I'm hoping that my parents' solicitors will sort out my financial situation, because at the moment I have no way of supporting myself. I'm sure if I made Wayfarers look through old personnel records they'd find evidence of having employed me, but my old job

177

has obviously gone, so it looks like I'm out of work at present.'

He slid his hand out from under mine. 'As I explained yesterday, finances are tight, but we'll manage for a while. The bigger problem is where you'll sleep if you stay with us.'

My eyebrows went up and I stared at him in surprise. I'd assumed that if I returned Calum would expect us to resume our relationship. A spark of hope ignited in my mind. Would he really mind if I continued a relationship with Matt? The flicker died as quickly as it came. As I'd said to Matt, such a relationship wouldn't work in reality and I knew I couldn't live like that.

I raised my eyes to Calum's but he was staring down at the table. He was looking decidedly awkward and as soon as he saw me watching him making fists with his hands, he relaxed and began to drum his fingers on the table top.

'I think it would be better, for the time being at least, if we had our own space. It will take time for us to adjust to being together again.'

'I think that's a good idea.' I had been more worried about that part of our relationship than I'd realised. In the brief time I had spent with Matt, my allegiance had shifted from Calum to Matt, in some deep sense that I couldn't quite understand. I was beginning to realise that a decision made with my head and heart didn't automatically mean my soul would simply follow suit.

'What did you have in mind?'

'As you know, I converted half the loft space into an office years ago. I had a look at the other half last night. It's a bit dusty and needs a good clean but there's an old bed up there I used to use if I was working late and had an early start out on the road.

'Grace used the room too, as a sort of hobby area,' he went on. 'Sometimes she'd be up there for hours at a time doing goodness knows what while little Abbey was napping in her cot or later on, at school. I'm sure with a bit of work it would serve as a temporary bedroom for you. Do you want to see it?'

I thought of Grace sitting in the attic room, working on whatever hobby she'd enjoyed and realised that I felt an uncanny affinity with Calum's deceased wife. Whether it was because he had almost lost me too, I didn't know, but it felt almost as if she was there in the room with me, nudging me to make the right decisions. I was about to say yes, when we heard a key in the front door, and the sound of footsteps outside in the hall. Abbey burst into the kitchen and planted herself in front of her father who had leapt to his feet in surprise at the sudden noise.

'Have you told him?' She was looking at her father though the question was directed at me. Her eyes were wild, her expression confrontational and I wondered if she'd taken something. I put a restraining hand on her arm but she shook me off.

'No, Abbey . . .'

She turned accusing eyes on me. 'You said you would.'

'Not now, this isn't a good time.'

Calum looked from his daughter and back to me. 'What is it that you haven't told me?' He glanced at his watch. 'Shouldn't you be at college by now?'

'That's the whole point, Dad. I don't go to college, I never have. They wouldn't take me and you never bothered to check, did you? You couldn't care less about me, just like you never cared a toss about Mum.'

Calum stared at her, disbelief showing clearly in his face. 'I'll put what you said about your mother to one side for the

179

moment. But what do you mean you don't go to college? Where have you been going every day?'

'Oh, I hang out on the streets, meet up with boys, drink cheap wine, do drugs . . .'

If Abbey's intention had been to shock her father then she'd succeeded big time. Calum went white and sank back down onto the chair. The energy seemed to drain out of him and I thought for a moment he was going to collapse. I stared from the angry teenager to the stricken father and was wondering what the hell I had got myself into when someone coughed discreetly from the kitchen doorway.

Dr Soram Patel was standing framed in the doorway. 'The front door was open,' she explained, peering at us all with interest. 'I hope I'm not interrupting anything?'

Chapter Twenty-Nine

Abbey was the first to move. She made a bolt past Dr Patel, slamming the door with a ferocity that shook the walls of the old house.

I pulled out a kitchen chair. 'Won't you sit down?'

Dr Patel sat delicately on the hard backed chair and placed a briefcase on the table in front of her.

'Would you like a cup of tea?' I tried to keep my voice even, despite the pounding of my heart.

'That would be very nice, thank you. Do you have any lemon?'

I looked questioningly at Calum who still seemed to be in shock. He shook his head imperceptibly.

'I'm afraid not,' I translated, 'would you like milk?'

'Black will be fine, thank you.'

After having made some tea, I tried to look relaxed and nonchalant while Dr Patel sat quietly, no doubt analysing us both for some research paper she was writing on dysfunctional families.

'I have brought the results of the tests you underwent at the police house,' she said at last.

This information sharpened my interest, dragging my mind back from Abbey and where she might have gone. I sat more upright, eager to find out something at last about my missing six and a half years. I watched as she opened the briefcase and extracted several sheets of paper. I wondered if she was ready to study my reaction to what she was about to tell me and told myself to keep my expression neutral no matter what she said.

'I'm afraid the tests were largely inconclusive.'

I felt my face drop. So much for the inscrutable expression. But Dr Patel continued talking.

'The blood and urine tests showed no evidence of drugs in your system. Your hair sample was clean too; no signs of drugs having been used in the last few months.' She leafed through the papers but hesitated and glanced towards Calum. 'Is there somewhere private we could go to discuss things in more detail?'

I was still a guest here, a stranger to this house, as it was now. Calum seemed to come to his senses, registering what was going on at last.

'I was going to work anyway. Give me a minute to fetch my case and I'll be out of your way.'

He left the room and Dr Patel lowered her voice. 'Your examination showed no sign of recent sexual activity, forced or otherwise, so we have to assume you were not kept as some sort of sex slave.' She leaned forwards and patted my hand. I tried not to flinch, whilst thinking how fortunate it was that Matt had kept to his own side of the bed the night he had come for me at the pub.

Calum walked past the kitchen with his briefcase and mumbled something about seeing me later. The doctor waited until the front door closed behind him before she went on.

'Your psychological tests were interesting.' Dr Patel continued in that precise voice of hers. Her English was perfect; almost too perfect in the way of someone who had learned it without the slang, her syllables clipped and slightly accentuated. 'DI Smith and I believe that you are telling the truth when you say you have no idea where you have been. We want to send a team to search the airfield again. You say you buried your parachute and helmet in a small depression when you landed and we are anxious to locate it. Whether you did that jump six years – or only a few days ago – the parachute was never located.'

My heart leapt with hope. If they found the chute where I'd left it on Monday evening, maybe they could do tests to prove it hadn't been lying there for over six years.

'You will let me know as soon as you find it?'

'Of course; but this is a long shot, you understand? The airfield was scoured very thoroughly during the original investigation in 2002.'

I found myself smiling at her. The fact they believed at least part of my story made me feel vindicated. Perhaps the thorough psychological testing had been worthwhile after all. I leaned back in the chair. 'So what happens next?'

'We wait for the results of the search. If we don't find anything, we will have to consider closing the case. I'm sorry. We are going out on a limb to have even sanctioned this second search with only a small amount of critical evidence.'

'Critical evidence?' I echoed. 'I thought all my tests were negative?'

'There were a couple of abnormalities that cropped up,' she explained. 'The swab we took from under your nails showed a trace of dirt. Tests have revealed that it is a match to the earth found in and around the airfield.'

I remembered being hurled onto the ground by the wind when I'd landed so I wasn't surprised to hear this.

'That of course, could have been picked up at any time. What interested us more was the pollen found on your clothing – your socks, to be precise.'

I stared at her, recalling how they hadn't returned my socks with the rest of my clothing when I'd been released from custody. I waited, willing her to go on.

'The pollen was a bit of an enigma; its presence certainly interested our forensic team. Apparently there was a particular type of grass which was native to the Kent area right up to 2004. Several years ago, a laboratory funded by the British Hayfever Association, cross-bred certain grasses in an attempt to combat the condition. As I understand it, the pollination period of different grasses overlap and so hayfever sufferers are exposed to a mixture of pollens. But the researchers were attempting to isolate and alter the genetic make up of one particular suspect grass that seeded uncommonly early in the season. Apparently they did too good a job of it. The genetic-ally modified species rapidly cross-bred and by 2004, had wiped the original variety out. The thing is, the original variety, which to scientific knowledge became completely extinct four years ago, was found in large quantities in the fabric of your socks.'

Soram Patel took a sip of her tea, and I watched as she rolled it over her tongue as if relishing the taste. But I soon realised it wasn't the tea she was savouring as much as her next piece of information. 'What was so strange and what's had our forensic people up all night with excitement, was the fact that the samples of this supposedly extinct pollen species were as fresh as if they had been growing only a few days ago. You have been somewhere in the last few days, Michaela, where a pocket of the original variety still exists. If we can find it, not only will we probably find where you have been held, but the agricultural scientists will be as delighted as an archaeologist finding a live, and perfectly healthy, woolly mammoth wandering in the woods.'

I must have looked incredulous. 'Are we still talking about a bit of wild grass?'

Dr Patel rolled her eyes and gave a short laugh. 'I must say I was thinking along similar lines until I had it all explained to me.'

'Wow.' I took a sip of my tea and mulled over the possibilities. 'How will anyone know this grass if they find it? Doesn't all grass look the same?'

'To us, maybe. But random samples will be taken back to the lab where they will be analysed.'

'That sounds expensive and time consuming.'

Dr Patel nodded. 'Unless we can narrow down the search, of course, which is why I'm hoping you can be more specific about the area you found yourself wandering ... I mean landed in.' She looked at me hopefully. 'DI Smith and I are sure you must have been held somewhere near that airfield. I need you to describe exactly what you remember.'

Resting my mug back on the table, I tried to think. The airfield had been bathed in darkness when I'd landed.

'There were trees,' I said suddenly. 'Trees to my right and way behind me in the distance, I could see them against the skyline. That's why I took the direction I did. I knew there weren't any trees by the hangars.'

Dr Patel was nodding and making notes. 'We'll have a look at the grass and have another search of those woods.' She looked up and smiled encouragingly. 'We'll find who did this to you, Michaela. We'll find who took six years of your life and traumatised you into blocking it out.'

Chapter Thirty

I washed up the mugs and spent the next couple of hours cleaning the kitchen.

The mindless manual labour was exactly what I needed. While Calum had tidied the place since yesterday, there was an underlying greasy coating to the fronts of the cupboards, the tiles and the walls. I scrubbed every inch of the kitchen, cleaned the fridge and was just considering stopping for a well-earned coffee break when I heard a key in the front door.

Turning, I found Abbey standing in the doorway clutching a Tesco carrier bag.

'We thought you might be hungry,' she said as she pushed past me to dump the bag on the table.

I glanced towards the door. 'We?'

Kevin appeared from the hallway carrying two more bags. 'We've got chicken and vegetable wraps, sandwiches, Pringles and fruit smoothies.' He put his bags next to Abbey's and began to rummage. 'Nice locally grown apples and . . . loads of chocolate.'

I filled the kettle and watched as the two of them emptied the contents of the bags onto the table top.

'I assume you were hungry when you bought all this?'

'Famished.' Kevin took a seat and stretched his legs out across the kitchen. 'How's it going, doll?'

'I've only been here one morning,' I said with a smile. 'I had a visit from Dr Patel, the police psychologist. She told me some interesting things.'

'Yeah?' He sat up a bit straighter, the half eaten sandwich poised in his hand. 'I've got some pretty random stuff to tell you, too.'

I reckoned his use of the term random meant fascinating or unusual and grinned at him. 'I can't wait.' Turning to Abbey, I gave her a questioning look. 'Dare I ask where you've been and how you met up with Kevin? I was worried about you, storming off like that.' I had to stop myself adding, *and you've upset your father who has a hospital appointment later.*

'No one has given a damn about me for the past six years,' she said caustically as she helped herself to a vegetable and bean wrap. 'You don't need to pretend you care now.'

'Abbs rang me,' Kevin explained. 'I gave her my mobile number and said to call anytime. Looks like anytime came up sooner than I'd thought.' He flashed Abbey an apologetic glance. 'She was pretty upset so I took her back to mine for a while.'

'God his place is such a tip,' Abbey said through a mouthful of food. 'You can hardly squeeze through for computers and TV screens and weird gadgets. There's like wires and plugs everywhere.'

Kevin thrust a selection of food towards me. 'Take what you want.'

I selected a chicken wrap and took a bite. The breakfast I'd shared with Matt in the hotel seemed a lifetime ago. We all munched in silence and for a few minutes the only sound in the kitchen was the rustling of plastic packaging and Kevin slurping at a raspberry and blackcurrant smoothie. I took a bottle of smoothie for myself and read the ingredients. 'This is pretty good. How long have these been around? Maybe I wasn't very adventurous, but the only smoothie I've had before was something I made in my blender with milk.'

Abbey rolled her eyes at me. 'I don't know whether to believe you or not. God, you talk like you've been on another planet for six years.'

'She's not the only one who's come back,' Kevin said, showering the table with bits of sour cream and chive Pringles as he spoke. 'That's what I wanted to tell you. I was listening to the news in the van, some guy from the RSPB was saying a flock of swallows had appeared in London after their numbers mysteriously declined back in 2002. It's the wrong time of year for them to have arrived of course, they should be heading south for the winter.'

My mind went immediately to the buffeting I had taken when the wind had hit me during the jump. Any small birds that had been in the air at the time would have been blown seriously off course.

'Several species of bees have also reappeared, the experts having thought their numbers were mysteriously in decline.' He stuffed another bunch of Pringles into his mouth and his voice came out muffled as he crunched.

'Maybe they were caught up in that strange wind I found myself in as I was doing the jump,' I mused aloud, trying to ignore his appalling eating habits. 'It was like being in the centre of a tornado.'

'Hmm,' Kevin murmured. 'The trouble is the weather was perfectly pleasant that day and the air calm and still. I don't know why you should have encountered anything more than a light breeze. The more you tell me about what you experienced, the more I'm inclined to reassess the feasibility of the alien abduction theory!'

Abbey snorted, but then brightened visibly. 'I could try asking the cards.'

'Ask them what exactly?' Kevin bit into an apple and continued in a muffled voice. 'If you could have found out where Michaela was from a pack of cards, you'd have asked your tarot friends about her long ago.'

'I have to ask a specific question,' Abbey explained, giving him a withering look, 'you can't just say, where is Kaela? The cards can only show an answer to a properly posed question.' She thought for a moment. 'Before we get sucked in to Kaela's story about not knowing where she was for six years, I could do a past, present and future spread for her.' She looked pointedly at me. 'The cards are incredibly accurate with things like that.'

I nodded, anxious to prove to her that I was telling the truth but glanced at my watch. Two o'clock. Calum's appointment wasn't until three thirty so it would be ages until he was home. Abbey seemed to read my mind. We both knew her father wouldn't give tarot readings the time of day. 'Where did Dad go anyway?'

'He said he had some calls to make today.'

'He's working?'

'Yes, I believe so.'

She put the remains of her wrap on a piece of clear, plastic packaging. 'He was pretty pissed off this morning, wasn't he?'

'More upset than pissed off,' I said gently. 'He worries about you, Abbey. I know you don't think he cares but he really does and you weren't exactly tactful when you broke the news to him about not going to college.'

'I know. I might have gone a bit overboard I suppose.' She scrambled for her cards.

She removed them from a little black, velvet bag and began to shuffle them while I tidied away the debris from our meal. When the table was clear, Abbey gave the pack to me and asked me to cut it. Kevin and I watched as afterwards she

189

carefully laid the seven top cards face down, in a sort of triangle shape.

'This is the horseshoe spread,' she told us softly as she concentrated on the cards. She tapped the card at the bottom of the triangle on the left hand side. 'This is card number one and it represents your past.'

I found I was holding my breath as she turned it over. The card had a pattern of three five-point stars sealed within three circles.

'What does it mean?'

'This is the three of pentacles. It represents the use of your skills and talents to have achieved an elevated position in your place of work, attributing to the financial comfort of your life. This card indicates that your achievements probably made your less-talented workmates envious of you.'

I thought of my career at Wayfarers and how I'd been trying for a promotion while Ingrid had been desperate for domestic security. Yesterday she said she'd hated me and I wondered if envy had had something to do with it.

'The pentacles are also sometimes known as discs or coins and would be the diamonds in an ordinary pack of cards. They relate to the Earth element. It's a very feminine suit, which is perfect for you, Kaela, as it shows the influence of earth signs Taurus, Capricorn and Virgo. The three of pentacles can also represent a move of house, which of course you did when you moved out from your parents and in here with Dad and me.'

I nodded. 'Considering any old card could have come up, I suppose that's a fairly accurate depiction of my past.'

Abbey placed her hand on the second card, which was above the first.

'This is the card which represents the present.' Abbey turned the card and sucked in her breath as she looked at it.

'What?' I found I was quite anxious. Somehow, sitting in

the kitchen watching Abbey's serious expression and complete concentration I found I had been sucked into her world and was on the edge of my seat.

'This is the ace of swords. It's a strong card showing the beginning of an unstoppable force.'

My mind went immediately to the strange wind that had caught me up and spun me round during the jump. No doubt Dr Patel and DI Smith would say the unstoppable force had begun when someone had kidnapped me and held me somewhere against my will. I swallowed and tried not to let my imagination run away with me. 'Is that bad?'

She tore her gaze away from the card and looked up at me. 'The swords are a strong suit. In ordinary cards they would be the spades, which is the Italian word for sword, of course. The suit is related to the Air element and is to do with strife, trouble and mental activity.'

'Astrologically swords are under the influence of Gemini, Aquarius and Libra,' Kevin put in.

Abbey and I looked at him in surprise.

Kevin grinned. 'I did a little research into tarot cards after I got home last night.'

'So you'll know,' Abbey pressed on, 'that as with all sword cards there is strife and hard battles to be fought.' She turned her attention back to me. 'However with the Ace it means that with your courage and intellect, Kaela, nothing will stand in your way for long.'

'So it's an OK card?' I asked, breathing out a sigh of relief.

'This card is your present, you're living it right now. Only you can tell whether it's OK or not.'

I didn't really have a choice in the matter. 'I'm learning to live with it,' I admitted. 'The reading so far isn't all that bad.'

'That's without the hidden influences,' Abbey warned as she turned the next card. 'This third card represents hidden influences at work which could prevent you from reaching your goal.'

I stared at the picture on the card. Seven goblets stood against a pale blue background in two rows of three with a single cup below.

'This is the seven of cups. In a regular pack the suit of cups are the hearts, associated with emotions.' She glanced at Kevin as if waiting for him to elaborate.

'The cups are ruled by the Water element and are associated with the astrological signs of Scorpio, Pisces and Cancer,' he quoted with a flourish.

Abbey grinned at him and I willed her to get on with the reading. I was itching to know the rest.

'The key word here is "choices". The seven of cups indicates an important decision you have to make.'

I immediately thought of the decision I was making to stay here with Abbey and Calum. Perhaps it wasn't too late to change my mind. 'Does it say which choice I should go for?'

Abbey shook her head. 'The choice is up to you, but the card cautions you to make your decision carefully, since all is not as it seems. The hidden influences are the different doorways of opportunity open to you, but you have to develop the intuition to know which one to take.'

'So there is an unstoppable force at work, but success is only certain if I make the right choice?'

She nodded. 'Exactly.'

I pointed to the fourth card, the crowning pinnacle of the triangle. 'What does this one mean?'

'Ah,' Abbey breathed. 'This is the card that represents obstacles you must overcome.' She turned the card over slowly, almost reverentially. I realised I was holding my breath. A card was revealed with a picture of a man hanging upside down by one foot from a scaffold. As I stared at it I felt a chill of foreboding creep through my bones.

Chapter Thirty-One

'That doesn't look too good,' Kevin observed, almost cheer-fully.

Abbey was furrowing her brow. 'It's not as bad as it looks. The hanged man represents a temporary pause in your life. It means you have to go with the flow, learn patience and accept the changes that are occurring. You will have to sacrifice something so that something else can be gained.'

I let my breath out slowly and thought of Calum and the changes I would have to make if I came back here to live permanently, the sacrifice of giving up Matt and the future he offered me.

'The card can mean illness, can't it?' Kevin asked.

I felt my heart flutter as if I'd been caught thinking out loud.

Abbey shook her head. 'Only in some cases. I don't see illness for Kaela, just a feeling of uncertainty and that she's walking a tightrope because of events around her.'

My palms felt sweaty and I rubbed them on my jeans. I was becoming quite uncomfortable with the way the cards were unfolding.

'I'm not sure I want to continue with this,' I whispered huskily. 'So far we've covered much of what has already happened. I don't know if I want to look any further. Maybe it's not a good idea to know what lies ahead.'

'You can't stop now! The next card depicts the attitudes of people around you,' Abbey cried, and I remembered suddenly that although she had been explaining my card readings so far in a calm and professional manner, she was still a young girl with a lot of attitude and little patience. 'It's lying right here ready to look at. Do you want me to turn it over or what?'

I looked at the card and then at the expectant faces of both Abbey and Kevin. 'Oh, alright, I suppose it can't hurt.'

I felt my face blanche as she flipped it over; it was a sword card again – the harbinger of battles and strife.

'Oh, no.'

'It's alright,' Abbey assured me hurriedly. 'The two of swords is good. It depicts balance and friendship at a time of adversity. The two of swords means you have an ally on whom you can depend.' Her brow furrowed as she concentrated on the card before her. 'This card emphasises what the previous cards have already told us; that you have a decision to make but there are no clues as to which direction to take. The balance aspect is between two equally matched opponents. Originally this would have meant a duel with swords.'

I pictured Matt and Calum duelling in the street. Again the accuracy and poignancy of the cards was worrying me.

'Shall I turn the next card?'

There seemed no point in stopping now. 'Go on then.'

'This card is the one that will tell you what you should do.'

At last, I thought, some actual help. I watched as she flipped the card over. The card appeared to show a picture of a row of fence posts.

'Wands,' Abbey breathed as she stared at the card, 'the nine of wands.'

'Tell me.' I was growing impatient now. 'What does it mean?'

'Wands would be clubs in an ordinary deck of cards. They belong to the Fire element and sometimes they're known as staves or batons or even rods. They are to do with creativity, work, growth and enterprise. The signs of the zodiac they are associated with are Aries, Sagittarius and Leo.'

'Yes, yes, but what does it actually mean?'

'It means resilience. It is a reassuring card to have now because it stands for self confidence, stability and strength. This card tells us that you have all you need within yourself to come good, Kaela. It's telling you to be patient and to remain vigilant.'

I groaned. 'It's all so cryptic. The reading seemed to make sense at first, but now I'm just getting confused.' I tapped the last card with my finger. 'Let's look at the last card then.'

'Ooh, this is a good one to end on,' Abbey said with relish as she turned the seventh card over. 'This card represents the eventual outcome of your life. It's the ten of cups, lovely. This is the "happy ever after" card.'

She picked up the pack and smiled at me. 'That was the best card you could have been dealt.'

But as she brandished the cards aloft, one solitary card disengaged itself from the pack and fluttered face up on top of Abbey's successful horseshoe spread. Kevin, Abbey and I stared at it. The card depicted a human skeleton riding a horse, brandishing a scythe aloft. And printed in neat letters beneath the ghostly horseman, was a single word, 'Death'.

'Bugger,' Abbey muttered, picking the card up quickly as if it were a naughty child appearing where it shouldn't, and shoving it back into the middle of the pack, 'now that is *not* a good omen.'

Judging by the looks on Abbey and Kevin's faces, we all heard the front door open at the same time and I looked with surprise at my wrist watch. How had it got to be five o'clock already?

Kevin scrambled hastily to his feet as Calum entered the room looking more tired and drawn than he had when he'd left this morning. The two men stared at one another.

'Hello, Calum,' Kevin said rather too innocently.

I watched uneasily as Calum's eyes narrowed. 'What are you doing in my house?'

'I brought your daughter home,' Kevin explained. 'She was in a bit of a state this morning.'

'I thought I'd seen the last of you and your parachute instructor buddy. He turned from Kevin as if dismissing his presence from the room and looked accusingly at me. 'I have never trusted those so called friends of yours from Wayfarers. They along with Matt Treguier were the last to see you six years ago in unexplained circumstances and inexplicably it seems that now, according to the police, the instructor was the first to find you again. Until we know for sure what happened, I'd rather they didn't have anything to do with either you or my daughter.'

'God Dad, he was just trying to help,' Abbey snapped. 'At least he was there when I needed someone to talk to.'

'How do you know him?'

Abbey glanced uncertainly at me.

'Matt and Kevin picked me up from outside the police station,' I said hastily. 'If you remember you said you didn't want me back and I had nowhere to go. They took me down to Brighton to find Ingrid – I thought I might be able to stay with her.'

'Yes, but how did my daughter get involved?'

'I went to see Susan,' Abbey explained. 'I knew Kaela would turn up at her mum's sooner or later. When she did, I begged to go with them to find Kaela's old friend.'

Calum sank onto the chair and put his head in his hands. 'I never thought to ask how you and Abigail got to Brighton yesterday. It never occurred to me you were with them . . .'

'I think I'd best be going.' Kevin was already edging towards the door. He looked pointedly at me. 'I'll be in touch.'

'Thanks, Kevin. And thank you for lunch.'

'All in a day's work, babe.'

Calum's head shot up at the familiarity of Kevin's words, but Kevin was already making his way out of the house. Calum fixed weary eyes on Abbey. 'I think we need to talk.'

'You might need to talk but I don't want to hear it.'

And with that she collected her velvet card bag and flounced out of the room.

I reached out and put my hand on Calum's. 'You've got to tell her you're ill. She doesn't understand . . .'

'She hates me,' Calum said with a groan. 'I just want to protect her but I can't get through to her.'

'Give it time. I'll talk to her tomorrow.' I looked at the lines etched into his face and felt a pang of concern. 'How did it go at the hospital?'

'I saw the consultant. He says the tumour isn't shrinking as much as he'd like. He wants me to have the prostate removed while the cancer is localised.'

'Will you consider it?'

Calum brought up his other hand and laid it over mine, stroking my skin gently with his thumb. 'Will you definitely stay?'

I thought of the tarot cards and how the choice was still there, waiting for me to make up my mind. I looked into Calum's eyes and found myself nodding. 'Yes, I'll stay if you're sure that's what you want.'

Calum tightened his grip on my hand and breathed out

a long sigh of relief. 'You are what I want. How could I ever have wanted anything else? Kaela, I think you just saved my life.'

The remainder of the evening passed in a blur. Calum showed me up to the attic room, which looked as though it hadn't seen the light of day for several years. It was full of dust and cobwebs, but the bed appeared sound and Calum seemed exhausted, so after taking up a duvet and quickly tucking on a bottom sheet, I returned to make an evening meal out of leftovers in the fridge.

Abbey refused to eat with us but took her food through to the sitting room on a tray, where I noticed she only picked at it half-heartedly whilst sprawled in front of the TV. Once Calum had gone to bed, I sat and watched the small TV in the newly cleaned kitchen and was about to go up to sort out the attic room when the doorbell rang.

Hurrying to answer it before it disturbed Calum, I found myself face-to-face with three teenagers – two male and one female. The girl had dyed hair very much like Abbey's and the two young men were sporting numerous piercings and tattoos. They had a bulging backpack with them and I found myself wondering what it contained.

'Abbs in?'

'I'll go and fetch her for you.'

As I turned to go I realised the trio had followed me into the house and were jostling behind me in the hallway. My instinct was to face them down but Abbey saved me from the possible confrontation by appearing in the small passage.

'Oh, hi, Cat. Hi, Oggs and Rumps.' Abbey turned to me. 'This is my best friend Catrina,' she waved at the girl. 'And this is Oggs – we call him that because he's always ogling the girls and Rumps . . . you know, like Rumplestiltskin.'

'Nice to meet you all,' I found myself saying rather too brightly. I turned to Abbey. 'You won't be too noisy, will you? Your father has gone to bed.'

Abbey frowned. 'It's a bit early, isn't it?'

'He's not feeling all that well.'

'Oh.' She seemed to digest this piece of information then shrugged and grinned at her friends. 'We'll be quiet as little mice, won't we, guys?'

The others sniggered.

During the next couple of hours the noise in the sitting room gradually escalated to fever pitch. By eleven thirty both the TV and the computer seemed to be simultaneously blaring out unintelligible noise which bore no resemblance to anything I'd heard in the past. Head pounding, I stuck my head into the sitting room to ask them to keep it down a bit and found Oggs standing on the sofa shouting drunkenly, waving a beer and Cat and Rumps lying in a tangle of gyrating limbs on the floor. Abbey stared at me with bleary eyes, her pupils dilated and told me drunkenly to piss off.

'I don't think so,' I told her, bristling slightly and thinking of Calum who was trying to sleep in the room above. I stood my ground. 'I think you ought to ask your friends to leave now.'

She glared at me. 'You can't tell me what to do, you're not my frigging mother.'

'No, but I'm here because you wanted me to be. Your father isn't well and I'm tired and want to go to bed. This just isn't a good time, Abbey, and I'd appreciate it if you could see your friends out now.'

'I'm not a kid any longer, I'll do what I like . . .'

Sighing, I marched over to the TV, switched it off at the mains, did the same with the computer and turned to face her. 'You're right, you're not a child, so stop acting like one. There's a lot going on at the moment and sometimes you have to take other people into consideration.' I smiled sweetly at the swaying trio who gawped at me in the sudden silence. 'It was great to meet you all, but I'd appreciate it if you left now.'

The three of them looked at Abbey who was staring at her feet. 'I think you'd better go,' she said sullenly.

After seeing them to the door, I returned to the sitting room to find Abbey lying on the couch gazing moodily at the ceiling. I was struck by how different she was from the girl who had so proficiently and coherently read my cards earlier in the afternoon.

'You've made me look like an idiot in front of my friends,' she complained.

'No, Abbey,' I replied wearily as I rubbed my aching temples. 'You did that all by yourself.'

'Turn out the lights before you go to bed,' I said over my shoulder as I mounted the stairs up to the attic. Yawning widely, I picked up the thick down duvet and climbed underneath. My exhaustion was due to worry, concern over Calum's illness, unease over Abbey's behaviour and a nagging doubt about whether I had made the right decision by becoming a part of this household once more.

Chapter Thirty-Two

I thought that sleep would claim me the moment my head touched the pillow, but the strangeness of my surroundings kept my brain from disengaging for quite some time. There was a stale, musty smell to the room that seemed both familiar and alien. I shivered under the duvet, wondering if it was possible for Calum to have kept me a prisoner in this room without his daughter knowing. I'd spotted a couple of packing boxes before I'd turned off the light and now I pictured them filled with all the things I would have needed over the space of six and a half years – clothes, toiletries, perhaps even some books.

Stop it, I told myself sharply as I plumped up the pillow and curled up on my side. First you suspected Matt and Kevin and now you're letting DI Smith and Dr Patel's theories run wild in your imagination. Go to sleep, Michaela Anderson, things will look better in the morning.

I awoke in the middle of the night. There was someone in the room with me, I was sure of it.

I let out a shallow breath, listening through the darkness for the sound of a muted footfall on the threadbare carpet. Through fear-filled eyes I peered into the darkness; my fingers clutching the down-filled duvet in the chilly night as if the soft feathers might offer some protection.

The moon came out from behind a cloud. I could see the faint silver light filtering through the edges of the blind on the skylight, and in that light I saw a shadowy woman dressed in grey and apparently watching me as intently as I was now watching her. The intruder moved towards me and I stifled a scream. Something told me that any sound would startle her and my instinct was to keep very, very quiet.

She drifted towards the bed and I held my breath, but she wasn't coming for me. My eyes followed her as she bent to run a hand haltingly over something in the corner of the room.

Lungs bursting, I knew I was going to have to exhale eventually and as the breath rushed from me, she turned to face me again and spoke so softly I could barely hear her. 'You must finish this for me, Kaela . . . finish it, for *us*.'

Had she said my name, or had it been the sound of my own breath escaping from my lips? I wasn't sure. But as I peered towards the corner of the room, I realised she was no longer there, and emboldened by her sudden departure I reached out with trembling fingers, felt carefully for the bedside lamp and snapped it quickly on. Blinking in the instant yellow glare, I stared round the room expecting to see goodness knows what, but it was empty, save for a pile of dusty packing boxes topped by an ancient sewing machine, several plastic containers and an old rocking-horse with a tattered mane.

'Idiot,' I told myself. There had been no one there – I had imagined the whole thing. Taking a sip of water from the glass by my bed, I took one last look around the room before turning off the light and pulling the duvet up over my head. I willed sleep to come, or morning to break, whichever would come first and rescue me from my demons.

* * *

With the morning came the unsettling memory of the dream. Yawning and stretching I looked around the small room, which was to be my home for the foreseeable future. I was thirsty and had finished my glass of water, but all I could think about was my nocturnal visitor. Had it been a dream, or had someone really been in the room with me?

Slipping out from the bed I padded barefoot across the faded carpet which looked as if it was as old as the house itself and pulled up the blind. Sunlight slanted into the small room illuminating the old sewing machine like an arrow pointing the way. Was this what the figure had been touching? The dust layering the top of the cover was undisturbed; no human hand had touched it in the night. What else could it have been? Berating myself for my stupidity, I was about to turn away when I saw that the wooden packing box the machine was standing on was slightly open. Peering through the gap I saw what looked like a pile of rags bundled inside.

A shiver ran through me. What was in the box? I took a deep breath and pulled firmly at the material, easing it out. What appeared to be a quilted bedspread lay in my arms. I stared at it, partly disappointed, partly intrigued. Mostly I felt relief that the box hadn't held a collection of my missing possessions after all.

I lifted the quilt over to the bed and spread the delicate fabric out on top of the duvet. It was beautiful. Carefully worked triangles, diamonds and hexagons of a myriad of fabrics made up a patchwork of squares, all sewn neatly together to form one large and exquisite, patchwork quilt. Running my fingers lightly over each square, I realised I recognised some of the pieces of material. There was a pattern using fragments of a dress I'd seen Abbey wearing in a photo taken when she was a baby; another was made from her old school uniform, and yet another was from a floral skirt I'd once found at the back of her wardrobe. The quilt was predominantly pink and cream, but other more colourful fabrics had been stitched into the whole. For all I knew each and every piece had been saved from various stages of the first eight and a half years of Abbey's life.

But it wasn't finished. There were jagged edges hanging open where new pieces were presumably to be fixed and I ran my hand lightly over the quilt, wondering who had made this.

Then I remembered the voice in my dream, 'Finish it for me, Kaela; you must finish it . . .'

And I realised with sudden inexplicable insight that this might be a life-gift Grace had been making for Abbey. Perhaps because of the accident, she hadn't been able to complete it. And now somehow, I felt my job was to finish it for her . . . this partially fashioned quilt could be a joint offering of love from Abbey's mother and me.

As if everything wasn't already weird enough, I thought with a smile as I picked the quilt up and held it to my cheek, inhaling the musty scent of a dead woman's perfume. I knew I was being fanciful in thinking that Grace had asked me to do this for Abbey, but so much of the life I had come back to was in tatters because of my strange absence. Maybe this was a chance to make some small thing right.

I gave a short laugh at the craziness of it all. Well, if this thing was required to heal Abbey, I told myself, then I would give it my best shot.

The house was silent as I made my way down the stairs and along the narrow landing to the bathroom. Calum and Abbey were obviously still sleeping so I decided to take advantage of the interlude to have a long, hot shower. I stood in the bath under the cleansing jets of the shower for quite some time, running everything that had happened through my head, trying to make sense of the pieces. My life had become a giant jigsaw and it was no wonder I'd dreamed of Grace I thought, as fine drops of water fell on my upturned face. I imagined the picture on the front of the jigsaw box reflecting an image of myself surrounded by shadowy figures – Calum, Matt, Kevin and Abbey, my mother and father, and a grey apparition with her features obscured. All around our heads, on the edges of the picture, were birds returning from a mysterious six-year absence and at our feet a strange circle of grasses which were supposed to be extinct. All the pieces were there; my ability to choose the way in which I assembled the jigsaw had been indicated by Abbey's cards and in my mind's eye I was holding a pink and cream quilt with a single heart stitched into the centre.

I was eating breakfast at the kitchen table when Calum popped his head round the door, smiled and came over to perch next to me.

'How did you sleep?'

'The bed was quite comfortable, actually,' I told him. 'I thought I'd give the attic room a bit of a spring clean today.'

'Great idea, it was rather dusty. I haven't slept up there for years.'

I looked at the dark circles under his eyes and realised that for all his veneer of cheerfulness he was probably in some discomfort.

'How are you feeling?'

He shrugged. 'The radiotherapy is making me tired, but I lay awake for quite a while thinking . . . you know how you do in the middle of the night.'

'Did you come to any conclusions?'

'Not really. I was thinking mostly about how happy I am that you chose to come back to us,' he smiled tentatively at me. 'I don't know why or how this happened, Michaela, but I do know you seem to belong here with Abigail and me.'

We contemplated one another for a moment and I found myself smiling at him. 'I'm glad I'm here with you both too, although I don't think I'm going to be given the "step-mum of the week" award by Abbey. I asked her friends to leave last night and she wasn't best pleased with me.'

'I thought it all went gloriously quiet rather suddenly,' he said, helping himself to some muesli. I passed him the carton of milk and he splashed it into his bowl. 'Do you know, I think I might actually be hungry for the first time in several months.'

'I thought you'd lost weight. We'll have to fatten you up. I thought I might go shopping later.'

He nodded, obviously pleased I was going to be looking after him. 'I'll leave you some money.' He tilted his head to one side. 'Are you alright for clothes and things?'

'I've got a few things to be going on with,' I told him, thinking guiltily of the brand new jeans and T-shirt I'd donned that morning and how I'd wistfully run my hands over Matt's choices before pulling them on. 'And on Monday morning I'm visiting the solicitor again to see if I can gain access to my bank account and funds.'

'Just get what you need and we'll sort it out next week then.' Calum took out several notes from his wallet and laid them on the table as he finished his breakfast. 'I'm going to try and work for a couple of hours this morning.'

'Are you continuing with the radiotherapy later?'

'I'm scheduled for another few treatments but I'll tell the consultant I'm ready to have that operation and see what he says.'

I nodded. 'I'll see you later then, I hope it all goes well.'

I kissed Calum goodbye at the front door, and imagined

us as an old married couple as I waved him off. Abbey was obviously still asleep and I decided not to wake her. I had plenty to think about, sorting out my financial status with the solicitor, looking for another job and in the interim, working out how to continue the work Grace had started on the quilt.

I was pulling dusters and cleaning sprays out from under the sink when the front doorbell rang. I paused in front of the open cupboard, wondering who on earth could be calling now. Surely not the police again. Had they found the para-chute, I wondered?

The doorbell rang again, this time longer and more insistent as if someone was holding the buzzer down with their finger. With a can of polish and a duster still in my hand I hurried to the front door and flung it open.

And there in front of me stood Ingrid.

Chapter Thirty-Three

The Ingrid standing before me was all wild, blonde hair and tired features, with the diminutive figure of her son at her side. I realised I was staring at her in astonishment, wondering what on earth she could be doing here.

Ingrid smiled thinly at me. 'Hello, Michaela. I hoped I'd find you here. Can we come in?'

'Ingrid!'

'I thought I might find you back with Calum, playing happy families,' Ingrid commented. 'Well? Are you going to leave us standing out here all day?'

To my shame, I actually found myself wanting to shut the door in Ingrid's face. There was a nervousness about her, as if she was the harbinger of bad news.

The day, which until then had been thinly sunny and pleasant, clouded over, dropping a grey overcast veil over everything. I looked at the child huddled against his mother, as a chilly wind whistled past, catching at his light brown hair and tugging at the grubby blanket he was holding.

I forced a smile as I stood back to let them pass. 'Come on through. I'm afraid it's still a bit of a mess.'

Ingrid squeezed past me with all the aplomb of someone who was familiar with where she was going. She'd been here many times over the years I reminded myself, as I followed her more slowly, wondering why she was here.

She sat herself on the sofa, dropping a small rucksack to the floor and leaving Tristan to stand close by. His expression was both guarded and watchful.

I deposited the cleaning materials on the windowsill behind me and smiled at him. 'Would you like some orange squash or some cola?'

'Cola makes him hyperactive,' Ingrid cautioned. 'He prefers blackcurrant but squash will do.'

'Can I get you a coffee?' I asked.

She shook her head. 'Don't bother on my account, I can't stay long. I have a favour to ask you.'

Resting a hand on top of the TV, I regarded her apprehensively. Only twenty four hours ago she had asserted that our friendship was over. Indeed she had even gone so far as to say she had never really been my friend at all. Now she was in Calum's sitting room asking for a favour. I decided to cut right to the chase.

'What do you want, Ing?'

'I've had a job offer, something that could change my life. I need to go to an interview today – it might take all day, and I can't take him with me.'

She motioned her head towards Tristan who kept his eyes downcast, his fingers working along the silken binding of the blanket, seeking reassurance.

'You mean you want me to have him?' I couldn't keep the surprise out of my voice. 'But he doesn't even know me.'

'It's only for the day, and I know you're OK with kids. Don't forget I saw you with Abigail when she was small and I know you can manage.'

I thought of my plans to clean the attic room and to go into the nearby town of Dorking later on and find a book on quilt making.

'I don't know, Ingrid.'

Ingrid's eyes narrowed. 'What happened to "I'm sorry I wasn't there for you" and "Is there anything I can do to help?" she sneered.

I felt my cheeks suffuse with colour; she was right of course. Pursing my lips I held up my hands in defeat and nodded my head. 'OK. If you're sure Tristan won't mind.'

She nudged the child. 'You'll be alright with Auntie Kaela, won't you?' she demanded. When he didn't respond she nudged him again. 'Tristan Matthew Peters, are you listening to me?'

Tristan nodded miserably and Ingrid beamed up at me. 'There. He'll be fine.'

Having received my answer, she shot to her feet with indecent haste. 'I'll be back for him before bedtime.'

'What time would that be?' I asked.

Ingrid shrugged. 'Some time this evening I suppose. He usually goes to sleep when he's tired enough but I'll be back before then.'

'Is there a number I'll be able to reach you on?'

She scribbled a number on the back of a scrap of paper and handed it to me. 'If he's any trouble, just give him a cuff round the ear and he'll soon behave,' Ingrid said as she headed for the door.

'Do you mind if I take him out with me? I was going to do some shopping later.'

'You can do what you like with him, he won't mind.'

I followed her into the hall just in time to see Abbey come yawning down the stairs. She was wearing a pair of skinny jeans and a cropped black T-shirt with a skull and crossbones across her chest. The T-shirt reminded me suddenly of the death card and something lurched uncomfortably in the pit of my stomach. Abbey stopped in surprise at seeing a visitor standing in the hall. I wondered fleetingly why she looked so different this morning, younger, fresher and prettier and then realised she wasn't wearing her dark, gothic style make up yet. I watched as Abbey's neat eyebrows knitted together.

'I know you, don't I?'

Ingrid shrugged and tried to retreat into the passage but Abbey inched down the last couple of stairs and peered at her. 'You used to come here after Kaela disappeared.'

'It was quite a while ago,' Ingrid said. 'I'm surprised you remember, you were only a kid.'

'You used to have dinner with Dad.' Abbey looked past Ingrid and questioningly at me. 'Who is she?'

'This is Ingrid. We used to work together.'

Abbey's eyes widened with sudden comprehension. 'The one from Brighton? The . . .'

I cringed, thinking she was going to say *hooker*, but she hesitated before adding, '. . . friend from work.' Abbey made even those words sound somehow disgusting and I found myself wondering just what Ingrid had been doing having dinner with Calum in my absence.

'I'll see you later then,' Ingrid said as she hurried towards the front door to let herself out, 'and Kaela?'

She pulled at the door handle and turned in the open doorway. 'Thanks.'

Abbey came to stand beside me as the door closed behind our visitor. 'What was she doing here?'

'She came to ask a favour.'

'What sort of favour?'

Abbey had followed me into the sitting room and stopped dead at the sight of the small child standing statue-like by the sofa. It didn't look as if he'd moved a muscle since his mother had left the room. She turned to me with a horrified look of disbelief.

212

'Oh my God, are you joking?'

'I'm afraid not. This is Tristan and it seems we have him for the day.'

An hour later Abbey, Tristan and I were getting along better than I could possibly have hoped for. Wanting to get on with cleaning out the attic room, I'd remembered Abbey's old rocking-horse and had taken Tristan upstairs.

After a moment's hesitation Tristan had climbed onto the horse, leaned his head against its neck with his blanket still dangling from his hand and had rocked contentedly ever since, while his eyes followed my every move. Abbey, who had apparently forgiven my expulsion of her friends the night before, had traipsed after us complaining that I was unbelievably soft to have agreed to minding the boy and deserved to be taken for a mug. She ensconced herself on my bed and sat with her legs crossed yoga style, first painting her toenails black and then simply watching as I dragged packing boxes about and attacked cobwebs and layers of thick dust.

I chatted while I worked telling the two of them about my job at Wayfarers. I told them a couple of stories about my child-hood and found myself unexpectedly tearing up when I recalled a story that included my father. Finding myself suddenly swallowing back tears, I suggested to Abbey that she go and fetch us some drinks and she trotted off with surprising amiability to do my bidding, appearing a moment later with three tumblers of orange squash and a packet of chocolate chip cookies.

Tristan's eyes lit up when he saw the cookies and although he was reluctant to get off the rocking-horse at first, he came and climbed up between Abbey and me where we sat on the edge of the bed. We sat in a companionable row and munched cookies, showering the newly-swept floor with crumbs.

Glancing sideways at my companions I wondered if they too, thought of this interlude as a kind of respite. I sighed as I saw Tristan reaching for another biscuit, remembering his watchful eyes as he'd observed his mother swigging back her vodka. He seemed to be quietly alert all the time, waiting for something to happen.

'What's that old sewing machine doing up here?' Abbey asked abruptly through a mouthful of biscuit, breaking into my thoughts.

'I think it belonged to your mother,' I told her. I watched as she hopped off the bed and went to run a hand tentatively over the glossy blackness of the machine. I had hidden the quilt wanting to finish it for her as the dream had indicated and offer it as a joint gift from her mother and me.

Abbey's fingers traced the outline of the machine in silence and suddenly her shoulders were shaking and I realised she was crying. I went to her and put an arm around her.

'I think your mother must have sat up here and sewed,' I said softly.

Abbey nodded through her tears. 'She used to sit me on the rocking-horse and I'd rock for ages while she worked away at this old machine. She'd sing as she worked and I'd try and join in even though I didn't know the songs.' She turned to me, her eyes wide. 'God, I can only have been about four when we did that, the same sort of age as Tristan. I'd forgotten all about it until I came up here.'

It was strange to think of the little pre-school Abbey sitting up here with her mother. 'This must have been a favourite place for her,' I agreed, remembering the dream again. 'Sewing was obviously a passion of hers.'

'Do you think Dad threw all the things she made away?'

'Maybe not everything,' I allowed, glancing guiltily at the box containing the quilt.

'He had no right!' Abbey stamped her foot and held her hands in tight fists at her sides. 'They weren't his to throw away. How could he have been so selfish?'

'When someone loses a person they love, it isn't always easy to see things clearly,' I tried to explain. 'If your father gave some of her things away it was probably because he was hurting. He's only human, Abbey.'

'If he'd just kept one thing,' Abbey said as tears rolled down her cheeks. 'Just one, I could have forgiven him. But there's nothing left of her and I hate him for it.'

And in that moment I realised I too was being selfish. I'd wanted to please Abbey, to be part of the joy of her finding out that her mother hadn't forgotten her. I'd wanted it to be a gift from both of us but realised now that I had no more business keeping her mother's quilt from her than Calum had to have disposed of everything else.

Glancing round at Tristan I was surprised to find he was still methodically munching biscuits. I had been worried Abbey's outburst might have distressed him, but he was watching us with a kind of detached interest. I wondered how often the boy had been dumped with strangers over the years.

'I think I may have found something belonging to your mother,' I said to Abbey, drawing the girl back towards the bed and sitting her down. 'I had a strange dream last night and this morning I felt drawn to look into the box below the sewing machine. I think your mother intended what is in there for you. I was going to try and finish it for her – for you, but now I think she may have wanted you to see it exactly as she left it.'

Lifting the machine off the box and placing it carefully on the floor, I felt like a magician about to perform some fantastic feat for my rapt audience.

'I believe your mother made this for you, Abbey.' I pulled

the quilt from the box, and walked over to her as she sat stiffly. 'I think it was meant to be a record of your life, only . . .' I swallowed the lump that had formed in the back of my throat. 'Only she didn't have time to finish it.'

Chapter Thirty-Four

Tristan and I watched as Abbey gathered the quilt onto her lap. After a few minutes she raised tear filled eyes to mine and smiled a deep smile of such happiness that I had to swallow hard so as not to cry.

'It smells of her,' she whispered. 'I'd forgotten what Mum smelled like, but it's here, caught in this quilt. Thank you, Kaela.'

'When is my mummy coming back for me?'

My gaze shifted from Abbey to Tristan and I glanced at my watch. It was almost midday.

'A few more hours,' I told him. 'She said she'd be back before bedtime.' I straightened up and rubbed my hands together. 'How about we pop down to the supermarket and buy some lunch?'

'Kaela?' Abbey's voice was tentative and I realised she wasn't ready to be jollied along just yet. 'Were you really going to try and finish it for me?'

I nodded. 'I'm really glad I didn't make a start on it though. I'm not much of a seamstress and I might have ruined all her beautiful work.'

'How did you plan to do it then?'

I looked down at my hands. She was questioning me about details I hadn't really considered. 'I thought I'd start by going to the quilt shop in Dorking – if it's still there after six years – and getting a book on quilt making.'

'Can we still go?' She was running one of the unfinished edges through her fingers, in much the same way that Tristan was fingering the silken edge of his blanket. 'I'd like to have a try at it.'

'I'm not sure we can today. I was thinking of going in by bus but I hadn't realised we'd have Tristan with us. It might be a bit much for him.'

'We could have lunch out,' Abbey suggested. 'Make a day of it. I saw Dad has left you some money.'

I looked at Tristan, doubtful that he would want to be dragged off when his mother had left him here. 'Is there still a bus that goes to Dorking?'

Abbey shrugged. 'I could always call Kevin. He'd give us a lift.'

My heart gave a small leap at the thought of seeing Kevin again, his connection with Matt had my heart in a flutter.

'You can't use him like a taxi service,' I found myself protesting half heartedly.

Abbey produced her mobile phone and dialled a number. She grinned when it was promptly answered. 'Twenty minutes will be fine,' she said into the phone. 'We'll be ready.'

'I can't imagine why he'd want to bother,' I said under my breath. I shook my head at Abbey's youthful acceptance that the world and everyone in it were at her disposal. 'Doesn't he have anything better to do?'

Abbey grinned. 'There is a catch.'

I groaned. It seemed there was always a catch. 'Dare I ask what it is that he wants?'

'He's asked me to do another tarot reading for him.'

A shiver ran down my spine and I rubbed my bare arms. I thought of the previous tarot reading and the single card

218

fluttering down. Abbey had never really explained the significance of that card and I realised its appearance was niggling away in my mind. I felt a warm hand brush against my arm and opened my eyes to see Abbey looking at me anxiously. 'Are you alright, Kaela?'

Both she and Tristan were watching me warily and I gave myself a mental shake. I crossed to the skylight and closed it firmly, shutting out the cold, grey sky. 'I'm fine,' I told them with forced cheerfulness. 'Let's get ready to go, shall we?'

After we'd descended the stairs, Abbey disappeared into her room for several minutes and reappeared with her eyes heavily outlined in dark eye shadow, her lashes thick with mascara. She pouted with newly mauve lips as she surveyed my face. 'You could do with some lipstick at the very least,' she advised me.

I was considering my response when I felt a tug at my jeans. Glancing down I found Tristan looking flushed and rather anxious. He was hopping from one leg to the other.

'I need a wee,' he whispered uncomfortably.

'Oh, er, come with me then.' I guided Tristan towards the downstairs loo, closed the door behind him and turned to Abbey. 'I don't have any make up. Everything I ever owned has gone.'

She looked at me with her head to one side. 'You could borrow some of mine if you like.'

I was about to say that I didn't think her choice of make up would be quite to my taste, when I realised she was waiting for my response with an intensity I couldn't place. It occurred to me that she was holding out a proverbial olive branch much as she had tried to do with her father that morning when she had offered to make the tea. I nodded slowly, shuddering at what I might end up looking like. 'That's really kind of you, Abbey.'

Tristan had emerged from the toilet looking much happier and followed as Abbey led me to her bedroom.

'Hang on a minute,' she cautioned, making eye signals towards the child. 'I need to clear a few things away.'

Tristan and I hovered on the narrow landing listening to drawers and cupboards opening and closing, and I wondered what she was hiding from our young guest.

'OK, you can come in.'

She had cleared up remarkably quickly. A quick glance showed a typical teenage room with posters on the walls and a dressing table full of discarded junk jewellery and cosmetics. There were still some items of black and purple clothing scattered across her bed, but otherwise there was nothing untoward.

'Here,' she said holding out an eye liner pencil and a tube of mascara. 'You can borrow these.'

'Thanks.' I applied a thin line of the pencil then brushed some mascara onto my lashes while Tristan watched quietly. I wondered how many times he'd watched his mother dolling herself up for an evening's work and what he must have seen in his few short years of life. I tore my thoughts away from him and Ingrid and blinked at myself in the mirror. 'Do you have any blusher or lipstick?'

Abbey held out a box which contained a set of four blushers, ranging from very pale to a tawny pink. I pictured the young girl experimenting with the different shades and decided to go for the darker of the colours on offer.

Lipstick was a problem as Abbey seemed to own either ghostly pale pinks or violently dark shades. I took the paler of the two and mixed it with a little blusher before applying it to my lips. Sitting back I contemplated the result with satisfaction. Abbey had been right; I did look better with a little colour on my face.

'Thank you, Abbey.'

Her reflection beamed at me from the mirror and I thought how pretty she was when she smiled, so different from the sulky teenager of a few days ago.

The beep of a car horn sounded from outside and I took Tristan's hand as we scuttled downstairs to fling open the front door. Kevin had obviously got tired of waiting in the car and was walking up the drive towards us. He seemed not to have noticed Tristan who was hovering behind me, his gaze drifted to something at one side of the steps which led up to the door.

'What's all this then?' he enquired as Abbey and I followed his gaze, peering beside the steps where there was an area partially covered by an overgrown shrub. 'Has someone come to stay?'

Tucked neatly under the bush were a battered suitcase and a clear plastic bag containing a duvet, a pillow and a small pile of toys.

I felt a swift stab of alarm; these were all items which looked as if they might be the meagre belongings of a four-year-old boy.

What the hell was Ingrid up to?

Chapter Thirty-Five

'Are these things yours?' I asked Tristan, who was lurking silently in the passage behind me.

He hung his head.

Kevin seemed to see the boy for the first time. 'Who's this?'

'He's Ingrid's,' I answered faintly. 'She asked me to mind him for her.'

He eyed the luggage and raised a quizzical eyebrow. 'For how long?'

I pressed a hand to my temple, feeling like a complete fool. 'She said it was just for today, so she could go to an interview.'

Kevin pushed past me into the house.

'Did he have anything else with him?' Kevin asked.

It was the second time I'd wondered just how sane and normal Kevin really was under his charade of awkward eccentricity.

I pointed to the backpack Ingrid had left at the side of the couch, 'Just that. Oh, and a mobile number.'

The memory of the number brought me sudden hope and I scrabbled about for the piece of paper. 'I'll give her a ring and ask why she's left him so much stuff.'

I left Kevin rifling through the backpack and dialled the

number with trembling fingers. The call went straight to voice mail and I left a brief message.

Abbey was watching me nervously. 'Has she left him?'

'No, no. She must just have wanted a bit more time and didn't want to risk me refusing to take him. Maybe she's gone off for the weekend.'

'Uh oh,' Kevin's voice came through from the sitting room. 'You'd better come and see this.'

My feet felt leaden as I walked into the room to see him holding out an envelope.

'It's addressed to you.'

I took the letter and turned it over in my hand. It simply said, 'Michaela' on the front in what I recognised as Ingrid's handwriting.

Perching on the edge of the sofa I tore the letter open and read it quickly, then a second time more slowly, trying to register the enormity of what she had written.

Dear Michaela,

I hope by the time you read this I am safely on the plane, because I couldn't bear to come face to face with you. You must think I'm a terrible mother leaving Tristan like this, but believe me, if you'd lived like I have, you'd know I'm doing the best thing for him.

It's no life for a child seeing all his 'uncles' coming round night after night. Not all of them were kind to him. I've wanted out for a long time but I couldn't see a way to do it. After you left yesterday I got to thinking, you were bound to go back to Calum or shack up with Matt and I know you're good with kids. You took Abbey on, didn't you? And back then she was only a few years older than Tris is now. I don't want him going into a home, not after what happened to me. I trust you not to do that. You

were my friend once, but if you don't want to do it for
me, do it for him. Please.

Maybe it would help if I told you that you are the next
best thing to being his mother anyway. He's where he
rightfully belongs.

I'm going to be living another kind of life from now
on, somewhere far away. Don't try to find me. Thanks.
Ingrid.

'Bloody hell.' I leaned back into the sofa and closed my
eyes for a moment. When I looked up, Kevin was holding
another piece of paper and a small booklet.

'It's the boy's birth certificate and his inoculation record.'
I put the letter on my lap and stared at him as he delved
back into the rucksack and produced a second, shorter note.
I took it with shaking hands, hardly daring to read it.

I give permission for Michaela Anderson to act as parent
and guardian to my son Tristan Matthew Peters while I
am out of the country. She is to have all parental rights
until I return.
Ingrid Peters.

I sat in stunned silence while Abbey snatched the note from
my hand. She read it quickly and her eyes grew round and wide.

'She can't do that, can she?' she asked in horror.

'Whether she can or not is immaterial,' Kevin snorted. 'She
has done it, hasn't she?'

'Shit,' Abbey said. She turned to look at Tristan who was
following the proceedings watchfully. It seemed she was about
to say something but closed her mouth and simply shook
her head.

'Put the TV on for Tristan,' I mouthed over the boy's head.

Abbey flicked the television on and followed me and Kevin through to the kitchen.

'What can I do?' I asked Kevin.

'As I see it you have three choices: contact social services and have him put into care, try and track Ingrid down and make her take him back or look after him yourself until she deems to return.'

'You can't put him into care!' Abbey shrieked in horror. 'We could keep him, couldn't we, Kaela?'

'He's not a puppy,' I told her indignantly. 'And your father may have something to say about having a small child foisted on him.'

I thought of the cryptic comment about the child being where he rightfully belonged and wondered what she'd meant by it. Abbey's mention of Ingrid continuing to visit Calum long after I'd disappeared rang in my ears. Could the boy be Calum's?

I sank onto a chair, feeling as if my body was actually dissolving round the edges with the worry of it all. I wanted to close my eyes and disappear again. Perhaps, I thought, if I closed my eyes really tightly, I might be able to return to my previous life, or failing that, hop another six years into the future where everything would have been neatly resolved without me.

As I worked out the timings in my head the guilty realisation hit me that when Calum and I had first become lovers, his wife Grace had been gone less than two years – that made me no better than Ingrid.

I felt a small hand rest on the knee of my jeans. Tristan had followed us into the kitchen and was looking at me, his face pale, blue eyes round and strangely hopeful.

I knew he couldn't possibly understand what was going on here, so I smiled kindly at him. 'What is it, Tris?'

225

'I'm hungry,' he said in small voice. 'Can I have some dinner?'

The simple request brought me back to earth with a bang. There would be time for recriminations later. Maybe Ingrid would change her mind and come back for him. In any event there didn't seem to be much I could do until I'd spoken to Calum. Right now there was the more immediate matter of lunch.

I glanced at Kevin. 'Are you still OK to drive us into Dorking? I expect we could all do with something to eat.'

'Sure thing, babe, whatever you want.'

I noticed the return of Kevin's jaunty use of the English language and wondered fleetingly if it was all an act intended to fool me into thinking he was harmless. As we went to get into the car, Abbey ran back to get Tristan's car seat from his belongings. Meanwhile Kevin leaned against the car and fiddled with his mobile phone, stealing sideways glances at me when he thought I wasn't looking.

'What is it, Kevin?'

He hastily put the phone in his pocket. 'Just checking a text, babe.'

I remembered what he'd said about wanting to video me for his website. 'You weren't filming me, were you?'

'You have fans, Kaela. Everyone wants to know what happened to you. I'm just giving a little interest back to my subscribers.'

'Space Dog,' I muttered under my breath as Abbey returned lugging the booster seat. 'I should have known you weren't in the area by chance. Have you been watching me?'

'Think of it as looking out for you,' he grinned. 'And I'd only just arrived in the vicinity when Abbey called. That's why I didn't see Ingrid come and go. I might have followed her if I had.'

'Pity you didn't,' I whispered as I fastened Tristan into the booster seat. I turned to face Kevin with a rueful grin, keeping my voice low so the child wouldn't hear. 'We would have known where to return him then.'

I climbed into the rear of the car next to Tristan and waited until Abbey was safely strapped into the front seat.

'What do you suggest for lunch?'

'We could go to the converted mill, at Gomshall,' Abbey said. She swivelled around to talk to me. 'Tristan will love it. Do you remember taking me there with Dad when I was little?'

'What a good idea,' I smiled at her, seeing again the excited little girl I once knew so much better than this teenager. 'Does it still have the mill stream running underneath?'

She shrugged. 'I haven't been there for ages, but we could go and see.'

'The mill it is then.' Kevin floored the accelerator and headed towards Dorking.

The mill was a huge success. Abbey took Tristan to see the now silent mill wheel and the stream through a glass window within the restaurant while we were waiting to be served. When the food arrived Tristan tucked in to his sausages and mash as if he'd never seen food before and we ordered sticky toffee pudding all round for dessert. I couldn't help but smile as both Tristan and Kevin wolfed the pudding down while Abbey and I picked delicately at ours. We must have looked like a family of four enjoying a day out. Although there was no way anyone could possibly guess that none of us were remotely related at all. Unless of course it turned out that the two youngsters were in fact half siblings . . .

I shook the unwelcome thought away. That was something I would be taking up with Calum later on – and I wasn't looking forward to that confrontation one little bit.

Chapter Thirty-Six

Despite my protestations Kevin settled the bill for our meal on the way out. Tristan looked tired and sure enough, by the time we arrived in Dorking he was asleep in his booster seat, mouth open, blanket in hand. Kevin volunteered to stay in the car and keep an eye on him while Abbey and I had a quick look in the quilt shop and bought some groceries.

The quilt shop was an Aladdin's cave of texture and colour. Although I'd never had much interest in sewing I could see how exciting this shop must be to those who did. Set in a street of ancient buildings, the shop had uneven floors and rickety steps and stairs taking the shopper into smaller rooms, over-flowing with everything one might need for the craft of quilt making. Ignoring the suspicious looks thrown in Abbey's direction I made my way to the book shelves lined along a back wall. I could hardly blame them, I thought as I took a sideways glance at the girl with her black and purple head bent over one of the books, the piercings standing out against her face.

'Look at this, Kaela,' she said suddenly. She was holding one of the books open and I looked over her shoulder to see a picture of a colourful patchwork. 'Isn't this the kind of design Mum was using?'

Shrugging, I had to confess that I didn't know, I couldn't tell one design from another.

'I'm sure it is,' she said, tucking the book under her arm. 'They've even used the same colour scheme she chose for me, mainly pinks and creams, and look here how the pieces fan out from the centre just like hers do.' She moved off to look at the fabrics and I followed her as she ran a black talon along the front of a rainbow selection of bolts of cloth. 'These would go well together, wouldn't they?' she murmured.

'Can I help you?' asked an assistant.

I was about to say that we were just looking, when Abbey turned to her with shining eyes and asked how much fabric one would need to make the quilt in the book.

I went off to look at packs of brightly coloured buttons. I had to confess that I had no idea what they were talking about. Eventually I wandered back and heard the assistant telling Abbey she would look at it and give her some advice on how to proceed. I paid for the book and some templates and threads that Abbey had selected and dragged her round the corner to the supermarket, very much aware of the time. Tristan might have woken up and forgetting where he was got worked up. As Abbey and I forged ahead with the shopping, I wondered just what I had got myself into.

As it happened Tristan didn't wake until Kevin turned off the car's engine outside the house. Then he raised his tousled head, stared blearily round him and began to cry.

As Kevin took in the shopping, and Abbey trotted ahead with the key, I dealt with Tristan.

'Shush, Tris, its OK,' I told him. 'Let's get you inside the house, alright?' I realised he'd dropped his tiny blanket and I retrieved it from the floor and thrust it into his hands. While he quietened immediately, his shoulders were still trembling as I hoisted him out and stood him on the pavement.

'I want M . . . mummy.'

'I know, sweetheart.' I found I didn't know what else to say. Should I lie and tell him his mother would return shortly? I doubted very much that Ingrid would change her mind and come back for him any time soon. Her obvious planning indicated long-term abandonment.

Sitting Tristan down on the sofa and putting the TV on for him I returned to help Kevin with the last of the bags, stowing the shopping away in the kitchen.

Kevin peered at his phone. 'I'd better be going. I doubt that Calum would be impressed to find me here again.' He gave Abbey a grin. 'Ring again if you want anything, princess. I won't be far away with my white charger.'

'Yeah,' Abbey replied. She was sitting next to Tristan, showing him pictures in the quilt book and she barely glanced up. 'See ya.'

I was putting the rest of the shopping away when I heard the front door open. Glancing at my watch I realised it was almost five o'clock. It seemed that Kevin had only been gone a few minutes and I had been looking forward to a short respite with a cup of tea.

Taking a deep breath I turned to face Calum as he appeared in the kitchen doorway holding a huge bouquet of flowers. He advanced towards me and thrust them into my arms.

'For you,' he smiled, 'a belated welcome home gift.'

'They are lovely,' I commented, trying not to wonder whether he had brought Ingrid flowers like these. Placing the bouquet on the kitchen counter I began to hunt for a vase, but Calum reached out and gripped my wrist, spinning me round to face him.

'Leave them for the moment,' he said. He studied my face with his blue eyes. 'You really don't look a day older. It's quite uncanny.'

'Calum, I . . .'

'Hush. I want to look at you, remind myself how beautiful you are.' He traced the outline of my face with his finger and I fell silent. I wanted to lean into him, close my eyes and go back to how things were before. I didn't want to suspect him of having a fling with Ingrid or fathering a child by her. I just wanted things to be normal again.

'How did it go at the hospital?' I heard myself asking.

He pulled back and grimaced. 'The consultant can't see me until next week but we'll discuss the operation then. Until I see him I have to continue with the last few radiotherapy treatments.'

'Is it very gruelling?'

'I'm a bit sore and constantly tired, but it's not terrible. I'm just weary of the whole thing.' He paused and looked round the kitchen. 'You haven't started cooking, have you? I thought we might go out for a bite to eat.'

'Calum, there's something I have to . . .'

I broke off in mid sentence as Abbey appeared in the kitchen doorway with Tristan at her side. They both stopped dead at the sight of Calum and I realised they hadn't heard him come in over the sound of the TV.

'Dad?' Abbey was looking at him in dismay as if she'd forgotten his existence.

But Calum didn't seem to register his daughter's presence. He was staring in surprise at the small boy standing next to her. He turned back to me with a puzzled expression. 'Who's this?'

'That,' I said, my earlier feelings of hurt and indignation unexpectedly surfacing again, 'is what I hoped you might be able to explain to me.'

The four of us stood in silence. I swallowed, wishing immediately that I hadn't challenged Calum in front of Abbey, but when I glanced apologetically towards her, I found her expression was showing neither surprise nor any sudden dawning realisation about what my question had implied. She had read Ingrid's letter too and the same thoughts had obviously crossed her mind. Abbey had been pretty good to Tristan today – almost as an older sister would care for a younger brother, I realised.

'Well?' demanded Abbey of her father, 'Why did Ingrid bring him to us?'

'Ingrid?' Calum looked nonplussed. I noticed he was tightly gripping the back of a kitchen chair.

'My supposed friend,' I told him grimly, 'who travelled all the way from Brighton this morning to drop her son "where he rightfully belongs".'

'I don't know what you're talking about.' Calum pulled the chair out and sank onto it looking suddenly exhausted. 'Why did she bring him here? And when is she coming back for him?'

Abbey and I exchanged glances. Did he really not know what we were talking about? Maybe if Ingrid had never told him she was pregnant and expecting his child, he truly might not have known of Tristan's existence.

I motioned to Abbey to take Tristan back to the sitting room, but the boy protested.

'I haven't got my drink yet,' he said, pulling his hand from hers. He looked pointedly at me. 'When is my mummy coming back?'

'I don't know, Tristan.' I'd decided to err on the side of truth and honesty. 'Would you like some blackcurrant?'

He nodded and I reached around the dumbstruck Calum to give him some. 'Abbey can carry it back into the TV room for you,' I told Tristan. 'Go and see if there's anything good to watch on telly.'

232

Calum turned to me as soon as the pair of them left the kitchen. 'What is going on, Kaela?'

Sighing, I pulled out the chair next to his and turned to face him. 'Ingrid arrived with the boy this morning. She told me she was going for an interview and asked if I would mind him for the day. I believed her Calum. I thought she'd be back this evening to collect him.'

'But . . . ?'

'But when we went outside we found the child's belongings heaped by the front step. I tried ringing her mobile number but she's not answering it. We went through Tristan's backpack and found these.' I reached across the table and handed them to him.

Calum read the two letters carefully and fingered the birth certificate and inoculation booklet as if deep in thought. When he looked up there was a wounded expression on his face. 'You think I'm the boy's father, is that it?'

I stared him down. 'Are you?'

'Of course not! The woman is unhinged if you ask me, always has been.'

'Abbey says Ingrid was in the habit of coming round here after I went missing.'

He went very still and I wondered if I'd caught him out.

'We saw quite a bit of each other when you first disappeared,' he admitted after a pause. 'Ingrid was in shock not just from the way you vanished into thin air but that she had lost her best friend and confidante. She, Kevin and your boss Graham were being hounded by the press; the instructor too, of course. The media tried to pin your disappearance on Matt and the pilot – and I confess – I believed they had something to do with it.' He gazed at me, imploring me to believe him. 'I mean what else could we think? Ingrid told me Matt had been chatting you up the whole time you were training for the jump . . .'

He trailed off as I let out a small snort through my nose. I had spent most of that training day watching Ingrid flirt with Matt. Had she been jealous when he rebuffed her advances? I recalled the look in Ingrid's eyes when Matt had helped me up into the plane behind her. She'd covered her annoyance with a smile but she must have seen him talking to me, possibly even seen him give me his phone number.

And in my absence she'd come to Calum and told him it had been me who had done the flirting. I felt disgust followed almost immediately by a small flush of guilt when I remembered that I wasn't totally innocent any longer where Matt was concerned. 'Go on.'

'We were thrown together by our mutual grief. She came by a few times to ask if I needed anything; she even cooked on a few occasions over the next year or so, but despite her eagerness to be with me, she didn't seem to take to Abbey. We met occasionally for drinks, but it gradually petered out.' Calum fixed his eyes on mine. 'I never slept with her, I swear it.'

Chapter Thirty-Seven

We eyed one another across the kitchen table. I wanted to believe Calum, but found I wasn't sure of anything any longer. I thought of how many times Ingrid had become fixated with someone and would do pretty well anything to snare them. She had never really understood that some men – especially the married ones – were out of bounds or simply didn't want her.

He pursed his lips. 'She actually tried very hard. When I eventually refused her she became quite abusive. I realised she was very highly strung and for a while was quite worried about what she'd do, but to my surprise, she just cut me out of her life. It was a relief to be honest.'

I looked away from Calum and sighed. I couldn't very well condemn him for finding comfort with another woman after spending sixteen months alone. I had run straight to Matt after Calum had rebuffed me, hadn't I?

'What are we going to do with Tristan?' I asked tentatively. 'I don't want to abandon him to social services.'

Calum picked up the letter and read it through once more. 'It seems that after you visited her, Ingrid wasn't sure whether you were going to come back to live with me or if you were going to "shack up" with Matt Treguier. If she hadn't found you here, chances are that she would have gone looking for you at his place.' He raised his eyes to mine and I read a hint of accusation there. 'That suggests that this letter was designed to make either or both of us look like the guilty party. And as it isn't me, I suggest you contact your friend Matt and see if he'd like to have his son stay with him.'

My mind flashed back to Ingrid's parting shot as I'd left her flat the day before; *A word of warning from your old pal . . . all men and I do mean* all *men, are complete bastards.*

I recalled the girlie T-shirt Matt had lent me on my first night in his flat and how easily I had accepted that he'd had many lovers over the years. If one of those lovers had been Ingrid, then what did it matter? If it happened, it would have been long before anything had happened between Matt and me. So why did the idea that he might be Tristan's father rankle me?

I glanced at my watch. 'It's rather late to move the lad on now,' I pointed out. 'I'm going to try Ingrid again and if I can't get hold of her, could Tristan stay here tonight, at least? We can track Matt down in the morning.'

'Do whatever you think is best.' Calum was slumped in the chair and looked to be on his last reserves of strength. 'I don't want to fight with you, Michaela, but I have no idea where the boy could sleep.'

I dialled the mobile number for the umpteenth time, not bothering to leave another message.

'Tristan can have my bed.' We looked up to see Abbey framed in the kitchen doorway. 'I'll sleep on the sofa.'

'Now why would you want to do that?' Calum asked her wearily. 'He has nothing to do with us.'

I wondered how much she'd heard of our conversation and if she still suspected Calum was the boy's father, but once again she surprised me.

'It doesn't matter whose he is. He's just a little boy whose

236

mother has abandoned him.' She glanced at me. 'I know what it's like to be without a mum.'

'Oh, for goodness' sake, he can stay if that's what you both want,' Calum capitulated abruptly. I could see that he was suffering and I nodded to Abbey.

'Why don't you take his things upstairs to your room and show Tristan where he's going to spend the night?'

As soon as she was gone I turned my attention to Calum. 'I know this is the last thing you need right now and I'm sorry Ingrid has put this on us. You look about done in. Do you still want to eat, or do you need to go and lie down?'

'I think I'll go and lie down for a bit.' He caught my wrist as I started to rise from the chair. 'I'm sorry too, Kaela. This has all come a bit out of the blue but I want you to know that I am glad you chose to come back here to me and Abbey.'

'Glad to be of service,' I quipped. Calum was looking ghastly. 'Come on, let's get you to your room and I'll make dinner. We can go out another night when you're not quite so washed out.'

I found I enjoyed cooking in my kitchen again. Now I had it clean and tidy, it was almost as if six years hadn't passed since I had last chopped and peeled and roasted things in the oven. By quarter to seven the four of us were sitting at the kitchen table tucking into breaded goujons of chicken with roast potatoes and vegetables.

'This is delicious,' Calum commented as he cleared his plate and sat back, replete. 'I'd forgotten what a good cook you are.'

Abbey and Tristan were still eating. If Tristan was distressed at his mother's abandonment he seemed to have forgotten it for the moment and I wondered whether he had been continually hungry in his mother's care.

An hour later I ran a bath for Tristan – who had neither

seemed nor smelled too clean since his arrival this morning. When I told Tristan his bath was ready, he hung back looking apprehensive.

'Come on, Tris,' I encouraged him. 'You must like bath time, it is such fun. Look,' I continued as Abbey dropped a bath bomb into the bath and stood back so we could watch it scatter blue bubbles into the water. 'Wouldn't you like to go in and play with it before it disappears?'

'I don't want to.'

'Well, let's finish getting you undressed at least.' I began to pull his T-shirt off over his head but stopped as he winced with pain. 'What is it, Tris?'

He looked at the thinly carpeted floor while I inspected his head and neck. There was a purple bruise behind one ear and the greenish yellow remnants of an older one across his bony little shoulder.

'How did you get this?' As I asked the question I remembered Ingrid telling me to give him a cuff round the ear if her son misbehaved. Had Ingrid done this? 'It looks a bit sore,' I commiserated, unwilling to try and coax the truth out of him. 'Why don't you finish undressing yourself? Would you rather Abbey and I wait outside the door while you play in the water?'

My instinct was to gather the poor child up and give him a hug, but I could see that he might not want to be manhandled by strangers. Having found a couple of empty shampoo bottles for him to play with, I started towards the door, but Tristan began to whimper, so I returned and hunkered down in front of him. 'What is it, Tris? Do you want me to stay while you have your bath?'

'I don't like water in my nose!' He began to cry in earnest and I put my earlier misgivings to one side and put my arms round him, pulling him close.

238

'We won't let water get into your nose,' I assured him. 'How about we don't even wash your face? You could sit in the warm water and play with these bottles.' I lifted him over the edge of the bath and although he clung tightly to my arm, he allowed me to lower him into the water. Grabbing one of the bottles, I filled it with warm water and swished it over his knees. 'There, isn't that nice?'

What had happened to the poor child during bath time with his mother I dreaded to imagine, but he was soon pouring the bubbly remnants of shampoo carefully from one bottle to the other. 'Would you like another fizzy ball in there?' I asked with a smile.

He nodded and Abbey, who had been standing quietly by the bathroom door, stepped forwards with the strongly scented green ball and handed it to him. Tristan's eyes lit up as he weighed the ball in his small hand.

'Can I put it in the water?'

'Of course you can. Let's watch it fizz and bubble up.'

He lowered the ball into the water and grinned as it exploded in a cloud of green bubbles. 'It looks like the sea,' he said. 'Mummy let me swim in the sea once but I didn't like it. It was cold.'

I wondered if I'd misunderstood the child's apparent fear of the water. Of course, living in Brighton he must have spent lots of time on the beach and by the sea.

After ten minutes he had had enough of the bath and wanted to be helped out. As I wrapped him in a fluffy towel I noticed Abbey was grinning at me from the bathroom door.

'Nicely done,' she whispered as I rubbed him dry. 'I just hope he won't pee himself or anything in the night.'

From the cloying smell of the pyjamas we'd found in Tristan's suitcase, I wasn't going to chance it, and found an old plastic decorating sheet to spread over Abbey's mattress, just in case.

It was almost nine o'clock by the time Tristan was tucked safely up in bed. Abbey and I returned downstairs to find Calum sitting on the sofa in the sitting room watching a programme on the TV. He made room for us to sit with him.

The drama was about a dysfunctional family, but none of us laughed. It was all a little too poignant and close to home. I found my thoughts returning to Matt and tried to put him firmly out of my mind. Agitated and unable to settle I left Calum to it and wandered into the hall to try Ingrid's mobile again.

After dialling I waited for a few moments and was about to replace the receiver when the ring tone ceased suddenly as if someone had answered the call. 'Ingrid? Is that you?' No one spoke. Fearful that she would cut me off, I tried again, my voice softer. 'Ingrid?'

'You'll look after him, right?'

Relief flooded through me. She was wavering in her decision to leave Tristan. 'He's asleep, Ing, but he can't stay here.'

'Promise you won't put him into care.'

'He needs his mother. Don't abandon him, Ingrid. Don't do to him what your mother did to you.'

I trusted my plea would appeal to her maternal instinct, but her next words dashed any vain hope I might have.

'That's exactly why I can't take him with me. I'm sorry, Kaela. The flight leaves tonight – and I'm going to be on it.'

Chapter Thirty-Eight

A cold wave washed over me at the determination in Ingrid's voice.

'I can't keep Tristan here, Ingrid. There's so much going on as it is.' I took a deep breath, keeping my voice low so that Calum and Abbey wouldn't overhear us. 'Look, can we meet? We need to discuss this face to face.'

There was a sob on the other end of the line. 'It won't make any difference.'

'What's this all about, Ing? Where are you going and how long are you going to be away?'

'I've met a man – Lewis – who's promised me a new life. We're going abroad and I'm going to be working for him. He's rich, Kaela. He can give me everything I've dreamed about, protection, security, a life free from hardship.'

'Why can't you take Tristan with you?'

'Lewis doesn't like kids. He's . . . rough with Tris. He gets angry with him and I'm not going to subject my son to what I went through at the hands of my mother's boyfriends. I can't do that to Tris, but if we stay here we're just not going to make it. He'd be taken away from me soon enough anyway.'

'What would you have done if I hadn't come back?'

'What I *was* doing; refusing to go with Lewis and drinking myself to death.'

My hands felt clammy as I held the receiver. I didn't want to be saddled with a child I barely knew. Ingrid was using emotional blackmail but whilst I was tempted to put down the phone and call social services, I realised that the pay off was a small boy's future.

'You told me once that your mother's abandonment was the worst thing you ever had to face – more debilitating than never knowing your real father. How can you even think of doing the same thing to your son?'

'Have you *seen* Tris's bruises?'

'If Lewis did that to him then you should ditch him. For God's sake, Ingrid, this is your little boy you're talking about here.'

'I'm sorry, Kaela . . .'

'Don't hang up! Please, Ing . . .'

I thought for a moment I'd lost her but then her voice sounded again, high pitched and whiney with suspicion and doubt. 'If I tell you where we are, you'll only bring him with you.'

I had, of course, been going to do just that. Taking a deep breath, I came to a decision. 'I promise I won't. Not tonight. But if you don't want me to call social services first thing in the morning then you have to agree to talk to me. You have to meet me half way on this, Ing, or it'll be Tristan who ultimately suffers.'

There was silence followed by a loud sniff.

'Alright, but you'll have to come here. I'm at a small hotel near the airport. Lewis has some last minute business to see to. He won't be back until around midnight.'

Thinking quickly, I asked the name and address of the hotel. 'OK, Ingrid, I'll get there as soon as I can.'

So, after telling Calum and Abbey my plans I rang for a taxi. Calum immediately asked why I wasn't taking Tristan.

'There won't be much she can do if you leave the child there with her. I mean he is her son. We'd be quite within our rights to call the police and insist she keeps him.'

'It's too late to get the poor child out of bed and bundled into a taxi,' I protested. 'And anyway, I gave her my word.'

'Then I'll take you,' Calum countered. 'Come on. Cancel the taxi and I'll take you and the boy and we'll hand him back to his mother where he belongs.'

'I promised her, Calum.' I fixed him with a steely glare, reminding him that Ingrid wasn't the only person I had given my word to recently. 'And I don't break my promises.'

I saw that Calum had got my meaning and immediately backed down. 'Well, it's up to you; as long as I don't have to be involved with the boy if Ingrid vanishes.'

'I'm hoping to persuade her to take him back.'

'Hmm, if I remember Ingrid, she's pretty darn stubborn once she's made up her mind.'

As it turned out, Calum was right. As the taxi dropped me off, Ingrid was waiting for me in the small lobby. She was wearing a very short skirt with high heeled shoes and a see-through blouse. Despite the clothes she looked drawn and puffy-eyed as she ushered me towards a tired looking sofa, half hidden behind a large rubber plant and took the seat next to me, swivelling so we were face to face.

'This is a waste of time,' she said abruptly. 'You shouldn't have come.'

I wanted to retort that she shouldn't have left her son, but held my tongue. I had come to try and make her see reason, not to antagonise her. 'I can't keep him, Ing. I've only just moved back in with Calum and I have my own life to sort out. You're not thinking clearly.'

To my surprise, Ingrid took both my hands in hers and

looked imploringly into my eyes. 'I've never thought about anything more clearly in my life.' She shook her head wonderingly. 'I still can't believe you're really back. You're the only real friend I ever had and over the years I dreamed about what it would be like if you hadn't gone missing . . .' she petered off as tears welled in her eyes. 'Where the hell were you while my life was falling apart?'

'Don't put this on me, Ing,' I murmured, shaking my head. 'The last six and a half years might have been bad for you, but I never even had a chance to live mine.'

'No one has ever stuck by me.' She slumped in her seat and continued as if I'd not spoken. 'They've taken what they wanted and then dumped me like a piece of old rubbish; my mum's boyfriends, my mother, the male carer who abused me in the children's home. I am bad to be around, Kaela. I try to please, try to be a good person, but I'm bad to the core.'

'You're not a bad person,' I told her. 'You've done your best. And you were a good friend to me.' I gave the hands that were holding mine a squeeze. 'I'd lived such a sheltered life before I started at Wayfarers, an only child with rather doting parents. You showed me what the world was really about and you were great to be with.' I gave her a broad smile. 'Do you recall the day you found me crying in the ladies room at work, because one of the secretaries had said I was a plain Jane? You took me shopping and to have my hair done and even showed me how to shape my eyebrows, remember?'

Ingrid managed a wan smile. 'You turned out to be a stunner, didn't you?' The smile faded. 'But then I was jealous of you.'

'Who could blame you for feeling insecure and needy after the childhood you'd experienced?' I gripped her hands more tightly. 'Don't do the same thing to Tristan, Ing. Don't do it.'

She pulled her hands from mine and leaned away from me. 'You are the only person in the world I trust enough to leave my son with. Lewis would kill him – and I need Lewis.'

We stared at one another and I realised her mind was made up.

'You're going, aren't you?'

'I have to.' She rose to her feet. 'It's that or I'll be dead and Tris will be put into care anyway.'

'But what will I do with him?'

'Believe in him, Kaela. Just believe in him like you believed in me.'

I scrambled to my feet and looked her in the eye. 'Will you come back?'

'I don't know; maybe one day, if things change.'

The front door to the hotel opened behind us bringing a gust of cold air into the lobby and I shivered. Ingrid's eyes went very round.

'It's Lewis,' she whispered. 'I've got to go.'

'Just one last thing.'

'Yes?'

'Will you tell me who Tristan's father is?'

Ingrid's eyes narrowed, as if I'd asked a trick question. She seemed about to say something and then pressed her lips tightly together. 'I won't do that to you, Kaela. I need you to be strong for Tris, and for once in my life I'm going to do the noble thing.'

'Ingrid!'

Ingrid reached out and lightly touched my arm.

'Thank you for everything,' she murmured.

I watched her cross the lobby with a sinking heart. The mystery of the boy's father hung heavy about my shoulders.

I hadn't said I'd take Tristan on but Ingrid had assumed she'd got her own way. Out of a lifetime of misery and let downs, perhaps it was as well that she didn't know I had far from made up my mind what I was going to do with her son.

Chapter Thirty-Nine

That night I dreamt of Grace again. She floated into the attic room and sat at the end of my bed, watching me as I slept. I could feel the slight weight of her pulling the duvet tight over my feet and convinced myself I could even hear her shallow breathing. Perhaps it was because Ingrid had asked me to care for her child that I dreamt Grace was asking me to watch over hers.

I pulled the duvet up to my chin and turned over in my sleep, realising it comforted me to think something Abbey and I were planning for the future was giving solace to someone from the past. The quilt represented the continuation of a thread that had been started several years ago. Now that thread was to be taken up and woven through the tapestry of Abbey's life and my own, and perhaps even into the next generation of Grace's descendants.

Despite all my recent trauma, I found myself smiling, safe in the knowledge that somehow, somewhere, there was a plan for us and that whatever had happened to me, no matter how difficult life seemed at the moment, I was part of that plan.

When I awoke chill and stiff in the grey light of morning I wasn't quite so sure about things. Sometime in the early hours

I'd thrown back the duvet and the cold of the old attic room had gnawed into my bones. Shivering, I put one foot onto the threadbare carpet and threw on my fleece jacket.

It was gone eight o'clock and I needed a hot cup of tea. I was about to make my way down to the kitchen when I decided to check on Tristan.

Abbey's room was bathed in a dull grey light which seeped under the hems of the closed curtains. It took me a second to realise that Tristan wasn't there. I crossed the room in two strides and felt the sheet; it was cold and damp. I scanned the room, but there was no sign of him. With my heart thumping loudly in my chest I scurried down the stairs and into the sitting room where Abbey was curled in a ball on the sofa, her expression relaxed in sleep. If I hadn't been so worried about Tristan, I might have stayed to study her a little longer, wondering at the innocence hidden beneath the normally darkly-painted face.

I gave the girl a little shake. 'Abbey, wake up! Tristan's gone.'

She sat up staring at me blearily and rubbing her eyes. 'What do you mean he's gone? Where is he?'

'I don't know. His bed's empty. He isn't in the bathroom either.'

'He's not crept in with Dad or something, has he?' she suggested as she tumbled from the quilt. 'Maybe the kid is used to sleeping with his mother.'

I had contemplated knocking on Calum's door, but had been reluctant to wake him. I knew how tired the radiotherapy was making him and had hoped he might lie-in. 'Would you check for me? I didn't want to disturb him until I'd looked down here.'

Abbey nodded and headed for the stairs, while I hurried into the kitchen.

Everything was as we had left it the night before. The

clean, now clutter-free surfaces starkly bare in the thin light from the kitchen window. And there, lying like a shadow, curled beneath the kitchen table in a nest he'd made from his own blanket was Tristan, fast asleep with a corner of his comforter rag lying moistly against his cheek.

Abbey returned to the kitchen still clad in her pyjamas smiling with relief as I put my finger to my lips and pointed to the slumbering form.

'What's he doing down there?'

'I think that's where he slept at Ingrid's,' I whispered. 'There was bedding under the kitchen table in her flat.'

'God, what sort of mother was she?'

'I know it seems bad, but I think she was trying to protect him. There was only one bedroom in the flat and if Ingrid had clients in there . . .'

We fell silent, staring at one another in grim understanding.

'Dad's sleeping like the dead too,' she said suddenly. 'I even shook him but he won't wake up.'

I felt my eyes widen apprehensively. A vision of the death card floating down from Abbey's hand imprinted itself on my brain with sudden, horrible clarity. Hurrying from the kitchen I ran up the stairs, my heart pounding. I'd known Calum was pretty sick, but could one die in one's sleep from something like prostate cancer?

I paused at his bedroom door, trying to calm myself and then knocked half-heartedly. No reply.

I rapped louder then walked into the dark room. All I could see was his still form outlined under the duvet. Creeping closer, I kneeled on the edge of the bed to get close enough to shake him. Still he didn't move.

Damn.

Scrambling off the bed I threw back the heavy curtains.

Grey light streamed into the room washing across his pale features and I stood at his feet wondering what on earth I should do. After a moment's hesitation I felt for a pulse in his neck and to my immense relief, felt the steady but faint throb of his heartbeat. Glancing at the bedside table my eyes came to rest on a bottle of pills. I had no idea how many he'd taken.

I tried once more to wake him, but there was no response. I had the vague idea he should be put in a recovery position but he was already on his side, so I left him where he was and hurried down the stairs to the phone in the hall.

'What is it? What's the matter?' Abbey was standing at my elbow while I dialled the emergency services and asked shakily for an ambulance.

As soon as the operator assured me help was on the way, I turned to face her. 'Your father isn't well, Abbey. He's taken some painkillers or something and maybe he took too many by mistake – I don't know. There's an ambulance on its way . . .'

She gave a strangled screech and bolted up the stairs behind me. I could hear her calling her father and I found her kneeling on the bed, pulling frantically at him.

'Dad, Dad, wake up!'

I was about to put a restraining hand on her arm when I realised it was not a bad thing to be trying to rouse him and for the next ten minutes we tried unsuccessfully to drag Calum back into a state of consciousness.

By the time the ambulance arrived, Abbey was hysterical and while the paramedics were strapping Calum onto a stretcher, I pocketed what was left of the bottle of pills and thrust Abbey's mobile phone into her hand.

'Abbey! I need you to calm down. Ring Kevin and ask him to come over and sit with you. I need you to look after Tristan for me.'

She continued to sob and I put an arm round her heaving shoulders. 'I'll go with your father and make sure he's alright, do you hear me? Can you look after Tristan?'

She nodded, looking at me with red-rimmed eyes, 'I can't lose him, Kaela. I've been so horrible . . . he thinks I hate him.'

'He knows you don't hate him, Abbs. And when he wakes up you can tell him so.' I gave her a little shake. 'Do you hear me?'

Abbey nodded and I gave her a half smile, imploring her to be strong. The paramedics were wheeling the pallid and horribly still form of her father out onto the landing, heading for the stairs. 'Everything will be alright. I'll call you from the hospital, OK?'

Hurrying down the stairs behind them, I grabbed some loose change from the phone table in the hall before following the stretchered form of my one-time lover out through the front door and, with a million emotions jostling in my head, down the drive as the paramedics loaded him into the waiting ambulance.

It was two hours before Calum regained consciousness and I was allowed in to see him. He was lying back against a mound of pillows with a hospital blanket folded neatly over him; the curtains pulled round us giving the illusion of some privacy. A saline drip pumped fluid into a vein on his left arm, but apart from that and the sickly yellow hue of his complexion, he looked to be firmly back in the land of the living.

'What happened?' I asked, taking a chair next to him. I neither kissed him nor touched his hand. I realised as I looked at him, that I was furiously angry.

'I'm sorry, Kaela.' He wouldn't meet my eyes.

'Sorry you did it, or sorry it didn't work?'

He pursed pale lips. 'I want you to know I didn't plan it. I took the pills to help me sleep and for the pain . . .'

'The doctors told me you'd taken enough to kill you several times over. If Abbey hadn't found you when she did, you would have died.'

He groaned. 'Abbey? Was it her who found me? I never thought . . .'

'We were looking for Tristan,' I continued, too angry to let him try to explain. 'The poor child had made a bed for himself under your kitchen table. Abbey thought he might have gone into your room and when she went to look, she couldn't wake you . . .' I broke off as my voice caught in my throat. 'How *could* you, Calum? How could you do that to your daughter, after all she's lost already?'

'I told you I didn't plan it. I wasn't thinking straight. I was so very tired and in pain, and I thought you'd only go back to that bloody instructor, and then I wouldn't be able to have the operation and I'd die anyway and I thought, what the hell? Why die slowly and in agony?' He took a deep raggedy breath and continued in a rush, as if by getting it out quickly, he wouldn't have to think about it for too long. 'The hormone treatment is already giving me . . . trouble. And the consultant told me possible side-effects of the surgery could be impotence and incontinence. Why would you stay with me then? What would I have left to offer anyone?'

'You have to think positively; neither of those things might happen and if that had been the worst case scenario, we would have coped. But no matter what, you would have had your daughter, who desperately needs you,' I told him coldly. 'You nearly died, leaving Abbey to think you thought she hated you.'

He shook his head in defeat. 'I thought she did hate me.

I've not been much of a father to her. I know she blames me for her mother dying and she looks at me with such contempt! She wouldn't have cared if I'd gone.'

I wanted to tell him he was completely mistaken, that he had never taken into account his daughter's unassuaged grief at her mother dying or the guilt she felt when I'd disappeared – that she desperately craved his love and affection. But at that moment the curtains were pulled apart and a bearded doctor of about my own age, appeared through the opening.

He held out a manicured hand. 'Good morning, Calum, I'm Dr Omar Nadal. I hear you've had a bit of a difficult night?'

'You could say that,' Calum responded apprehensively.

'I'd like to have a bit of a chat with you about everything.' The doctor glanced at me. 'And you would be . . . ?'

'Michaela Anderson,' I held out my hand and he shook it limply, 'Mr Sinclair's partner.'

'Right. Right, I see. I need a chat with, er, Mr Sinclair here and wondered if we could have a few minutes in private?'

'Fine, I'll wait outside.' I found I was irritated by the doctor's uninvited use of Calum's first name. It wasn't a psychologist Calum needed, I thought as I walked swiftly through the busy casualty department, it was a jolly good shake-up and a few home truths.

Finding an unoccupied row of blue plastic chairs lining a wall, I sank onto the nearest one and put my head in my hands, feeling suddenly exhausted.

Oh, God, I thought desperately. *If Mum's right and there is a God out there, then help me, please.* Closing my eyes tightly, I brought my hands down from my face and knotted them together in my lap in silent prayer. *I don't know what I've done to deserve all this, but if you exist, then please give me the strength to stay with this family who only last week were my whole world; to be there for Abbey and Tristan and even Calum – though the selfish bastard doesn't deserve it – and help Abbey with Grace's gift, even though I'm probably not supposed to believe in ghosts; and not to think of Matt, when I love him and want him with an intensity that is probably sinful in the extreme. And if you don't mind*, I added, thinking that if I was putting in requests to the Almighty I may as well go the whole hog, *I'd like my mother to get better because I need her. Amen.*

Chapter Forty

I stayed with my eyes closed in prayer for several minutes wondering if, when I opened them I might just find I had travelled back six years to a time when everything was normal and uncomplicated. But the long, empty corridor looked much the same as it had minutes ago and I realised that nothing could ever be the same anyway, not after I'd had a glimpse of my future.

My mind went to Abbey's tarot readings and I gave a little shiver. Wasn't the same true for the cards? Wasn't it better to leave the future to stretch safely into the unknown ahead of us?

'Kaela!'

Shaken from my reverie I looked up to find Abbey walking towards me, all tight black clothes, skinny legs and attitude. 'Where's Dad, Kaela? Where have they taken him?'

I'd rung home from a hospital pay phone to tell Abbey that her father was out of danger and she'd cried so much that I'd been unable to tell her any more. Now, here she was coming towards me with such a grim look that it could only mean trouble.

'He's still in the casualty department, but the doctor told me they will probably keep him in for the rest of the day and maybe tonight, pending a report by the psychiatrist on duty.'

'He did it on purpose then, actually tried to kill himself?'

'He says not. It wasn't planned apparently.'

She plumped down on the chair next to me. 'How could he do that, Kaela?' she asked, dismissing my small defence of her father with a sneer. 'Maybe he didn't plan it, but he did it all the same, didn't he? Do we all mean so little to him?'

'I think he was confused and overwhelmed,' I replied carefully, wishing I didn't want to agree with her so readily. 'He's been ill for some time and didn't want to worry you over it.'

She tilted her face to mine and I could see anxiety lurking beneath the fury. 'What's wrong with him? Is this illness why he couldn't work properly?'

'Yes. He has prostate cancer, Abbey. He needed an operation but he wouldn't have it because he was concerned that you wouldn't cope. I think he was afraid of dying and leaving you on your own.'

'But that's exactly what he just tried to do! It doesn't make sense.'

I pressed my fingertips to my forehead as I thought this over. Was it my fault he'd tried to do this? If I hadn't come back he wouldn't have done it, I was sure of that. He was relying on me to look after his child if anything went wrong. Just like Ingrid. *Just like Grace.*

'If he thought things through at all, I think he was hoping I'd hold things together,' I said carefully. I tried to look at Calum's actions from someone else's point of view and found myself wondering how Abbey's mother would have handled this. 'But I don't think he was really thinking rationally.' I found I was speaking my thoughts aloud; 'I think he never got over your mother dying. He should have got help for both of you back then, instead of struggling along alone and then taking up with me on the rebound.'

256

Abbey was silent for a moment or two, digesting what I'd told her.

'Is he going to die anyway, because of . . .' she struggled to say the words, 'the cancer?' she asked quietly.

'I don't think so. From what he's told me, the operation should cure him. I think he's just frightened.'

'It's weird,' she observed, 'talking about Dad as if he's a child or something. I always thought Dad was strong.'

'We're supposed to think of our parents as strong,' I smiled sadly, thinking of my own father and how he'd always been there for me and Mum, a tower of strength and responsibility. 'Then one day we grow up and realise they are people, just like us and that they can make mistakes and even die.' I thought of my mother languishing in a home for the mentally confused. I wished I could talk to her now and let her stroke my troubles away as she had when I was a child. 'Your father has problems but hopefully he'll get some help now.'

'Kaela?'

'Yes?'

'I'm glad you came back.'

I looked at the girl sitting beside me and put aside my doubts. I sighed, 'So am I, Abbey, so am I.'

The psychiatrist on duty recommended that Calum be kept in the hospital overnight and a bed was found for him on the psychiatric ward. Abbey refused to visit him despite my murmurings that it might be a good thing.

'He decided not to see me again the moment he took those pills,' she said stubbornly as we walked towards the hospital entrance. 'If we hadn't gone looking for the kid he would have died and that would have been that.'

'People make mistakes,' I reminded her. 'Everyone is entitled to a second chance, Abbey.'

She didn't appear to be listening and when I glanced at her, I saw she was waving towards a coffee shop just off the entrance hall. Kevin was sitting at a table with Tristan next to him.

She stopped suddenly and I nearly bumped into her as she turned and fixed me with her steady gaze. 'Are you going to use what Dad did as an excuse to have your second chance, Kaela? Are you going to leave us?'

I was stung by her insight. I'd told Abbey all of ten minutes ago that I was glad I'd come back, but was it for her sake rather than Calum's? I found I wasn't sure.

'I'm angry with your father at the moment,' I hedged. 'When I see him again tomorrow we'll make a decision. Both of us have to want to be together for this to work.'

'But it doesn't involve just you and Dad,' she pointed out. 'Why don't adults ever take their kids' views into account?'

'Because children grow up and leave and make their own lives and if those adults stay together for the sake of the children, what's left when the children go? Life is too precious to waste, Abbey.'

'You should try telling that to Dad,' she muttered, turning away from me. Kevin rose to greet us and I watched as Abbey gave him a grin and stopped to ruffle Tristan's hair. She was more relaxed around Kevin than she was with anyone else, I realised.

'We are in your debt yet again,' I said as Kevin pulled out a chair for me. I studied him as I sat down. If I went on the premise that I hadn't aged in the six years that he had grown from a gangly teenager of nineteen to a chunky young man of twenty five, theoretically we were now the same age. So why did I feel Kevin was a bit of an enigma? I felt older, wiser than him socially but he was more knowledgeable and more worldly-wise than me.

'Would you like a cup of tea?' Kevin asked as he pushed a banana milkshake towards Abbey and mopped up a spill from Tristan's fizzy drink. I noticed he was drinking a milkshake himself and smiled. Maybe Kevin was simply Kevin and I was trying to over analyse him, I thought.

'I'd love one, thank you.'

Kevin returned a moment later with tea in a polystyrene cup, which he placed in front of me.

'Will Calum pull through?'

I nodded. 'He's being kept in overnight for observation and psychiatric evaluation, but he'll live.'

'And this sprog here . . .' he glanced down at Tristan then uncertainly towards Abbey as if afraid his questions might upset her. 'Did he say whether the boy has anything to do with him?'

'He says Tristan isn't his.'

'And yet after that denial, he tried to top himself,' Kevin observed. 'Do you believe him?'

'I'm beginning to wonder whether it's any of my business,' I replied tiredly. People were pushing past our chairs, jostling for a place in line at the counter. It was like having a personal conversation in the middle of the morning rush hour.

'Dad thinks he's Matt's,' Abbey commented as she took a slurp of her milkshake.

Kevin caught my eye while both the youngsters weren't looking and I felt myself blush. 'Ingrid could have been making the whole thing up,' he offered. 'In her line of work the boy could have come from anywhere.'

'I was going to visit Matt today.' I took a sip of the tea so I wouldn't have to see Abbey's expression. 'Calum thinks I should see if Matt knows anything about the boy . . . at least that's what he intimated last night.'

'How will you get there?'

'I thought I'd take Calum's car. I used to drive it and he certainly won't be needing it today.'

'I'll give you a lift home if you like.'

'Thanks. Will you wait there with Abbey and Tristan until I get back?'

'Of course, if that's what you want, doll. Your wish is my command.'

I sneaked a questioning look at him to see if he was joking. He was doing rather a lot for us and I wasn't entirely sure why but he had already turned to Abbey who was apparently keeping her counsel about my proposed visit to Matt.

'You can show me that thing with the cards, toots. You did promise me another tarot reading after all.'

I gave an involuntary shudder at Kevin's words, recalling the death card as it had fluttered down in front of us.

'And you can tell me more about your numerical sequencing, *Space Dog*,' Abbey was picking up the challenge again.

I put a restraining hand on her forearm. 'Abbey, are you sure it's a good idea to continue with those things?'

'Don't tell me you're still sceptical about the cards?' she quipped.

'Quite the opposite,' I told her as my thumb nail carved a deep gouge out of the rim of my polystyrene cup. 'I found the cards scarily accurate. And that's why I'm worried about that last one – you know the death card. It gives me the creeps.'

She wrinkled her brow, obviously surprised at my worries over her predictions, but her young skin smoothed out and she smiled. 'Oh, that. You don't need to worry, Kaela. The card only very rarely signifies death; it much more commonly means transformation, not death as we know it but a major change in life.'

Good grief, I thought wearily, unsure whether this news was better or worse. Hadn't I had to cope with enough changes already? What other major upheavals could there possibly be?

Chapter Forty-One

An hour later I was motoring merrily along in Calum's old Volvo. I watched the damp scenery whiz past, clusters of trees decked out in their autumnal regalia on either side of me dripping from the day's drizzle, but still acting as a balm to my ragged nerves. It was a relief I realised, to have left my worries behind and with Calum safely tucked up in hospital, and Kevin watching Abbey and Tristan, I buttoned all my worries and fears firmly into the back of my mind and concentrated on pretending I had not a care in the world.

When I eventually left the main road and headed off down a country lane, the first doubts began to creep into my head. Suppose Matt wasn't there? What if he was there, but didn't want to see me? Worse still, what if he *did* want to see me and got the wrong idea about why I'd come? Perhaps I should have rung ahead, I decided. But what would I have said? I could hardly have asked if he was the father of Ingrid's child over the phone, could I?

My nerves began to jangle and all at once my relaxed mood evaporated and I began to feel sick. Perhaps this hadn't been such a good idea after all, I decided as I rolled down the window and gulped several mouthfuls of fresh air.

I missed the turning into Matt's road and had to turn the car in someone's drive and head back the way I'd come.

When Matt and Kevin had taken me back to see Calum on Tuesday and returned with me later from the police station I believed I'd memorised the way, but my thoughts had obviously been taken up with more absorbing questions.

I knew I must be within a stone's throw of Matt's house, so drawing into a grassy lay-by, I turned off the ignition and decided to walk up the quiet residential road.

It was pleasant out in the damp windy air and I was just beginning to enjoy the short walk when I recognised the familiar open gateway. I hesitated, no longer sure if I shouldn't just turn round and head home. But I'd come this far, I told myself; did I want to see him or not?

Setting my shoulders and taking a deep breath I set off up the path, rounded the bend and stopped dead in my tracks. Matt was standing in his driveway, next to a silver convertible that stood with its black roof up. But it wasn't the car that drew my attention, it was the occupant, who was tall and slim with black, shoulder-length hair and long brown legs. She stepped out from the car – which must have come in from the opposite direction to the one I'd walked from – and threw her arms round Matt's neck.

I watched as if from afar as Matt kissed her on her smooth mocha-coloured cheek. I wanted to turn and run, but my feet seemed glued to the ground. And then, with his arms wound tightly round the woman and with his face pressed to hers, he glanced up. Our gaze met and I saw his grey eyes widen in surprise, but then I was running, running away from someone on whom I had no claims whatsoever and who I knew I never could have.

What the hell had I been thinking? I asked myself as I ran along the edge of the grass verge. I had made it perfectly clear to Matt that I was staying with Calum. What did I expect?

I blinked back tears. Matt was entitled to see whoever he pleased.

Still, it hurt that it hadn't taken him much time to seek solace elsewhere. So much for love at first sight, and his waiting six years for someone who meant something special to him, as he had put it. Maybe Ingrid had been right, I thought, when she'd summed up the whole of the male species. When I thought of how difficult the decision to go back to Calum had been for me, it was galling to know that Matt had simply leafed through his address book to find an instant replacement.

The Volvo was in sight when I heard his footsteps pounding behind me, and feeling foolish to be running away, I stopped and turned to face him. He drew to a halt a couple of paces from me. I stared at him; this man with plain brown hair and a slightly prominent nose, who made my blood sing in my veins when I looked at him. I wanted to slap him and hug him at the same time, so I thrust my hands into the pockets of my jeans and tried to stare him down. And in that moment it dawned on me with a terrible certainty that I was completely and utterly in love with him.

Damn.

'Michaela . . . I didn't expect to see you. I thought, I mean Kevin rang this morning and said Calum was in hospital. Why aren't you there?'

'I think it's blatantly obvious you weren't expecting to see me,' I retorted. 'And I'm not there with him because I'm incredibly angry he's in there at all. But don't let me keep you.' I balled my hands into fists in my pockets. 'I can see you have pressing matters to attend to.'

He looked blankly at me then laughed suddenly as the penny dropped and he realised to what I was alluding.

'Are you jealous, Michaela?'

'Certainly not. What you do and who you see is no concern of mine.'

'Why are you running away then?'

'I'm not . . . well not now anyway.'

The laughter was still in his eyes, but now he was studying me as if deep in thought. He dropped his voice to a husky whisper, 'What *are* you doing here?'

'I . . . I . . .' I stammered. I found I couldn't finish the sentence. I didn't want to ask if he'd fathered a child with my one-time best friend. I thought of the dark beauty waiting for him in his driveway and it didn't seem to be my business any more.

'I made a mistake coming here. It wasn't fair.' I turned to go but he reached out and grabbed my hand.

'Michaela . . .'

He was looking at me in such a way that my heart started leaping in my chest. I was still panting slightly from the run and he seemed to be having trouble breathing too. My hand felt as if it had been super-glued to his and I was suddenly no longer standing at the edge of a quiet road with a sky above my head and grass at my feet, I was immersed in a bubble that held only two people and that bubble might as well have been the whole universe.

Infinitely slowly, he drew me towards him. My feet seemed to move forwards of their own accord until we were so close that I could feel his breath upon my face, the heat radiating from his body. His eyes were fixed on mine and I found I simply couldn't look away. He lowered his chin at the same moment I tilted my face to his and when our lips met, I closed my eyes and leaned into him, pressing myself against him. He wound his arms round me and held me close. We were still standing there, folded together when someone tapped him sharply on the shoulder.

'Sorry to interrupt, Matthew,' said a female voice, full of sarcasm, 'but I don't think I've been introduced to your friend.'

We both turned at the sound of her voice and I found myself looking into a pair of intelligent eyes, which were staring back at me appraisingly, as if weighing me up.

I felt myself blushing, embarrassed to have to meet one of Matt's girlfriends and somewhat appalled by my own lack of self control. I could picture this gorgeous creature looking completely at home dressed in the T-shirt I'd borrowed from Matt on my first night and knew with sudden certainty that it belonged to her.

Pulling myself from Matt's embrace, I muttered an apology and something about leaving, but Matt was having none of it. He tightened his grip around my wrist and turned to face the woman.

'Simone, this is Michaela.'

She tilted her head to one side as she continued to scrutinise me. 'I saw your picture in the papers six years ago, of course. You really haven't aged at all have you?'

'I told you,' Matt replied, beaming as if showing off a prize specimen. 'She's exactly the same as the last time I saw her, before she jumped from that aeroplane.' He turned to me, 'Michaela, meet Simone. My older sister.'

'Not so much of the older, thank you,' Simone said, punching his arm playfully. 'A couple of months is nothing in the grand scale of things.'

I found myself struck dumb. How could this sultry beauty of obvious African descent be Matt's sister?

'Close your mouth, it doesn't become you,' Simone commented with a smile. 'And before you ask, no, neither of us was adopted. Also, interesting as it is to be having this nice chat in the middle of the road, I think we should adjourn to

266

Matt's house. I've been in the car for the last four hours and need the loo and a cup of tea, in that order.'

She walked away up the road and I found that my feet and legs did indeed still work, despite all feeling to the contrary, as Matt pulled me along in her wake.

'I didn't know you had a sister,' I commented lamely, trying to make up for my lack of diplomacy.

'I suppose you thought those night-things and toiletries belonged to a stream of live-in girlfriends,' he said with a laugh. 'I know you're bursting to know more but I'll let Simone explain, she's so much more articulate than I am.'

Matt put the kettle on while I slid onto one of the kitchen stools and leaned weakly on the central counter, wondering as I did what good could possibly come of my being here. Seeing Matt, being with him again was simply prolonging the agony. However much I might try to convince myself that it was Calum who had broken the bargain of our staying together, I knew that in his present state, he would probably need me now more than ever.

Simone came into the kitchen rubbing hand cream into her slender hands. She motioned to the stool next to mine and I pulled it out so she could slide in.

'Thanks.'

She was looking at me again in that piercing, almost X-ray type vision of hers that studied first my face and hair, and then swept down my body to the tips of my toes.

'I can see why he's been besotted with you for the past six years,' she commented. She accepted the mug of tea her brother handed her and smiled. 'It must be like a fairytale ending for him that you have surfaced again, from nowhere, and landed in his lap, so to speak.'

'The problem is it's not quite the ending I'd envisaged,'

Matt said as he took the stool on the other side of his sister. 'She's being all heroic and insisting on staying with her ex boyfriend and his daughter.'

Simone looked appalled. 'Why on earth would you want to do that?' she asked me.

'To me it hasn't been six years,' I tried to explain. 'I left Calum on Monday to do the parachute jump and now it's only Friday. He's ill, he's got prostate cancer. If I don't stay with him he won't have the operation he needs because he doesn't want to put his daughter Abbey through it.' I paused and took a sip of the tea, deciding not to tell her about what Calum had tried to do the night before. Not wanting to look at either Matt or Simone directly while I dropped the next bomb shell, I stared fixedly at a bowl of apples in front of me. 'And now there is an added complication.'

I waited, thinking one of them might say something, but they remained silent, so I ploughed ahead. 'Ingrid – that's my best friend, or at least I thought she was – has done a runner and left me with her little boy, Tristan.'

Tristan *Matthew* Peters, I thought as the child's full name came back to me in a blinding flash. How could I not have noticed before? It seemed she'd even named the boy after his father. How stupid did that make me?

Chapter Forty-Two

I took another sip of the tea and swallowed, trying not to choke.

'Abbey and Kevin are minding Tristan for me now, but I'll have to go back and take care of him.'

'Ingrid always was a user,' Matt commented drily.

'How long has she left him with you?' Simone helped herself to a biscuit from the packet Matt had placed in front of us.

'I'm not sure exactly,' I hesitated, glancing at Matt, 'but I think it's going to be pretty permanent. She's left me his birth certificate and inoculation records.'

Simone slapped her mug onto the counter with a bang and looked incredulous. 'Have you contacted social services?'

'I don't want to put him into care. Somehow I feel he's my responsibility.' I fumbled in the pocket of my fleece and drew out the letters Ingrid had left for me. Simone read them through and handed them on to Matt.

'How did you interpret that cryptic bit about you being the next best thing to the boy's mother?' Simone asked.

'I thought at first she meant that Calum was Tristan's natural father,' I admitted. 'Abbey had already told me Ingrid used to visit him after I disappeared and I put two and two together, but he denied it.'

'He would, wouldn't he?' she said shortly.

'I believe him. Calum said she made quite a play for him when I went missing but he rejected her. After that she cut him out of her life completely. He also pointed out that when Ingrid wrote that letter she didn't know if I was back with Calum or whether I was staying here with Matt.'

'You think it's me,' Matt said suddenly as the light rather belatedly dawned. 'You came here today to confront me with this, didn't you?'

I felt myself blush. 'I didn't know what to believe. I still don't. Kevin thinks Tristan could be anybody's, with the lifestyle Ingrid has been leading, but I know her – well, knew her. She only ever wanted stability and someone to take care of her. I'm sure she didn't become a prostitute until after she'd had Tristan. I think she only did it to give him a more comfortable upbringing than he would have had on benefits alone.'

Matt slipped from his stool, brushed past his sister and came to rest his hands on my shoulders. 'I'm not saying I wasn't tempted. Ingrid was pretty and sexy and she did her best to snare me, but I was grieving for you, Michaela. I know you'll say I barely knew you, but I've already explained my feelings.'

I thought of the photograph in his bedside drawer as he went on.

'We met up occasionally and talked about you – I thought she was missing you as much as I was. It was comforting to speak about you with one of your friends. She used to tell me about the things you'd said and done and it made me feel as if I'd really known you, like she had. But in the end I realised that wasn't what she wanted and told her it wasn't a good idea to meet up anymore,' he paused, remembering. 'She was pretty damned angry. She called me a miserable bastard and told me to go to hell . . .'

So that's what Ingrid meant when she'd said all men were bastards, I thought. She had been rebuffed by both Calum and Matt. Maybe she had had a short fling with a complete stranger – or even a one night stand. And that made Tristan someone else's problem, not mine.

'Look, I'm getting a numb backside sitting on this stool. Why don't we go into the sitting room and talk about this in more comfort,' Simone said, rising from the stool next to mine and picking up her mug as she departed.

Matt was still gripping my shoulders, but he seemed to come to his senses at his sister's words, and let go of me reluctantly so that I could follow Simone into the light and airy sitting room.

Simone had ensconced herself in a wide cream armchair, with her feet raised on a matching footstool. She looked relaxed and at home here and I wondered where her home actually was.

'Four hours is a long journey,' I commented, taking a seat on the sofa. 'Do you visit Matt often?'

'I work in Norfolk, though home for us proper, is Kent. I come back all the time as our parents live about twenty minutes away, just outside Dover.'

I nodded in understanding, though I was still puzzled by her use of the term 'our parents'. How, I wondered, could the two of them be natural siblings?

'We're both descended from the Vikings,' Matt said with a laugh, as if reading my thoughts. He took the seat next to me. 'With a bit of this and that thrown in along the way.'

I didn't know what to say, but Simone took up the story.

She was obviously used to having to explain their very different appearances.

'Matthew and I have the same father,' she said as she sipped at her tea. 'Dad's family originated in the far north several centuries ago and made their way south through France, settling in what was to become Normandy. His ancestors then came across with William the Conqueror in 1066 and settled here in Kent. We think the family surname came from the place in Normandy that they were from – there is a town there called Treguier.'

I didn't like to mention that she didn't look much like a Viking to me with her café-latte skin and jet black hair, but noticed as I gazed at her that she had smoky grey eyes, very similar to Matt's.

'Our father's job took him to the other side of the channel; he deals in diamonds and spent much of his early career in the Netherlands and Luxembourg. He also,' she said with a smile, 'spent the majority of the seventies travelling to and from South Africa where he made frequent visits to the company's diamond mines.'

'Ah,' I said, sensing the connection and waiting for her to go on. It was a relief to have something to think about for a while, other than my own problems. I sank deeper into the sofa and began to relax, intrigued by her story.

'Dad fell in love with a local African girl. I gather she was very beautiful, and reportedly she was a wonderful singer too. I was born in 1977, just before he was due to return permanently to the UK. Days before Dad left there was some sort of conflict between warring rebel tribes. Although South Africa now only produces about fifteen percent of the world's diamonds, in those days there was a much bigger interest. My mother . . .' Simone paused and took a steadying breath, '. . . was killed in the conflict. Dad was devastated and after

272

several months of battling the immigration services, brought me home to England.'

'Meanwhile,' Matt took up the story, 'my mother, Dad's English wife Doreen was expecting me. Despite Dad's infatuation with Simone's mother, he and my mum had a happy marriage. Dad discovered Doreen was pregnant only a few months after Simone's mother had told him she was expecting his baby. Mum knew nothing about his affair of course and wasn't happy when he insisted he had to make one last visit to South Africa at about the time she was due to give birth. She had just brought me home from hospital and was awaiting Dad's return, when he turned up with Simone.'

'Good grief,' I exclaimed, turning to Matt, 'what on earth did your mother do?'

'After the initial shock, she eventually forgave him and took me in,' Simone replied. 'Mum brought both of us up together, as if I was her own child. There are only a few months between Matthew and me in age so it must have been like bringing up twins. Doreen is one special lady.'

'Are your parents still together?'

'Happily married and planning a world cruise when Dad retires properly in a couple of years,' Matt told me. He paused and gave me a strange look. 'Whoever little Tristan belongs to, he deserves a fair chance at life. Children shouldn't be held accountable for the manner or circumstances of their arrival into the world.' I wondered for a moment if Matt was admitting to being Tristan's father after all, but he went on, 'I don't know who the boy's natural father might be, but Ingrid obviously wanted you to raise him for her.'

'But having to care for Tristan gives me another reason to stay with Calum,' I pointed out, slightly panicked. 'The child would have to be brought up in a settled home environment. I think he's already had a pretty raw deal; he's covered in suspicious looking bruises and it seems he'd rather sleep under the kitchen table than in a proper bed.'

And much as I liked Tristan, I found myself thinking again of the tie he would represent. I was still young. Deep down I knew I wanted to have a few more adventures, see the world and continue with my career. Perhaps not quite as big as *this* adventure I told myself with an inward smile, but adventures nonetheless. Hadn't I already put my life on hold once to care for Abbey? I thought of Doreen and what she had done for Simone and felt guilty that I was even a tiny bit tempted by these strange circumstances I found myself in to abandon my responsibilities. But by some fantastic stroke of fate I'd been given another chance. Could I give up my dreams of a career and the excitement of travel a second time? Did I really want to?

'Good Lord,' Simone commented, 'poor little chap.' She turned to stare at me and once again I found her direct gaze unnerving. It felt almost as if she'd known what I'd been thinking and I felt myself blush under her scrutiny. 'I thought going to a predominantly white girls' school and having to prove myself time and time again was hard enough,' she went on. 'Despite my parents' acceptance, I found I couldn't change the majority's perceptions of someone who was slightly different from them. I was verbally bullied at school, not just by the other pupils but by some of the teachers too. People fear anyone who isn't the same as them, and the more my parents protested, the more I was looked upon with suspicion. At least,' she said with a sigh, 'I was never beaten or physically abused like your Tristan might have been.'

'Tristan will undoubtedly need lots of love and care,' I said, nodding. 'But so does Abbey and so, come to that, will Calum when he leaves hospital.'

'You do seem to have tumbled back into some pretty

problematic circumstances,' Simone observed matter-of-factly.

I almost laughed at the understatement.

She didn't know the half of it.

'Has Matt told you what happened to me?' I asked Simone.

'Michaela, my brother has been obsessed with your strange disappearance and talked of little else for the past six and a half years,' she told me dryly. 'Believe me when I tell you, phone lines have been zinging since your return. That's mainly the reason I'm here.' She grinned at her brother. 'Apart from wanting to see my kid brother of course.'

'She makes me sound unhinged,' Matt said with a wry smile. 'But Kevin and I never believed you'd been kidnapped. He had his wacky theories about an alien abduction, and although I didn't believe that, we were drawn together by our joint belief that something weird and unexplained had happened to you. The only other person who didn't think I'd murdered you was Simone – and my parents of course.'

'I wondered why the two of you were such good friends,' I confessed. 'You and Kevin are such different characters.'

'He saved my life,' Matt said quietly. 'The press were hounding me day after day. Every time I left my house they were there with their microphones and their intrusive questions. When I did eventually give them an interview, they cut it and invented things to make it look as if I was some kind of monster. Then Kevin gave them the alien abduction theory to sink their teeth into and that took the heat off me. He is a good guy.'

'I gather from DI Smith that you knew him before we did our charity jump?'

Matt nodded, 'He was besotted with Ingrid and didn't

want to look like a fool in front of her. He came for some lessons and a test jump the week before the rest of you arrived.'

'I thought that must have been the case.' I found I was heartily relieved by his easy admission of what DI Smith had seen as evidence of his guilt.

'The police latched onto it, used the fact I already knew him – when Ingrid and your boss Graham swore blind that Kevin had told them he'd never met me before – as grounds to keep me at the police station for endless interrogations. They were convinced that prior to your jump, Kevin and I had planned to do something hideous to you.'

'I'm so sorry.'

'Don't blame yourself Michaela,' Simone said shortly. She sat up and placed her empty mug on the coffee table. 'What happened to you wasn't anyone's fault. My brother and I have been trying to prove it ever since, partly to clear Matthew's name and partly because I find the whole scenario totally fascinating.'

'You do believe me then?' I asked her, leaning forwards to put my empty mug next to hers. 'You believe that I have no idea where the last six and a half years have gone?'

'Absolutely. And Matthew tells me he assured you he would try to find out what really happened to you?'

I nodded, feeling foolish. I hadn't really taken Matt seriously. 'I don't see how either of you could help.'

'Now that,' Simone said, 'is where you are wrong, Michaela. My brother has a hotline to someone very influential in the world of science. Both he and I firmly believe that it is through science that we will find the answer to the conundrum of your missing six and a half years, and subsequent astonishing reappearance.'

I was sitting on the edge of my seat now. 'Who?' I asked.

'Who does he know who could possibly find the answer to where I've been?'

Simone fixed me with her lovely eyes, crossed her long shapely legs with a dramatic flourish and grinned, showing pearly white teeth. 'Me,' she said. 'He knows *me*.'

Chapter Forty-Three

'I'm a quantum scientist,' Simone told me happily as she chopped red cabbage and tossed it into a pre-heated pan. We had moved back to the kitchen when Simone had announced she was hungry. Both she and Matt insisted I join them for a late lunch, and having missed breakfast in my rush to get to the hospital earlier this morning, I was only too happy to accept. Apparently Matt had already been braising some duck in the oven prior to his sister's arrival, and now stood to peel and slice potatoes before putting them to simmer on the hob.

I sat on one of the stools and listened as they worked. I'd offered to help but it seemed my assistance wasn't required. To be honest, I was glad for the rest and the two of them operated together with all the efficient familiarity of siblings who had cooked together on many occasions.

'I made it my business to excel at school and when I began to get A grades in maths and the sciences, the teachers began to look at me differently.' She chopped two apples that Matt had neatly peeled for her. 'Suddenly I was no longer the shy mulatto, the outsider, but a possible star pupil who could represent the school on an international level. I went on to get a degree and masters in the sciences and then a PhD. I now work for a large scientific organisation which is co-funded by the government and various private sponsors.'

'Our parents were – still are – immensely proud of her,' Matt put in as he tested the potatoes with a fork, 'I, on the other hand, mucked about at school and ended up spending my parents' allowance on driving fast cars, learning to freefall from aeroplanes and eventually becoming a pilot.'

Matt rested the fork on the work surface and came to stand behind me, his hands lightly around my waist. I wondered if he needed reassurance that I was happy with him just the way he was and pushing aside all thoughts of Calum, I crossed my arms around my waist, laying my hands on top of his. I wasn't just happy with Matt's accomplishments, I was genuinely proud of him. It was comfortable being linked together like that and I gave a contented sigh, leaning my head back against his chest.

We watched as Simone worked, and I found myself wondering if there was anything she wasn't good at. She was beautiful, self-assured, smart and could obviously cook. Sneaking a glance round at Matt, I wondered if he'd grown up somewhat in her shadow and thought wryly, that if either of them had had to struggle to overcome narrow-minded bigotry and prejudice, it might just have been him.

'The organisation I work for – Subatron Industries – is only one of several government-funded research companies whose sole aim is to try and understand the nature of the universe,' Simone went on. 'You couldn't know of course, because you were still missing in September, but last month scientists made headlines for experimenting with atomic particles in a Super Collider otherwise know as a particle accelerator – and trying to recreate the conditions immediately after the Big Bang. We thought it might possibly create a tiny black hole but the press got hold of the notion and blew it out of proportion until the public were panicked into believing it could be the end of the world.' She gave a derisive laugh as she threw the apple pieces into the pan with the cabbage. 'The amount of energy it created would have been minuscule, smaller than a mosquito and no danger to anyone. But it proved to the people at the top – those funding the research – how quickly public fear of the unknown can cause mass panic,' she sprinkled brown sugar and cinnamon into the mix, 'and how right they were to keep their previous experiments totally secret.

'For years there has been an ongoing experiment into the existence of something called Gravitons,' she explained blithely, ignoring my expression of incredulity. 'In Louisiana, America, there is a gravitational wave observatory, which exists solely to record the existence of gravitational waves that travel through space. It is hugely costly, but in lay terms,' she glanced at me to make sure I was keeping up, 'the organisation and their scientists are trying to understand how gravity worked at the beginning of time and how the conditions that brought about the Big Bang arose.'

'Er, so what are these things called Gravitons?' I asked, trying to keep the scepticism out of my voice. 'If scientists are trying to prove their existence surely that means they have no proof as yet that they even exist? And what does this have to do with my disappearance?'

Simone beamed at me. 'Let me tell you about this recent experiment and then you will understand everything.' She went to the sink, washed her hands and returned to sit on the stool next to mine. 'When protons of matter and anti matter are smashed into each other at great speed, the force of the gravity is transmitted by a particle called a Graviton. The only way we know that a Graviton exists is because when all the pre-measured parts involved in the collision are meas-ured in the lab after the collision, there is a part missing – unaccounted for – and that missing energy is the Graviton.'

'The total parts before and after the collision should be the same,' Matt interjected. 'But every time this Graviton escapes; simply vanishes into an extra dimension which is beyond our comprehension.'

'Exactly,' Simone continued. 'We know our world as three dimensional; we know up and down, north, south, east and west, but it is the unseen dimensions that scientists are trying to discover in these experiments.'

'So Gravitons spend their time in these extra dimensions,' Matt spoke again. 'And both Subatron Industries and the lab in Louisiana are trying to prove the existence of naturally occurring Gravitons in space.'

'Let me show you what causes these gravitational waves,' Simone interrupted her brother and took several apples from the fruit bowl. She spread a loosely meshed dish cloth out on the work surface and dotted the fruit about on top of it. 'The apples represent neutron stars. These neutron stars orbit each other churning up space and time.' She dragged one of the apples in a circle round another one, making the dish-cloth ripple. 'Think of space as a giant mesh which is affected by everything moving within it, like this dishcloth moves when I rotate these fruits. Now, when violent cosmic events occur, like the smashing together of atoms, it makes gravitational waves appear . . .' she moved the cloth with her finger so that it bunched up and spread out again, taking the other apples with it, 'space and time stretches and contracts just like this when disturbed. You saw the other apples move within the cloth when I disturbed it?'

I nodded.

'So you see that space and time can actually be distorted, taking with it all the planets in that particular location.'

Matt must have guessed I was struggling to understand what his sister was trying to explain. 'Don't worry, the quantum theory even had Einstein stumped,' he said kindly. 'We have to think a bit outside the box on this and the whole concept is so huge our scrappy little human brains can only just scrape the surface.'

'Are you saying that you think I was the victim of some kind of scientific experiment?' I asked guardedly.

'Not an experiment exactly.' Simone took the pan with the cabbage off the hob. 'More the discovery of a major galactic event having happened in space. Six and a half years ago – on 15th April 2002 to be precise, the top secret laser gravitational wave observatory in Norfolk – the sister observatory to the one in Louisiana – gave a reading which indicated for the first time in scientific history, the actual presence of Gravitons.'

'The day I did the jump,' I murmured.

'And vanished,' Matt confirmed.

Simone nodded. 'Scientists working on the project believe that on that day some violent occurrence – perhaps a neutron star exploding, triggered a shift in space and time. The trouble is there was no visual evidence of anything at all having happened because all the stars within our limited field of observation move in synchronisation with us. In fact, we only know about it because the computers in the gravitational wave observatory registered the fleeting presence of Gravitons. Some of our sponsors insisted it was a malfunction of the equipment; others were convinced that it was the most exciting breakthrough of the scientific age. But apart from that one reading there was no evidence that anything untoward had occurred. Lunchtime, I think,' she said as she tossed a pair of oven gloves at Matt. The conversation seemed to be on hold. 'You deal with the duck while I mash the potatoes. Michaela, could you fetch the plates and cutlery?'

*   *   *

282

We ate in a small dining room just off the sitting room. The duck was delicious, but my appetite was sorely diminished. I was still struggling with the concept of a space/time distortion.

'The problem Subatron Industries is facing,' Simone commented between mouthfuls, 'is that unless they can prove their equipment actually works, they will in all likelihood lose their funding.'

'What about the gravitational wave observatory in Louisiana?' I asked as I pushed the red cabbage around my plate. 'If the readings in Norfolk were accurate, wouldn't they have recorded the same result there?'

'As luck would have it, they were offline that day,' Simone replied, wiping her mouth on a serviette. 'There was a malfunction with their computer and engineers were working on it when the Norfolk observatory got the Graviton reading.'

'So there's no proof that any of this happened?'

'Only that one reading and the insistence of our scientists that as this was exactly what the lab was set up for, we should trust in our equipment.' She frowned and I could see she found the lack of proof galling. 'If the people in charge aren't going to believe the readings when something actually happens, I don't see the point of keeping it up and running. The trouble is, nor do our sponsors.'

'Oh.' I was beginning to see where she was coming from. 'You think that if you can prove I vanished at the precise time of the Graviton reading – and have now miraculously reappeared, it might give credence to the accuracy of the read-out and influence your sponsors to keep backing the project?'

'Exactly,' she fixed me with that sharp look of hers. 'At the moment you might be our only hope of averting the possibility of Subatron's closure.'

'What I don't understand is why this thing would only have happened to me. I mean, out of the whole world, why was I the only one to have been affected by this ripple in space and time?'

'Actually you were the only one to be *un*-affected by it,' she corrected. 'We think it was because you were floating freely and weren't fixed to the Earth at the time of the gravitational wave. Had you been on the ground you would have been swept up in the wave like everyone else. We believe the plane you jumped from was big enough to be caught by the wave, as was the rest of Earth, which means you were the only thing bigger than a bird or insect in the entire known universe that didn't move in time with the ripple. Because you were effectively small and unattached to anything, you simply slipped through the hole in the fabric.'

I felt a sinking feeling creep over me. I understood that governments had spent millions on funding for this project with the very purpose of finding such evidence, but it all sounded like science fiction to me.

'In my opinion you haven't so much lost six and a half years, Michaela. It is the rest of us who have lived through six and a half years in the blink of one of your eyes.'

Chapter Forty-Four

I rested my knife and fork down neatly on the plate as if by keeping my movements small and tidy I could keep normality within my grasp. I was beginning to feel decidedly nervous about Simone's revelations and it obviously showed because Matt reached across the table and gave my hand a squeeze.

'I know it sounds incredible,' he said, 'but Simone's theory is backed up by a lot of well thought-of scientists and proven scientific facts. As we told you, the gravitational wave observatories are jointly government and sponsor funded.'

'I'd like to take you back to Subatron's headquarters with me for a debriefing and physical examination if you are willing,' Simone said softly. 'We already know about the return of several rare birds and swarms of bees after an absence of six years, but you are the only one who can actually describe what happened to you. Will you come with me and talk to our scientists?'

I must have continued to appear alarmed by the prospect as Matt gave me an encouraging smile. 'If you decide to go with Simone I'll come with you, if you like.'

'When would you want me to go?'

'What about right now?' Simone's eyes lit up as she sensed my capitulation.

'I can't go today! It's mid afternoon and I have to get back to Abbey and Tristan this evening.'

Matt frowned at his sister. 'You're scaring her, Simone. There's no rush, if we go sometime this weekend, Michaela will have had a chance to think over everything and make plans to have Abbey and Tristan cared for.'

I smiled gratefully at Matt. As long as he was there to keep his somewhat intense sister in check, then I didn't see the harm in it.

Partly to assure myself of the normality of the rest of the world, I called home after the meal to check on Tristan and see how Kevin and Abbey were coping.

'We're fine,' Abbey told me. 'Tristan started crying soon after you left, but Kevin and I took him out to the shops to buy up half a toy store and he and Kevin have been constructing a Lego jet fighter. I think Kevin has been having the most fun but Tris seems OK.' She paused. 'When are you coming home?'

'I'm not sure. Matt's sister is here and she's been telling me all sorts of fascinating things about my disappearance. I may stay another half hour or so, but then I'll start back.'

'Should I get Tris some tea? Do you think you'll be home before his bedtime? I've taken the bedding off my bed and washed it – it felt a bit damp and I thought I may as well sleep in my own bed tonight if the kid's going to camp out under the table anyway.'

'Well done, Abbey.' I was impressed. 'And yes, I think you'd better give him his tea; it will take me some time to get back. Hopefully I'll be home in time to help you get him ready for bed. I don't expect he'll be best pleased that he's spending another night without his mother.'

Leaving Matt would have been harder this time if it hadn't been for the promise of seeing him again at the weekend.

'I don't know what I'm to do about Calum,' I told Matt as we paused at his gate. 'I can't abandon him while he's so ill and I dare not tell him the truth about my feelings for you. Then there's Abbey and Tristan . . . Not to mention my dreams about Grace's spirit haunting me.'

He placed a finger on my lips and kissed the tip of my nose. 'Things will work out, you'll see. If you can survive being all alone while the universe churns like a cauldron all around you, you can survive anything. Be strong Michaela, and do what you have to do – for now, at least.'

We kissed one last time before I gave Matt's hand a final squeeze and headed off down the road to retrieve my car.

The journey back seemed to take forever. I wondered if my heart was standing still in time back at Matt's house, as Simone believed my body had done when the Gravitons had been registered at the wave observatory. The thought should have been amusing, but I felt leaden inside.

My head seethed with all the scientific information whizzing round in it as I tried to recall exactly what I'd witnessed during the jump.

By the time I drew the car up outside Calum's house, I felt both physically and emotionally exhausted. All I wanted was a long, hot soak in the bath and a very early night. But there was Kevin to thank for giving up his day and Abbey to talk to and Tristan to get bathed and ready for bed. I braced myself as I walked up the drive to the house. The front door key was on the ring with Calum's car keys and I opened the door without knocking, kicking off my boots in the hallway and calling out, 'Hello. I'm back!'

I stopped stock still in the sitting room doorway, as if my borrowed socks had velcroed themselves to the threadbare carpet, at the sight of the visitor sitting primly on the sofa. DI Smith was admiring a beautifully made Lego aeroplane.

She handed it back to Tristan who was sitting on the rug at her feet. Kevin glanced up from the floor where he was scraping up loose bits of Lego, and pulled a face at me which I took to mean, *Sorry, we couldn't prevent her from coming in.* Abbey was eyeing the DI with apprehension and suspicion and I wondered if she was thinking of the stash of marijuana she had hidden somewhere in her bedroom. I suppressed a shudder. I wanted to back out the way I'd come, climb into Calum's car and disappear, but I held my ground and looked the DI squarely in the eye.

'What are you doing here so late on a Friday evening?' I asked.

'I have some very good news for you,' she said with a self-satisfied smile. She didn't get to her feet, so I forced myself forward with what I hoped was a look of nonchalance and rested my hand against the nearest chair.

'Yes?'

'We have had something of a breakthrough where your case is concerned.' She gave a pause for effect while I swallowed nervously. 'We have apprehended a man who we believe was involved in your abduction and six-and-a-half-year imprisonment.'

I felt my mouth drop open.

'We have also located the place where we believe you were held against your will.'

My legs wobbled beneath me and I sank onto the chair, my knuckles rammed against my mouth in disbelief.

'There is a small, dilapidated caravan partially hidden – we initially thought abandoned – in the woods near the airfield. The place was searched of course, during the main investigation, but while hunting for the location of this unique patch of grass, our search teams entered the caravan and this time pulled up the rotting linoleum flooring of the vehicle.

Beneath the floor we discovered a large pit dug out of the soil. It was lined with bracken and grasses, and was full of as-yet unidentified bone fragments.'

'No!' I spluttered. So much for Gravitons and ripples in space and time . . .'I don't believe it. I would have remembered if I'd been kept somewhere like that.'

'We know you were there at some point quite recently,' DI Smith went on, her small eyes gleaming behind her glasses, 'because fresh samples of your blood, which match the DNA samples we took from you at the police station, have been found in that hole, along with your missing helmet and parachute.'

Chapter Forty-Five

'Who is this man you have apprehended?' My voice was croaky even though I had recovered from the initial shock.

'I don't want to tell you too much about him at this stage, as we would like you to identify him from a line-up tomorrow morning.' The DI was sitting on the edge of the couch now with her hands on her knees. 'I can tell you we believed him to be a vagrant who has apparently been seen in the area, on and off over the last few years. He was interviewed at the time you went missing, but he seemed harmless enough. After sifting through police records however, we find he has a record dating back to over twenty years ago.'

'What had he done?'

'He was cited at that time for lewd behaviour and theft. The theft was of women's underwear. On another occasion the RSPCA brought proceedings against him for the mistreatment of a dog.'

'Nothing about kidnapping then.' It was a statement rather than a question, as I tried to get my mind round this disturbing development.

'No, but Dr Patel believes that in some cases inappropriate behaviour can escalate into actual crime if left unchecked.'

'What about the parachute?' I was watching Tristan wave the newly-built fighter jet round his head. He was totally absorbed and making little zooming noises. 'Is there any way you can tell how long it had been down there?'

'The parachute is undergoing further tests as we speak, but I think we have to assume it has been down there since you first went missing, because where else could it have been all this time?'

She smiled triumphantly. 'If you can positively identify our suspect tomorrow we can throw the book at him and lock him away where he can't harm anyone ever again.'

And close the case and move on to other things, I thought somewhat uncharitably as my fingers traced the thin outline of the now healed cut on my hand. My mind went to Simone and her Gravitons and the huge sums of money the government were spending on trying to find out whether they actually existed. Which scenario did I want to believe, I wondered?

I ran a hand shakily across my face. The DI's findings couldn't be ignored. I knew that eventually I would have to confront this new and unsettling development.

'OK,' I conceded. 'I'll come and see if I recognise anything about your suspect tomorrow. What time are we going to do this?'

'I'll send a car for you at ten o'clock.' DI Smith managed an encouraging smile. 'You'll feel better once this is all over.' She rose to her feet and I saw her out. Closing the door behind her I leaned heavily against it, my legs feeling almost too weak to hold my weight. I'd have to ring Matt, I thought and tell him I couldn't go anywhere with him and Simone, not tomorrow at least.

Kevin appeared at the end of the passage. 'I ought to be going,' he said apologetically, 'I'm so sorry, Kaela.'

I raised my eyes to his. 'Sorry? What for?'

'For getting it so wrong,' he said. 'Matt and I were convinced it was something else altogether; OK not the aliens, I'll admit that was a bit far-fetched, but Matt's sister had a fascinating theory. I have to confess I was sucked into the idea myself.'

'I met Simone today at Matt's,' I said with a tired smile. 'I wanted to believe her theory too. It sure beats being abducted by some horrible old man with a passion for women's knickers.'

Kevin gave a short laugh but stopped as Abbey appeared at his shoulder.

'Have you told her about Susan?'

'What about her?' I asked, pushing off from the door and advancing on the two of them as alarm bells went off in my head. 'What's happened to Mum?'

'Dr Hewitt from Acorn Lodge rang to say your mother wanted to see you,' Abbey told me. 'Apparently your previous visits registered with her at last and she believes you were really there. They have changed her medication and she's much more lucid.'

'Why didn't you ring me at Matt's?' I wrung my hands together, upset that I hadn't gone to her.

'He only rang a couple of hours ago,' Abbey said quickly. 'Kevin phoned Matt but he said you had already left. And then DI Smith turned up and waylaid you before we had a chance to tell you.'

'You're going to have to get a mobile,' Kevin advised. He had his car keys in his hand. 'Do you want me to run you over there now?'

I glanced at my watch. It was seven o'clock, a couple of hours before the nursing staff would be starting the ritual of preparing Mum for bed.

'Thanks, Kevin, but you ought to get off home, I can take Calum's car. And you've done so much for us already.' I turned to Abbey. 'Will you be alright getting Tristan ready for bed on your own, after all?'

'Yeah, I don't mind. If he plays up I'll give him a drag on a spliff.' She grinned at me as my face paled. 'Only joking, I'm clearing my room out tomorrow. What with the kid here and the police sniffing around, I think it might be time to get clean.'

I smiled, despite the tension of the day. This older Abbey was hard to get used to. 'That would be really good – for all of us as well as you – well done, Abbey.'

I sat on the floor and pulled my boots back on while Abbey watched.

'Kaela?'

'Yes?'

'What did Matt say about Tris? Do you think he's his?'

I shook my head as I stood up, amazed to find that I'd forgotten all about the question of Tristan's parentage. 'No. He says not.'

'Good.' She seemed satisfied with my answer. 'OK, bye, Kaela. And give my love to your mum.'

Nodding, I followed Kevin out into the dark night.

It only took ten minutes to get to Acorn Lodge. I walked up the dark path to the front door and rang the bell. Autumn had really set in now and a faint mist hovered over the flower borders on either side of the path. I inhaled the musty scent, thinking of the river which wasn't far away and wondering where I had smelled that smell before.

The door was answered by Dr Stephen Hewitt himself.

'Ah, you got my message then. Come along in, your mother will be overjoyed to see you.'

'Abbey told me you have changed my mother's medication?' I followed him up the stairs to my mother's room.

'Yes, we monitor our patient's progress very closely. Some care homes simply dish out pills month after month, year after year, but we adjust the dosage and medication regularly. If early signs can be trusted, the new pills seem to have worked wonders with your mother. She is now willing to believe you have returned and is extremely anxious to see you.'

'She grew rather agitated on my previous visit,' I murmured as he put his hand on the door to Mum's room. 'Will she be alright if I just walk in on her?'

'On the two previous occasions you visited she thought she was hallucinating, and that upset her,' the doctor assured me. He gave my shoulder a quick pat. 'She'll be fine, go on in and see her for yourself.'

Mum was sitting on the edge of her bed turning a photograph over in her hands. She glanced up when she heard her door open and focused her eyes on my face. I watched as recognition dawned across her features, filling her eyes with light and hope.

'Michaela?' she whispered as if afraid to raise her voice in case I vanished like a wraith in the mist. 'Is it really you?'

I crossed the room and stood before her, holding out my hands. 'It's me Mum, I'm back.'

She rose from the bed with a wail and flung her arms around me clutching me to her chest. Through her tears she repeated my name, alternately patting my back and combing my hair with her fingers and I could feel her heart beating through the fabric of her thin top.

'My little girl,' she murmured again and again. 'You've come back, you really are here.'

We sank onto the edge of her bed and twisted to face one another but she wouldn't let go of my hands. 'I knew you weren't dead,' she said as tears ran down her face and dripped off the end of her chin. 'I kept trying to tell everyone. I would have known if something terrible had happened to my little girl.'

'I'm alright, Mum. Nothing terrible has happened to me at all.' I wondered whether to tell her Simone's version of what had befallen me or DI Smith's. 'Do you remember anything of my last visit?' I asked her.

She shook her head. 'I thought I saw you many times over the years, but the doctors kept telling me I had to accept that you were gone. They said I couldn't move on unless I grieved for you.' She turned desperate eyes on me. 'But how could I grieve when I didn't want to believe the worst? They encouraged me to paint, to express my grief through my art, but it never felt right, it felt as if I was betraying you.'

'I'm so sorry for what you've been through,' I whispered, my voice breaking with emotion. 'Something weird happened to me during the parachute jump and there was nothing I could do about it.'

'Did you go to the place between worlds?' she asked hesitantly. 'I dreamed of you there a few times, but you weren't dead, Michaela, you seemed to be so full of life, but . . . waiting.'

'The police still think I was kidnapped and held against my will,' I confessed. 'But you remember Matt – the parachute instructor?'

'How could I ever forget? He was the last one to see you before you vanished from our lives.'

'He has a sister who is a scientist. She thinks my disappearance is to do with a glitch in space and time. She thinks I haven't been anywhere for the past six and a half years.'

She let go one of my hands and wiped her face on her sleeve. 'Calum thought you were dead,' she said in a tremulous voice. 'He came to visit often, and his daughter Abbey came to see me too. Sometimes I was well enough to know who they were. Calum was having trouble with her you see.'

295

'I know. She's a bit better now that I'm back and she has Kevin to spar with too, which she appears to enjoy.'

'Kevin? That spotty-faced youth who did the jump with you?'

I nodded. 'He's grown up a bit in the last few years.'

'They were given a hard time by the press,' she said, a faraway look coming into her eyes. 'I never did think they were involved, but your father spent a lot of time with them, trying to get to the bottom of things.'

'I'm sorry about Dad. I can't believe he's gone.'

She shook her head. 'Nor can I, it's like there has been a void in my life since . . . it happened. There's been this empty space inside of me all this time that only you or he could fill.' The tears started again. 'I've missed you both so very much.'

Chapter Forty-Six

I stayed with Mum until the carer came to help her to bed, and then made my way back to the car. It was only as I was driving home that I realised my mother had intimated that it had been not just Abbey but also Calum who had been a visitor at the home. Why had Calum visited my mother? What could he possibly have wanted with a mentally sick woman?

The question bugged me as I drove back through the mist, and later as I climbed into bed, it bothered me more than the question of where I'd been for the last few years.

The next morning I rose early to shower and wash my hair, and after setting out breakfast for Abbey and Tristan, I stuck my head out of the front door to check the weather before deciding what to wear that day.

Suddenly a mass of people were swarming up the drive and microphones were thrust under my nose, as photographers jostled and snapped and called my name.

'Michaela! Michaela Anderson! What can you tell us about your disappearance in 2002?'

'Miss Anderson! What do you feel about the man in police custody?'

'Michaela, would you tell our readers exactly what you remember about your abduction?'

I held a hand up to shield my eyes from the flashes and realised they had herded me down the steps and surrounded me at the side of the drive like a pack of hounds.

'I . . . I don't know. I can't really remember anything.'

'Did your captor abuse you in any way?'

'No, no, I don't recall being held by anyone.'

I was being nudged this way and that as members of the press vied with one another to get closer.

'Miss Anderson, can you explain . . .'

The reporter didn't finish the sentence as DI Smith appeared as if from nowhere. She was clad in a severe navy trouser suit and she elbowed the press out of her way, grabbed my arm and pulled me back into the house, kicking the door shut behind us with the heel of one of her sensible blue court shoes.

'I thought we'd kept the lid on your reappearance to good effect until now,' she said cheerfully, guiding me into the kitchen where Abbey looked up from her breakfast in surprise.

'What was all that about?' she asked. 'What's going on?'

'What's going on is that someone has at last leaked the story of Michaela's reappearance to the media. They are out there in force – newspaper reporters and TV crews en masse.'

'It's true,' I murmured, sinking onto a chair, feeling stunned. 'The garden is heaving with them.'

'You've been lucky to have evaded them for this long,' DI Smith said with a grimace. 'Now that the press have got wind of the fact that we have a suspect in custody, I'm afraid you won't be left alone until they have their story.'

'Should I talk to them?'

DI Smith gazed at me, her pale eyes disconcerting behind the rimless glasses. 'What would you say?'

'Well, I er . . .'

'Exactly. So we block them for the present until you have

identified our suspect and then we will prepare a statement for you to read on our terms, not theirs.'

'What if I can't identify the suspect?' I asked uneasily. 'I mean, I really don't remember being held by anyone.'

'Dr Patel feels that you may be in a state of denial at present, but seeing your captor will hopefully unlock your memories and the last six and a half years may come flooding back to you.'

I glanced at Abbey who was looking as dubious as I felt. I saw she was fingering her tarot cards anxiously.

'Not according to the cards they won't,' the girl muttered.

'Fortunately,' DI Smith said rather cuttingly, 'the police don't deal with the mumbo jumbo that appears in tarot cards.'

'That's because the police are narrow-minded fascists,' Abbey responded rudely. Tristan looked up anxiously at the sound of Abbey's raised voice and cowered in his chair, and I thought of the bullying Lewis.

'Abbey, you're upsetting Tristan,' I cautioned. 'Look, will you be OK if I go with the DI and get this identity parade over and done with?'

Abbey glanced at Tristan and lowered her voice. She seemed to struggle between her desire to be hostile to the DI and her instinct to protect the boy. 'We'll be fine, won't we, Tris?'

'When I called last night I assumed that the boy was a temporary visitor.' The DI looked at Tristan.

'I'm looking after him for a friend.'

'Well, I think there should be a suitable adult here with these two,' the DI said, including Abbey in her rather scathing glare. 'Is Mr Sinclair here?'

'Calum's in hospital,' I told her quietly, 'he's not been well.'

'I'm not a kid,' Abbey's voice was petulant, 'I am almost seventeen!'

'I'm not happy about leaving you or the boy alone, especially with the press outside.' She turned to me. 'I think we'd better take them with us.' Removing a radio from a belt around her waist, she spoke into it and a moment later two burly police officers entered the room. 'Is there a back way out of here?' she asked Abbey.

'Might be,' Abbey retorted unhelpfully.

'There used to be a removable panel in the wooden fence at the rear of the garden,' I said, gathering some of Tristan's toys and stowing them in the backpack Ingrid had left with us. 'Have you got a coat or something, Abbey? It's quite chilly outside.'

'Stop fussing, Kaela, I'm not a child any more, no matter what this *detective* seems to think.'

After I'd finished dressing, the police officers escorted us out through the back door and down the garden, ferrying us to two waiting patrol cars in the lane behind the house. Just as the cars were moving off, a cry went up in the nearby road and the press began to run in our direction.

'Put your foot down, Bob,' DI Smith instructed and the car screeched away from the kerb and out onto the open road.

We arrived at the police headquarters twenty-five minutes later and were driven round to the back entrance where we were shepherded swiftly into the police station. Abbey and Tristan were taken to the police canteen for drinks and biscuits and I was shown into a small room where I sat anxiously awaiting DI Smith's return.

The room was small and bare save for two chairs on either side of an empty desk, and the stark environment did nothing to dispel my increasing anxiety. Sandwiching my hands between my knees, I chewed my lip and tapped my feet nervously as a multitude of questions niggled their way into my head. What if I didn't recognise the man DI Smith had in custody? Bloody hell, I thought in panic, what would happen if I did?

Dear God, I thought, if indeed there was a God, what had I done to deserve all this? It occurred to me that I didn't have to be here. I wasn't under arrest, was I? There was nothing to stop me from simply walking out of this horrible room, collecting the children and making my way home to Calum's house.

I was about to get to my feet when the door opened, and DI Smith came in looking rather pleased with herself.

'We have recently adopted a new type of identification process,' she told me, holding out a hand, which indicated I was to follow her into the corridor. 'To save witnesses the trauma of a live parade and the problems of holding onto suspects long enough to arrange the timely – and I may say costly task of organising an identity parade – you can now make your identification via a video line-up.'

'So I won't have to face this guy in the flesh at all?' I trotted along behind her.

'No. You will be asked to look at several similar-looking head and shoulder images selected from a database.'

'I won't be able to see how tall he is, or what he sounds like, though?'

'No, I'm afraid that is one problem with the system.' She opened a door off to our right and motioned me to go in ahead of her. 'If you would prefer to have a live identity parade we can arrange it for a future date, but there is always the risk of our suspect not turning up.'

'No, no,' I said hastily, looking round the sparsely furnished room where an officer stood ready with technical equipment. However worrying I was finding this, I didn't want the prospect of a live identity parade hanging over me for days or weeks to come. 'I'd rather get it over with now.' For all the good it would do, I thought bleakly.

I sat at the table and was shown fifteen-second shots of a range of shabby men, mostly unshaven and looking fairly desperate. If they were actors, they were doing a good job, I thought wryly as one shot after another flashed before me. I tried to imagine any of them stealing women's underwear or harming an innocent dog, but all I could feel for them was compassion. And not one of them looked in the slightest bit familiar.

'I'm sorry.' I turned to face DI Smith. 'There is no one in that line-up I remotely recognise.'

The DI set her lips in a straight line and fixed me with her steely glare.

'Are you absolutely sure, Michaela?'

I nodded.

'That is a great pity, but it may be that we won't need a positive identification to make a case, especially as there is medical evidence of your psychological trauma and amnesia.' She took a deep breath. 'Not only have DNA tests proved that traces of your blood have been found in the hole under the caravan floor, but early this morning our suspect was banging on his cell door, begging to talk to me.'

'And?' I felt sick to the stomach but the question had to be asked.

'Our suspect Danny Hill has now confessed to your kidnap, physical assault and six-and-a-half-year imprisonment.'

Chapter Forty-Seven

I sat in stunned silence on the way home in the police car. Abbey kept throwing me sideways glances and I knew she was desperate to ask me what had happened. Tristan was fortunately looking importantly out of the patrol car window, apparently in heaven at being given a ride in a real police vehicle.

After a moment or two Abbey's hand sneaked out and took mine and I felt her give me a light squeeze. Surprised, I managed a thin smile of thanks and patted her hand before succumbing once more to the misery in my heart. All I could picture were those unshaven, sad old men in the pictures. I could almost smell the sour, whisky-laden breath, the unwashed odour of their bodies. The thought that one of them had held me in a stinking pit under the ground for over six years, had probably touched me – I shuddered at the thought and bit back tears of revulsion and self-pity.

We re-entered the property the same way we'd snuck out and fortunately the press and camera crews were nowhere to be seen. Before we'd left the station the DI had asked if I wanted an officer to stay with us, but I'd refused. I wasn't going to sit all day imprisoned in my own home because of media interest in my plight.

Once back in the house I tried to do a few chores, but the

enormity of what I'd learned at the police station gnawed at me, making simple tasks impossible. After twenty minutes I gave up, walked upstairs to my room and slumped down on the bed.

Could a sane person block out six and a half years so totally? Not a flicker, not a whisper of a memory existed. 'Oh, God,' I groaned. 'Why did this have to happen to me?'

I wanted to stay in the attic room forever. The thought of picking up the threads of my life and continuing as if nothing had happened, filled me with a sudden all-consuming fear. Was I even capable of looking after Tristan and Abbey? How could I live with the terrible shadow of those missing years hanging over me?

As I sat huddled and miserable, I got to thinking of Grace and the hours she must have spent in this room. Had she had a premonition that her life was to be cut short, I wondered? Is that why she'd started the quilt for Abbey? I realised suddenly that as my thoughts had wandered, my heart had stopped racing and my hands felt less clammy. At least I was alive, I reminded myself. Grace would never have the chance to live again, to breathe fresh air and feel the sunlight on her face – but I did. Standing up, I brushed invisible cobwebs from my clothes. I would be strong for Grace's sake, for Abbey, Tristan, Calum – and for myself.

My new determination was tested the minute I saw Abbey. She was sitting on the couch with Tristan, watching something on the TV, and when I suggested that she and Tristan come with me to visit her father at the hospital, her expression changed almost immediately to one of anger and hurt.

'No way I'm going to see him! Not after what he tried to do. God, Kaela, he must really hate me to try and take the easy way out like that.' She stomped round me working herself into a fit. 'Do I mean so little to him?'

'He's ill, Abbey,' I explained once again. 'I told you he said he didn't plan it. I think he was feeling low and it was the middle of the night and the pills were just there . . . and don't forget how scared you were, thinking he was going to die.'

'That's no excuse! He's never loved me, not since Mum died. I *do* hate him and I don't care if I never see him again!'

I held up a placating hand. 'Alright, alright. Look, if I go alone will you be alright here with Tristan? The press are still hanging about at the front.'

She calmed down at the mention of the boy's name. 'We'll be fine, won't we, Tris?'

The boy looked at her adoringly and I realised that a strong bond was growing between the two of them.

'You can play with your Lego and I'll carry on with my sewing,' she told him.

'Sewing?' I remembered the quilt book and the thread we'd bought in Dorking. 'Have you started on something?'

She smiled secretively despite her earlier outburst. 'I've worked out how to thread Mum's sewing machine. It still works fine.'

'Well OK, if you're sure. Can you make some lunch for you both?'

'I'm sure Tris would like spaghetti hoops and toast, so we'll have that.'

'I'll see you both later then. Keep the door locked behind me.'

To get to Calum's car I had to run the gauntlet of the media and was surrounded by reporters and TV anchor men and women the moment I left the house.

'I have no comment to make,' I said over and over, as I shoved my way through the sea of bodies and climbed behind the wheel. 'DI Smith will be releasing a statement later.'

I drove off before the reporters could ask any more

questions and switched my concentration to navigating the Saturday traffic until I eventually drew up to the hospital car park. After turning off the engine I leaned against the steering wheel to collect my thoughts, bracing myself for the forthcoming visit. If I'd thought this morning's trials had been hard, talking to the man I was supposed to spend the rest of my life with was going to be doubly difficult. Not only was I still angry at what he had tried to do, despite the excuses I'd offered to Abbey about him being ill, I was also aware, for the first time since I'd been back, that whatever foundation of love we had been building together before my jump, it was probably nowhere near strong enough to support us for the rest of our lives. The moment I had kissed Matt yesterday morning, I'd realised that keeping the promise I'd made to stay with my one-time boyfriend was going to be almost impossible.

I decided to spend only a short time with Calum before going over to visit Mum again. I knew she would be anxious to see me, and I thought that if she seemed well enough we could do something normal like going shopping together for an hour or two and choose some new items for her wardrobe. Perhaps she could also come with me to the solicitors and tell the obstructive Mr Archibald Brent that I was indeed her long, lost daughter.

Calum was sitting propped up by pillows in bed, eating a hospital lunch of white fish in a cheese sauce with mashed potato, from a tray on his lap.

He looked up, his fork poised in his hand and his expression changed immediately from boredom to one of pleasure and relief. 'Michaela. You came back.'

'Yes.' I gave him a brief smile. 'I thought you might like some company – and we need to talk.'

'I know.' He rested his fork down on the plate and held out his hand to me. 'Look, I can't tell you how sorry I am for what I did – it was cowardly in the extreme. I know you're angry with me. Do you think you can ever forgive me?'

I sighed as I took the seat next to the bed, ignoring his hand, which he dropped back onto the bedside table. 'It's not just me who has to forgive you, Abbey is incredibly hurt and angry with you.'

'She's always angry with me,' he said tiredly. 'She's blamed me since her mother died. Nothing I ever do is right.'

My earlier intentions to be kind to him vanished. 'She's only a teenager and you are the adult. Grow up, Calum! Abbey is desperate for your love and you have to make the first move to reconcile this thing between you.'

'There may not be time, Kaela.'

'What do you mean?'

'I mean I've had a psychological assessment and Dr Nadal thinks my depression stems directly from the fear of this operation I'm supposed to have.'

'I could have told you that,' I said somewhat coldly.

'He thinks the sooner it's done and dusted, as he puts it, the better.'

I stared at him and he pushed the tray away testily. 'Dr Nadal contacted my oncology consultant and recommended that I be put on the list for a cancellation. They have got back to us already.'

'And?'

'I'm having the operation first thing on Monday morning.'

We stared at one another while I digested the ramifications of this information.

'Are they keeping you here until then?'

'No, they need the bed. They are sorting out my discharge right now. I was going to give you a ring after lunch.'

307

My heart sank. The fact that I wasn't immediately over-joyed about taking Calum home with me confirmed all my doubts about what we had left between us, but I gave myself a mental shake and forced a smile.

'That's very good news. And,' I said, fixing him with a stern look, 'it will give you a whole day with your daughter.'

It was almost another hour before a doctor was found to discharge Calum and write a prescription for some new drugs. Because of his fragile state of mind, they would only give him enough to see him through the next two nights, and I found I was heartily relieved by that decision.

On the way home in the car we discussed Abbey once more.

He was leaning back in the passenger seat, looking grey and drawn. 'I just can't get through to her,' he said wearily, 'believe me, Kaela, I've tried.'

'It didn't help that you destroyed all evidence of her mother's existence.' I pursed my lips disapprovingly, as I negotiated the early afternoon traffic. 'She thinks you never cared about Grace and you don't care about her.'

'I agree that in hindsight it wasn't a kind thing to do, but it's too late now.' He glanced sideways at me. 'What can I do?'

'It isn't too late yet,' I told him firmly, thinking that if I could pull myself together after all that had happened, so could he. 'With your operation looming, you have to resolve things with her now. Tell her you love her. Tell her she is important to you. Could you give her something special of yours? Something that means a lot to you that she knows she will be holding for you for when you come out of the operation?'

He fell silent beside me and I wondered if it had been cruel of me to remind him that he could die on the operating table.

'Do you think giving her something special will be enough?'

'I think it will go a long way to making things right. But you have to talk to her too, make sure she knows you love her.'

We continued the journey without talking, both lost in our own thoughts and were almost home when I remembered my plan to visit my mother.

'Damn.'

Calum's gaze flicked towards me. 'What's the matter?'

'I'm going to have to drop you home and go straight back out again. I'd planned to go and see Mum. They've changed her medication and now that she's accepted I'm truly back, she's making huge steps towards recovery.'

'That's really good news, I'm so glad.'

The mention of my mother seemed to jerk Calum out of his brooding silence.

'Susan was very kind to Abbey and me after you went missing. Early on, in the first weeks and months after your disappearance, she came round regularly to help with Abbey. I don't think we would have coped without her.'

I thought of my mother trying to keep some sort of second-hand contact with me by becoming more involved with my new family. I had to give it to her. Although she and my father had initially disapproved of my moving in with an older man, she had always been solicitous to Calum and accepting of my decision to make my life with him and Abbey.

'I'm glad my parents continued to see you both,' I told Calum, 'and that you allowed them to keep in contact with Abbey. I think it must have meant a lot to them.'

Whilst talking I had turned the car automatically down our street, but hit the brakes when I spotted the press vans still lined up along the kerb.

'Oh no, I'd forgotten them,' I groaned. 'Don't they have homes to go to?'

Calum sat bolt upright and was staring anxiously at the

people loitering around clutching microphones, sound booms and cameras with enormous zoom lenses. 'Has something happened? What are they doing outside my house?'

'No, no. Everyone's alright,' I did a three point turn and headed back the way we'd come, intending to take the back road home. 'The police have arrested someone for my kidnap and the press have got hold of the story of my return, that's all.'

'That's all?' he spluttered. 'Pull in over there.'

I yanked on the steering wheel and headed into a parking space at the nearby supermarket and sat facing him.

'Now tell me exactly what's been going on,' he demanded. 'I can't believe you didn't mention this, Kaela. What do you mean they've arrested somebody? Who? When?'

Sighing, I closed my eyes momentarily to think what exactly I was going to tell him. Did I mention my visit to Matt and the meeting with Simone? Should I just tell him what DI Smith believed – the unthinkable thing that had almost sent me over the edge? In the end I decided to tell him everything except my confused feelings for Matt. When I had finished he sat looking at me with open astonishment.

'You've been rather busy while I've been at death's door, haven't you?'

'I've just been trying to get to the bottom of what's happened to me,' I told him. 'It's been a lot to deal with and you haven't exactly helped.'

His shoulders sagged and I wished that I hadn't burdened him. The poor man had just come out of hospital, he had a possibly life-threatening illness and a serious operation looming ahead of him, not to mention a lifetime of mistakes to put right with his daughter.

'Let's get you home,' I said a little more kindly. 'You must be exhausted.'

'I don't know what to say. I don't even know what to think any more.'

I reached out my hand and rested it tentatively on his. 'I think we should just take one day at a time, Calum. Look, I'll put off my visit to Mum. I can go over to see her tomorrow afternoon. I've decided to go with Simone to Norfolk in the morning. Despite DI Smith's findings I have to investigate every possibility. But in the meantime let's see the children and have some quiet time to ourselves, what do you think?'

'Yes.' He nodded. 'Let's go home.'

After taking the back way home, Calum followed me silently through the gap in the fence. Just as we reached the back door to the house, he caught my wrist and pulled me round to face him.

'I'm sorry, Kaela,' he said softly. 'Sorry for everything.'

I gave him a wan smile, remembering how close I'd come to giving up. 'You'll be OK, you know. Everything will turn out alright.'

Chapter Forty-Eight

The house when we arrived back was in pandemonium. Loud music blared from the sitting room as we stood in the doorway and looked on aghast at the party, which appeared to be in full swing.

Two of Abbey's three friends from the previous night were sprawled on the floor with cans of drink in their hands, while the one I remembered as Oggs had hoisted a giggling Tristan onto his shoulders and was jigging him round the room in a strange kind of dance. Abbey was twirling with him and laughing with abandon, the fabric of her jagged-hemmed skirt fanning out round her. As she turned and caught sight of her father, she stilled in her tracks, her scratched and tattooed arms falling to her sides. It was like watching a joyous and colourful balloon suddenly deflating.

So much for a quiet couple of hours sewing and making Lego with Tristan, I thought grimly.

Calum stalked across to the computer and turned it off. 'What the hell is going on?' he asked his daughter.

'I've invited some friends round, what does it look like?' she retorted in the sudden silence, which was interrupted only by the faint background noise of the TV.

The two I remembered being called Cat and Rumps sat up and stared around in surprise. Calum snatched the cans out of their hands and looked about to explode when he peered more closely at the drinks, and then thrust them silently back to their owners.

'See?' Abbey said sarcastically. 'Energy drinks, that's all. Did you think I'd have alcohol with Tris here?'

We all froze in a confused kind of stare-off and then a small voice piped up from the sofa, where he'd been unceremoniously dropped, 'I want more music.' He lifted skinny arms in Oggs's direction. 'Carry me again, Oggy, that was fun!'

Calum muttered a stilted apology and nodded. 'Well OK then. I'm sure the noise has been giving the press something to think about anyway – take their attention off Kaela for a while.'

'Yeah, they asked loads of questions when we arrived,' Oggs said helpfully.

'What did you tell them?' I asked, suddenly nervous.

'Oh, only about Abbey's theory that you were taken by Satanists and made to act out all sorts of rituals and weird rites for six years . . .'

'What?' Calum looked at his daughter, appalled.

Abbey had the decency to appear embarrassed but Oggs went on, oblivious to the tension in the room. 'They loved it when I pointed out she'd been missing for exactly six years, six months and six days; I mean, they hadn't even *noticed* the obvious connotations of the triple sixes.'

'Shut up, Oggs,' Abbey said faintly.

'Yeah, shut up, Oggy,' Tristan echoed. He held up his arms with more insistence. 'I want you to carry me again!'

An hour later peace returned to the household. Abbey's friends wandered off after devouring the recently purchased contents of the kitchen cupboard and after bringing their drinks cans and empty crisp packets out to the kitchen at

313

my request. Finally, we settled in for what remained of the afternoon.

'I have to ring Matt,' I told Calum apologetically. 'He and Simone are supposed to be picking me up tomorrow morning. I have to tell them the journey may well be a waste of time now that the police have a confession for my kidnapping.'

'Go ahead.' Calum waved me towards the phone in the hallway. 'Do whatever it is you have to do.'

I was relieved when Simone answered Matt's phone. I had been nervous about having to speak to Matt, with the possibility of Calum listening in from the other room; worried that perhaps my voice or body language might give my deepest feelings away. After I explained about the suspect and the confession made by the vagrant, Simone merely murmured, 'Uh uh, OK,' and 'leave it with me.'

'So you still think it's worth coming for me tomorrow?' I asked hopefully. 'I mean, if the man's confessed . . .'

'Yes. We'll see you as planned.'

Abbey had vanished up to the attic room to sew as soon as her friends had left and taken Tristan up with her, so Calum and I sat companionably side-by-side on the recently vacated sofa to watch TV.

Later we ordered an Indian take away, which was brought by a nervous delivery boy who'd had to negotiate his way through the dwindling crowd of media outside.

Abbey and Tristan joined Calum and I to eat the chicken tikka with rice and curried vegetables at the kitchen table. And later, after another attempt by Abbey and me at bathing Tristan, the boy curled up in his bedding under the kitchen table and slept with the sound of the dishwasher whirring through its cycle nearby. It turned out to be a remarkably relaxed evening and neither Abbey nor Calum mentioned anything about his possible suicide attempt, his earlier unfortunate effort to take belated control over her friends or the subject of what she had told Oggs about her Satanic theories. I decided not to dwell on the ramifications of the Satanic cult matter either, believing it best to enjoy the apparent truce between father and daughter.

However, any hope I had of an earnest talk ensuing between the two of them soon evaporated and after a while Abbey asked me to come up to the attic room to show me what she had been doing over the last couple of days. Watching the slim legs climbing the stairs ahead of me, I found myself thinking of Simone. Abbey and Simone weren't so very different, I thought. One might be a quantum scientist and the other a college dropout, but both had lost their mothers at an early age and disguised the need to prove themselves with a great deal of attitude.

Entering the attic room I saw, lined up on the top of my duvet, several beautifully crafted squares, each one made from diamond shapes in varying fabrics and stitched carefully together to form squares. I could see the blacks and mauves of various items of Abbey's clothing and ran my finger along the painstakingly created quilt pieces in awe. 'These are fabulous! You are a natural, Abbey. Did you learn how to do these from the book we bought?'

'Sort of,' she said, suddenly bashful, obviously unused to praise. 'I have looked at the book, but when I sit up here I can feel the presence of my mother sort of guiding me, telling me what to do.'

I could understand that, I thought. I'd fancied I had felt Grace's presence often enough myself over the last couple of days. I smiled to myself then realised Abbey was studying my expression carefully.

'You actually believe me, don't you?' she asked with a degree of wonder in her voice.

'I've never believed in ghosts, but whatever she is – a dream in my case and perhaps a half remembered memory in yours – she brings a feeling of peace.'

'I wish I'd known her properly,' Abbey murmured sadly.

Be careful what you wish for, my mother had said. But sometimes when wishes were made, the universe seemed to know exactly what was required of it. Through the quilt, Abbey was getting to know her mother, even though she was long dead. Perhaps, I thought, out of the distress and confusion of a human life, good things could happen and shattered lives could be rebuilt.

I put my arm round her and gave her a hug. 'I think you know your mother already, she's a part of you, Abbey. Her talent at sewing and her love for you will always be inside you.'

For the briefest of moments she relaxed against me but then I felt her stiffen, as if the contact was unwelcome. 'You always say the right things, don't you?'

It was an accusation.

I sensed the return of aggression in her voice and drew back. I realised that six years of perceived rejection and consequent rebellion couldn't be swept under the carpet so easily.

She was looking at me challengingly. 'You haven't said anything about what Oggs and I told the reporters.'

'There didn't seem much point. What's done is done. You can't unsay it even if you wanted to, and if I made any sort of comment to the press to try and quash this 666 thing, it would only give them quotes to use against me and ultimately fuel the flames.'

'Why do you always have to be so nice – so bloody level-headed?' She'd got up and was facing me down as I sat on the edge of the bed. Her eyes were full of anger and confusion.

I put a hand to my head. 'I'm just trying to do the right thing, that's all.'

'Was this quilt really my mother's? Its not some project you've dreamed up to make me toe the line, is it?'

'Of course not! I wouldn't have had the know-how or the time – you can see how much work must have gone into it.'

She seemed to wilt suddenly. 'How can you like me when I'm such a bitch? I told Oggs that stuff about the Satanic angle because I knew he'd spill it to the media. He never could keep anything secret . . .' she looked at me uncertainly. 'I wanted to cause you trouble, Kaela. I did it to hurt you.' She paused before continuing. 'I thought Mum would be pleased if I didn't accept you. I thought she'd resent you being here, taking over her life . . .' A tear rolled down Abbey's cheek. 'But after feeling her presence – I'm not so sure. I think I've let her down, and you too.'

I reached out and pulled her alongside me. 'You've had a tough time, Abbey. It takes time to change. Don't beat yourself up about it.'

She was looking at me sideways as if weighing me up. 'It's just all so odd – you turning up out of the blue after all this time; Dad suddenly ill and this present from Mum appearing like this, when I've wanted it for so long.' She hesitated again. 'I feel it must mean something, like there is a reason for it all. And I think Kevin may have been right all along.'

'What do you mean?'

'I'm beginning to think these triple sixes; the number of the beast, and the representation of the goddess Isis, who I thought was so important,' she glanced at the scars of the ancient symbols on her arm, 'don't mean as much as Kevin's special number.'

I frowned, recalling their numerical sparring, 'What, you mean the number fifty-two?'

317

She nodded, her eyes downcast.

'What made you change your mind?'

'Well, he's right, isn't he? I mean there being fifty-two days in the year and fifty-two cards in the pack are quite important markers . . .'

'And?' I prompted.

'When I said I'd felt Mum's presence – you know, about how to proceed with the quilt, I felt a compulsion to count the sections she'd already completed.' She raised her darkly outlined eyes to mine. 'I thought there might be multiples of the number six, or maybe something to do with the Fibonacci sequence. But there are fifty-two pieces in that quilt, Kaela. Not one more or one less, but exactly fifty-two.'

Chapter Forty-Nine

Simone and Matt came for me at five the next morning as planned. Having prepared things for my disparate family, I left Calum, Abbey and Tristan snoring in their respective sleeping areas and climbed into the front seat of Simone's silver convertible Mercedes, that Matt had generously vacated for me on their arrival.

Fortunately Matt had merely offered a brief, 'Hi,' and a warm smile before settling in the rear seat behind his sister. Even that small interaction had sent my whole body a-quiver, and I had glanced guiltily back towards the house in case Calum should have risen and was watching us from his window. In his present fragile state of mind I didn't want to give my erstwhile boyfriend anything extra to brood about in my absence.

As Simone gunned the car along the main road, I swivelled my head to return Matt's greeting and almost immediately my good intentions were tested as I found myself wishing I was sitting next to him in the back seat. He had that 'just woken up' look and I wondered if he'd been asleep while his sister drove here from Kent. I wanted to run my hands through his tousled hair and feel his freshly showered skin against mine. The thought made me blush and I chided myself inwardly for my weakness. Today was business, I told myself firmly and I should simply be grateful Matt had decided to come with us at all. When Simone smiled beside me, I hoped she hadn't read my thoughts.

'It's going to be a beautiful morning now that the rain has let up,' I observed some time later when the dawn began to break and the sky became streaked with pink and silver. 'What time do you think we'll get to Norwich?'

'We should be there around eight if there are no obstructions.'

'I'm a bit nervous about all this. Do you think there will be anything I can tell your colleagues that they don't already know? Especially with the confession the man in custody has made?'

'I told you not to worry about your vagrant. I'm banking on this visit being a huge success.' Simone kept her eyes firmly on the road. 'It had better be, I've missed choir practice to deliver you there today.'

'Oh, do you sing?' I asked in surprise. I remembered what she had told me about her mother having a lovely singing voice but hadn't had Simone pegged as a singer.

'Simone has a beautiful voice,' Matt piped up from the back. 'She's part of the Kent gospel choir. You should come and listen to her some time.'

If I had trouble imagining Simone letting her hair down enough to sing in a choir, I certainly hadn't envisaged her glorifying the gospels with her voice. 'But doesn't a gospel choir belong to a church?'

'Usually, though not always,' Simone answered with a tinkly laugh. 'But I like the atmosphere in a place of worship. It's so peaceful, don't you think?'

I lapsed into silence again. I'd been under the misguided impression that someone like Simone who dealt in the

320

sciences, believed in evolution and such things as the Big Bang, wouldn't have much time for religion.

Looking out of the window, I watched as the dawn became daybreak and the traffic increased on the road in front and behind us. Here was I, who had once been brought up to believe in God, finding myself constantly doubting His existence after everything that had befallen me and those I loved. And yet whenever I was truly scared or fearful for my life, I found myself praying and entreating Him for assistance.

I shifted uncomfortably in my seat and tried not to think of the questions that had always bothered me about religion, such as the existence of wars, starvation and disease. I knew that every pre-programmed concept I had ever accepted was being sorely tried by the sudden disappearance of a large chunk of my life. Even my mother, in her depressed state, had been talking of places beyond and between and not the heaven she had always relied on so heavily.

'I'm so confused by everything,' I murmured. 'I wish I knew all the answers.'

'I've come to the conclusion that we're not supposed to know everything,' Simone said softly. 'I've spent years experimenting, using mathematics and advanced technology, searching for answers to every question that has popped into my head. I truly think we're not evolved enough, either biologically or spiritually to see the bigger picture. The trouble is the piddly little brains we humans are blessed with.'

'Speak for yourself,' Matt remarked from the back seat, followed by a wide yawn. 'I'll have you know that my brain is spectacularly large and well developed.'

'Did you know,' Simone asked, ignoring her brother, 'that tests on human brains using electronic measuring devices prove without doubt that there is an area of the brain especially designed for this type of connection to our deep inner selves – our souls, if you like? Electrodes fixed to subjects' heads show different parts of the brain lighting up during various activities, and there is an area which *only* lights up when a subject is praying or in deep meditation.'

'Meaning what?' I sneaked a sideways glance at her lovely profile, unsure what she was getting at.

'I believe it means that we humans have a part of us that is designed to search for something more infinitely powerful than ourselves – a supreme deity if you like. Each religion has a different name for the creator but you'd be surprised, if you studied the subject carefully, how alike most of them are.'

'So, you mean any God will do, according to where and by whom we were brought up?' I knew my attempt to sound nonchalant had fallen well short, but she didn't seem to take offence at my doubtful tone. In truth I found I simply wanted to hear her talking, to keep my mind off my own problems and the thought of where she was taking me.

'Any *name* for the creator will do,' she corrected happily. 'My research has led me to the conclusion that we humans simply have trouble comprehending what He or It is.'

Snuggling down in my seat I crossed my arms and closed my eyes, realising she was in her stride, and waited for her to go on.

'In the early days of mankind's existence, a human's need to worship was aimed at the creatures which kept him alive; the animals and birds he hunted and ate, which are depicted in cave drawings around the world. Later humans looked to things a little further away but which were still beyond their comprehension, like thunder and lightning, the sun and the moon, the seasons and the natural environment which surrounded them. The Greeks and Romans even invented gods for emotions, such as love and war.'

Typical, I thought, that Simone had done the research into past human beliefs as well as present ones.

'As we evolved, so did our brains' ability to see a little further. Historical events which seemed inexplicable at the time – and were therefore deemed to be divine – were dutifully recorded for posterity. Science has since proved that many events mentioned in the Bible were actually possible and probably true. The parting of the Red Sea was, in all probability, caused by the sucking out effect prior to a tsunami in the region at about that time in history, for example. Noah's Ark was a localised flood which geologists have found evidence of actually having happened, but which appeared to the limited knowledge of the people at the time, to encompass the whole world.'

'So you're saying none of these events were miracles, but simply explainable geological events?' I opened one eye to look at her.

'Oh, they were miracles alright, but brought about by real geological events, because geology itself is part of the bigger picture – the creator's picture, if you like. Everything was created from atoms, which formed particles of dust, which balled together to make planets. Geology, astronomy, physics, chemistry, biology and advanced mathematics show quite clearly that there is a precise formula to everything we know.'

'What, like Phi?' I thought of the shells in the picture on the wall in the rape suite and for a moment, the predicament I was in came flooding back. She nodded. 'Exactly. There are precise measurements and patterns to all things. Phi is just one of them. There's also the signs of the zodiac, distances between constellations, numerical sequencing . . . they are all part of the same ultimate design.'

'It's a lot to get my head round.'

'That's what I meant about humans having still undeveloped brains. It is difficult to understand things in much the same way a flea might have trouble understanding that the dog they are living, feeding and breeding on is not an entire planet slumbering within the far distant universe of its basket.'

Simone was in her element now and I stopped trying to interrupt as she took a breath and continued. 'The flea might think that when the dog shakes its coat, after having a swim, it is because of something one flea might have done to upset another; or something one of them did to upset the dog. We humans can stand back and see it is only one dog in a pack of many and then only a tiny part of a much wider picture.'

I could have been deeply offended by her analogy if I hadn't been so intrigued.

'So you're saying that some higher power does exist, but that we as humans are trying to pigeonhole Him – or It – to something within our limited understanding?'

'Exactly. And in my opinion, science might one day prove the existence of a supreme being. In fact it could be that science is religion's greatest ally.'

'You would say that, you're a scientist,' I said, relaxing the hackles that had risen with her rather condescending analogy and breaking into a smile. I formed a mental picture of a group of scientific fleas dressed in little white lab coats, trying to persuade the rest of the colony that the dog they were residing on wasn't the be all and end all of the universe.

We fell silent and a gentle snoring from the back told me that Matt had gone back to sleep. Staring out through the windscreen I watched the Mercedes eat up the miles as we sped northwards and I chewed my fingernails nervously at the thought of our destination. Firmly putting all anxieties about what I was going to find at Subatron Industries out of my mind, I concentrated instead on trying to reconcile all Simone had said.

It wasn't so much what Simone believed that had put my back up, I realised – I was finding her theories quite fascinating. It was more the way she was so positive about everything, when so many religious leaders and probably other scientists must have completely different views. I wondered again what she'd said about not fitting in well at school and whether perhaps it hadn't been her mixed race parentage that had alienated her from her peers, so much as her apparent belief that she was always right.

Despite that, I needed to know more. My world had been turned upside down and I wanted answers, lots of them.

'What about wars and starvation and disease?' I said, my mind going to Calum and the illness he was battling. 'Where do they fit into the bigger picture?'

'What people don't understand is that although the Creator made this startlingly beautiful world for us, it is a living world, still expanding out into the universe, still moving, breathing and rumbling beneath our feet.' Simone wrinkled her nose as she spoke. 'As a species we have been incredibly successful, settling in even the remotest parts of the planet, and sometimes some of us are caught up in natural disasters such as floods, earthquakes and eruptions when the dog shakes his coat. We have to battle viruses and disease and sometimes human lives are cut alarmingly short, but each life still has their own special purpose, their own reason to be here for however short a time they are given.' She took a deep breath before I could comment. 'But where we differ from fleas is that we humans are evolved enough to know good from bad, right from wrong. We make conscious choices every minute of every day – and those decisions are what separate us from the rest of the Almighty's creatures.'

'As humans it seems to me we often make the wrong choices,' I murmured, thinking not just on the scale of world wars and vicious conflict, but of what Abbey had said about adults taking second chances at the expense of their children. I felt a shiver run down my spine. 'Are we all inherently bad, do you think?'

'I believe we are born inherently good,' Simone said firmly. I was struck again by her certainty. 'As babies, our souls are pure and completely free of sin. I think we are born in this challenging world the Creator provided for us with a body full of the varied genetic make up of our forebears, to gather information and to learn from everything we experience. We might inhabit bodies that have a tendency to greed or honesty, bad temper or a gentle nature, selfishness or sweetness. We may inherit hormones that make us unpredictable, maternal or sexually precocious – or even prone to mental illness, but we can't blame our genes for everything we get right or wrong; it is what we choose for ourselves and our treatment of others that make us who we are.'

'You make life sound like a struggle between our spiritual selves and our physical bodies,' I commented.

'Isn't that the truth of what we all have to contend with every day of our lives? If there was no conflict and strife and Earth was like the place some of us call heaven, there would be no choices to be made and no growth for our spiritual selves to achieve.' She braked when a truck cut into the lane in front of us and once the danger was over, relaxed again, flashing me a sideways glance. 'When I sing I feel I am glorifying everything our creator stands for; the universe as we know it, stretching away into eternity, the ground at our feet and the history of everyone who has gone before us.'

'But where does that leave your quantum mechanics and the third dimension?'

'Ah, but that is the best bit of all. That very elusive part of Graviton energy we have recorded as missing in the lab, disappears into that extra dimension, if we can find those missing Gravitons, we will have found the world between worlds.'

Chapter Fifty

'Look,' Simone said suddenly, 'there's a service station up ahead. Do you want to stop for a coffee?'

'We'll have to wake sleeping beauty in the back there.' I tried to stop my head reeling from her highly investigated opinions, and peeked round at Matt who was slumped back in his seat with his eyes closed.

'It's about time he woke up anyway.' Simone set her indicator flashing and turned the car off up the slip road. 'If you ask me my brother's been snoozing for far too long. Matt needs a serious wake-up call; something or some*one* to keep him focused and give him some positive motivation to reach his potential.' She was off on another tangent, her brain never still. She turned her dark eyes in my direction and raised her eyebrows ever so slightly.

I stared back at her. 'You mean me?'

Simone inclined her head, which I took to be an affirmative, as she manoeuvred the car into a parking bay and lined the car up with the white lines, on the first attempt.

'Wakey wakey, time for coffee and doughnuts,' she called into the back as she turned off the engine.

Matt roused himself and peered round. 'Are we here already?'

'No, we're stopping at a service station,' I told him quickly before Simone had a chance to speak further. 'Your sister has a hankering for caffeine and sugar.'

'Ah, and what our sweet, opinionated Simone wants, Princess Simone always gets.' Matt rubbed the bristles on his chin as he opened the door and stepped out into the car park.

I thought he looked endearingly rumpled in beige cargoes and a white open-necked shirt and I wished I had the right to put my arms round him, but Simone was already striding away to the cafeteria.

'Come on you two, we haven't got all day!'

We both scurried in her wake. 'Is she always like this?'

'I'm afraid so.' Matt found my hand and held it fast, and my heart soared as we trotted along behind her. 'It's the product of being super-intelligent. The rest of us are merely cloddish irritants in her eyes.'

'She's been enlightening me on the Creator and the workings of the universe.'

'Oh, God.'

I giggled. 'It actually makes quite a lot of sense.'

'First lesson of the universe,' he said with a wry grin, 'Simone is nearly always right.'

After the stop Matt took over the driving, while Simone sat in the back seat with her eyes closed. We kept our voices low and I told Matt about Calum's probable suicide attempt and the impending operation.

'How awful, I'm really sorry, Michaela. Why didn't you say something on Friday? Kevin told me Calum was in hospital, but I assumed it was something to do with his illness. When you said you were angry, I thought you meant about his situation in general.'

'I hadn't really taken it in myself,' I confessed. 'I suppose I was shocked and really disappointed with him. Abbey's angry with him too. I mean he obviously wasn't thinking about us when he did it, was he?'

'Maybe he wasn't thinking rationally at all. Everything must seem a bit overwhelming to him at the moment.'

We lapsed into silence for a while. I pictured the death card that had slid unbidden out of Abbey's pack and wondered if it could mean Calum was still in possible danger. I wanted to tell Matt about Abbey's predictions but wasn't sure if Simone was listening in. I was sure she'd have strong opinions on the subject of divination and wasn't sure I wanted to hear them.

When Matt eventually drew the car up at the guard house of what appeared to be an old army base I slunk down in my seat, suddenly nervous and wishing I'd never agreed to make this journey. There was nothing I could tell them that would shed any light on where I'd been, I was sure of it. And no one had bothered to mention that Subatron Industries was housed on property owned by the MOD. Simone climbed out of the car and showed the soldier guarding the gate a pass. She spoke rapidly to him and waved a hand in our direction while the guard consulted a clipboard. As soon as Simone was back in the car, he opened the barrier and waved us through.

After bypassing all the barracks and main buildings, at his sister's instruction Matt took the car gingerly down a track, which threaded through rows of conifer trees and eventually pulled up in front of an expensive-looking smoked glass and chrome building, which was well set back from the road.

'Here we are then,' Simone said cheerfully as Matt parked, 'my place of work.'

I sneaked a look at my watch and realised it was spot on eight o'clock. Simone appeared to have a sound judgement of travelling time as well as everything else, it seemed.

At the front door, I watched apprehensively as Simone

pressed various security numbers into an electronic pad, before passing through security with ease.

Entering a lift, we took the elevator to the third and topmost floor, stepping out behind Simone into a deserted corridor with closed doors leading off on both sides. She strode ahead of us and opened the fourth door on the right, standing back to let us pass through.

'My office.' I detected the pride in her voice and I couldn't say I blamed her. The office was wide and roomy, with soft-pile blue carpeting, a squishy-looking leather sofa along one wall. On one side of the room a long dark mirror filled the wall. I found myself wondering if it was a one-way mirror with people studying us from the other side. 'If you'll take a seat, I'll let my boss know you're here.'

As soon as she left the room I turned nervously to Matt. 'Have you been here before?'

He shook his head. 'From what Simone's told me in the past, they don't usually encourage visitors.'

We exchanged apprehensive glances, but Simone returned before we could say any more. She had a middle-aged man at her heels who smiled broadly at us and held out a welcoming hand.

'This is Dr Robert Jacobson, my boss,' Simone said.

'Welcome, welcome,' he beamed. 'As Simone says, I'm in charge of this facility. It was good of you to spare us a couple of hours of your time, Miss Anderson.' He was wearing checked trousers and an open-necked polo shirt and would have looked more at home on a golf course. He turned to Matt. 'Ah, Simone's brother, I assume? She's told me so much about you.'

He waved an effusive hand towards three hard-backed chairs. 'Do take a seat. Simone, could you organise some coffee and biscuits do you think?'

I felt her bridle at his words and despite the strange circumstances I suppressed a laugh. I wondered when she had last been asked to make coffee like a mere office assistant, and whether she even knew where the coffee machine was kept. She stalked off while Matt and I took two of the chairs and Dr Jacobson seated himself in Simone's swivel chair.

'Well, now, Miss Anderson – or may I call you Michaela? I hear you have been having rather a strange time of things lately?'

I nodded. 'Michaela will be fine. I assume Simone has told you my story?'

'Oh, yes, and her opinion as to what she thinks happened to you of course. Simone is an extraordinarily talented young lady, but she does have firm beliefs, doesn't she?'

I caught Matt's eye and he suppressed a grin.

'Might I also assume she told you about our work here at Subatron Industries and how crucial your contribution might be? Now,' he continued without waiting for an answer to either of his questions, 'I was rather hoping you would tell me exactly what happened to you from the moment you jumped out of that aeroplane, right to the present time. Just so you know, what you tell us will be recorded for posterity.'

Simone arrived back in the room with four coffees and a packet of custard creams, which she placed with exaggerated care onto the table in front of us. Dr Jacobson helped himself to one of the coffees and made a contented, clucking sound. 'We will have to add coffee-making to the endless list of your accomplishments, won't we, Dr Treguier?'

'Don't get used to it,' she replied shortly as she took the chair beside her brother. She turned to me. 'Where have we got to?'

'I'm about to tell Dr Jacobson what happened to me.'

332

She crossed her legs and leaned back as far as the hard chair would permit. 'Do go on.'

I started by recounting my jump from the plane to when I'd landed on the deserted airfield, my walking to the Royal Oak to when I'd called Matt and had my suspicions about having lost six years, to when it was confirmed.

'What about the cut on your hand?' Dr Jacobson asked, leaning forwards. 'I gather you snagged the side of your palm on a piece of metal when entering the aircraft and that it was still bleeding when Matt picked you up at the pub?'

I held up my hand, showing him the faint purple line that on Monday had been an open wound.

'Hmm, a pity we have nothing more than a photo to illustrate this.' The scientist turned my hand over in his and shook his head in apparent disappointment. 'That could very well have been the evidence we needed.'

'A photo?' I asked, snatching my hand away from him. 'How did you come by a photo of my hand? No one except those of us in the plane knew that I had cut myself.'

Dr Jacobson pushed the printout of a colour photograph across the desk. I stared in disbelief; it was me, with my hand held out to shield my face. A picture of Kevin, with his fancy mobile, sprang to my mind. I remembered him asking if he could film me. I'd held my hand out to stop the photo, hadn't I? Which meant . . . had Kevin taken the photo anyway? And if so, how had Dr Jacobson gained possession of it?

'One of the most trusted employees of Subatron Industries has been keeping a close eye on you since your return, Michaela.'

I glanced suspiciously at Matt, then remembered that it wasn't he who had been so attentive to Abbey and me, appearing at the drop of a hat to our aid whenever we needed him, asking questions, watching over us both . . .

My heart sank as I realised that nothing and no one was ever what they seemed. My shoulders slumped as I mumbled his name out loud, the disappointment heartfelt and undisguised.

'Kevin.'

Chapter Fifty-One

Disappointment turned quickly to anger and I rounded on Matt.

'Did you know Kevin was spying for these people? Did he make reports to you as well as them? I suppose you all had a good laugh at what I was going through, not to mention poor Abbey. My God, she trusted him – we both did.'

'It wasn't like that . . .'

'So you did know!' I pushed my chair back and glared at him. 'No wonder Kevin was the first person you called after I turned up on Monday evening. He was working for your sister's company all along.'

Matt sprang to his feet and tried to catch my hand but I swatted it away. 'I've just been a commodity, haven't I? A lab rat to be studied and watched for adverse reactions after having been caught in your hypothetical cosmic event! Did you think I might mysteriously disappear again, was that it? Were you told to keep a close watch on me, to see how I behaved?

'Isn't it bad enough this thing happened to me at all? Have you any idea what it was like to come back after one measly day to find my relationship with Calum in tatters, my job gone, my father dead without a chance to say goodbye, my mother in a home, Abbey grown up and Ingrid having a child I hadn't known existed, who was subsequently dumped at my door? And now I find I have been lied to by Kevin, who I believed liked me and Abbey and . . .' I swallowed as I faced Matt again. 'And you? How *could* you?'

'Michaela.' Matt tried to take my hand again but I shrugged him off.

'Leave me alone! You don't have to pretend you care about me anymore.'

'We'll give you few minutes,' Simone said from behind her brother. Glancing up I saw that her face had paled, her eyes filled with concern. I wondered uncharitably if we should add 'actress' to her many talents, as she took her boss's arm and towed him into the deserted corridor, closing the door behind them.

Matt and I stood facing each other. Struggling to bite back my tears and half choking on the words, I repeated wildly, 'How could you, Matt?'

'Please, Michaela.' He was shaking his head. 'It wasn't planned, I promise you.'

'No, of course not, how silly of me. You just happened to choose Kevin as the first person you told about me, after you collected me from the pub. He just happened to work for the company who had been studying the phenomenon of my disappearance, a company your sister just *happens* to work for too.' I rounded on him angrily. 'Do you think I was born yesterday? Do I look like a complete idiot to you?'

'Michaela let me explain.'

His voice was firm but there was a hint of desperation in it. I stood with my back to the glass window, my arms folded protectively across my chest. 'It had better be bloody good.'

He held out his hand again and this time when I ignored it I could see the indignation reflected in his eyes. 'Come and sit down.'

'I'd rather stand.'

'Please yourself.' He walked to the window and stood without touching me, looking fixedly out through the glass as if trying to get himself under control 'Michaela, I promise you that what has happened between us is genuine . . .'

'Pahh!' I interrupted him with a derisive snort. 'I'm not sure there's any point in this; I don't believe a word you say.'

He held up a hand in defeat and returned to perch on the corner of his sister's desk, facing me. 'Just hear me out, OK?'

I continued to glare at him.

'Everything happened as I told you on the day of the jump.' He fixed his eyes firmly on my stony face. 'It was true I had met Kevin the week before, but he had sworn me to secrecy. He wanted to be good at the static line jump to impress Ingrid . . .'

'I know all this . . .'

'Let me finish, Michaela, please.'

I nodded and he continued carefully, 'When your company arrived at the airfield for the charity jump it was business as usual. Only when I met you, something strange happened. I know I talked recently of love at first sight and I want you to believe that was all true.'

I raised an eyebrow but he ploughed on regardless.

'There was something about you, something I couldn't quite let go of. You know what happened with the police, the subsequent witch-hunt by the media and me having to hide your fleece jacket when my boss came in. Kevin offered to take the jacket away with him, he reckoned it was a decent repayment for me not having given him away over that extra lesson.'

He took a deep breath before continuing. 'As it happened, all the airfield personnel's lockers were searched by the police soon afterwards. If Kevin hadn't taken your fleece back to his car it would have been found in my possession and there would have been reasonable grounds to assume I was implicated in your disappearance.'

'So you owed him one.'

'Yes. And when Simone started getting all excited about the exact timing of your disappearance, wanting to know if there was anything of yours the police hadn't already taken, I told her about the fleece. She contacted Kevin, who by then was getting warnings from Wayfarers about his poor time keeping. He came here to Subatron Industries in person to give her the fleece, but they found nothing untoward on it or in it so I asked if I could keep it.'

Uncrossing my arms, I pulled out a leather swivel chair and sank onto it as Matt continued to perch on the corner of the desk.

'Why did you want my fleece?' I asked, watching his expression intently.

'I told you why. I know it sounds strange now, but I wanted something of yours to remind me that I'd met you.'

I wanted to believe him, but I couldn't let Matt off the hook that lightly. 'Tell me how Kevin came to work for Subatron Industries.'

'Once Kevin had made contact with Simone they found they could work together studying the circumstances of your disappearance. Because of his involvement in the case Kevin was able to glean first-hand accounts of where the police were with their investigations and pass it on to her. When Wayfarers sacked him, Simone found him employment in the IT department of Subatron Industries. Kevin continued to keep his finger on the pulse of your disappearance by running the Space Dog website and coming up with theories like the alien abduction thing to keep the case alive.'

'And then I turned up and fell into your lap, so to speak and you called Kevin, and he reported back to Simone?'

Matt nodded. 'Kevin was asked to keep an eye on you.'

I contemplated him minutely from the other side of the desk. 'Were you involved with Subatron Industries too?'

'Hell no, I'm a pilot, Michaela. Flying is what I know best; it's what I do.'

'And what we had together?'

Matt rose to his feet and came round the desk. This time when he put out his hand, I placed my shaking fingers into his and looked up into his face.

'I love you. I have loved you since the moment I first set eyes on you.' He pulled me to him and I allowed him to fold me into his steady embrace. Burying my head against his chest, I let the tears come and he held me against him while I sobbed for all that I had lost and for what Matt and I might never have together. But mostly they were tears of happiness that he had loved me enough to wait six long years for me.

A while later, Matt held me away from him and brushed my tears from my cheeks with his thumbs. 'Do you feel up to talking to Simone and her boss again?' He kissed the tip of my nose.

I sniffed, nodded and wiped the rest of my face with the heel of my hand while Matt went to the door and called Dr Jacobson and Simone in from the corridor.

Dr Jacobson studiously avoided looking directly at either Matt or me as he made his way to the safety of the swivel chair. Simone however came over, draped an arm lightly round my shoulders, and gave me a brief squeeze.

'You've got one of the good guys in Matt, Michaela. Don't throw him away.'

'I'm beginning to realise it,' I told her with a wan smile.

'Right, to business,' Dr Jacobson announced rather too heartily. 'What else can you tell us about what happened to you on the 15th April 2002? Any little thing that might seem insignificant could be important. And I'd like you to describe exactly where you think you were during the strange wind you mentioned. Were there any visual clues as to your whereabouts, unusual scents or sounds?'

An hour later the four of us were back in Simone's office after various tests including a full body scan, a calculation of my body mass index, swabs from inside my mouth and a phial of blood from my arm, both of which were going to be tested for any abnormalities.

Once back in the office, Dr Jacobson asked yet more questions, made notes and kept the tape recorder running in front of me.

'What of the police investigation?' he asked at last, sitting back from the desk and rolling his shoulders as if they had stiffened while he'd sat hunched and attentive. 'What was it exactly that made them decide to research the area around the airfield after all that time?'

'I think it was the pollen,' I said, stretching my legs out in front of me to gaze at my feet.

The scientist fell very still and I could feel the sudden tension emanating from both him and Simone. 'What pollen?'

'The police forensics experts found some grass pollen on my socks.' I looked from Dr Jacobson and anxiously round to Simone and Matt who had until that moment been sitting in a relaxed fashion alongside me. Simone now sat bolt upright on the edge of her seat and even Matt was looking interested. 'They said it was a conundrum because that particular species of grass was thought to have become extinct in 2004.'

Dr Jacobson was rather red in the face as he leaned towards me. 'You might have mentioned this earlier, Michaela. Tell me, do the police have samples of that pollen?'

'I think so, I mean they told me they had found the stuff

and that it was really fresh, as if it had been growing only a day or so before they took the sample.'

Dr Jacobson pushed the chair back and scrambled to his feet giving me an exasperated look. 'Simone, we have some urgent strings to pull. I want that sample in our lab by the end of the day, do you understand?'

'Yes, sir.'

He turned to me, swallowing his annoyance. 'Is there any other little gem you would like to share with us?'

'Well, there is also the blood on the parachute.'

'Tell us.' He sank onto the chair again and leaned towards me expectantly.

I blushed, realising that what I was about to say was going to cause a second sensation. 'When you mentioned the cut on my hand earlier, I was so angry about Kevin and Matt . . .'

'It doesn't matter now.' Simone had paused at the door ready to leap to her boss's bidding. 'What about the cut, Michaela?'

I found I was nervous about giving my reply and flicked an anxious glance in Dr Jacobson's direction. 'When I gathered up the parachute on landing so it wouldn't blow away, blood from the cut on my hand must have got smeared onto it. DI Smith says they've found the parachute in the pit under the vagrant's caravan. The thing is, like the pollen, the blood was fresh, only a day or so old. That's why they are convinced I was held down there and only recently escaped. As far as the police are concerned it's the only scenario that makes sense, which it does – if you're thinking one dimensionally, of course.'

Chapter Fifty-Two

Dr Jacobson stared at me. 'The blood and the pollen both being fresh after all this time may very well be enough hard evidence to tip the scales in our favour.' He straightened up, all business now that he had what he wanted. 'OK, Matt, I want you to take Michaela back to her home and keep an eye on her, do you understand?'

'I don't think her boyfriend would be very happy to have me there.'

'Very well, contact Kevin and ask him to keep a twenty-four hour watch.' He turned his attention to me again. 'Do not talk to the media, do not tell anyone the details of your visit here today.' He began to hurry from the room but turned in the doorway. 'And, Michaela . . . well done.'

The journey back to Surrey seemed to pass in half the time it had taken to get up to Norfolk. Matt drove his sister's car with careful precision and I found myself wondering what it must be like to be a passenger in a plane he was piloting. Simone, I was sure, would have been furnished with another car by Subatron Industries and we tried to keep our thoughts off what she was up to.

Matt and I spent the journey revelling in one another's company, as if neither of us had a care in the world. We both knew these three hours alone together were precious so we concentrated on the here and now, deciding to leave the future where it lay as yet undisturbed by the passage of time. I rested my hand on his knee and every so often he would lay his on top of mine and the chemistry would shoot through us. We talked non-stop, sharing our hopes and dreams, our loves and joys. At one point Matt asked me what I would have liked to do with my life, if the decision had been solely down to me.

'I'd like to have a family eventually,' I mused, 'but first I'd travel. I've always wanted to see the world. And I'd have adventures . . . like canoeing up the Amazon and climbing Mount Kilimanjaro, and skiing in the Rockies and maybe swimming in one of Iceland's hot springs.'

'Those things are right at the top of my list too,' he murmured, 'how about white water rafting down the Grand Canyon and scuba diving off the Maldives?'

'Definitely; and what about the simple pleasures like sitting toasting crumpets in front of an open fire in a cottage in Wales, or walking along Hadrian's Wall on a warm spring day?'

'And making love on a white sandy beach while the waves lap at our feet.'

I sighed not wanting to break the spell, but both of us knew those things would have to wait. They were pipe dreams and I had made a promise to Calum. Matt echoed the sigh and we lapsed into a brief companionable silence knowing that even if things went wrong with Calum, I would still have Abbey and Tristan in my life and my mother to support.

'We'd have to be filthy rich to do all those wonderful things anyway,' Matt pointed out.

'Nah,' I said, embracing the fantasy again, 'we could do it on a shoe string. I could work nights as an exotic dancer and you could do shifts as a night watchman and we'd meet in the mornings at breakfast time, to make love, and count our earnings before going to our day jobs.'

'In that order, I hope.'

'Definitely,' I smiled happily at him. 'And both would far exceed what we could ever have dared hope for.'

We turned off the main road and stopped for a late lunch where we lingered over our after-meal coffees and tried to pretend that our paths were not about to branch in two different directions.

Once back in the car we fell silent and suddenly we were turning into the top of the road where I lived. The bubble burst and all my responsibilities crowded back onto my shoulders. The press turned in our direction to see who was arriving and the crowd began to surge in our direction.

'Damn, we should have gone round to the back. Can you reverse and go the other way?'

'Too late,' Matt groaned. 'They'll be right round the car by the time I've turned.'

'I'd better hop out and draw them off before they recognise you too.' I opened the door and stepped out to face the advancing scrum. 'Go, quickly . . . and Matt.'

'Yes?'

I wanted to tell him I loved him, but it seemed so pointless. 'You'd better go.'

By facing the press and taking up their attention, I gave Matt a few precious minutes to slip away, hopefully unrecognised. Dr Jacobson's warning not to talk to the media rang in my ears as cameras flashed and a microphone was thrust under my nose.

'Sally Vale from World News,' the woman introduced herself quickly. 'Can you comment on recent reports that you were held by a group of Satanic worshippers, Michaela?'

I shook my head as I tried to slide past her. 'I'm sorry I have nothing to say to you.'

'Was your stepdaughter involved in your disappearance? She has been reported as saying you were forced to participate in black magic rituals in a pit near the airfield where you were last seen . . .'

'It's all nonsense,' I said as I shuffled closer to the sanctuary of the garden gate. 'No such things happened.'

'Over here, Miss Anderson,' called a voice and as I turned a camera flashed.

'What are your feelings on the breaking news that the police have released the suspect Danny Hill from custody?' Sally Vale was still hard on my heels as I inched closer to safety. I stopped dead and turned to stare at her.

'Danny Hill?' I had heard that name before. It was the vagrant DI Smith had been holding for my kidnap.

Sensing a story from my surprised expression the reporters pressed closer. 'We are receiving reports that the chief suspect in your case has been released without charge; what are your feelings about his early release?'

'That was quick,' I murmured as I pushed at the gate, which opened with its usual familiar creak. Stepping through, I closed it firmly between me and my pursuers.

Once indoors I stood for a moment, my back pressed to the front door and took several deep breaths.

'Kaela!'

I looked up as Calum rounded the corner into the hall, where he stood contemplating me anxiously.

'I thought I heard the front door. How did it go?' He advanced down the passage and took my hand, towing me back towards the sitting room, his eyes searching mine in the slightly brighter light. 'I missed you.'

'It was a strange day,' I confessed as I peeled off my fleece jacket. 'The place in Norfolk is very hush-hush and a bit spooky. There was hardly anyone there, it being a Sunday, I suppose.'

'Were you able to help them in any way?'

'I think so. I told them about that pollen the police found on my socks and they got very excited. What with that and the blood on the parachute . . .'

'Hang on a minute. What blood is this? Not yours, I hope?'

I tried to remember exactly what I'd told him when I'd picked him up from hospital and realised I might not have mentioned the blood.

'I cut my hand when I climbed into the aeroplane,' I explained, holding up my hand. 'When I landed I rolled the parachute up to prevent it from blowing away, and this old tramp must have found it and hidden it.'

'So why were these scientists so excited about it?' Although he was still interested I could see he was tiring.

'Because the blood samples, like the pollen, were fresh, as if they'd only been produced a day or so ago.'

'Which surely indicates that you were held by the vagrant until a few days ago?'

I shook my head. 'That could be true of the blood I suppose, but definitely not the pollen, because the particular type of grass that pollen comes from has been extinct since 2004.'

He shook his head as if it was all beyond him.

'Where are Abbey and Tristan?' I asked, realising that the house was far too quiet.

'Kevin came by and took them both out for a pizza.'

Kevin. I wasn't sure exactly how I felt about him right now. I had thought he was our friend and now it turned out we were merely a job to him.

'How long have they been gone?'

Calum glanced at his watch. 'They should be back at any time.'

I realised there wasn't much I could do about Kevin until the trio returned. 'I have to ring DI Smith and see what is really going on at the station. Is there anything you need before I make the call?'

Calum shook his head and closed his eyes. 'I'll just rest here,' he said, 'you go ahead.'

My call was put through to DI Smith who informed me none too happily that she had been obliged to give up her Sunday to deal with the present crisis.

'We had him, Michaela.' I could hear the anger in her voice tinged with a hint of apology. 'We were about to charge him, when our chief intervened and told us we had to hand the entire investigation over to another department. They've thrown out all charges against our suspect Danny Hill, and he is now free to return to petty crime and vagrancy.'

'That means new evidence must exist which shows he was innocent,' I pointed out. 'I wasn't able to make a positive identification of him, after all.'

'Miss Anderson,' DI Smith's voice took on a firmer tone. 'In my opinion, there is probably an unseen political agenda or a stab for extra funding somewhere behind this. I don't know why the powers that be are trying so hard to get Danny Hill off the hook, but I have been in this job for many years and I know a true confession when I hear one. Think what you must, but I will go to my grave knowing that we had the right man in our grasp.'

Chapter Fifty-Three

I didn't have time to dwell on the possibility that I had somehow been duped by a huge organisation because the front door opened and Tristan came trotting in with a helium balloon held aloft, all smiles with streaks of chocolate ice-cream running down his face.

Abbey and Kevin appeared in the sitting room doorway a moment later, laughing and joking companionably like old friends. I knew that verbal sparring had indicated a liking for one another, but Abbey was vulnerable and searching for love and acceptance. In Kevin she had found both in abundance. Hadn't he come running every time she had asked it of him? I hoped and prayed that watching us had been more than a job to him. If not, Abbey was going to be badly let down.

Ignoring Kevin, I gave Abbey a smile and stooped to wipe Tristan's mouth with a tissue. 'Hi! Have you had a good time?'

Tristan nodded. 'Kevin bought us really big pizzas. I ate loads and I got this free toy.' He rummaged in the pocket of his trousers and brought out a cheap, plastic fortune-telling spinning top. 'I'm going to be rich one day.'

I raised my eyes to Kevin's and he had the decency to look away. He must know by now that I knew.

I realised Calum was watching his daughter too. At first I thought he was going to object when Abbey got out her cards, but he didn't say anything; he simply sat and watched her quietly. As I looked at Tristan bounding around the room, I blessed the decision I'd made to keep Ingrid's child at my side. If there was one single thing I could alter, it was this relationship – or lack of it – between Calum and his daughter. And with the operation scheduled for tomorrow morning, there wasn't much time to change things.

Desperate to get Calum to put things right with his daughter, I motioned to Calum to join me in the kitchen for a cup of tea. He seemed relieved and, as if at a complete loss, he settled on one of the kitchen chairs while I rummaged in the cupboard for cups.

'Have you thought any more about talking to Abbey?' I dropped tea bags into the pot and went to the fridge for milk.

He shook his head. 'I thought about it, but I think she's avoiding me. When she got up this morning she stayed in her room until Ingrid's boy began to cry, then made them both something to eat and took him up to your room to sew, or whatever it is she does up there. I was going to talk to her but your friend Kevin turned up to take them out and the opportunity was gone.'

'Calum, she's going to feel terrible if you go for this operation tomorrow without having made your peace with her.' I poured boiling water into the pot. 'It's often the things you don't do that you regret the most.'

'You saw her with Kevin.' He wiped a hand across his face. 'And he's old enough to be her father. I'm not what she wants any more.'

'*You* are her father, Calum. No one can replace that. And anyway Kevin is only eight years older than her. They have their strange beliefs in common; he's a good friend and she needs that right now. It's you she needs acceptance and unconditional love from.' I placed a cup of tea in front of

349

him and took a seat. 'Think of her Calum, not yourself for a change.'

'I have got something I'd like to give her, like you suggested,' Calum muttered hesitantly. He fiddled with the handle of the cup. 'It's something I should have shared with her long ago.' He looked up at me fearfully. 'Do you think it's too late?'

I reached out a hand and placed it on top of his. 'While there's breath in your body, it's never too late.'

'I'll have a chat with her when Kevin leaves,' he promised, nodding, 'yes, I'll . . .'

But he got no further because Abbey let out an anguished scream. Calum and I leapt to our feet and hurried through to the other room. Abbey was curled on the couch with her face in her hands; the floor covered in scattered tarot cards. Kevin was trying to console her by patting her awkwardly on her arm, but she continued to sob wretchedly.

'What's happened?' I asked him.

'It's that bloody death card,' Kevin explained quietly. 'No matter how many times Abbey shuffles and cuts the cards, it keeps appearing.'

'It must be a coincidence.' I bent to pick up the dropped cards but Abbey whimpered for me to leave them where they were.

'I thought when it first fell from the pack that it was indicating the changes we're all experiencing, you know with you back, and Dad ill, and Tristan and everything.' Her tears forged dark tracts in her eyeliner as she looked up at me with huge, fear-filled eyes. 'But now I believe someone is going to die, Kaela.' Her eyes flickered uncertainly towards her father. 'It's going to happen, whether we like it or not.'

Predictably it was hard to settle Tristan for sleep that evening. I phoned the home and spoke to my mother, telling her I'd have to postpone my visit until the morning because I couldn't leave Tristan. When she asked about Tristan I realised I hadn't mentioned him to her previously and promised to explain it all tomorrow.

When Tristan eventually fell asleep, I transferred him to his nest under the kitchen table, where he wriggled into a comfortable position, with his well-chewed cloth popped into his mouth.

My earlier hopes that Abbey's distress would be the catalyst for Calum to speak to his daughter were shattered when Calum stalked up to his room after the announcement about the death card.

'I hate him.' Abbey stood up from the couch, kicked at the fallen cards and stormed out of the house. Kevin dithered in her wake, looking anxiously at me and then towards the front door, which was still reverberating from the hearty slam she'd given it.

'Don't worry about your brief to look after me,' I told him. 'Go after her.'

It seemed Kevin needed no second telling, and that at least gave me hope that his feelings for Abbey were genuine. I turned to find Tristan standing in the kitchen doorway watching the proceedings in white-faced alarm. He had obviously been woken by the slamming of the door.

'Come and watch the TV for a few more minutes,' I told Tristan, switching the TV set on. 'I'm going up to see Calum and when I come down you'll be nice and tired again and can try to go back to sleep.'

Calum was sitting on the edge of his bed staring into space when I entered his room. 'The cards were talking about me, weren't they?' he said bleakly.

Perching next to him, I prised one of his clammy hands from his knees. 'Since when did you ever believe anything the cards foretold?' I asked him, surprised by the fear I could see in his eyes. 'Come on, Calum, the operation will be a complete success and you'll be a new man again in a week or two.'

'I know it's unmanly and irrational to admit to being so scared, Kaela, but I don't want to end up reliant on a life-support system, with bags and tubes running out of me.'

'That's unlikely to happen. Anaesthetics are really good these days and the surgeon probably performs this kind of operation routinely. To them tomorrow's operation is just another simple procedure, which will be over before you know it.'

'I hope you're right.' He raised his worried eyes to mine. 'Where's Abbey? She's upset – I ought to go to her.'

I shook my head. 'She's run off, but Kevin has gone after her. I don't suppose she'll get very far.'

'Oh, God,' he murmured. 'I've made a mess of everything, haven't I?'

We sat side by side for a while and then I suggested we go down to keep Tristan company. 'He's had rather a disturbing time since Ingrid left him,' I commented as he slowly got to his feet. 'The poor child will think all families are crazy.'

'I was meaning to talk to you about him,' Calum whispered as we headed down the stairs. 'I don't think we have any right to keep the boy here. I mean he's not related to any of us, is he? I was thinking we should contact social services.'

'Don't you dare,' I cautioned, stopping dead in front of him, so he almost tripped over me down the stairs. 'I promised Ingrid I'd take care of him, and I will.'

'You did nothing of the sort,' he pointed out. 'She just dumped him on us and left.'

'I want to give him a proper life,' I insisted, realising that I actually meant it. 'The poor little boy has had a rough start.'

'Abbey has looked after him more than you have,' he argued. 'You've hardly been here.'

'Things have been difficult, I know. I haven't even been to see Mum this weekend. But things will settle down. And anyway,' I added. 'Looking after Tristan has been good for Abbey, too. It's made her think of someone other than herself.'

'Well,' he relented slightly, acknowledging the truth of this. 'Maybe we'll see how it goes.'

Tristan gave us a mournful gaze as we entered the sitting room.

'I want Abbey,' he said miserably.

I pulled him onto my lap and Calum softened enough to reach out and pat him. 'She'll be back soon. Abbey will want to be here in the morning to see me off.' Calum turned anxious eyes to me. 'She will, won't she, Kaela?'

I gave a great sigh as I hugged the boy to me. 'I sincerely hope so.'

Chapter Fifty-Four

In the morning Abbey still wasn't back. I tried phoning Kevin but there was no answer, and I was determined not to let my fears flood my mind. She was almost seventeen, I reminded myself for the umpteenth time and Kevin was probably looking after her. Wrapped in an old dressing gown of Calum's I pottered round the kitchen making tea and laying out breakfast things, while Tristan watched me from his bed under the table.

Realising that Tristan hadn't asked for his mother for some time I marvelled at the child's resilience.

'We're going to take Calum to the hospital,' I told him as I finished my cup of tea. 'And then you can come with me, while I visit my mum who's a nice lady called Susan.'

Pushing back my chair, I held out my arms to Tristan who obligingly clambered onto my lap. As I held his slight form I realised I was no longer thinking of him as a burden thrust upon me by my one time friend, but as someone I actually cared about. I gave him a hug, which he dutifully returned and kissed the top of his head as he slid to the floor to retrieve his comforter cloth, which had come loose from his grasp.

'Go and start getting yourself washed and dressed, Tristan,' I told him. 'We have a busy day ahead of us.'

Calum was sitting on the edge of his bed, clad in clean

chinos and a blue polo shirt when I knocked and entered his room to see how he was getting on. His freshly washed hair was still damp and he smelled of shampoo and shower gel. Perching beside him, I slid an arm round his waist.

'You'll be alright, you know.'

He turned agonised, sunken eyes to me, and I wondered if he'd had any sleep. 'Is Abbey back?'

I shook my head. 'She didn't come in last night, but I'm sure Kevin will have found her.'

'I should have talked to her. I need her to know I love her; she is my little girl.'

'Oh, Calum,' I sighed.

'I've got this for her.' He opened his hands to reveal a small blue, leather box.

'What is it?'

He handed it to me silently and I opened the box slowly, pushing the lid back on tiny hinges. Nestled against folds of creamy satin was a silver locket, slightly tarnished with age and engraved with two beautifully entwined letters; G & C. Grace and Calum, I realised.

'Go on, you can open it.'

Removing the locket from its case and pressing the clasp back with trembling fingers, I opened the locket to find two black and white photographs on the open locket staring back at me. One was a young looking Calum, with his shock of dark hair, and the other was a pretty girl, with lighter hair and delicate features.

'Grace,' I breathed.

'I couldn't throw it away. I was going to give it to Abbey when she was eighteen, but now . . .'

I remembered Abbey's tearful protests that her father had kept nothing that belonged to her mother.

'It's beautiful.'

'Will you give it to her for me? If anything happens today and I can't give it to her myself . . .' his voice trailed off and I could feel his body actually trembling next to mine.

'You can give it to her when you wake up from the operation,' I told him firmly. 'Yes, yes,' I assured him in response to his pleading expression. 'If anything should go wrong, I will make sure she gets it.' I found his hand and squeezed it. 'But you're going to be fine, Calum. I'll find Abbey and when you're back on the ward this afternoon, we'll be there waiting for you.'

While we were waiting for Calum to go to the operating theatre, I made small Lego vehicles with Tristan which I'd had the foresight to bring with us. The ward was light and bright, with a faint smell of antiseptic and stale food. It had five other beds in it, all occupied by men of varying ages. Calum sat stiffly under the smooth covers clad in a hospital gown, with his newly fixed plastic name tag round his wrist, while nurses came and made notes on his chart.

Every time the door opened into the ward, he glanced up and I knew he was hoping Abbey would come to see him. Kevin still wasn't answering his phone and I was becoming increasingly uneasy about what might have become of her.

Come on, Abbey, I thought time and time again. Where the devil are you?

When two porters eventually came to transfer Calum to the operating theatre he turned anguished eyes on me, but I nodded encouragingly and smiled. He held a shaking hand out to clasp mine and motioned for the porters to wait a moment. Bending my head close to his, he whispered, 'I'm sorry for everything I've put you through. I do care about you, Kaela. And don't forget to tell Abbey that I love her.'

I felt my eyes mist over but kept my tears in check and

tried to give him an encouraging smile. 'You can tell her yourself. I'll see you later, OK?'

And then he was gone, whisked away on the squeaky-wheeled trolley, leaving Tristan and me to collect our belongings and head out of the ward into the late October sunshine.

Acorn Lodge was a hive of activity this Monday morning. Two men wearing white overalls were up a ladder fixing a lighting fixture in the front porch and the front door was open, revealing a girl in a pink nylon tabard, vacuuming the reception area. I knocked on Dr Hewitt's partially open office door and found him poring over some ledgers with his secretary. He looked up and smiled when he saw me.

'Aah, Miss Anderson. Your mother is expecting you.' He raised an eyebrow and glanced questioningly at the child by my side.

'This is Tristan. I'm looking after him for a friend. How is my mother this morning?'

'Susan is vastly improved. Now you are back and her depression has begun to lift, we have been able to reduce her medication still further over the weekend. She has a couple of visitors with her already, but she is looking forward to her morning out with you.'

'Visitors?'

'Abigail is here with a young man.'

My heart soared. So this is where Abbey was hiding; I should have guessed. I remembered that she and Calum had made a habit of popping in to see my mother over the years when anything had been troubling them.

'Come on, Tristan,' I grinned. 'Come and meet my mum, Susan. And Abbey is here too!'

With Tristan at my heels I made my way to Mum's door,

which was standing ajar and I could see Kevin sitting in Mum's armchair and Abbey perched on the dressing table stool. Mum was sitting on the bed, bent double, pulling on her trainers.

Two pairs of eyes met mine as I walked into the room. Kevin looked embarrassed and so he should, I thought. But Abbey's eyes held a different story. There was apology, mixed with fear in her eyes, and I knew she was having second thoughts about having let her father go for his operation without having made peace with him.

Mum seemed to sense Abbey and Kevin's distraction and I watched as her eyes found mine and lit into a joyful smile. She stood up as I reached her, and threw her arms round me, drawing me into a tight hug.

'Michaela,' she murmured into my hair, 'my beautiful, darling daughter.' She pushed me back and held me at arm's length, studying me minutely as if memorising my every feature. 'Each time I see you I allow myself to believe a little deeper, that you are really back and not an illusion.'

'I'm sorry I didn't come to see you over the weekend.' I shot Kevin an accusing glance. 'I've found out all sorts of mysterious things about my disappearance, people I thought I knew and trusted have turned out to be something quite different altogether.'

'Michaela,' Kevin began apologetically. 'I want you to know . . .'

But I didn't want to hear it, I turned instead to my mother and pointed to Tristan who was hovering awkwardly in the doorway. 'This is my friend Ingrid's child, Tristan. You remember Ingrid, don't you?'

My mother let out an anguished squeal and clutched her hand to her mouth. 'How could you bring him here Michaela?' she gasped. 'How *could* you?'

358

Mum dropped down onto the edge of the bed, where she rocked back and forth ever so slightly, her eyes fixed on Tristan, whose bottom lip began to tremble. He let out a small sob and now thoroughly alarmed, I signalled to Abbey who sprang to her feet and gathering Tristan in her arms, carried him swiftly from the room.

'What on earth is the matter?' I asked my mother, sitting myself next to her and putting an arm round her quaking shoulders. 'He's just a little boy.'

'He's not just a little boy,' she croaked. 'You said yourself that not everyone is what they seem. No one can be trusted, Michaela, not even those closest to you. That child – is your own half brother.'

Chapter Fifty-Five

At first I thought my mother was having a relapse and was simply confusing Tristan with someone else, but as she continued to moan and talk about my father's betrayal, everything suddenly became alarmingly clear.

'She started coming round to see us.' My mother groaned as if she were in physical pain. 'Ingrid seemed such a sorry little thing, all blonde curls and big, blue eyes. We took her under our wing and she did things for us too, like helping to organise the "missing" leaflets and handing them out, and eventually she all but moved in with us.'

My mother turned to me and took my hand, squeezing it repetitively in hers. 'I liked her, but she was never a replacement for you, Michaela. No one could ever have stepped into your shoes, but looking back I can see how hard that girl tried to do so.'

I remembered Ingrid telling me how much she'd wanted what she'd thought I had – respectable parents living in a decent area.

'Leonard was beguiled by her.' It seemed that now the flood gates were open, my mother couldn't stop until the whole story was told. 'I didn't realise until it was too late, because he was never the same after you went missing. He couldn't rest at night and he stayed away from me when he heard me crying myself to sleep. He said he simply couldn't bear to hear my pain.'

'I'm so sorry, Mum.'

'It wasn't your fault, my darling. I know you would never have done that on purpose, but in a way that made it more difficult, because we had to wonder if something unthinkable had happened to you.'

'I can't believe Dad did this.'

My mother gave me a sad little smile. 'It wasn't so much what he did to me, but what he took for himself. He said he wanted some happiness back in his life and Ingrid made him happy. I know he was a handsome man and could be a bit of a flirt, but I trusted your father implicitly. I never questioned where he was or why he and Ingrid were sometimes gone so long, canvassing or leafleting together.'

'How did you find out?'

'He told me eventually. Almost a year and a half after you'd gone missing, Ingrid found out she was pregnant. I think she did it on purpose to keep Leonard in line because he said afterwards that it was almost over between them by then. He'd begun to see through her conniving ways and wanted to stop seeing her. She had other ideas. She told him she was pregnant and gave him an ultimatum; he was to tell me he was the father of her baby, or she would tell me herself.'

My mother had stopped squeezing my hand and a far away look had come into her eye. 'He told me that last morning. Ingrid was six months pregnant and apparently it couldn't wait any longer. My grief had already left me a shadow of my former self and that was the very last straw. I was devastated, Michaela. I told him to get out and never to come back, but I didn't mean it. I would have had him back, no matter what he had done.' She gave a heaving sob and buried her face in my shoulder. 'He thought he'd lost me and he left the house with my hurt and anger ringing in his ears, and that morning he suffered a massive heart attack . . .'

I could barely breathe my chest felt so tight. I wanted to shout at the world, to stamp and cry, but I just sat there and held my mother. It hadn't been my loss alone that had sent her toppling over the edge, or even the unthinkable act of my father's betrayal, it was because she had never had a chance to tell him, even after his infidelity, that she loved him.

'Oh, Mum,' I whispered as we clung to one another, locked in our mutual grief. 'How terrible for you; I'm so very sorry.' The words Ingrid had thrown at me rang in my ears, 'All men, Kaela, and I do mean *all* men . . . are complete bastards.' I had just never for a single moment imagined that bitter and sweeping statement could include my own father.

My mother dried her eyes on a tissue that Kevin who was standing in the corner, handed to her. Abbey, who had crept back into the room, and who presumably had heard everything, was sitting wide eyed, rocking Tristan on her lap. I hoped the boy had had no notion of what was being said. The boy, I thought in amazement – my brother.

'If this has taught me one thing,' my mother was saying in a choked voice, 'it is never, ever to leave things unsaid. Life is too short and much too precarious to remain proud or angry. I never had a chance to say goodbye to Leonard and I will never forgive myself for that.'

I glanced at Abbey and saw that she was ashen-faced and not far from tears. She had allowed her father to go into an operation without telling him she loved him.

'Maybe you could take Tristan home,' I cautioned Abbey, glancing anxiously at my mother again. 'Will you meet me at the hospital later?'

Abbey sniffed and nodded. 'When will he be out of surgery?'

'They told me to go back after midday, when he was out of recovery. He should be awake again by then and up to having a couple of visitors.' I turned to Mum. 'Do you feel up to coming to the solicitor with me first?' I asked her gently. 'I have an appointment with him in half an hour and we can just make it if we hurry.'

'Yes, of course. I don't know what Mr Brent was thinking of, making you wait for proof of your identity like that.'

'I gather he was a friend of Dad's,' I murmured. 'I think he was trying to make me suffer for what I put you and Dad through.'

'Well, I'll vouch for you today and we can reopen your bank accounts and sort everything out for you.'

'Thanks, Mum, that will be a weight off my mind.'

I called to Abbey who was walking Tristan to the door. 'If all goes well, I'll be at the hospital around twelve thirty.'

She nodded again as she and Kevin disappeared out into the corridor.

'I'd like to come with you to see Calum.' My mother was pulling on a jacket. 'He came to visit me in here, and we had long talks about just about everything. He became a good friend and I'd like to repay the compliment, if I may.'

'Of course, I'm sure he'd like that.'

It was actually closer to one o'clock by the time Mum and I stepped out of the lift and made our way along the corridor to the men's surgical ward. We had stopped off after the brief, but productive meeting with Mr Archibald Brent, to have a coffee and buy a few items of clothing for both of us.

Despite the time constraint it had been like old times, browsing through the women's clothing section, though after my mother's enforced incarceration and my six-year absence, we found fashions had changed and ended up giggling like a couple of schoolgirls over the latest accessories, and buying similar outfits to be on the safe side. It was wonderful having my mother back again; she had always doubled as a friend and confidante, and I hadn't realised how much I'd missed her wise counsel in the last week. On the way to the hospital I found myself telling her about Matt. 'I feel really deeply for Matt, but I know I should stay with Calum, especially as he is so ill.'

'Your father and I were never quite sure about Matt's possible involvement in your disappearance. I am pleased he's innocent and I can see why you are attracted to him; but are you sure it's not Calum you want to spend the rest of your life with?'

I was left pondering over this, as we entered the surgical ward. As we approached the reception desk, the ward sister seemed to square her shoulders. It was as if a veil came down over her face as she recognised me.

'Miss Anderson. Would you come along with me to a side room please? The doctor has been waiting to see you.'

'What's happened? Is Calum alright?'

'Please, the doctor will answer all your questions.' She opened a door onto a small carpeted room which had armchairs lining the walls. Abbey was sitting in one of the chairs looking pale and wan and I hurried to her as she rose to greet me.

'Kaela, there's something wrong with Dad, but they wouldn't talk to me until you arrived,' she blurted. 'They won't let me see him.'

I glanced uneasily at my mother, then back to Abbey. 'Where's Tristan?'

'Kevin's at our place keeping an eye on him. We bought more Lego and they're making a pirate ship or something.' She held out a hand to Susan. 'I'm glad you're here too.'

We turned as the door opened behind us and a doctor came in. He glanced round at us and his eyes settled on me. 'Miss Anderson?'

'Yes,' I replied. 'And these are other family members, Abbey and Susan.'

'I'm Dr Gordon, the surgeon who performed Mr Sinclair's operation. Please, sit down.'

We gingerly took seats and waited impatiently for him to go on.

'Is Calum alright?' I asked again.

'The operation to remove the prostate went well. We were pleased that it was still intact and that there was no evidence that the cancer had spread.' He removed his hat and twisted it in his hands as he continued. 'However, I'm afraid there was a problem during the operation, which no one could have foreseen.'

Susan's hand flew to her mouth and Abbey's eyes grew round and fearful.

'Mr Sinclair had a violent reaction to the anaesthetic. I'm very sorry to have to tell you that we have been unable to bring him back to consciousness. He is at present in a state of coma.'

I thought of Calum's earlier apparently unfounded fears. This is what he had been so afraid of. Was it possible he had known that this supposedly simple operation was going to result in this? 'Where is he?' I managed shakily. 'Can we see him?'

'We have moved him to another room where he is receiving the best possible care. You have to understand that some-times the body can repair itself. A coma is an unpredictable state that could last days, weeks or possibly months. His breathing is steady and his pulse stable, so at present he isn't on a ventilator. If there is no change by tomorrow morning, the medical team will discuss the best options for an ongoing treatment plan.'

Abbey was crying openly and I went to her, her trembling hand encompassing my own. My mother took my other hand, and linked together the three of us followed the doctor to see Calum.

The room was in semi darkness, with a curtain drawn across the only window, and a bed in the centre surrounded by a blood pressure monitor and a saline drip. Calum had an oxygen mask over his mouth and nose, and his chest rose and fell gently as if he was in a deep and dreamless sleep.

The nurse brought in a third chair and Abbey, Susan and I sank wordlessly down in a circle round him, willing him to wake up. All I could think of were the words Calum had uttered as we'd sat on his bed together this morning, 'I'm afraid, Kaela. I don't want to end up on some life-support system with bags and tubes running out of me.' It seemed that fate had dealt him the cruellest of blows.

Chapter Fifty-Six

Abbey got to her feet, kissed her father's brow and whispered, 'I'm so sorry, Dad. I wish I had come to see you this morning. If I could undo the fact that I wasn't there for you, I would, a hundred times over.'

Remembering the locket, I got to my leaden-feeling feet and went to ask the nurse about Calum's possessions. She handed me a plastic bag – the sort that bereaved widows were handed in films with their loved one's effects within. The sight of it made me feel cold inside.

Finding the locket I handed the rest of his belongings back to the nurse and returned silently to Calum's side room. I had the idea of fulfilling his final wish of giving the locket to Abbey, but the sight of the two heads bowed together over the bed, held me back. Mum, ever the faithful believer, was clasping her hands tightly and whispering prayers to her God. Abbey had her tarot cards in her hands and was shuffling them rhythmically and mouthing incantations to the major arcane. I thought of all that Simone had told me about the part of our brains designed only for prayer and meditation and about our true creator, residing somewhere in an unseen dimension. Perhaps that was where Calum's consciousness was now, I thought with a faint smile; flying with atoms and Gravitons in a place we could neither see nor understand.

Taking my seat, I was struck by the fact that while they believed in such different things, they were still united in their love for Calum. Perhaps that unity was all that was required, I thought. Maybe unity was what the whole human race was crying out for. 'Can you picture your painting, Mum – the one you did of the world between worlds? I think Calum is there now and if we pull together, you never know, we might just be able to get through to him.'

I put my mouth close to Calum's ear. 'Remember what you told me that day at the beach; keep your head above the water, you have to fight. Please keep trying, Calum.'

There was no response and I knew that despite my best endeavours, I should be preparing myself for the worst.

So the three of us sat like three spell-casting witches round Calum's bed with fingers entwined and brows furrowed, lost in our own hopes and thoughts.

Nurses came and went, checking Calum's blood pressure and temperature, the daylight which had been filtering into the room, through thin, checked curtains, faded into evening, but none of us moved, and I felt my chin drop onto my chest as I began to doze. And in my dream-like state I became aware of the faint aura of a misty figure standing in the corner of the room. Somewhere deep within me I knew with a strange certainty that it was Grace, come to guide her husband's soul as it slipped from our plane towards the other side. She held out wraith-like hands to him, beckoning him, and in my mind's eye I saw Calum's life force lifting from his slumbering form and hovering as if indecisive, in the room above our heads.

'Don't go,' I entreated sleepily as tears prickled beneath my closed lids. 'Please, Calum, for Abbey's sake don't go yet.'

Something cool and peaceful seemed to pass through me

and I shivered involuntarily, sliding my hands from Abbey and my mother's to rub them over my arms. The movement broke the spell and consciousness gradually returned to my partially slumbering mind.

'What's going on?' The voice came from somewhere in the room, muffled and croaky, jerking me to full wakefulness. My eyes flickered open.

It took a moment to realise that the voice was Calum's, as I stared at him, trying to stop myself from letting out a startled sob.

'Calum?'

He pulled the oxygen mask to one side and peered at the three of us; blinking in the dull light. 'You all look like you're at a wake.'

'Dad!' Abbey shrieked, letting go of my mother's other hand and throwing herself on top of her father. 'Oh, Dad, you're back!'

'Abbey?'

'I'm here, Dad,' she cried.

He hugged his daughter to his chest, his eyes filling with tears. If we had any doubts that he was fully back with us he quickly dispelled them with his next words, which seemed to tumble out of him in a rush, 'I love you, Abbey. I am a complete idiot to have let you think otherwise; you are and always will be my little girl.'

I slipped the locket out of its box and into his hand and he smiled up at me. 'Kaela, my trusted friend, thank you.'

I watched as he handed her the locket. 'I was going to give this to you on your eighteenth birthday, but I see now that you should have had it a long time ago.' We watched as Abbey opened the locket and after looking at it for a moment, she threw herself on her father again, the tears cascading down her face. When at last she released him, his eyes found Mum

369

who was standing back in the shadows, and his face creased into something soft and glowing. 'Susan? Is that you?'

Calum held out his hand and I watched as my mother moved towards him, threw her arms round father and daughter and clasped them both tightly to her.

'You have both been such good friends to me all these years, and I want you to know I am better now, and will be here for you for as long as you need me,' she murmured tearfully.

After dropping my mother off at Acorn Lodge, I headed for home with a quiet and thoughtful Abbey sitting beside me. She was wearing her mother's locket round her neck and every so often, her hand would sneak up to caress it, to check it was still there; a tangible reminder of her parents' love for each other and for her.

Kevin was waiting with Tristan in the kitchen when we slid in through the back way. My little brother had a completed Lego pirate ship in his hands and was zooming it round above his shoulders like an aeroplane. He smiled when he saw me and grinned harder when he spotted Abbey. Crouching down in front of Tristan I made a pretence of admiring the toy, whilst studying his features closely. The bruises were fading, he had a little more colour in his cheeks and I fancied I could see something of my father in him. Suddenly the tears were pouring down my face. Ingrid might have thought my father was a bastard, and maybe his dealings with her had shown poor judgement, but he was still my dad and I had loved him.

'Don't cry, Kaela,' Tristan said kindly. 'Kevin has cooked us a whole chicken and it smells really nice. You can have some of mine if you like.'

*   *   *

That night I couldn't sleep. Everything should have been wonderful. Before Abbey, Susan and I left the hospital, Calum had told me how over the years I had been gone, a deep bond of friendship had grown between him, my mother and Abbey. We had sat hand in hand while he told of how he had visited Mum in the home to pour out his heart to her.

'At first Susan was the nearest thing to you I had left, my only real connection to you after you vanished,' he'd told me. 'She seemed better after my visits and I felt more able to cope with Abbey, even on the days when she wasn't lucid, it helped just to see her.'

'Susan filled in as the mother figure I needed when I was missing you so much,' Abbey had agreed. 'She's been like a sort of stepmother to me.'

'Thank you so much for looking after them both, Mum,' I'd said later as I reluctantly dropped my mother off at Acorn Lodge. 'We'll soon have you out of the home and moved into somewhere of your own as near to Calum and Abbey's house as possible.'

Because that, I realised was what they would all want.

The attic room seemed unnaturally quiet and empty of Grace's presence tonight. I hoped that now Grace's husband and child were reconciled she could venture further from this earthly plane and continue her own spiritual journey in peace. It occurred to me as I tossed and turned that everything we'd been through had been a journey of discovery. And whilst the voyage had seemed at the time to be random and rudderless, all the pieces had been there, waiting to slot into place like a giant jigsaw coming together to form a map. Even Kevin's obsession with the number fifty-two had alerted Abbey to the importance of the number so she had recognised the message from her mother, sewn into the fifty-two pieces of the quilt.

I scrunched my eyes closed and wondered if my own spiritual journey had also been mapped out. I'd come to realise in the hospital that the name we gave to our creator wasn't as important as the intention with which we prayed. Perhaps because Abbey, my mother and I had all wished so selflessly for the same thing, our prayers had been answered by Calum's miraculous recovery.

But something was still bothering me. There was a piece of the jigsaw still missing. As I pulled the duvet up to my chin and willed sleep to come I realised I still didn't know, not for sure, what had happened to me in those missing six years six months and six days. And it was a truth I desperately needed to discover for myself.

Chapter Fifty-Seven

Well before daybreak I pulled on some clothes, left a note for Abbey and snuck out of the house, careful not to disturb Tristan who was sleeping peacefully in the kitchen under a fold-away bed Kevin had procured for him while the rest of us had been with Calum at the hospital. I smiled as I took an affectionate look at my baby brother and wondered how long it would be before he was comfortable enough to sleep on a bed instead of under it.

Wary of encountering any die-hard members of the press, I went out through the back garden, pulling the fence panel closed behind me. The Volvo was parked round the back.

As I slid behind the wheel of the car, I wondered whether I should have called Matt. Calum had told me that just like his feelings of deep friendship for my mother, we also could and would only ever be good friends. I was free to go to Matt now – Calum had made that clear. It was as if during those long hours when his soul had been elsewhere, he had understood his path in life more clearly and was now a stronger, more understanding person than he had been before.

But something held me back from contacting him, and as I headed towards Kent I realised it was the same thing that had prevented me from sleeping. It was the unknown factor of where I had been and what had actually happened to me. Was it fair, I asked myself, to embark on a new relationship when for all I knew, I had unresolved issues which might surface at any time and create problems between us? If some filthy old tramp had truly kept me captive all that time, goodness knows what horrors could suddenly surface from my subconscious mind.

All I wanted, I told myself firmly, was to look at that place in the woods. I wanted to see, feel and smell the underground pit that DI Smith had described to me and find out if it stirred any hidden memories. It would give me a kind of closure. If seeing the place didn't bring any memories rushing to the fore, I would accept Simone and Dr Jacobson's offering of the gravitational wave theory instead, and simply get on with my life.

The airfield was as dilapidated as it had been when I'd landed in the dark the previous Monday evening, and the early morning light did nothing to make it look more appealing.

Standing on the cracked, weed-straggled paving with my back to the hangar, I shaded my eyes and looked into the distance, where a line of trees stretched off to my left, beyond the long, rough grass of the old airfield. I had landed in that general area, facing this way, I was sure of it and those trees had been on my right then. I set off through the field of dew-sodden grass, humming tunelessly to myself to keep my resolve from wavering.

The distance to the trees had been deceiving and I found I was breathing heavily as I walked, concentrating on where I was putting my feet, careful not to twist an ankle on one of the many grassy hillocks.

When at last I drew level with the trees, I followed a broken barbed wire fence along the perimeter of the wood for half a mile or so, until I spotted an area that looked tramped and flattened.

The space was marked by a wide square of police tape and within this area, towards the far side of the clearing with its back pressed into the undergrowth was a small, weatherworn caravan. Its windows were cracked and grimy, the outer walls covered with green leaf mould and the whole thing tilted at a precarious angle where it had been hoisted from its previous position and tossed to one side.

In the centre of the gloomy clearing I saw the outline of a deep, dark indentation. Taking a ragged breath I tried to calm myself, fighting the overwhelming urge to turn and run away from this place of horrors. I had come to see this and so I must look, mustn't I? I crept forward until I was standing on the very edge of the hole. Some of the leaf mould gave way under my boots and tumbled into the depths and I stepped quickly back, but not before I saw that the hole was roughly hewn out of the ground, about two metres deep and the width and breadth of a double bed – almost as big as the discarded caravan itself. A battered ladder, which looked like the rusty steps to a swimming pool, leaned up along one wall and I assumed this was how the vagrant had descended into his treasure trove from the floor of his van where he had been living.

Glancing nervously round the clearing, I contemplated climbing down into the hole, but every instinct in my body resisted such a notion. Everything about this silent place was sinister and terrifying and after a moment of indecision I backed away, the bile rising in my throat as I thought about the bodies of all the little creatures that had been found imprisoned in its depths.

And then I heard a shuffling noise, somewhere nearby and my breath seemed to freeze in my lungs.

Keeping as still as possible, I raised my eyes to the caravan, from where the sound had come and just caught the slightest of movements from within. Danny Hill had been released, I remembered with alarm. Could that be him, returned to the only home he knew? Moving one foot at a time I shuffled backwards, away from the pit and the caravan. I had just reached the edge of the clearing and what I considered to be relative safety when a hand shot out from behind me and grabbed me roughly by the hair.

Instinct and fury clicked in almost simultaneously and I lashed out with both hands, trying to release myself from his grasp. The person who had me, was highly trained and not only evaded my attempts to disable him, but twisted me deftly to the ground, where he shoved me face down into the rotting vegetation with my arm jerked painfully behind my back.

'Stop it, you're hurting me!'

I could smell the body odour of my captor, even though the decaying vegetation was crushing my face. Heavy breathing accompanied his attempts to quell my feeble struggles, and vicious brambles pricked and stabbed through my fleece jacket, puncturing the skin on my upper arms and neck.

'Did you take my pretty things?' he asked from above and behind me. It was a petulant voice and I shuddered as I realised I was at the mercy of someone who may not have a grip on reality.

'I was just looking.' My voice was muffled in the undergrowth. 'I only wanted to see what was in the hole.'

He jerked my arm again and I yelped with pain.

'Who took my things then?' When I didn't answer him he rolled me sharply over until I was on my back looking up at him. 'I want my pretty things back.'

'I haven't got them.' My voice sounded shrill and panicky

and I took a breath, trying to keep it soothing and believable, understanding that if I annoyed him things could get very unpleasant indeed. He was a big man, probably somewhere in his late forties. His face was deeply pockmarked and lined, with whiskers on his cheeks and chin and a khaki woollen cap pulled down low over his forehead. He stared at me with angry, red-rimmed eyes.

'Who took them?'

'What sort of things were they?'

'Pretty things,' his voice softened as he spoke of his treasures, 'flying and crawling things, things with bright, fluttering colours and smooth feathers, soft fur.'

My mouth felt dry and my eyes darted past him for a means of escape but I kept my voice level as I wriggled up with infinite slowness until I was resting on my elbows. 'Birds, do you mean; birds and butterflies?'

'And things with soft fur,' he confirmed, nodding. He let go of me and sat back on his haunches, studying me carefully. 'They were all stored safely in my special place. They couldn't get away . . . except the bigger thing,' he said thoughtfully. 'That escaped. I told the police the pretty thing had escaped, when they asked me about it.'

'Tell me about the thing that escaped.' I tried to keep him talking as I surreptitiously inched myself into a sitting position and he didn't try to stop me.

'I watched the big thing spiralling, falling from the sky with its white wings spread outwards and I wanted to keep it for myself.'

Was he talking about me, I wondered? Could the white wings be the silk panels of the parachute? DI Smith had said they'd found the parachute in the pit, so he had definitely found it at some point and decided to keep it. The question was whether that had been six years ago, or last week.

'It sounds very pretty,' I said carefully, though my heart was racing. 'Did you keep it for a long time before it got away?'

'There was a strange wind,' his eyes had taken on a far away look as if he was remembering. 'The pretty thing tumbled onto the grass, it was winded, I think. I wanted to look at it but it was getting to its feet, struggling to get away.

'What did you do?'

'I had to hit it – I didn't want to hurt it, but it was getting away. When it lay still, I dragged it back to my camp.' He stared round at his battered caravan and swallowed hard as if the sight of his ruined living quarters was upsetting to him. 'I put it in my special place and kept it for a while.'

'What did this particular thing look like?'

'Tawny down, soft skin.'

'But it got away?'

He nodded sadly. 'I gave it food and water and kept it safe. I thought I could keep it forever, that maybe it wouldn't fade like the other things. But I brought it out of my special place to look at it properly, and it got away.'

I was petrified of making him remember too much, but at the same time was desperate to know the truth. He didn't appear to have recognised me as this 'pretty thing', but something he'd said when interviewed by DI Smith, had apparently made her think he had been talking about me.

'Did this particular pretty thing have a name?'

He pursed his lips as if thinking about his answer then nodded. 'I think it was called . . . Michaela.'

Chapter Fifty-Eight

'Oh no.' I slumped backwards against the soft earth and tangled undergrowth. It had been me. The man I assumed was Danny Hill had seen me land and had restrained me and somehow dragged me to that terrible pit beneath his floor. And having escaped once, I had come right back and fallen into his clutches a second time. What sort of fool was I?

He was looking at me strangely as if sensing my sudden fear and dismay.

'You're pretty,' he said. 'I could keep you.'

'You can't keep people,' I told him as I struggled to regain some sort of composure. 'The police wouldn't allow it.'

He began to look angry again. 'I think they took my other things. I'm going to have you.'

'But the police know about your special place now.' I hoped that reasoning with him might bring him to his senses, but his next words filled me with dread.

'They won't be able to find you, you'll be in little bits like all my other pretty things. They always end up in tiny pieces.'

Cold, unadulterated fear washed over me. I was wriggling backwards now, trying to put some distance between me and this confused and dangerous man.

I watched as he drew an evil-looking knife from a leather sheath round his waist, his eyes locked on mine.

'I won't let you run away.' He advanced on me with menace now showing clearly in his deranged eyes. Still on the ground, I had no chance to evade him and as he raised the knife in his hand, I shielded my face with my arm; flinching from the inevitable pain of the strike. As I closed my eyes, I heard the swish of the knife slicing through the air – but the pain never came. There was the muffled sound of a strangled grunt and a thud and when I dared to open my eyes, Danny was lying on the ground at my feet and there in front of me with a lump of wood in his hand, stood Matt.

For a few seconds I remained where I was, too stunned to move. Danny's cap had fallen off and I could see blood on the back of his head. Matt threw the wood down, reached round the prostrate figure of my attacker, took my hand and pulled me to my feet where he enveloped me in a bear-like embrace.

'I thought for a minute there I was about to lose you again,' he murmured into my hair as I trembled against him.

'How did you know I was here?' The tears were pouring down my face, as I clung tightly to him. I felt drained and emotionally wrecked. 'If you hadn't come, he was going to . . .'

'Ssh, I know,' he said. 'Abbey called Kevin and told him you'd left her a note. There wasn't time for him to get down here himself so he rang me and here I am.'

Danny groaned at our feet and Matt pulled me quickly away through the trees, putting distance between us and my attacker. 'I called the police,' he panted as we ran. 'They should be here soon. We'll let them deal with Danny Hill. This time they'll have something solid to charge him with. Even if they can't pin your abduction on him, he'll go down for assault with a deadly weapon at the very least.'

We had reached the edge of the woods and stopped to catch our breath when we heard the police sirens in the distance.

I tried not to think of the deranged man lying in that clearing, or what he'd tried to do to me and Matt was talking to me, trying to keep me calm. We were walking very quickly now, anxious to put distance between us and the madman with a knife.

'I really did think Simone was right with her theory,' he panted, as we trotted arm in arm through the long grass on the edge of the field. 'I hoped for your sake she was. The alternative seemed pretty grim.'

'But I'm still not convinced Danny had anything to do with my disappearance,' I gasped. 'I think he found a large bird of some sort on Monday night. I need to believe it, Matt.' I found I was still shaking uncontrollably. 'It may have been injured or disorientated by the same gravitational wave I was caught up in. He trapped it and tried to keep it in his pit but it escaped. I think his confession was a confused affair of talking at cross purposes with an over zealous DI Smith . . .'

Matt stopped walking and I grabbed a quick rest, bending forwards with my hands on my knees; sucking in ragged breaths.

'Maybe we'll never know the whole truth, Michaela. Perhaps you should believe whichever theory you can live with the most easily.'

As we paused we saw police officers running towards us from the far end of the field, but before we even had time to register our relief at their arrival, a wild whooping cry from our right had us spinning in our tracks. Danny Hill was standing on the edge of the wood, his gaze focused angrily on us. He had obviously recovered from the blow to his head and had tracked us from a distance within the safety of the woods he knew so well. I let out a squeal of fear and grabbed Matt's arm, but Danny stopped short, his head turned in the direction of the running police officers. What horrors he was envisaging at the sight of the advancing, uniformed men we couldn't know, but he let out another long animal howl of fear and began to run towards us.

The knife glinted in his hand as he advanced and Matt grabbed me, pulling me further into the field. But there was no cover; no where to hide. And then my boot caught in a hillock and I went sprawling into the wet grass.

'Michaela! Get up!' Matt was pulling at my hand whilst trying to shield me with his own body. I tried to claw my way to my feet, but he was still attempting to drag me along and I couldn't stand up. I could see him looking behind us, his eyes wide with horror and then suddenly he dropped my hand, pushed me squarely behind him and turned to face our enemy. I thought of a fox, realising it had lost the race to outrun the hounds, turning to face the howling pack in a final act of defiance.

A picture of the death card swam before my eyes and a terrible premonition ran through me. 'Please God,' I whispered under my breath, 'not Matt.'

'I want what's mine.'

'She's not yours,' Matt replied firmly.

The man made a guttural groan and lunged at Matt, who deftly sidestepped him. Danny regained his balance, brought the knife up again and flailed at Matt a second time. This time the blade nicked Matt's arm, tearing the fabric of his jacket.

'No!' I cried out, as I scrambled to my feet.

'You won't get away with this,' Matt was saying, his eyes locked on the knife. 'The police are coming for you – look, there's too many of them to fight.'

Danny made another thrust with the knife which Matt avoided by leaping backwards.

'Police! Put down your weapon!'

382

I turned to see three of the police officers panting towards us, but they stopped when they saw Danny wielding the knife inches from Matt's face.

'Give it up,' Matt cajoled as he continued to evade the knife's lethally sharp blade. 'There's nowhere to run to.'

Danny glanced over his shoulder. His knife seemed to hang in mid air as his bloodshot eyes focused at last on the uniformed officers.

'Matt!' I screamed his name as Danny flew at him, bowling him over so the two of them were a tangle of limbs on the wet ground. 'Stop him!'

The police officers dashed forwards, but it was too late. Matt half rose, grappling with Danny's knife hand for dear life, before Danny's booted legs kicked out and Matt fell sideways and back. Having gained the upper hand, Danny knelt astride him and raised the knife. But seeing that the officers were almost upon him he paused. For a split second, time seemed to stand still and then, as if in slow motion Danny brought his arm across his own face, from his right to his left, bending his elbow as it went, and sliced the knife deeply along his throat in one fluid, purposeful movement.

For a long moment he seemed to kneel there with the knife still gripped in his hand, while blood spurted upwards and outwards from the crimson gash in his throat. Then his knees buckled and he went down sideways in the slick, wet grass.

'Matt!' I knelt at Matt's side while the officers pulled Danny's body off him. He was covered in blood. 'Are you hurt?'

Matt sat up and staggered slowly to his feet, holding onto my shoulder for support, as he considered this question with a dazed look on his face. When at last he shook his head, I stared across to where my supposed captor was lying deathly still and suppressed a gasp. Protruding from the pocket of his jacket was a single long grey feather.

I hardly dared believe it. Matt was alive and apparently unscathed. And no memories whatsoever had surfaced of those missing six and a half years.

'I wasn't held by him.' I was shaking as much as Matt was. 'I would have remembered.' And all I could see in my mind's eye was Abbey's 'death' card detaching itself from the tarot pack and fluttering to earth like the big, grey bird Danny must have seen.

One Year Later

There was a ghost standing in the corner of the room. It had dark circles where its eyes should have been and in its hand was a can of Budweiser. I watched, amused, as Abbey dressed as a witch, with a long black skirt and pointy hat, snatched the Bud out of Kevin's hand and whisked him on to the dance floor, where ghost and witch gyrated to the music.

It was Halloween and Abbey's eighteenth birthday party. I nudged Matt and pointed out where Mum and Calum were standing at the bar; she dressed as a sort of devil woman in a slinky red and black dress and he as Count Dracula, in a black high-collared cloak with purple lining. I thought they both looked happy. Calum's operation had been a complete success and only a week before Matt and I had left for our trekking holiday in Peru, Calum had been told he needn't return to the hospital for any checks for another six months.

Tristan, looking a picture of health and energy, was racing round the dance floor, letting off party poppers with a couple of friends who had been invited from his class at school. He was dressed as a wizard in an outfit Abbey had made for him on her fashion and textiles course at the local college. She was adept with needles and sewing machines and had made not only her and Tristan's costumes, but mine and Matt's as well.

Simone and her parents were sitting at one of the tables, nibbling at the Halloween themed food and sipping frothing drinks from tall glasses. She waved when she saw me and Matt arriving. Having come directly from the airport we had dumped our backpacks in the hall's cloakroom and changed into our outfits in the loos. Matt was resplendent as a warlock, and I was in a green and black floaty arrangement.

'How was the trip?' Simone had come over to hug us both and we followed her back to her table. She was wearing a skin-tight black cat suit with the bones of a skeleton painted in luminous paint on the front and she looked fabulous as ever. 'I kept an eye on your company manager while you were away.'

A few weeks after Danny Hill had killed himself and the police enquiry into my disappearance was officially closed, Matt had confessed that for the past two years he had actually been the part-owner of the air freight company he had told me he only flew cargo planes for.

'Dad wanted to invest his retirement package in some-thing unusual, so he's part backer for Subatron Industries and a major shareholder in Diamond Freight – that's the name of my company.' Matt had taken my hand in his, and explained how he hadn't wanted me to know of his improved circumstances because he'd wanted to be sure I loved him for himself. I'd assured him that I would have followed him to the ends of the earth even if he'd been a pauper. He'd given me this news over a candlelit dinner, where he'd also produced a huge, diamond ring and a proposal of marriage.

'I still have to look after Tristan,' I'd told him. 'He's my responsibility now.' Because although we'd found an old photo of his mother for him to keep and we talked about her often, Ingrid had seemingly vanished for good.

But Mum, after getting to know Matt and Simone's parents and hearing the story of how Doreen had brought up her husband's illegitimate daughter as her own, had promised to help as much as she could with Tristan's upbringing. This coupled with Abbey and Calum looking after him whenever Matt and I went on one of our adventures, suited Tristan just fine – he thought it was all rather cool.

Tristan turned and spotted us from amongst the crowd on the dance floor and raced towards me, his arms out-stretched. I gathered him up and swung him round and he reached his arms out to Matt so we could have a joint cuddle. On lowering him to the ground, he scampered away to his friends and Matt and I made our way into the mass of bodies, where we danced to the strains of the Monster Mash until our feet ached.

'I'm glad your father and the other investors have continued to back Subatron Industries,' I called to Simone who had joined us in the dancing and was being flung about by an energetic and star-struck Oggs. It had taken almost a year for the enquiry into whether the Norfolk laboratories readings and my evidence would be enough to keep most of the backers on board. In the end they had decided that whilst the evidence was inconclusive, it was enough to show that the equipment had in all likelihood been working correctly and that it was worth continuing the funding.

I thought of the unlikely path that had brought me to this point in my life and decided that if the theory of my missing six and a half years was good enough for Subatron's share-holders it would have to be good enough for me.

'We're hopeful there will be another violent galactical event in the near future,' Simone called back as Oggs put her into a fast spin.

That night as Matt and I lay in bed, we talked of Abbey and her close friendship with Kevin. At eighteen now, she was still completely infatuated with the new slimmed-down and much fitter version of the man who had once been the gangly boy I had known. Despite the age gap, Kevin seemed to be content to wait for Abbey to grow up, while they continued to spar over numbers and patterns and he remained her knight in shining armour, only ever a phone call away.

'Love is a powerful thing,' I mused as we lay in a tangle of limbs, my head resting on Matt's bare chest, 'a mother's love particularly. Quite apart from the fact that losing me nearly killed my mother, look at what your mother did for Simone and what my mum is doing for Tristan, not to mention the strange thing with Grace and her desire to see Abbey happy, even from beyond the grave.'

'It doesn't always follow,' Matt said sleepily, 'Ingrid wasn't a very good mother, was she?'

'She cared for him until something better came along,' I reminded him. 'She trusted I would bring him up as my own when she left him with me.'

'She knew he was your brother, of course.'

'Yes,' I agreed, 'she did.'

And then Matt moved beneath me and for a while we were too absorbed to think any more about everything that had befallen us. When at last we lay back, breathing heavily, both covered with a thin sheen of perspiration, Matt gave me a playful nudge.

'Did the earth move for you?' he asked with a grin.

'Yes,' I said with a laugh as I snuggled closer to the man I loved with all my heart. 'Do you know, I do believe it did.'

IN CONVERSATION WITH MELANIE ROSE

If you were stranded on a desert island, which book would you take with you?

I'd take my *Roget's Thesaurus*. It is my constant companion providing a wealth of fascinating words at my finger tips. And unlike a novel, I'd never get bored with re-reading it.

Where does your inspiration come from?

My inspiration comes from real-life experiences, either my own or other people's. My work with under-privileged and sick children has made me aware of our spirituality. I believe everything has a purpose and that physical death is not the end. I study people and how they react to situations and I wonder constantly, what if? And then I write about it.

Have you always wanted to become a writer?

I've been a writer since I could first hold a pen. Writing is as necessary to my emotional well being as breathing is to my physical self.

What's the strangest job you've ever had?

Being the parent of four boys is the strangest job I've ever had. I am one of three girls so bringing up our lovely sons has been an inspiration – I never know what's round the

389

corner. Keeping everyone happy is a bit like juggling a hundred plates at the same time.

When you're not writing, what are your favourite things to do?

I enjoy keeping up with friends and family because people are important. I love off road cycling, badminton, swimming and skiing. Whatever keeps me outdoors and away from the kitchen. I also watch documentaries on TV because I like to soak up random information to store away for my next book.

What is a typical working day like for you? Have you ever had writer's block? If so, how did you cope with it?

A typical day starts with writing as much as I can on my laptop before I'm even out of bed and up for the school run. I make lists so I can organise the household and after the chores I check and answer emails before getting back to writing again. Fortunately I can pick up where I left off fairly easily. When I checked the statistics on my last novel I found I'd picked it up and continued with it over 663 times, yet I wrote the whole thing in the equivalent of eight days if I'd worked on it full time. Fortunately I've never had writer's block, just a million things forcing themselves between me and my keyboard.

Do you have any secret ambitions?

I'd love to have enough land to rear pigs and would experiment with rare breeds. I think pigs are intelligent, handsome, fascinating creatures.

What can't you live without?

I couldn't live without pens and paper. I could probably do

without a computer if the world as we know it ended, but I'd still need to write my thoughts down.

When you were a child, what did you want to be when you grew up?
I've only ever wanted to be a mum and a writer, so I guess I'm pretty lucky.

Which five people, living or dead, would you invite to a dinner party?
The five people I'd invite to a dinner party would be David Attenborough because he has an amazing wealth of knowledge; Andrew Marr, because he knows such a lot about history I could listen to him all day; Ghandi because he was a wise enlightened soul; Whoopi Goldberg because she's terrific fun and I think quite a deep thinker (I loved her in *The Colour Purple*) and Julie Walters because she's not only a talented actress but she'd bring us her brilliant sense of humour.